LEGENDS

OF THE

HASIDIM

LEGENDS
OF THE
HASIDIM

*An Introduction
to Hasidic Culture and Oral
Tradition in the New World*

JEROME R. MINTZ

PHOTOGRAPHS BY THE AUTHOR

The University of Chicago Press

CHICAGO AND LONDON

The University of Chicago Press, Chicago 60637
The University of Chicago Press, Ltd., London
© 1968 by The University of Chicago. All rights reserved
Published 1968. Second impression 1974
Printed in the United States of America
ISBN: 0–226–53102–3 (clothbound), 0–226–53103–1 (paperback)
Library of Congress Catalog Card Number: 68–16707

To Betty

ACKNOWLEDGMENTS

I would like to express my warm thanks to the many people who have helped me in the research and writing of this book. Dr. Henry Fischel of Indiana University is due special thanks for knowledgeable counsel. I extend deepest thanks to Rabbi Solomon Goldhaber and Rabbi Zev Sirota for their many kindnesses. I am grateful to Dr. Godfrey Cobliner for advice given me early in my fieldwork. My thanks go to Israel Friedman for the references from his unpublished bibliography of dissertations on Jewish themes and for his valuable aid. Rabbi J. Rubinstein kindly aided in establishing the vital statistics for many of the Rebbes. Dr. Isaiah Trunck of the YIVO Institute for Jewish Research read the manuscript with care and made many valuable suggestions concerning Yiddish orthography and offered other points of information.

I am indebted to a number of my colleagues at Indiana University. I extend thanks to Dr. Richard Dorson, who has always encouraged this research. Dr. Richard Antoun, Dr. Hillel Barzel, Dr. Maurice Friedberg, and Dr. Linda Dégh read portions of the work and made helpful suggestions.

I am grateful also to Dr. Joseph Dan of Hebrew University and to Dr. Francis Lee Utley of the Ohio State University for reading and criticizing the manuscript. Thanks go also to Mildred F. Mintz, Dr. Dan Ben Amos, Dr. Berel Lang, Dr. Raphael Patai, Dr. Natalie F. Joffee, Dr. Irwin Smigel, Dr. Hope Lichter, Dr. William Mitchell, Rabbi Rothenberg, Rabbi B. Shafran, Naomi Mintz, Suzanne Van Meter, Benjamina Feinberg, and Danna D'Esopo. I am grateful to Dr. Charles Eckert, who gave helpful suggestions concerning the photography done for this study, and to Dr. Margaret Mead for her advice and for permission to consult the Jewish materials of the Columbia University Research in Contemporary Cultures. In this connection thanks go also to the American Museum of Natural History.

Indiana University has been generous in supporting my research. I am also grateful to the Ford Foundation and to Harry Starr of the Lucius N. Littauer Foundation for the financial assistance granted to me.

There are many hasidim without whose help this book could not have been written but whom I may not name for fear of causing them some embarrassment. I am deeply indebted to them. I would like also to express my appreciation of the hospitality I received in the hasidic community. The hasidim have kept their traditional generous and warmhearted ways despite the hard blows they have been dealt. They are to be envied their sense of purpose and their comradeship. They made me welcome and I shall always be in their debt.

I am most thankful to my wife, Betty, for her encouragement and her counsel in helping me to prepare this work.

CONTENTS

ILLUSTRATIONS

FOLLOWING PAGES 150 AND 310

INTRODUCTION

The Present Study

This work is both a study of the contemporary hasidic community in New York and a collection of hasidic oral tradition. Part I, the study, is an attempt to describe and analyze a culture through its oral tradition. Its aim is to provide an integrated description of both the culture and the themes in the oral tradition. The study relies on the analysis of the tales collected and on data obtained through customary anthropological methods—participant observation, interviews, photography, and the collection of life histories. Part II consists of the collection of tales recorded in New York City, for the most part in 1959–61 and the summer of 1963. The bulk of the tales collected are legends—stories believed by the narrators to be true. Most tales are based therefore on actual experiences or observations which have been cast into narrative form in accord with traditional models and established points of view. The tales, presented completely and accurately, enable the reader to evaluate the analysis for himself.

The study of man through his oral tradition was established half a century ago by Franz Boas, who proved that the events, materials, and customs of daily life are reflected in tales. Since Boas' time the relation between oral tradition and culture has been examined by anthropologists, folklorists, psychologists, and historians, who have introduced varying approaches, techniques, and methods of study.[1] The particular methods of fieldwork and

[1] See Boas, "Tsimshian Mythology," *Thirty-first Annual Report of the Bureau of American Ethnology; Kwakiutl Culture as Reflected in Their Mythology*, Memoirs of the American Folk-Lore Society, vol. 28. For types of other studies analyzing oral tradition see Benedict, *Zuni Mythology*, 1: xi–xliii; Malinowski, "Myth in Primitive Psychology," in *Magic, Science, and Religion*, pp. 93–143; Jacobs, *Content and Style of an Oral Literature;*

analysis employed in this study are spelled out in more detail later in the introduction.

While the analysis of a culture through its oral tales is an accepted anthropological approach, the literary and interpretive treatment of hasidic tales have understandably led some historians and critics to doubt that hasidic legends, so central to Hasidism,[2] could be used to present a rounded portrait of hasidic life. In 1933, in a rich critical study of Hasidism, Torsten Ysander noted that the tales depict the literary and philosophical rather than the pietistic aspects of Hasidism and therefore render a false perspective.[3] One must agree with Ysander with regard to tales included in many literary collections in which the tales have been reshaped and severely edited for modern tastes—the material presents an erroneous impression.[4] The inadequacy of using literary collections to

Fischer, "The Position of Men and Women in Truk and Ponape," *Journal of American Folklore*, 69 (1956): 55–62; Parker, "Motives in Eskimo and Ojibwa Mythology," *Ethnology*, 1 (1962): 516–23; "The Wiitiko Psychosis in the Context of Ojibwa Personality and Culture," *American Anthropologist*, 62 (1960): 603–23; Vansina, "Recording the Oral History of the Bakuba—I. Methods," *Journal of African History*, 1 (1960): 43–51, 257–70; *Oral Tradition*.

[2] In his work, *Major Trends in Jewish Mysticism*, Gershom Scholem wrote: "The revival of a new mythology in the world of Hasidism . . . draws not the least part of its strength from its connection between the magical and the mystical faculties of its heroes. When all is said and done it is this myth which represents the greatest creative expression of Hasidism. In place of the theoretical disquisition, or at least side by side with it, you get the Hasidic tale. . . . To tell a story of the deeds of the saints became a new religious value, and there is something of the celebration of a religious rite about it" (p. 349).

[3] Ysander, *Studien zum B'seštschen hasidismus*, p. 11.

[4] Ysander was referring to the works of Martin Buber. Interestingly enough, Buber himself critically appraised his early efforts at retelling hasidic tales, saying: "I did not yet know how to hold in check my inner inclination to transform poetically the narrative material" (Martin Buber, *Hasidism and Modern Man*, p. 22). A later statement concerning the method he employed for preparing the tales of his great collection again finds Buber the artist, albeit restrained, shaping and reconstructing the tales that he found. "One like myself, whose purpose it is to picture the zaddikim and their lives from extant written (and some oral) material, must above all, to do justice simultaneously to legends and to truth, supply the missing links in the narrative. In the course of this long piece of work I found it most expedient to begin by giving up the available form (or rather formlessness) of the notes with their obscurities and digressions, to reconstruct the events in question with the utmost accuracy (wherever possible, with the aid of variants and other relevant material), and to relate them as coherently as I could in a form suited to the subject matter. Then, however, I went back to the notes and incorporated in my final version whatever felicitous turn or phrase they contained." (*Tales of the Hasidim*, 1: viii.)

The problem of an English reader in obtaining reliable and accurate texts describe hasidic life, however, does not apply to the content of tales collected from oral tradition and faithfully presented. As I believe will become evident, in oral tradition the tales contain the full scope of life—mundane beliefs and values as well as the humble distillation of mystical and philosophical beliefs.

The tales included in this collection were recorded in a variety of places—in homes, in stores, and at ritual ceremonies. A number of them were taken down with a pad and pencil, but the great majority were recorded on tape, often at traditional hasidic gatherings. Therefore, the collection includes many examples of tales collected in their "natural state." In all, stories were collected from fifty-nine storytellers from thirteen different courts.[5] Each tale is identified by narrator, court, and language used.

The Function of Hasidic Storytelling

For more than two hundred years a rich oral tradition has flourished in hasidic courts, first in eastern and central Europe and now among the hasidim who have emigrated to Israel and to the United States. The Baal Shem Tov (1700–60), the founder of Hasidism, revealed his teachings partly in the form of tales and parables; in addition, legends which testified to his holy powers gained cur-

---

is rendered virtually impossible by well-meaning but misguided editors. In his justly famous reservoir of hasidic tradition, Louis I. Newman, very straightforwardly, tells how he selected and edited some of his material: "For the benefit of those readers who may wish to compare these aphorisms [of the Bratzlaver Rebbe] with the original, the following remarks must be made: (1) Only those thoughts with special merit for a modern reader have been utilized. (2) The constant repetitions of the same idea have been omitted. (3) Kabbalistic references have been ignored. (4) References to sexual offenses, to the Evil Eye, to the Powers of Satan and his hosts of unholy beings, and similar themes have been omitted. (5) The constant emphasis upon the influence of the Zaddik and his powers of mediation has been minimized and utilized very sparingly. (6) While ideas intertwine, some have been dropped for the sake of clarity. (7) Entire subjects have been left out of the quotations from the Bratzlaver, for the reasons stated, but a large part of the meritorious material has been presented. This applies to the various items quoted in this work from the Bratzlaver." (Newman and Spitz, *Hasidic Anthology*, p. 316, n. 1. See also p. lxxxvii.) See also Levin, *The Golden Mountain*, p. xvi.

    [5] The term "court" (*hoyf*) is used throughout this study to describe any group of hasidim attached to a particular Rebbe. While contemporary courts have a less unified economic, social, and geographic structure than they enjoyed in Europe, the word still conveys the temper of the social setting and its dynastic qualities.

rency. Both served to draw followers to him. Like many religious leaders the Baal Shem Tov preferred to teach by word of mouth. He wrote nothing down and was skeptical of attempts to record his teachings.[6] The Baal Shem Tov's disciples perpetuated the tradition of expounding their credo in oral tales and parables, and like their teacher each Rebbe attracted a store of wonder tales testifying to his profound powers.

Storytelling won an established place in the life of the earliest hasidim and it became part of the Shabbes ritual. On the Shabbes, the men met three times to pray and to share communal meals. At those times, particularly at the third meal when the Shabbes was waning, the Rebbes often wove their teachings into an extended metaphor or parable or told an illustrative tale. The hasidim added a fourth communal meal, the melaveh malkeh, at which it became customary to gather at the Rebbe's table to hear stories of hasidic saints and sages.

Another ritual occasion, the meal held on the yohrtsait (anniversary of the day of death) of a famous Rebbe, played a significant role in the growth of hasidic storytelling. At the meal the hasidim celebrated the new elevation of the deceased's soul with song, dance, drink, and with tales which recalled the Rebbe's deeds. The hasidim were called on to use their memory and imagination to glorify the deceased tsaddik.

To a great extent storytelling continues in the New World because it has remained part of the integral structure of hasidic religious and social life. Tales are exchanged casually at the besmedresh or in any social situation, but storytelling has also maintained its unique ritual significance, and so the hasidim continue to gather to tell stories on the yohrtsait of the Rebbes and at the melaveh malkeh at the close of the Shabbes. These gatherings may be held in the besmedresh or shtibl or in someone's house. As in the past the hasidim partake of a simple meal of rye bread, herring and onions, salt, fruit, potatoes, and tea. Brandy, often homemade, is offered, and blessings are exchanged; the singing is strong. The association with the Shabbes strengthens the sacred character of

[6] A legend of the Besht tells that the Besht encountered a demon with a book in his hand about which he said that the Besht was the author. The Besht questioned his own followers to find out who was writing down his words. When one of his disciples showed him the collection of sayings he had been keeping, the Baal Shem Tov examined it and said: "There is not one word here that is mine." See *In Praise of the Besht*, no. 159 (tale numbers refer to the English translation; the tales are not numbered in the Hebrew edition).

the storytelling, as in the tales themselves the mere mention of the Shabbes renews a chain of associations—the fellowship, the special dishes, and the meetings with the Rebbe.

If the Rebbe presides at the meal he may fill the glasses and offer his blessings, although these tasks are often done by the gabai (the Rebbe's assistant). The Rebbe also leads the storytelling. If the Rebbe is not present, an honored elder or a learned visitor may be called on to begin the evening with a tale. The storytellers usually vary. One story recalls another and the tales range from miracles to humorous anecdotes.

The melaveh malkeh itself may be seen as an outlet for the rigor and tensions of the long Shabbes day. Coming at the end of a day of sacred prayer, the melaveh malkeh retains the heightened atmosphere of the Shabbes, and yet in some ways presents a sharp contrast. The services during the day are customarily in the form of prayer dialogues held directly with God; the speakers in the prayers are often prophets and kings; and the language and tone are awe-inspiring. In contrast, in the tales told at the melaveh malkeh it is the familiar figure of the Rebbe to whom petitions are addressed, and he in turn may appeal to a court in heaven, the counterpart not only of the Sanhedrin but also of the communal structure of the hasidic community. Rather than a strong-willed deity issuing decrees, the Rebbe and the Heavenly Court debate and wrangle, and sometimes the Court delivers wry decisions (T1). The language of the tales is simple and direct, enriched only by practiced retellings. The characters in the tales too are less austere: merchants, peasants, Rebbes, and secret tsaddikim rub shoulders. During and after the telling of tales there is conversational byplay, with the Rebbe sometimes commenting on the deeper or the more obscure meaning of the tales. Questions are raised and alternatives are discussed. And the evening ends by most hasidim smoking cigarettes, perhaps tossed out wholesale by the Rebbe.

There are other significant factors which have helped keep the oral tradition a vital element in hasidic life. Since oral tradition has played a key role in the development of earlier talmudic and kabbalistic works, as well as in preserving the teachings of the Baal Shem Tov, its status in the hasidic community is extremely high. Storytelling is the primary source of entertainment in a society that bans the theater and frowns on secular books. Moreover, in addition to perpetuating the Baal Shem Tov's delight in tale-telling, the hasidim have also retained his suspicion of the printed word. Skeptical of an editor's motives in publishing a collection of tales, the hasidim continue to regard printed stories as usually amended in some way according to the editor's personal whim. For fear of identifying events that they personally witnessed with the fictionalized aura of printed tales, some hasidim have discouraged tales of their teachers and Rebbes from reaching print, and they often refuse to tell such stories to any but those who share the same loyalty. Still another motive in keeping silent is the fear of supernatural punishment for breaking a great confidence. One narrator noted: "He was not allowed to mention what happened while the Rebbe was alive. If he told, nothing good would happen to him. He was allowed to tell when the Rebbe went away from this world" (H71).

Some contemporary Rebbes caution their followers not to read any of the printed legends since they contain falsehoods and serve only to cause doubt and confuse the mind with several variants of the same story. Instead, the Rebbes advise that their hasidim listen only to the Rebbe, who heard the authentic tale from his father who in turn received it from his father. When the Ropchitser Rov died in 1827, his son, the Dzikover Rov, is reported to have said, "The world tells of many miracles performed by my father, but I know only three of them" (T28, T29). The Rebbes wrought miracles, the hasidim say—but not the ones printed in books.

As marks of authenticity, the name of the Rebbe concerned is almost always cited in the legend, and, almost as often, the name of the hasid who was involved or who passed along the tale. In concluding his tale a hasid notes: "The only way to know if a story is true is if it has testimony from witnesses—that is, true witnesses. This story has been passed by hundreds of people. I heard this story from Rabbi Bernstein from Montreal and from other people also" (H24).

Good storytellers are accorded special status. They are known to preserve the history of the court and the wisdom of the Rebbe. They are accepted as teachers of both adults and children. The storyteller, even though not necessarily directly involved in the tale, often witnessed the events that he reports and was in contact with the great Rebbes, and these factors lend a glow to his personality. By repeating the stories of the Rebbes, the storyteller becomes in a sense the Rebbe's spokesman and disciple, and a sage of sorts as well. The Stoliner Rebbe, who always seated one elderly hasid at the head of the table because he had been with the Rebbe's father, said: "Blessed are the eyes that looked at the eyes of a tsaddik" (TA13).

As the reader will see, the tales themselves serve multiple functions in hasidic culture:

1. They are a record of the historical circumstances of the hasidic movement and of individual courts.

2. On a more personal level the tales serve as family history, recording the experiences of forebears who were in contact with the Rebbes of the past.

3. The tales serve as a technique of social control by making acceptable and unacceptable behavior explicit. In the legendary tradition, the commandments furnish the background texture of custom and conduct, and the consequences of breaking the commandments are among the vital threads of conflict and drama. The tales make it clear that lawbreakers are punished and that their transgressions lie at the root of their misfortunes.

4. The tales validate the power and the righteousness of the Rebbes. They affirm as well the special relationship existing between the Jews and God.

5. The tales also testify that the Rebbe affords his followers protection from chaotic fate and that he can intercede on their behalf before the Court of Heaven. For the hasid who suffers from being childless or from illness in his family or from insufficient income, the tales affirm that the Rebbe can bring about an end to his trials.

6. Storytelling has the further function of helping the individual establish his place among his fellows. The righteous man possesses the means, through his prayers and good works and with the aid of the Rebbe, to reverse ill fortune. Recounting how he received aid is positive testimony that he is righteous and has been proven worthy.

7. Storytelling therefore also provides the individual hasid with the opportunity to tell that he shares in the mystique of the relationship existing between the Rebbe and his hasidim. (This is not to say that there are no guidelines for the telling of such tales. There is a sense of balance concerning reported events, and the reception of the audience is related to one's prestige in other areas of life. If someone of dubious status monopolizes the time, relating too many occurrences in which he and the Rebbe saw eye to eye, his statements, like those of any man who has overreached himself, are likely to be regarded with a tolerant but skeptical eye.)

8. The tales ostensibly serve as guides of conduct. The hasidim consciously use stories as the pleasantest way of introducing religious practices to the young.

9. The tales are also a prime source of entertainment. In the absence of a creative theater and literature, storytelling continues to provide within the religious system the central outlet for creativity.

10. In their role as entertainment the tales ease the unrelenting piety. The scope of the tales includes not only wonder stories but numskull tales and jokes as well. On occasion the law is parodied and the Rebbe is turned into a comic figure.

Storytelling is, however, more than the total of the personal and social functions we have outlined. It is more than entertainment, or the means to reassure the community, or a way to gain status, or a historical chronicle.

11. The telling of tales can be a mystical expression on various levels. To tell tales of the tsaddikim is one means of glorifying the tsaddikim and of contacting their piety and power. And, as noted in *In Praise of the Besht*, when one tells stories in praise of the tsaddikim it is as if one were engaged in *ma'aseh merkava*—the mysteries of the heavenly throne and the chariot.[7]

12. In this light, the hasidim believe that tales, like prayers, contain the potential to be active agents. The Rebbe often tells a tale to a troubled petitioner in which an identical problem was solved. This in itself may simply be reassuring. But the Rebbe may also conceal a prayer in the tale, or the tale itself may be considered a prayer. The tale may have the power of renewing the event it describes, thereby bringing about a successful conclusion once again (H61). Storytelling has been used to shape desired ends, and therefore can be conceived of as the powerful, even magical, equivalent of action.[8]

[7] Ma'aseh merkava: literally, the lore of the Chariot. See Ezekial i and x. See *In Praise of the Besht*, no. 194. See also Scholem, *Major Trends*, pp. 40–79.

[8] See *In Praise of the Besht*, no. 114, in which the Baal Shem Tov is asked for the secret of how to pray for a sick person with folktales. Buber cites a tale of how a disciple of the Besht was cured of his lameness while acting out how the Baal Shem would tell a story (*Tales*, 1: v–vi). For another example of the power of storytelling, see Scholem, *Major Trends*, pp. 349–50.

Such belief is widespread. Writing of the function of myth among the Navahos, Kluckhohn says: "Myths and rituals constitute a series of highly adaptive responses from the point of view of the society. Recital of or reference to the myths reaffirms the solidarity of the Navaho sentiment system. In the words of a Navaho informant: 'Knowing a good story protects your home and children and property. A myth is just like a big stone foundation—it lasts a long time'" (Clyde Kluckhohn, "Myths and Rituals: A General Theory," *Harvard Theological Review*, 35 [1942]: 45–79; reprinted in *Reader in Comparative Religion*, p. 149).

The Scope and Sources of the Tales

Most of the tales included here are the result of the interaction of
imagination and experience. As we shall explore in subsequent
chapters, an intimate relationship exists between hasidic tale and
hasidic law, ritual, social structure, and daily life. The tales have
come into being through diverse social needs, and as can be seen
from glancing at the present collection, hasidic tales include exempla, parables, legends, and jokes. They range from philosophical
expositions (W1), to historical accounts (N1), to wonder stories
(H22), to numskull tales (S18).

THE REBBE

The central figure in the tales is the pious, wonder-working
Rebbe. The charisma of the Rebbe and the role he plays in the
society have generated a continual flow of legends concerning his
life and activities. As the Rebbe is thought of not only as a spiritual
guide but also as a means of circumventing the evils of barrenness,
poverty, sickness, and oppression, each court nourishes a store of
wonder tales testifying to the profound powers of the Rebbes of
their dynastic line. The tales preserve not only the wonders performed but also the Rebbe's distinguishing personal characteristics
and his philosophical point of view. Thus tales still popular depict
the intellectual bent of Rabbi Shneur Zalman (T17), the warm
nature of the Berdichever (H17), the humble self-sacrifice of the
Sassover (T4), the timidity of the Dzikover (H49), the wit and
humor of the Ropchitser (S5–8), and the splendor and secret piety
of the Rizhyner (T43).

The Rebbe interacts with diverse characters both from within
the court as well as from the world outside. The canvas of the tales
is crowded with village folk: the rabbi, the shohet (ritual slaughterer), the coachman, the rich man, the protective mother, the
grass widow, the gabai (the Rebbe's assistant), the talmudic student, and the host of the faithful of the synagogue. Most commonly, the Rebbe is seen answering the needs of his pious followers, performing miracles for the sick and the needy, and resolving
their problems and questions. The Rebbe also matches his prowess
against emperors and generals, landowners and government
officials, skeptical misnagdim (literally, opponents), and, as he

faces the disciples of the haskala (the enlightenment), against cynical doctors and lawyers.

HISTORICAL EVENT AS A SOURCE FOR THE TALES

The Weltanschauung of the hasidim has always encouraged the creation of legends encompassing wonder, piety, and magic. In many instances the creative stimulus has been a historical event or a local happening. These tales concern the history of individual courts and the history of the hasidic movement, and they touch as well upon the larger historical circumstances. Accounts tell how the Besht won Rabbi Dov Baer to his cause (T3), how Reb Mikhel came to Zlochev (T11), and how the Rizhyner escaped from Russia (H37). Other tales record how Napoleon won and lost his battles (N1–4), and in modern times how Rommel was defeated (N23) and how the Israelis won at Sinai in 1956 (N37).

It is apparent that although the tales mirror events, the refraction of folk tradition is often somewhat oblique and reflects a particular world view. Although details in the stories accord well with our historical knowledge, it would be difficult to write a satisfactory history based on the tales alone. On occasion, time is telescoped in the tales and there are conversations between individuals who lived in different centuries (T1). One may question the usefulness of such material in understanding the past; but careful study will show that the tales can provide striking and unique insights into the study of culture and history. In the tales events are most often seen through the eyes of the hapless common man rather than from the customary vantage point of the statesman or general planning grand strategy; and the details in such accounts are often of a kind found only in diaries and letters or in interviews. Therefore, while the legends of the hasidim do not contain a well organized body of historical materials, the tales illuminate attitudes and behavior about which little is known.

Hasidic tradition, for example, preserves the reactions of the hasidim to the spate of laws produced in eighteenth- and nineteenth-century Russia, which were designed to expel the Jews from farms and villages and to deny them the right to lease land, to keep taverns, to settle in rural areas, to move out from the Pale of Settlement, to live near the border, and to trade or reside in the interior provinces of Russia. Of primary importance to the hasidic storyteller, however, is that the Rebbes were capable of miraculously turning aside such decrees (T12, H34). In other instances the tales reflect the fact that few Jews could afford to live within the requirements of the discriminatory laws, and their reaction simply was to circumvent them. Characters in the narratives accept as their prerogative the right to smuggle goods across the border, and one tale tells of a wonderful miracle that occurs when the chief of police drowns while waiting in ambush to nab a Jewish smuggler (H42). The tales also make clear that if an injunction could not find support in the Jewish code of laws it lacked moral sanction in the Jewish community. Breaking the secular law was not considered morally significant, and so on Passover, one tale notes, the Berdichever Rebbe reported with pride to God: "Bread which by Your word alone is forbidden cannot be found; but despite all the soldiers of the tsar, one can obtain silk everywhere" (H17).

Other examples of this sort may be seen in tales reflecting the harsh conscription laws of the tsars. In the first half of the nineteenth century, army service in Russia (except for Russian Poland) lasted for twenty-five years, and it continually robbed the poor, both Jew and Christian, of their young. If one survived, the army meant a life of bitter unrewarding toil, danger, and exile from one's family to the remote parts of Europe. When the Christain youth was pressed into service, the women sang *soldatka*, laments akin to dirges for the dead. The Jewish family too mourned as for the dead, their grief sharpened by the knowledge that their young son faced forced conversion.

Episodes in the tales enumerate the few alternatives open to recruits: they could try to raise the necessary funds to purchase a certificate testifying to membership in one of the three classes of the merchant guild; they could nullify their usefulness as soldiers by self-mutilation; they could try to bribe the examining army officials; and they could turn to the wonder-working Rebbe. The tales indicate that they often tried all four. Hasidim wandered through the countryside trying to raise money to redeem poor recruits (H19). There was a desperate science of self-mutilation as well as a core of "specialists" who claimed they could induce ruptures, swellings, and other temporary or permanent disorders (H51, H52).[9] Bribery functioned as a subsystem of government and the Jew used it to survive the network of discriminatory regulations. In the tales, ironi-

[9] The Russian government recognized the problem of self-mutilation and the disappearance of recruits and set harsh penalties against the community as a whole. See Dubnow, *History*, 2: 146–48, 356–57.

cally, it is a catastrophe when a Jew has to appear before an official
or doctor who cannot be bribed and who insists on fulfilling the law
(H57). For his part the wonder-working Rebbe could advise the recruit when it was best to appear for examination, when to hide,
when to pay a fine, and when to wait for supernatural aid (H52,
H56, H58).

One of the underlying purposes of the conscription laws had
been to convert the younger generation of Jews.[10] Most of the
recruits taken in Nicholas' time (1827–56) were forcibly converted; and even when in 1856 the harsher measures of Nicholas'
laws (under which recruits as young as twelve could be legally
impressed, and children as young as eight were often taken) were
abolished, it was still stipulated that Jewish children who had been
converted must be returned to Christian rather than to Jewish
families. Most Jewish children did not survive the first forced
marches away from their homes and the barracks tortures leading
to conversion, and many of those that did later died in the Crimean
War (1853–56) and in subsequent campaigns.[11] But the tales
relate a rare miracle—the sudden appearance of Jews forcibly
converted and long considered dead who were miraculously awakened. They are drawn back to their people by the secret strength in
their souls and by the powers of the Rebbe (H45, H46).[12]

Although the focus of this work is on the contemporary community, the content of historically centered tales is often of great
relevance. This is due to the enduring hasidic conceptions of the
historic process. The hasidic view of history seen in the tales is not
the interplay of social, religious, political, and economic forces of
the sort commonly accepted by western historians. History was and

[10] Dubnow, *History*, 2: 20.
[11] Dubnow, *History*, 2: 22–29, 149–50.
[12] These tales continue to have great impact because the hasidim still
work at restoring children separated from their parents during World War
II and converted to Christianity. Some also claim that poverty-stricken
families in Israel have given their children to Christian missions. A handbill
(n.d.) circulated by the Pidyen Shvuyim Committee reads in part (itali-
cized words translated from the Hebrew): " 'Please save me, get me
out of here!' Dear friend: The imploring eyes of the Jewish child in the
missionaries churches Eretz Yisrael cry just that. If one saves just one
Jewish life, say *our sages, let their memory be blessed*, it is considered as if
he had rescued an entire universe. Is there any greater accomplishment than
to save a Jewish child from conversion. To date we have, *thank the Lord*,
rescued and found strictly orthodox Jewish homes for over 850 children.
There are still approximately 2,000 children found in the missionaries. Our
aim is to rescue them all, *with the help of God*."

is considered first to be an expression of the will of God, and the
tales are exempla of that view. On an equally functional level, as
we shall see in subsequent chapters, historical events are generally
attributed to one of three causes: the power of hasidic Rebbes to
master circumstances and force a conclusion favorable to the Jews;
the inexorable procession of events toward the coming of the
Meshiah; and the toll exacted on the Jewish community as a whole
for its failure to fulfill the commandments.

In sum, the material in the tales accords well with our historical
knowledge gained from other sources; it provides as well insights
into the hasidic world view and into specific social attitudes.

OTHER SOURCES FOR THE TALES

The overwhelming majority of the tales appear to be new hasidic creations based on actual experience and observation. However, some tales included here apparently have been borrowed from
non-Jewish sources (although perhaps entering Jewish tradition
earlier than the rise of Hasidism) and reshaped in accord with
Jewish values. In Europe the bilingualism of the Jews has always
kept channels open to the storehouse of non-Jewish folk tradition,
and other folk beliefs, legends, songs, and tales have intermingled
with Jewish tradition. At times well-known aspects of village life
are interwoven with stories of far-off places, and familiar characters of the kitchen, barnyard, tavern, and market play their parts
alongside generals, emperors, princes, and sultans.

The present collection includes some widely known tales which
have been adapted by hasidic storytellers. Much as the international tale type of the grateful dead man (types 506–507c) [13] was
changed in the Book of Tobit to encompass the pious Jew, the
Persian demon Azarias, and the archangel Raphael, in this collection in the widely known tale of the trickster, "the man in the
sack," the cast has been altered to include Cossack and Jew, and
other Jewish figures such as the talmudic student, the far-seeing
Rebbe, and the grass widow (I12, I13). The framework of "The
Good Precepts" (H20) is widely known; the hasidic version, however, includes new material about the foresight of the Rebbe, the
value of learning, the need for children to learn about religious
practices, the fear of the authority of the nobility, and the dread of

[13] Aarne and Thompson, *Types of the Folktale*, pp. 172–75.

induction into the army with its consequent dissolution of cultural values. Known to both Jew and Christian was the legend of the mark burned on the wall by a dead soul, but while a non-Jewish tale collected recently (M6) indicates that the soul is a vengeful spirit of the dead, in the hasidic version in this collection the soul is that of a talmudic student who erred and must choose between Gehenna and reincarnation (H26). Even the most exotic stories of kings and courtiers have been reshaped by hasidic beliefs and values. Their naïveté and their affinity for debate, for example, prompt a young prince, trying to explain to his royal father his decision to leave his servants behind, to say, "I don't like too many servants. I have arguments with them" (H10).

The tales which blossomed in an eastern European environment might be supposed to have diminished in scope and in importance once they reached the New World. But this has not occurred. Hasidic oral tradition thrives in Brooklyn much as it did in Karlin and Warsaw. The tales set in Europe survive and continue to be told. Moreover, hasidic life has been renewed, and new traditions based on the experiences and observations of the present generation in America are being circulated as well. Williamsburg and Korea (HA49) have served as locales for miracle tales. During the Middle Eastern War in June, 1967, the predictions and blessings of a Rebbe in Brooklyn were significant to people in both Brooklyn and in Israel (N38–40).

Methods of Fieldwork and Analysis

In both the research and writing of this work, I have related analysis or oral tradition with data obtained through interviews and by participant observation. The following steps were taken in gathering the data and in preparing the analysis. Initially tales and cultural data were collected during interviews with informants from more than a half-dozen hasidic courts in New York City. The tales were generally elicited as part of discussions on a wide range of subjects. Some were collected while gathering life histories. Additional tales were collected at ritual ceremonies. When fifty tales were collected, a preliminary analysis was made to guide further collecting and interviewing. By analyzing the tales for their significant themes, and by examining the motivations, attitudes, and values of the characters portrayed in the tales, it was possible to make inferences concerning the beliefs and mores of the culture. At that time the following synopsis of the points was made.

1. Identification as Jews
   Separateness as a means of pre-
      serving culture
   Dangers of conversion
   Brotherhood of Jews
   Importance of commandments
   Suffering as a sign of covenant
   Comparison of Jew and gentile
   Resurgence of dormant feelings
      of Judaism
2. Proof of Rebbe's powers
   Foresight (practical and spirit-
      ual knowledge)
   Wonders
   Realistic appraisal
   Hidden knowledge
   Wisdom
3. Transmigration
   Gilgul (reincarnation)
   Dybbuk (metempsychosis)
   Gehenna
   Dangers of being reborn
   Mitsves for world to come
4. Wonderful events, objects, and
      feats
   Journeys
   Dreams
   Visions
   Objects
   Events
5. Relationship to authorities
   Trickster
   Outwitting authorities
   Counselor to kings
   Hidden teacher
   Napoleon
6. Meshiah
   Forcing the Meshiah to come
   Signs of the coming of the
      Meshiah
7. The philosophic inner world
   Ethics
   Divine plan
   Suffering
   Punishment

The purpose of this preliminary synopsis was to determine which areas warranted further investigation. Even a single tale could suggest a number of different problems. For example, the tale in which Rabbi Shneur Zalman's disciple appeared to him after death to ask if he should choose purgation in Gehenna or be reincarnated (H26) indicated the dependence of the hasidim on their Rebbes, the reward of Paradise awaiting the righteous, the purgation necessary for every misdeed, the dangers of rebirth, and the fear of breaking a commandment.

Other factors were taken into account in the process of analysis. Repetitions were seen as one means of determining the significance or currency of a belief. Obscurities and contradictions were included in matters to be investigated. Those aspects seemingly anachronistic were considered in their function and role in the present and in the past, so that, for example, an effort was made to measure current belief in magic and in supernatural beings.

After grouping the themes and ideas present in the tales, scores of questions were composed to ask informants on each point to test assumptions and to elicit further information. The overall consideration was to gather informants' interpretations of a number of areas of hasidic life that were highlighted in the tales.[14]

Whereas one of the purposes of the interviews was to test for the presence of the traits noted in the tales, the tales were also utilized as a means of eliciting additional information from informants. At times the tales presented a natural and convenient means for initiating discussions on a variety of subjects, particularly when it was otherwise difficult to obtain information or where avowed attitudes and actual practice appeared to differ. Using the inferences gleaned from the tales it was possible to present informants with questions concerning values and attitudes implicit in the oral tradition. The narratives were therefore used as a mirror of belief and custom, and also as an investigative tool, serving at times as a means of obtaining value judgments.

To ensure a more complete portrait of the culture, other sources were utilized in composing an overall interview guide. The points in the preliminary analysis were examined in relation to the social and historical circumstances of the culture as obtained from written records. Fortunately, the history and philosophy of Hasidism have been extensively examined by Simon Dubnow, Gershom Scholem, Martin Buber, Solomon Schechter, A. S. Aeščoly-Weintraub, Lazar Gulkowitsch, Torsten Ysander, Jacob Minkin, and others.[15] The works of these scholars provided a base on which to begin the present study. In addition, specific points of information were noted in the interviews conducted by the Columbia University Research in Contemporary Cultures, which had been used to prepare the volume *Life Is with People*.[16] Also useful were the materials developed by Abram Kardiner and Ralph Linton, described in *The Individual and His Society* and *The Psychological Frontiers of Society*.[17] (These materials were used to suggest what data might

---

[14] After interpreting the mythology associated with the Kula, Malinowski notes: "All these additions and comments I obtained in cross-questioning my original informant." (*Argonauts of the Western Pacific*, p. 325.)

[15] For complete citations, see the bibliography. A useful bibliography of recent works on Hasidism, primarily in Hebrew, can be found in "Hasidism," by Tishby and Dan, in *Encyclopaedia Hebraica*, 17: 820–21. An earlier bibliography of hasidic writings is in Newman and Spitz, *Hasidic Anthology*, pp. 535–48.

[16] Mark Zborowski and Elizabeth Herzog, *Life Is with People*. The interviews are kept under Margaret Mead's supervision at the American Museum of Natural History in New York.

[17] See bibliography, p. 454.

be included rather than as a method of interpretation.) The interview guide was therefore based on the analysis of fifty tales, on the interviews, on interviews made earlier on a similar subject by other researchers, and by Kardiner's chart of the sentiment system.

Interview Guide

Background
     Country of origin, mother tongue, year arrived, occupation
Family life and relations
     Household composition, number of children, pets
     Spouse: number of meetings before marriage, who introduced, reasons attracted, yihus (family background)
     Parents: authority, discipline; relationship between parents; comparison of own marital relationship with that of parents; comparison of roles of parents; comparison of roles of Rebbe and father
     Brothers and sisters: relationship, rivalry, affection, whereabouts, occupations, orthodoxy, relationship with parents
     In-laws, brothers-in-law: relationship, attitudes, orthodoxy
Child development and socialization
     Maternal care: feeding, quieting, kissing, constancy of attention or abandonment, help in learning processes (walking, talking), handling, fondling
     Weaning: age, method
     Language spoken to child
     Cleanliness: toilet training, washing
     Preparation for prayer
     Punishment-reward systems.
     Masturbation: attitude of elders
     Preparation for sex roles: sex demarcation (haircut, earlocks), preferential treatment, playing with opposite sex
     Sibling attitudes: rivalries encouraged or suppressed
     Participation in society: premature or deferred
     Honesty to children or practice of deception
     Introduction to school, besmedresh
     Menstruation
     Adolescence
Value System and Attitudes
     In-group
          chosen people
          friends (before and after marriage)
          court fellowship
          fellowship of hasidim
          brotherhood of Jews
     Out-group:
          misnagdim (opponents)
          gentiles

backsliders and renegades
government (comparison of Europe and U.S.)
apikoyrsim (skeptics)
reform and conservative Jews
anti-Semites
Areas of Conflict
Temptation
Shame
Rebellion
Self-imposed restrictions (fasts, mikveh, tefillin, spoiling the taste of food)
Anti-Semitism
Maintaining customs in an alien environment (peyes, beard, kaftan, yarmelkeh)
Secular education
Leadership
Personality of Rebbe
Character of dynasty
Moral teachings
Tales
Emphases: song, dancing, prayer, learning
Moods
Miracles
Exaltation
Help in attaining parnosseh (livelihood), gesund (health), nahes fun kinder (joy from children)
Activities at the tish (communal meal)
Goals
Marriage
Position
Education
Goals for children
Belief, Custom, and Superstition

Gilgul (reincarnation)	Kimpetzettel (childbirth amulet)
Dybbuk (metempsychosis)	Yetser Hora (Evil Urge)
Sheydim (spirits)	Werewolf
Einhora (evil eye)	Opsprekher (good eye)
Kapores (scapegoat)	Lilith
Baal moyfes (magician)	Magic objects
Magic flight	Mikveh: attendance, properties
Meshiah	

The types of interviews employed varied according to the informants, the situation, and the kind of information sought. Some interviews were unstructured, others were structured; some were

sharply focused, some were quite casual. The interview guide
suggested the areas that were intended to be covered, but not every
subject was discussed with each informant. Nor were all subjects
equally pertinent. In all, more than 150 adults were reached,
although extensive interviews were held with only about 50 hasidim. Unfortunately, very few women were interviewed and oppor-
tunities to observe infant care were limited. (The law prohibits a
woman from being alone with a man other than her husband or
father.) Several of the distinguished Rebbes were visited; however,
of primary concern were the beliefs held by the people rather than
those espoused by the leadership. As already indicated, life histories were recorded to study the culture as it was reflected in
individual life experiences. (The names of informants referred to
in the text have been changed. In addition, no informant's photo-
graph appears in the book.)

An aspect of my own attitude in interviewing should be made
clear. While I was respectful of the religious principles espoused
by the hasidim, and conducted myself in accord with those principles, I did not pretend to be an orthodox Jew. Although I always
wore a hat, I did not grow a beard nor did I wear a kaftan (long
coat). To pretend to be orthodox would have prevented me from
asking many important questions which an orthodox person would
be expected to know.[18] My stance was that I was an interested student of religion but that I was not cognizant of all of the articles of
faith. It was surprising to me at first how well this was received.
The hasidim were eager to make the conditions of my environment
responsible for my lack of religious belief and practice. This is
particularly clear to them since they number among them some
who were not completely orthodox before being converted to Hasidism, as well as others who were temporarily deprived of their
religion during the war.

Since I am Jewish, many hasidim took special pleasure in initiating me to the value of orthodoxy. However, although it would have
pleased my hasidic friends to have me put on phylacteries and become an observant Jew, I persisted in refusing to accommodate
them. It is one thing to say a simple prayer before or after eating,
or to join in the dancing, or to observe negative taboos out of a
sense of courtesy and common sense, but it would be an obvious

[18] To understand the problems involved in pretending to be completely
orthodox, see Bernard Sobel, "The M'lochim: A Study of a Religious
Community"; see also Poll, *Hasidic Community of Williamsburg*, pp. 267–78.

deceit to pretend to commit oneself to a new and consuming way of life. Furthermore, part of my relationship with some hasidim consisted of a dialogue. We discussed and debated various points. They were interested in convincing me of the merits of their religious way of life. I never was wholly convinced and the resistance that I offered encouraged them to press their case harder.

When I began this study I first sought out students at the Lubavitch yeshiveh. The students were very helpful in directing me to others in the community, in securing invitations for me, and even at times in arguing on my behalf to convince a reluctant informant to talk to me. Subsequently, one hasid would refer me to friends and relatives, or would suggest someone known only by reputation. Often I had to initiate contacts myself, particularly at a court I had never before visited. On those times I would go to the besmedresh during the week and on the Shabbes. Usually, I would wait on the edge of the activities until a chance contact enabled me to engage someone in conversation. Often, however, it was the hasidim who approached me. Sometimes it was because they needed a letter translated or a mystifying American custom explained. They were also curious to learn who I was, why I was there, and even what I believed in. (At the first Shabbes service I attended at the Satmar besmedresh, I sat in front of a fourteen-year-old boy whose first words of greeting were: "When was the world created?") In short, I was a representative of the outside culture, made less forbidding to them by my desire to know their beliefs, as well as an object of curiosity and interest.

In presenting the results of my work I have tried to make the interview material and the tales lead the discussion and provide examples. The tales are used therefore in much the same way as are interviews and observations—as pertinent and revealing data. I have made every effort to verify the assertions made on the basis of the tales through my interviews. One must note, however, that because I have concentrated primarily on those areas relevant to the content of the tales in this collection, there are omissions of important aspects of hasidic daily life as well as of hasidic philosophy and history. It should also be clear that this is not a comparative work. My task as I saw it was to describe the hasidic community and its traditions, and to reserve societal and folkloristic comparisons for another occasion and perhaps for other writers. Analogues in a few well-known collections of hasidic tales have been cited when it seemed particularly appropriate, but extensive comparative notation and analysis have not been attempted. These constitute a vast and separate undertaking far removed from the purpose of this work.[19]

This study makes no pretense of being more than an introduction to aspects of hasidic culture. I am acutely aware of the limitations of a single investigator attempting to study and describe a complex and historically rich culture. It should be said as well that the riches of the tales have been fully but not completely explored. Ultimately, the tales speak for themselves.

[19] Motif numbers and type numbers have been assigned in the notes to the few tales with parallels listed in Stith Thompson's *Motif Index of Folk Literature* and Aarne and Thompson's *Types of the Folktale*. To avoid misleading the reader, tales and motifs in this collection that are not recorded in those works have not been given new motif and type numbers. The world of the legend is largely uncharted and there are no satisfactory comparative indexes. Concerning the present state of legend study, see Hand, "Status of European and American Legend Study," *Current Anthropology*, 6 (1965): 439–46.

PART ONE

THE HASIDIC PEOPLE

. . . curiously, for all our wide acquaintance with the teachings of prophets and rabbis and philosophers, it must be said that we really know little about the Jewish religion—that is, the religion, not of the intellectual elite, the most advanced exponents of the faith, but of the common people—the masses—for whom religion is no bare logical exercise, no social doctrine or philosophical or even theosophical system, but a sorely needed source of strength in the everyday task of combating a perennially hostile world.

Joshua Trachtenberg,
"The Folk Element in Judaism,"
The Journal of Religion, 22 (1942): p. 173.

I

THE HASIDIM IN EASTERN

AND CENTRAL EUROPE

The hasidim are orthodox Jews who have established their own unique customs, traditions, and mores within the framework of orthodox Judaism. All orthodox Jews abide by the same laws regulating their social and religious conduct. Despite this essential unity, however, there are distinctions to be made between the hasidim and other orthodox Jews in terms of particular traditions and customs, intensity and emphases in belief, varieties of rabbinical allegiance, and social structure and organization.

The founder of the hasidic movement, in the mid-eighteenth century, was the Baal Shem Tov (Master of the Good Name),[1] called "the BeShT" in abbreviation, whose teachings espoused fervent fulfillment of the law and joyous piety. The hasidic movement may be said to have crystallized when groups of the ultraorthodox separated themselves from established congregations (and

---

[1] To ease the cankers of illness and poverty, the folk often turned to the ministrations of baale shem, "masters of the Name." The baale shem were said to perform wonders because of their knowledge of the secret names of God. They were healers and prognosticators; they gave blessings and amulets, promised insurance against fire and other ills, and, as masters of Kabbala, exorcised demons. The Baal Shem Tov, whose name was Rabbi Israel ben Eliezer, began his career as a baal shem in the Carpathian provinces of Podolia and Volhynia. He was said to be distinguished by his very name, the Baal Shem Tov, from the host of baale shem who lacked his holiness. Concerning the baale shem and the use of the Name, see Dubnow, *History*, 1: 202–3; Aeścoly-Weintraub, "Le hassidisme," in *Introduction à l'étude des hérésies religieuses parmi les Juifs*, p. 24; Trachtenberg, *Jewish Magic and Superstition*, pp. 52–53. For early tales concerning the Besht's use of holy names, see *In Praise of the Besht*, nos. 20, 231; concerning his use of amulets, see no. 107. Regarding the name Baal Shem Tov, see Buber, *Tales*, 1: 11–12; Newman and Spitz, *Hasidic Anthology*, p. xiii. There may have been others for whom the term Baal Shem Tov was used. See Scholem, "Baal Shem," *Encyclopaedia Hebraica*, 9: 263–64.

25

from other pietists who were, to use Scholem's term, "crypto-Sabbatian in character"),[2] and followed the Besht and his disciples, the Rebbes (or tsaddikim, righteous men), rather than the ritually ordained rabbis and established community leaders. Largely through the efforts of Rabbi Dov Baer, who assumed the leadership of the movement after the death of the Besht, and other disciples, Hasidism developed particular beliefs, social forms, and rituals.

The core of hasidic faith has been said to consist in their belief that the presence of God permeates and sustains all living matter and in the intense enthusiasm that they impart to their every action.[3] (The Hebrew word "hasidim" means "pious ones"—those who are especially dedicated to fulfilling the divinely appointed laws.[4]) The scope of hasidic devotion extended to all aspects of life, infusing holiness in work, in eating, and in social intercourse. To recapture the fire of their devotion each time that they prayed, the hasidim made the hours of prayer more flexible. The services of the cantor, so important in the large synagogues, were dispensed with and any righteous man could be called on to lead the services. Believing it to be a more perfect vehicle for prayer, the hasidim popularized the use of the Sefardic liturgy (with the modifications made by the sixteenth-century kabbalist Rabbi Isaac Luria) in place of the more standard Ashkenazi liturgy. Aspects of the ritual, such as the purificatory powers of the mikveh for men, assumed special significance. Dancing too was conceived of as service to the Almighty, a form of prayer. As a symbol of their passion for God, hasidic men danced joyfully every Shabbes rather than only on the Festival of the Law.

In the wake of their emphasis on other forms of divine service, talmudic learning, long the yardstick of piety, diminished somewhat in importance. One must add, however, that hasidic learning involved mystical revelation—the inspired Rebbe was believed able to penetrate more deeply into the text than was the dry rabbinical scholar (T3). Whereas the rabbi searched the text to establish the

[2] See Scholem, *Major Trends*, p. 331.

[3] See Scholem, *Major Trends*, pp. 347–48; Schechter, *Studies in Judaism*, p. 167. More explicitly, hasidic devotion is expressed in the doctrines of *kavana* (concentration toward God), *devekut* (communion with God), and *hitlahavut* (purifying fire). For discussion of these doctrines see Scholem, *Major Trends*, pp. 335–36; Minkin, *Romance of Hassidism*, pp. 92–95; Buber, *Hasidism and Modern Man*, pp. 74–125; J. G. Weiss, "The Kavvanoth of Prayer in Early Hasidism," *The Journal of Jewish Studies*, 9 (1958): 163–92.

[4] See Jacobs, "The Concept of Hasid in the Biblical and Rabbinic Literatures," *The Journal of Jewish Studies*, 8 (1957): 143–54.

weight and reason of the law, the Rebbe's exegesis provided a way of life.

A major source of the mystic faith of the hasidim was to be found in the Lurianic Kabbala, esoteric learning which the six-teenth-century mystics had meant for only a select few. The hasi-dim, however, in an outpouring of religious emotion, sowed kab-balistic mysteries among the population; equally as important, they transformed the role of the isolated mystic into that of community leader. The youthful mystic might for a time isolate himself, but he would emerge prepared to be a *Rebbe*—a leader of the people. One tale of Reb Mikhel of Zlochev relates that immediately after his wedding "for three years he was in solitude, and his food was delivered through a window. After three years he came out and he was a Rebbe" (T11).

The acceptance of Hasidism and the new wonder-workers was far from universal. The misnagdim, those who upheld the accepted rabbinic and community structure, considered hasidic innovations to be dangerous and even heretical. The adulation of the Rebbes and the lessened value of scholarship and learning seemed to strike at the very heart of orthodoxy. The conversion to Christianity in 1759 of Jacob Frank, the heir of Sabbatai Zevi's charisma, under-lined the danger of any deviation.[5] Bitter disputes broke out be-tween the opposing groups of hasidim and misnagdim which re-sulted for a time in the condemnation and excommunication of the hasidic movement. Within two generations of the inception of

[5] In the century before, Sabbatai Zevi, the false messiah, had been proclaimed the redeemer, but Zevi had disillusioned most of his followers by converting to the Moslem faith in 1666, the year prophesized that the Redemption would take place. Some, however, had remained faithful to him, and there was a renaissance of Sabbatianism under Jacob Frank (1726–91) contemporaneous with the emergence of Hasidism. Frank, like the Baal Shem Tov, had been born in Podolia. He lived among Sabbatians in Turkey from 1752 to 1755. Upon his return to Podolia, Frank initiated his followers into Sabbatian doctrines (these included the concept of a trinity consisting of God, the Meshiah, and the Shekhina, who was the female figure of the trinity; the major departure from Jewish thought was the belief that the Meshiah had already come in the person of Sabbatai Zevi). He was de-nounced to the authorities by orthodox Jews and in turn he denounced his opponents. In 1759, after a series of public debates with orthodox Jews, the Frankists were called on to prove their assertion that their doctrines were akin to those of Christianity, and in the following year the Frankists were converted to the Catholic faith, with King Augustus III acting as Frank's godfather. See Dubnow, *History*, 1: 211–20. Although Scholem has estab-lished ties between the early hasidim and secret Sabbatians, in later tradition, the Besht's death was seen as the result of his struggle with the forces of Sabbatai Zevi. See *In Praise of the Besht*, no. 247. In one account, the Besht detects a foul odor emanating from a book concerning Sabbatai Zevi (H4).

Hasidism, however, the disciples of the Besht and Rabbi Dov Baer
had won over a great portion of eastern European Jewry.

In the later stages of Hasidism, each hasidic group evolved into
a dynastic court (hoyf), comprising the Rebbe and his followers.[6]
As the Rebbe's power was inherited by his sons, in succeeding
generations the number of Rebbes multiplied and dynastic courts
were established in villages and towns throughout eastern and
central Europe. These courts were often like self-sufficient manors,
with their own artisans, storekeepers, and ritual slaughterers. The
name of the village or town became the identifying name of the
court and of the Rebbe as well (e.g., the village of Bobov—the
Bobover Rebbe). The centers of court life were the besmedresh
(the house of study and prayer) and the Rebbe's house. The
court's economic life depended largely on the business and the
donations derived from the Rebbe's visitors. Each court too had a
corpus of oral tradition testifying to the holiness and profound
power of their Rebbe. Although a basic core of law and teachings
united all the courts, some differences in philosophy and practice
were inevitable. Some courts became famous for their talmudic
learning, their system of mysticism, their majesty, their vigorous
prayer, their restraint, or perhaps their refusal to concede a single
point to the changing times. In subsequent generations the circle of
influence of each dynasty centered in a particular region (for
example: Ger in Poland; Lubavitch, Karlin-Stolin, and Rizhyn in
Russia; Belz in Galicia; and Sziget in Hungary).

The End of Hasidism in Europe

For over one hundred years the hasidim extended their hold over
eastern and central European Jewry.[7] In the latter half of the
nineteenth century and the beginning of the twentieth century, as
new social movements espousing religious, political, and economic
change gained strength in Europe, the hasidic movement entered
into a losing struggle against these new Hellenisms. The hasidim

[6] For a description of court life, see Zborowski, and Herzog, *Life Is with
People*, pp. 166–88.

[7] Simon Dubnow, the outstanding historian of Hasidism, records four
major epochs in the history of the hasidic movement: 1. origins (1740–81);
2. growth and expansion (1782–1815); 3. the strengthening of tsaddikism
and the struggle against enlightenment (1815–70); 4. decline (1870 until
contemporary times). *Geschichte des Chassidismus*, 1: 69–70.

sensed the danger of the growing Zionist movement and of the swell of immigration to the New World, for both augured the death of orthodox law and custom. Emigration, worker's movements, secular schools, and new intellectual ideas drew away the sons of the hasidim. Attacked earlier by the misnagdim as despoilers of the law, the hasidim came to be considered by those of the haskala, the enlightenment, as fanatics absurdly clinging to outmoded customs and superstitions. The hasidic world was further disrupted by World War I, which made a battleground of hasidic villages and uprooted many courts.[8]

Despite the changes in the environment the religious way of life persisted. Jewish life in eastern Europe continued in many ways to be semiautonomous and self-contained.

In the old country there was the community life, there was a kehilleh [community]. As in our town, so it was in every other town. And this kehilleh was in charge of all the public things. Like the cemetery. It belonged to the community. Somebody died, God forbid, he had to settle with the kehilleh. Somebody wanted to get married, he had to get a certificate from the kehilleh. A child was born, he had to get a certificate from the kehilleh. Everything had to go through this kehilleh. The people, the members of this kehilleh, were elected by votes. And there was a president and vice-president and secretary. It was like a little government. And this kehilleh was responsible to the government, to the city hall, for things, and they worked together. And this kehilleh had the right to tell you how much tax you had to pay to the community. To the Jewish community, I'm talking about. For example, they said that this man had to pay so much a year to the kehilleh. The kehilleh paid the Rabbi, they paid the shohtim, they supported Talmud Torahs, they maintained the mikveh—all the general things which belonged to the city.*

The larger centers for study and prayer, the besmedresh (house of study) of the hasidim and the Beit ha-Kneset (synagogue) of the misnagdim, were also supported by the kehilleh. The social matrix of the hasidic community, however, often depended on the smaller shtibl, the room or hall that served as the center for prayer and learning.

[In our town] the shtibl was never closed. The doors were always open twenty-four hours a day. Whenever you came into the shtibl you always found people, starting from thirteen-year-old boys up to eighty-

---

[8] For an account of the court of Belz during World War I see Langer, *Nine Gates to the Chassidic Mysteries.*

* Material quoted from interviews is marked by an asterisk (*).

year-old men. You would always find people learning, davening, talking, and even sometimes eating together in a group, wash together and
eat together, and then, while eating, talk about hasides. So this is what
a shtibl is like. It was not a yeshiveh, but you'll find many many great
scholars who never went to a yeshiveh, and who came out from those
shtiblekh.

A shtibl . . . I don't know how to describe it . . . it was . . . most
of the people that I knew, if you would ask him which is your home,
which do you consider where you really feel that you belong, I would
say that, I can't quote percentages, but quite quite a big, big percentage
would say that the shtibl, this is the home, this is the home. And
the house? All right you have to go home to eat something, I mean. But
the home—where he feels himself that *this is where I belong*—was the
shtibl. I recall that in wintertime there were many many nights that
my father did not come home. He used to stay in shtibl. He was
learning. He was dozing off a little, and talking, but most of the time he
was learning. He used to stay in shtibl, period. All night. Yes, I
remember it. And he used to come home to his supper content. He used
to have a piece of bread, a plate of kasha. This was his supper and back
he went to the shtibl.*

If religion remained the hasid's anchor to life, his economic
status often left him floating between heaven and earth.

My father did quite a few things but he did not make a living,
unfortunately. At one time, I must have been very little, but I remember that he was a merchant. He did not have a store on a street. There
was a big market—an open market where people used to come with
their stands and display their merchandise. And all the farmers from
around the city used to come in. At the same time they used to sell their
products that they brought into town, like chickens, butter, cream,
ducks—farm products. They used to bring in potatoes with a horse and
wagon. In wintertime, they also used to bring in a certain kind of stuff
that you use to warm up the house. We used to call it in Polish "torf."
It is earth, dried-out earth. They used to bring this in and at the same
time they used to buy stuff that they needed. Most of the merchants, as
far as I remember, were Jews. They used to sell to the farmers. And
my father had a stand. He had a stand with goods. Material, like
remnants, and they used to buy it by the yard. My mother was more the
business lady than my father. Even though my father used to do the
buying. He used to go to Warsaw to bring the merchandise. But as far
as selling, I would say that my mother was more like the saleslady. My
father was the buyer. But this did not work out. I don't know why, but
they had given it up.

Then he used to sell tickets. In Poland the government had a legal

lottery. So he used to go around selling those tickets. And he used to
split them. Most were poor people who could not afford to buy a whole
ticket by themselves; he used to sell a quarter to this person, a quarter
to this person. And each one had a quarter, if this number won. Say
there were four people, it would make it easier to sell. On Sukkes night
he dealt with esroygim [a type of citrus fruit]. Before Passover he dealt
with matseh shmireh [guarded matseh]. He used to sell the flour. They
used to cut the wheat, they used to bring it into the mills to have it
ground, and they used to sell it to the hasidim because the hasidim
mostly used metseh shmireh for Pesakh.[9] Each family went to a matseh
bakery and stood by the baking process, and how many pounds he
needed he took home. Most ate shmireh, but for the family they used
plain matses. So before they started to bake the plain matses they used
to bake a couple of pounds of shmireh for themselves. And so he sold
the shmireh flour.

Well he was a shadkhen [matchmaker] too. I remember him talking
to the parents of one fellow, to the parents of the girl. People used to
come into the house and discuss things and sometimes I remember even
that he had to go out of town to talk.

But from all this he did not have enough to support his family. You
shouldn't think that the whole town was poor. As I say, my father
happened, unfortunately, he happened to be poor. There were quite a
few rich people too.

We [parents and five children] lived in one room. We lived in a
three-story house and we had one room. About three families lived
there. Some other families I think had two rooms. We had one room
because we were living downstairs. The front was a store, and in the
back was a room. There were two beds. There was like a wooden
couch. By day it used to be used like a bench; at night you took off the
top and put straw sacks and we used to sleep. And there was another
big bed, I think, we opened like a folding bed. There were two beds for
the parents. And with each parent some of the children slept too. There
was a stove which you had to light with coal. It was like built from
bricks. We had enough potatoes, potato soup, potatoes and bread.
Meat—we couldn't afford to eat meat. Occasionally mother used to buy
some liver which was cheap. In Europe liver or lungs—this was the
cheap cut. Herring, a piece of herring, bread. Chicken was for the rich
people.

I remember many times that my mother, when she got a loaf of
bread, she used to first take off a piece of bread and hide it from my

[9] Although Jews are enjoined to eat matseh during Passover, they also
eat at the seder on Passover eve a portion of matseh shmireh. This is matseh
which is guarded from the time the wheat is cut (to protect it from damp-
ness) through the baking process (to ensure that it does not leaven). The
poor could usually afford only six pieces of this matseh, three pieces to be
used at each of the seders.

father. Otherwise, if she wouldn't have done it, nothing would be left, because he surely would have eaten up the whole loaf of bread.*

The center of hasidic life remained focused on the absorption of the traditional learning of the past. The sons of the poor and the well-to-do went to the yeshiveh to study.

When I was ten years old [in 1909] I was sent to Lubavitch in the state of Mogilev in White Russia. Lubavitch is situated in the plains. It is a city near fertile land—black earth. My father had a grocery store which he took care of in the winter. The rest of the year my mother took care of the store. My father was in charge of loggers. They floated logs down the Dnieper to the Black Sea to Kiev, Odessa. He left in the beginning of spring and came back at the end of summer. I attended Lubavitch [yeshiveh from] 1909 to 1912. The Rebbe had one son and on Friday night he would have the son face him and he would tell his hasides. Later he would talk to the students. There were scores of students. On Friday night you're not allowed to write and we would repeat it until we knew it by heart. On Saturday night one would talk and the others would criticize the memorizers.

I slept at a house with ten lodgers. My father paid no tuition but he paid for the room and gave me some money. We used to have eating days. We would go to three or four homes to eat. My cousin was starving to death. His father was a poor teacher, and my cousin was so timid I had to go out and get him eating days. He had three, and when I left I gave him four and so he was eating seven days.*

Three decades later, in 1939, just before the outbreak of World War II, the picture was precisely the same.

All the yeshives took in poor people without any money. I don't think my father ever paid tuition. Because when I first started to go to school it was like a Talmud Torah. It belonged to the city, the community, and the community supported it. And of course those who could afford it I guess paid tuition. But from poor children they did not take. They couldn't take, even if they wanted to. In the shtibl there was no tuition, there were no expenses. When you became older and you studied by yourself, there was no tuition again. The yeshives that I went to did not have any kitchens. All the boys who studied there from out of town used to eat every day in a different house. Essen tag—eating days. Monday you eat with this man, Tuesday with this man. Some of them, some men make you feel like at home. It wasn't a question so much of the food. It was the way they treated you, the way they accepted you when you came into the house, the way they made you feel.

I remember one family who happen to be now in Israel. They are quite old, and they were exceptionally nice to me. The man, when I knew him, was among the most beloved people in this town. First, he was a rich man. Second, he was very good-hearted. He always did favors for the poor; he always worked for the poor people, raising money, giving them some money. He was very lovely. Talking to him just made you feel good. He was a smart man. He had married his second wife when I started to eat with them. She was sort of a relative to him. She was a very poor girl, as I understand, and when he became a widower, she married him. And she was also as kind as he was. In fact they had a maid in the house. But she always made sure, the woman, that she used to be present when I came in to eat, and make sure that I'm getting the right treatment. They really made me feel at home. They were very, very friendly. It's quite a few years. This was in 1939 in this town of K. And it is a miracle that those two are alive now and are now residing in Israel. In fact, I do send money occasionally to them to help them out. And I wrote them once that, "I don't know if you remember," I wrote them, "but this is from a man who used to eat in your house one day a week, and it was one of my best days, in your house." *

Undoubtedly, hasidic life in Europe would have remained essentially the same for generations to come had it not been for the Nazi invasion.

The first day of Rosh Hashoneh I remember the Rabbi of the town and a group of Jews went to look for the Jews who were killed from the German bombs and were still lying under the houses. They were trying to take them out and bury them according to the Jewish law. The Rabbi announced that you were not allowed to daven in any shul on Rosh Hashoneh. He wouldn't allow any Jews to daven before we took care of those people who were buried underneath the houses. And that day already the Germans took all the group, and the Rabbi and my father were among them, and they took them to the market, and it was a big market, and they cut off their beards on one side of their faces to make it look awful. And they beat them. The Rabbi's clothes, I remember, they took off his clothes, rabbinical clothes, traditional, and they put it on one of the laymen. And they changed clothes—just to make him look ridiculous. And then they took his hat, his shtraiml, his Shabbes hat, a fur hat, and they collected garbage in it. And then the troubles began. *

The hasidic world of eastern Europe ended in the death camps.

As we were very near the German border, we were affected right away. The Germans came to our town on the second day of the war. It's hard to explain. It was like the world turned over. There was such a big difference from one day, from hour to an hour. They came right away with guns ready to shoot. We were hiding in the cellar. Then we went upstairs. The Germans were in town so we went upstairs already. We had a little coffee. Right away they wanted to shoot us. They didn't care, they were just barbaric. And we didn't understand this. Why were they going to shoot us? What did we do to them? We were pleading, you see, you know, no guns or nothing. We're just innocent people. And we felt right away that something is going to happen. We should have run away maybe. We were very wrong to stay. But we heard right away that they were going so fast. Later on we saw that there was no use in running away; they took over all of Poland in a few days.

So we stayed and then the trouble started. Gradually they started pushing us closer together. First, you were not allowed to live on this street, in this street, and not in this street. Then they made a ghetto. We moved on a back street, somewhere on a back street. They put two or three families together in one apartment. First they took away the store. My father had to go to work cleaning the streets. Everybody had to work for them.

The first week they shot my cousin. And they made up a story that the Polish army killed a German, and they took two people, a gentile and a Jew. And they shot them in the middle of the street because somebody killed one of them. You couldn't shoot at them. I mean, it scared the people.

On a Sunday they took my father to a camp to work. We knew at the beginning what camp, D., a German town. They took him away and we didn't hear from him anymore. From the beginning they didn't want people to get scared. They made it sound like only working camps. Your father will come home. They wanted people shouldn't be against it. Slowly, slowly they took us away.

And then one night they took all the Jews. They took us all away. We had a very good hiding place in our house under the stairs. So we all went to the hiding place. Three days we were there without bread, without water even. And then my mother said that she heard that nobody was there, no more Jews. So me and my cousin, a girl, we went out separately. Of course we knew that all together they would take us to Auschwitz to get burned. So they thought maybe we, as young people, would be taken to a labor camp. I remember how my mother was crying. Maybe she will see me, we told each other under the stairs lying there. She kisses me and she hopes maybe we'll see each other once more. And we went out and they took me to a labor camp. And a day later I heard from other people my mother went out from the hiding place and they took her to Auschwitz.

I was very young then. I was one of the youngest kids in the camp. Maybe my body didn't ask for so much for food. You see I was used to it. I didn't eat too much. Some other people, stronger people, their bodies needed more food. They couldn't take it. They broke. I was frail and didn't eat so much and sometimes they had pity on me, even more pity since I was very young.

I worked very hard. I liked it. Nobody chased me, but I did my day's work very honestly. There was a law that when you saw a soldier you had to greet him, take off your hat. And I didn't see the soldier, a German soldier. I didn't greet him. He came over to me. Why didn't I greet him? I thought, it's bad, already it's bad. I fell to my knees. I begged him. "You see I'm working very hard and I didn't see you." It was no excuse. He didn't want no excuse. He took my number. Everybody had a number—no name. He took my number off and he'll report me to the head of the camp. And it came in the night they call out my name and a few more, and they gave us to the straf [punishment] commander. There were special guys—kapos. If somebody did wrong, they took care of these people in the night. Instead of going home to eat, they took you to the barracks to eat, away to the side, out on the fields, and they gave you such a lesson nobody came home afterwards. In this camp the kapos were mostly Polish, mixed with Russians and Jews. You had to pay for your sin. Special payments for your wrong doing. Special people had special murderers. And they called us, five or six Jews, and they called us out. They started to give us pushups, and ran us around, and hit us with sticks. What I went through in two hours it's impossible to imagine. I was the youngest. I thought if somebody said, go left, run left, jump. I was always the first. I took their attention off of me a little bit. And this little bit of attention, how much I got hit . . . you still got hit, somebody instead of right, he went left. And I knew that this was my last chance to stay alive. So I put all my mind to it I should follow very fast and do everything right. They see I did everything so exact and right. How much I got hit I still didn't get as much as other people. And I survived. I came home. The others didn't come home anymore. The rest didn't survive. They took them to the hospital or they finished them off. They hit them with sticks. They beat them to death. I came home to the barracks to sleep. They gave me a double portion of soup because I stayed alive, because I came home. I was the first one to get a double portion of soup. "You survived," he said, "another portion of soup." This was the prize. A double portion of soup meant to me like a hundred thousand dollars today.

After the war, you see we hoped right after the war the Jews would find better conditions to live. After the war we were very much disappointed. You see I forgot all religion then. I was not religious at all. I was so young that I forgot about everything, forgot even the aleph bes. I forgot everything completely. So much trouble, so many beatings. I forgot everything. I didn't know what I was already.

Then we wanted to go home, to go home to see the home town once more, to see if something was left over in memories, some pictures maybe from our parents. You know, everybody saw some memories.

Maybe a relative was left over, maybe someone hid himself in the town. You know.

I went home to C., maybe I'll find some relatives. And there I saw it was no use. You see, we thought in the camp when we come out at least people would greet us in our home town. Give us back our belongings, our houses, our businesses. There were so few Jews left over. I was afraid to mention I'm a Jew then, understand? And I saw it was no good. I couldn't even go up to my apartment. I went to the first floor to our house and I sat down and started crying on the steps. I . . . I . . . couldn't walk up. We lived on the second floor. I couldn't walk up to see my apartment. I couldn't, I couldn't see it anymore. I couldn't and I ran away. I sat on the steps and was crying. And I didn't walk up any more to see the apartment. I ran away to Cracow. It was the same troubles—nothing to eat, nowhere to sleep, nowhere to go. We heard already the Polish people started killing Jews again, pogroms and everything the same thing it used to be before. They hate us again. We got very disappointed. So, I was very young. I ran away on the train.

In Italy I saw the Rebbe for a very short time, maybe only a few minutes. I still didn't feel right after I came to Italy. I was sick then. It's very hard when your mind is so occupied with eating, with sickness. You are still running away. You are happy to see a face; you are very happy. But it was still the war though it was even '46–'47. We were still not free to think about these things, not so free as now. I felt closer and closer to the Rebbe. He knew my family very well. He didn't know me, but he knew my family. He was very happy that he saw me. He said he was coming to America, and he'll send me papers. And a friend of mine also went to America, and he reminded him. And this way he sent me papers and I came to America. He brought me over to his yeshiveh.

I was a very young fellow. I was maybe nineteen when I came to America. When the Rebbe sent for me I felt not only like I have a relative behind me—I have a father behind me. I was missing a family life. Somebody who cares about me. Not only spiritual, but physical. I have somebody who thinks that I'm alive. Somebody wants me to be near him. I'm still a human being. This point itself felt very good. Somebody sends for me. Somebody knows I'm not lost. Somebody wants to keep the name of the family alive, still remembers my family. I felt that I have a home.*

II THE SETTLEMENT OF THE
NEW YORK COMMUNITY

The hasidic Jews who survived the war made their way across Europe to Israel and to the United States. Some hasidic Jews settled in London and in Montreal, but for most Jerusalem and Benei Brak in Israel and Brooklyn, New York, became the end of the European exodus.

A number of the important surviving Rebbes served as the heart of the new settlements: the Satmarer Rebbe and the Klausenberger Rebbe took up residence in Williamsburg, the Lubavitcher Rebbe and the Bobover Rebbe moved to Crown Heights, and the Stoliner Rebbe settled in Boro Park. Some hasidim also moved to the older Jewish settlement on Manhattan's Lower East Side, where such Rebbes as the Boyaner had resided for over three decades. Most hasidim maintained their loyalty to their Rebbe, or to the heirs of the rabbinic dynasty; in some cases, where the court had been virtually wiped out or where the center was in Israel, new allegiances were formed. Some hasidim, without a Rebbe, formed independent shtiblekh of their own, and while they visited one Rebbe or other from time to time, they did not maintain any firm bonds. In all, the hasidim say that about forty courts, many of them numbering less than fifty families, began to function in the metropolitan area.

The arrival of the hasidim in the forties and fifties differed from previous settlements of hasidic Jews in America. Although hasidic Jews had been part of the earlier waves of immigration to America in the last century, for the most part they had come as individuals, leaving behind their Rebbe and the majority of the court. As most Rebbes had remained in Europe during this earlier period, the focal point of hasidic life had been missing. Many customs practiced with strict regularity in Europe were slowly discarded. In time orthodox Jewish women in New York gave up wearing shaitlekh (wigs), which in Europe had served to mark Jewish women since the Middle Ages; few women continued to attend the mikveh, and the number of mikyes decreased. Only a small percentage of children persisted in wearing yarmelkehs. Instead of attending the yeshiveh, most children went to a secular school during the day and at best enrolled for an hour's work each afternoon in a Talmud Torah, where the rigorous learning of the yeshiveh was lost. The curricula of those yeshives that remained changed to include secular subjects and even sports. The children were gradually absorbed into the secular world, and by the nineteen thirties orthodox congregations had slipped away, leaving only shrinking pockets of orthodoxy in the city's Jewish ghettos.

To keep their religious beliefs intact and to survive as a community the new hasidic immigrants were aware that they had to counter the acculturating pressures that had reshaped the lives of the earlier immigrants.

Williamsburg, Crown Heights, and Boro Park

The hasidim of Williamsburg settled in the midst of an older religious community composed of German, Austrian, Czech, and Polish Jews who had fled Europe when Hitler came to power.[1] The older community was orthodox, but most followed the more restrained western European pattern of dress and worship. There was but one mikveh for the entire community and few of the women wore wigs. Except for the rabbis, most of the men were clean-shaven. Their children studied in the yeshiveh, but they often continued on into one of the city colleges as well.

Although the hasidim who came to Williamsburg were members of a number of separate courts from different parts of eastern Europe and were sometimes sharply divided on points of belief, practice, and the personality of their leadership, they were united in their desire to maintain the integrity of the community, and they formed a rapidly expanding core of extreme orthodoxy. The hasi-

[1] George Kranzler's *Williamsburg, A Jewish Community in Transition* is a prime source in this work for information concerning the Williamsburg community before the arrival of the hasidim and during the first years of the hasidic settlement.

dim of Williamsburg were numerically dominated by those of
Hungarian origin who formed the Satmar and the Klausenberg
courts. The Satmarer hasidim acquired an old mansion on Bedford
Avenue for their use as a besmedresh; the Klausenberger hasidim
converted the last movie operating on Lee Avenue into a besmedresh (and the Rebbe's residence as well).[2] Other less populous
courts converted a number of small houses, rooms, and cellars into
shtiblekh. The hasidim came to form the majority in several blocks
of the brownstone houses in the neighborhood. Hasidim opened
stores on Lee Avenue, the main business artery, drawing business
away from older established retailers. Three additional mikves
were built.[3] Hungarian and Yiddish became the common languages
of the street. As hasidic influence intensified, many previous residents found the atmosphere too confining and moved elsewhere.[4]
Some members of the older community who remained adopted the
new standards, and the sons of the clean-shaven Williamsburg
residents began to grow beards.[5] By 1951, on many streets in
Williamsburg, it became difficult to catch sight of a young boy
who was not wearing a yarmelkeh and peyes or a woman who was
not wearing a shaitl.[6] The trend toward acculturation had been
sharply reversed.

Despite their rapid and initially successful resettlement, the
hasidic community in Williamsburg is still in the process of adjust-
ment. Since the first influx the neighborhood has undergone considerable change. In 1954 construction of the Brooklyn-Queens
expressway through Williamsburg replaced ten blocks of housing
in the center of the hasidic settlement. A low-cost housing project
displaced other families and further ate into the continuity of the
neighborhood. Some Rebbes also decided to move. In 1957 the
Squarer Rebbe moved from Williamsburg to the newly founded
village of New Square in Spring Valley, and late in 1959 the
Klausenberger Rebbe left for Israel with a few close adherents.[7]
(Both Rebbes, however, left the majority of their followers be-

---

[2] This took place in 1951. See *ibid.*, p. 29.

[3] *Ibid.*, p. 133.

[4] *Ibid.*, p. 120.

[5] *Ibid.*, p. 134.

[6] Kranzler observed that as early as 1951 on one block only three children
remained who did not wear skullcaps, and the parents of these children had
made plans to move away (*ibid.*, p. 111).

[7] "Hasidic leader moves to Israel," *New York Times*, Jan. 3, 1960.
Approximately fifteen families from the court have joined the Rebbe in
Israel; most of these families left with the Rebbe in 1959. In 1967 one
family of the court migrated to Israel.

hind.) Adding to the sense of instability, the Satmarer hasidim, who are the core of the Williamsburg settlement, began to consider a plan to develop a community near Newark, New Jersey.

More recently, however, Williamsburg has shown signs of maintaining its religious population. The Satmarer hasidim have not moved and have indicated that they would prefer to remain in Williamsburg.[8] While the city housing projects tore out significant sections of the older housing, arrangements were finally worked out to rent apartments on the lower floors of the project to orthodox Jews (so that they could use the stairs on the Shabbes) and to provide the houses with fully automatic elevators. In addition to those still residing in the old brownstones, some six hundred orthodox families, including hasidim and misnagdim, are now housed in the two city projects in the center of Williamsburg, and still other families have moved to another housing project nearby.[9]

The other hasidic settlements, in Brooklyn's Crown Heights and Boro Park, less populous than Williamsburg, developed into hasidic centers more slowly. The largest and most influential court in Crown Heights is that of Lubavitch, a court formerly in Russia. The besmedresh and the yeshiveh of the Lubavitcher hasidim have been located at 770 Eastern Parkway since 1940 when the Lubavitcher Rebbe arrived in the United States. The court's growth can be traced back fifteen years earlier when Rabbi Jacobson, one of the Rebbe's adherents, emigrated to America and began to develop a strong following for Lubavitch. The number of Lubavitcher hasidim who took up residence in the middle-class apartment houses and once elegant homes in Crown Heights was gradually swelled by those who trickled in from behind the Iron Curtain as well as by American students attracted to Lubavitch. When the Rebbe died in 1950, his son-in-law, who succeeded him, became the leader of an expanding court with an entrenched American tradition.

In recent years the racial pattern in Crown Heights has shifted and many of the older white residents have relocated elsewhere. The Lubavitcher hasidim, on the other hand, seem determined to remain. They have enlarged their besmedresh twice within the past five years and anticipate further expansion in the future in the building adjoining their yeshiveh.

The Bobover hasidim, who were originally located in Galicia,

[8] Weinberger, "The Miracle of Williamsburg," *The Jewish Observer*, 2: (1965): 18.
[9] *Ibid.*, p. 19.

settled near Lubavitch, on the opposite side of Eastern Parkway. The Bobover Rebbe, who had spent the war in a concentration camp, moved to Brooklyn Avenue, and his hasidim rented apartments near the besmedresh and yeshiveh. Few of the Bobover's followers had survived the war, but the court was increased by displaced persons from other courts whom the Rebbe was helping to resettle. The Bobover hasidim constructed a new school building with the intention of remaining in Crown Heights; the increase in the crime rate, however, encouraged them to sell the building to the city and initiate plans to move away. They purchased several acres in Flushing, Queens, where they intended to develop housing and industry for two hundred families. Zoning laws, however, forced them to abandon the project.[10] During 1966–67 the Rebbe and most of the court relocated in Boro Park, a quiet Brooklyn neighborhood of apartment houses and two-family homes. The older inhabitants of Boro Park are first and second generation Italians and Jews; the neighborhood has more recently attracted hasidim displaced from Williamsburg and Crown Heights. In June, 1967, a new Bobov yeshiveh and a besmedresh were opened a half block from the Rebbe's residence on forty-eighth street.

The Stoliner hasidim, another court earlier located in Russia, were among the first to settle in Boro Park. The Stoliner hasidim brought their Rebbe to Boro Park from Israel, where he had gone after his release from a concentration camp. The court is largely composed of American-born young men, some of whom are the sons of Stoliner hasidim who had emigrated to the New World earlier in the century, and a few older hasidim who had lived in Stolin. Until this year their besmedresh and yeshiveh consisted of two reconstructed stores on Sixteenth Avenue, with living quarters for students above. They are now building a larger yeshiveh in Boro Park. A besmedresh and a yeshiveh are also maintained in Williamsburg.

Boro Park promises to rival Williamsburg as the center of hasidic life in America. The neighborhood is undergoing a period of rapid change. Yeshives and synagogues are being constructed, real estate prices have spiraled, and apartments and houses are at a premium.

[10] Ground-breaking ceremonies for this Queens project were held on June 27, 1965. The court was then trying to raise two million dollars to build the besmedresh and school. Each member of the court was taxed one thousand dollars; other fund raising devices were to be used to raise the remainder of the money. The homes were to have been privately financed and privately owned.

The growth of the courts has continued so that at present the hasidim estimate that they number between 40,000 and 50,000 in New York City. The individual courts range in membership from over 1,300 families in one court (Satmar) to several courts of between 100 and 500 families (Stolin, Bobov, Klausenberg, and Lubavitch). Many other courts are still smaller. It is difficult to ascertain the exact membership within each court, and it is virtually impossible to estimate the total membership since branches of the court have congregations not only in different neighborhoods but also in Israel, Canada, England, South America, and behind the Iron Curtain.[11] Moreover, definitions of membership and allegiance vary. Each court has a core of followers who emulate the Rebbe in dress and outlook. They spend as much time as possible near him, absorbing his teachings and attitudes and functioning as dedicated disciples. They share in the responsibilities for the besmedresh and the yeshiveh. Each court also counts a number of admirers who do not partake fully of the community life but may tender financial support and usually seek the Rebbe's counsel and his blessing. But the numbers of those influenced by hasidic beliefs far exceeds the actual membership of the courts. The hasidim, by their strict adherence to orthodox law and custom, have already significantly affected the larger contemporary Jewish community.

Some hasidic courts continue to think of the possibility of forming independent, self-contained communities, insulated from the modern world. The implications of this step warrant a close look at New Square, the first attempt to found a hasidic village in America.

---

[11] On January 3, 1960, the *New York Times* reported that the Klausenberger Rebbe was the leader "of some 3,000 Hassidic Jews in the United States" alone; some days earlier (Dec. 21, 1959), the *New York Herald Tribune* stated that the Klausenberger Rebbe "is believed to have about 650 followers in New York, Montreal, and Mexico City." So far as the entire community is concerned, on November 6, 1963, the *New York Times* reported speaking "to a chief spokesman for the Brooklyn Hasidic community, which has 15,000 families and is the largest settlement outside of Israel." On October 30, 1967, the *New York Times* noted: "The Lubavitcher Rebbe is Menachem M. Schneerson, who as the rabbi of rabbis is the leader of an estimated total of 250,000 people, the world's largest Hasidic group." Hasidic leaders are usually ambiguous on such matters. The Lubavitcher Rebbe, asked the number of his followers, replied: "How many Jews are there in the world?" Weiner, "The Lubavitcher Movement I," *Commentary*, 23 (1957): 232. Poll estimated the Hasidic community of Williamsburg to number between ten and twelve thousand in 1959. *Hasidic Community*, p. 30.

New Square

New Square is a suburban village of 126 families (as of 1967) located in the Rockland County Township of Ramapo, two miles west of Spring Valley. It is an hour and a quarter drive from the center of New York City. In 1954, when the original organizers purchased 130 acres, their goal was to establish a community of hasidic Jews under the leadership of the Squarer Rebbe. New Square promised that the residents could partake of a completely religious life free from the temptations, distractions, and dangers of the city. Their children would grow up in a protected island of orthodoxy "away from the goyim and the half-Jew." Initially the men would have to travel to the city to work but eventually they planned to develop shops and small industries within the village. Building multiple garden apartments would reduce the price of the land and enable the developers to charge low rents. With these inducements the community could then expand and attract more settlers.

Construction of the houses began in 1956, and the first families moved in a year later. By 1958, sixty-eight houses were completed and occupied. At the outset the villagers encountered financial and contractual difficulties, and a lien was placed against the property which prevented the sale of additional plots of ground.[12] The villagers found that the zoning regulations prohibited the establishment of shops and factories or the construction of two-family houses (notwithstanding, the Rebbe's residence and office became two attached houses). Lack of funds halted the completion of the besmedresh, which had been begun in 1957. School facilities soon proved inadequate to handle the growing number of school children. And no one had the time to devote himself wholeheartedly to the management of the community's business affairs. The internal disputes drove out one of the community's chief organizers, who had also been named president.

In the following five years conditions greatly improved. In 1961, the village was incorporated.[13] This meant that the village could petition to rezone and thereby permit the erection of multiple dwellings as well as stores and factories. With the lien lifted,

[12] See Peter Krell's articles in the *Rockland County Leader*, September 17 and 24, 1959.

[13] "Hasidic Jews Win on Forming Rockland Village," *New York Times*, July 14, 1961.

during 1962–63 seven additional houses, some designed for two families, were constructed. Since 1963, ten additional houses have been built, some able to house three families. Although there were business enterprises functioning in the community during its first five years, they are now legally sanctioned. By 1963 New Square had a grocery-bakery and a fish store as well as a display-card printing shop, a cap manufacturer, an electrical contractor, and an engraver. Since then the community has added a butcher, a bookbinder, a wig manufacturer, and two bakers (one who sells bread and cake in New Square and in nearby Monsey, and another who sells cookies wholesale in New York City). At present the stores and workshops are located in the basements of the houses; however, one street in New Square has been zoned for commercial development, and a two-story building is being constructed which will house a half-dozen businesses.

The village has acquired other signs of organization: the school principal serves as town clerk, and one resident, a lawyer with a practice in the city, serves as village judge, a necessary office since the unique character of the community attracts visitors of all sorts—the pious, the curious, and the vindictive. Unfortunately, the besmedresh, which was in use and near final completion, burned down; a new besmedresh is now under construction. The planning board of Rockland County has been several years in formulating a plan for the further development of New Square, although little progress has been reported.

There are still many nagging problems, but the community has demonstrated its ability to survive. By 1963 the community had increased from the original sixty-eight families to eighty-five families with a total population of 620. At that time residents said that only four families had left the village since its founding. In 1967 the number of families had increased to 126, with a total population of 812. (Three families were said to have left the village between 1963 and 1967.) In addition to attracting new residents, the village is also growing from within. The children raised in the village are now reaching maturity, and there were more than ten marriages in the year 1967 alone.

The members of the village are in a sense zealous pioneers. While all the villagers were of course orthodox before they came to New Square, not all were members of a hasidic court. None of the villagers was a follower of the Squarer Rebbe in Europe. They joined the experiment in New Square after becoming attracted to the Squarer Rebbe or to the idea of living in a completely hasidic village.

The structure of the community incorporates features of the Old World and the New World. The Squarer Rebbe is the head of the community and his views temper all decisions affecting village life. He appoints all religious functionaries, but there is also a village mayor and a justice of the peace, and a great many matters affecting village affairs in relation to the township are initiated by someone other than the Rebbe. The besmedresh and the yeshiveh are in large measure dependent on the contributions that the Rebbe attracts, while the economy of the village is tied to New York City, where a large percentage of the residents work. Many of the men ride to the city each morning on an old bus that the community purchased. The bus contains an ark, so that they are able to recite the morning prayers during the trip, and one section of the bus is curtained so that women may ride as well. On its return trip in the morning the bus carries back the city-dwelling followers of the Rebbe who wish to consult him. Each year the Rebbe also spends two to three weeks in Williamsburg, where he is besieged by members of his court. These ties to the city affect the social organization since the residents are less dependent on the community than were villagers in a European shtetl.

Other aspects of the community structure of every hasidic court account for a number of continuing problems. There are a large number of salaried religious functionaries who present a formidable financial burden. Besides the Rebbe himself there are the Rebbe's gabai and his cook, the executive secretary of the yeshiveh, the principal of the yeshiveh, the principal of the girls' school, the rabbi and the assistant rabbi, the shohet, and the fund raiser (the latter receives a salary rather than the customary percentage of money raised). The rosh ha-kohol, the head of the community, the shul, and the mikveh—who is, incidentally, the mayor as well— does not receive a salary, nor do the gaboyim who take care of the besmedresh and arrange the services. The community must also pay the salary of the hasid who drives the bus. There are few people in the village who are not employable (in 1963 one person was retired, one person received welfare because of illness, and one new immigrant was unemployed; in 1967 three other persons received welfare due to illness). Despite its other obligations the village maintains the tradition of encouraging scholars. In 1963 there were five batlonim (scholars, idlers) who spent all of their time studying in New Square. Three were young men, newly married (within the previous three-year period), who were supported by their fathers and/or fathers-in-law (one of these was the Rebbe's son); two were mature men who receive outside support for their continued study. In that same year New Square introduced the practice, common to hasidic courts, of giving newly married men a stipend to enable them to study for a year or two after marriage. In 1967 there are twenty young married men in New Square who receive stipends of thirty to forty dollars a week.

In addition to these continuing expenses, there is a mounting financial deficit because the village, like all hasidic courts, maintains its own school system. The enrollment of 425 requires a staff of thirty-two teachers, seventeen for the girls and fifteen for the boys. Most of the staff are residents of the village and the salaries paid are a severe financial drain. As in European hasidic courts, support for the yeshiveh depends in great measure upon the entire community and on outside contributions rather than on individual tuition fees. In New Square as in all hasidic courts the older students (over sixteen) pay little or nothing; other tuition fees are paid on a sliding scale and some children attend without charge. However, in addition to the funds required to meet the needs of their own community, each family must pay an educational tax to the township of between twenty and twenty-five dollars a month. In sum, New Square is dependent on outside aid, and the structure of the community indicates that this aid will have to continue if the community is to survive.[14]

It is questionable whether there will be other villages of this type. While the Rebbe promises to continue as the unifying force for such communities, as well as an important source of revenue, his talents are not usually those of director or financial wizard. In general, the hasidim have few sophisticated men of the business world who can turn their energies to directing such enterprises. A move to the suburbs means an additional financial burden as well as longer hours spent in traveling. To offset these problems, projected suburban communities would like to develop small industry to employ their people in the village; the question, however, is

[14] Offers of charity have been made because of the established piety of the Rebbe and also because of the nostalgia aroused by the village. Donations helped complete the exterior of the besmedresh in 1960, although the interior had not yet been completely finished at the time of the fire in 1966. A $100,000 donation was given to construct a yeshiveh for boys, and the building was completed in 1963. The same donor gave a similar sum for the girls' school.

whether sufficient industry could be developed. Moreover, it is difficult to convince many hasidim now living in the city that a return to village life would be of benefit to them. Subtle changes have to some extent already taken place. While the hasidim have maintained their religious life in the city, they have been able to cast aside some of the burdens of living under the close scrutiny of village neighbors, as well as the Rebbe, and many would be reluctant to relinquish this liberty. In addition, many American-born hasidim have a distinctly New World cast to their thinking:

First of all, I don't like to be looked upon by my neighbor what I'm doing. It's an automatic thing that you are one big family, and everybody does the same. And I'm an individualist. I mean I can't just go along exactly with the group. I like to be able to be independent. I want to do this, I want to do that. I don't want to do this. I want to daven when I want to daven. I want to send my children to which yeshiveh I like. I mean I want to be independent even though maybe if I have a choice I would send them to that yeshiveh.

I know two people that I know personally, very close friends, they like the Rebbe, they go to the Squarer,[15] but they couldn't get used to the ghetto living. It's sort of too small-townish. If I move out to Monsey, it's right near Square, they have a nice yeshiveh there. There I'd probably enjoy living because it's all different types of religious people and I would enjoy it.*

---

[15] Unfortunately, the Squarer Rebbe passed away unexpectedly on March 31, 1968 (the second day of Nisan), while this work was being printed. The Rebbe's son was proclaimed as his father's successor at the funeral.

III COURT LIFE

The Besmedresh

As in Europe, the besmedresh is the central point for the activities of the hasidic court. It serves not only as the place of study and prayer but is also the hub of hasidic social life—a place of rest, meditation, conversation, politicizing, children's play, and story-telling. Although the besmedresh is used for prayer and all other community activities, there is no attention given to its architecture, and the besmedresh may be a renovated house or movie theatre, a single room, or a basement. The only adornment may be amateur-ish frescoes of the ancient Temple in Jerusalem. The floor is bare, and the curtain shielding the holy ark may be in need of a cleaning. Roughly furnished with heavy tables and benches, it is much used and often appears disorderly by western standards. A hasidic tale wryly explains this state of affairs as a misunderstanding of a Biblical text: reading Jacob's reaction to his vision of heaven ("how awesome is this place") the hasid jokingly mistranslates, "how *awful* is this place—it's in such a state of disrepair that it could only be a shtibl" (S29). Whatever its aesthetic deficiencies, the besmedresh provides both the place and the atmosphere for lively, informal communal exchange.

Like all orthodox Jews, the hasidim meet at the besmedresh for three daily prayer services—at any time from dawn until noon for the morning prayer (shahris), and at dusk for the afternoon prayer (minheh) and the evening prayer (mairev). The morning prayer appears to be the most solemn as the talis (prayer shawl) and tefillin (phylacteries) are worn.[1] Since only ten men are required

---

[1] The tefillin consist of two small leather squares attached to leather thongs. Inside the tefillin are parchment slips containing passages from the Scriptures (see chap. 5, n. 3). While reciting the prayers the worship-

for a minyen (quorum) to begin services, there may be several
morning services, sometimes overlapping. During the week, when
the strict Shabbes prohibitions are not in force, the scene is one of
ease and bustling activity: collections for charity are made; someone may be selling yarmelkehs, books, or pens; another may be
passing out political or religious broadsheets; men are studying
aloud in pairs or in groups; small groups may be chatting, ex-
changing jokes and confidences, and smoking cigarettes before
prayer; and children may be racing through playing tag. Many
of the men come to the besmedresh early in the morning before
prayers or return late in the evening in order to study and discuss
the talmudic writings.

The attitude of the hasidim toward the besmedresh, or the
smaller shtibl (the difference between the two depends largely on
the number of members and the size of the room—or, at times, on
the proportion of representation of the total community) has not
changed in the shift from eastern Europe to Brooklyn, New York.

In the old country a besmedresh belonged to the whole city, to
everybody. All the hasidim from every group, from every movement,
used to come to the besmedresh to daven minheh, mairev. Or when, let's
say, like when a Rabbi of a different town came to our city for an
appeal for certain things, he didn't come to individual shtiblekh. He used
to announce that he was going to speak in the besmedresh. The
besmedresh was for everybody. The besmedresh belonged to everybody. Here in this country each hasidic group, like Lubavitch, you
come in here in a certain way it is like a shtibl. You come into the
Bobov besmedresh, you come into Satmar besmedresh, you come into
any besmedresh of the Rebbes, this is like a shtibl in the old country.*

The hasidic besmedresh is under the control of the Rebbe,
although he delegates authority to others. The Rebbe designates
those who will serve as the gaboyim in charge of the besmedresh
and the mikveh, and he may indicate who will function as the rov
(rabbi) to decide on ritual and legal matters.[2] The hasidim will not

per places one case on the left biceps, inclining it toward the heart, and then
winds the thongs tightly seven times around his arm and three times around
his middle finger. The second case is set on the center of the forehead and
held tightly by the thongs.

  [2] The rov is generally supported by the members of the besmedresh and,
if he teaches there, by the yeshiveh. In addition, the rov earns his livelihood
by selling esroygim (a festival fruit) during Sukkes, and by selling to non-
Jews the membership's supply of food that is ritually unfit for use during
Passover. Those who ask the rov to decide on a question of law may pay
him a fee.

employ a cantor; one of the hasidim serves as baal tefila, the leader of prayer. A hasidic besmedresh that has no Rebbe will elect a group which control the functions of the besmedresh.[3] The monies supporting the besmedresh are provided by membership fees, by donations, and by charging for seats for the High Holy Days.[4]

The Shabbes

For the hasidim the week is sharply divided by the Shabbes into holy and profane days.[5] The Shabbes is a time set aside for intense prayer and for a host of religious and social activities—sitting at the Rebbe's table, partaking of elaborate family meals, supervising the study of children, visiting friends, resting, promenading on the avenue, and, finally, storytelling. At dusk on Friday evening, the courts draw together for prayers. Street noises are subdued, stores have long been closed, and only the cars of passersby are driven through the streets. Most of the men dress in long black silk kaftans, some wear colored robes, and others don knee-length white or black stockings. In Hungarian and Galician courts a married man wears a shtraiml, a round fur hat consisting of twelve spokes of fur which form a circular border.[6]

On Friday afternoon before prayers the men go to the mikveh to purify themselves for the Shabbes. The mikveh is a small rectangu-

[3] In non-hasidic circles, shuls are usually organized along corporate lines. A board of directors is elected, and they hire a rabbi, a shammes (beadle), and a cantor to serve the congregation. Other officers, such as the gaboyim who lead the services and head the various committees, are voluntary functionaries elected by the membership. The shul is supported by donations from fund drives and appeals, and from the sale of tickets for the High Holy Days.

[4] If a hasid cannot afford to pay he is still assured of a seat for the High Holidays, customarily the same seat he has every Shabbes: "Many times I didn't pay and they gave me the same seat." * Moreover, there is no system for taking tickets and no one is turned away.

[5] Similarly, the temper of the year is determined by the holidays. Time is calculated by the proximity of the holidays and a great deal of effort is spent in preparation for them. They are emotional peaks of the year for the community in terms of its social life as well as its relationship with the Almighty.

[6] The style of hats worn on the Shabbes varies. The fur hat worn by Polish hasidim is more cylindrical in shape, but there are very few Polish hasidim in New York and that style is rarely seen. While in Hungarian and Galician courts every married man may wear a shtraiml, in Russia and Poland generally only the Rebbe and the rov wore fur hats.

lar pool deep enough so that one may dip under the water and be completely immersed while standing. It is usually located in the basement of the besmedresh. Many hasidim go to the mikveh every morning, and others attend at least every Monday and Thursday when the Torah is removed from the ark and read. The symbolic purpose of the immersion is to disperse unholiness and profanity and to promote holy thoughts. On certain instances the mikveh is seen as a curative rite (H14). On Friday afternoons there is always a throng of men waiting to dip themselves in the pool in preparation for the approaching Shabbes.

From Friday evening until Saturday night any activity which might be construed as work is scrupulously avoided. Children's activities are more closely supervised so that they will not violate the Shabbes. Until the close of the Shabbes, when there is a sense of physical release from the special obligations and the special joys, the courts are sacred communities.

In the folktales the approach of the Shabbes establishes a mood of expectancy: in the shtetl (village) houses fresh sand is placed on the dirt floors (H4); travelers are offered shelter and hospitality (H5). At this holy time miraculous encounters and revelations seem commonplace (H9). The Shabbes too augurs the adventures of hasidim who travel from far away to see their Rebbe and must spend the holy day in a strange village. The journey, often undertaken with insufficient funds, initiates encounters with travelers and innkeepers, the rich and the needy, the pious and the impious (H61). When they arrive at the hasidic court the assembly of the full congregation on Shabbes eve sets the stage for an event of special significance or for the arrival of a stranger with an extraordinary story (H54). The Baal Shem Tov often began a quest just before Shabbes, and as the day might be waning, he would employ his charm for rapid travel so that he and his followers would arrive at their destination before nightfall (H9, H10). The presence of the Besht and his followers in a village on Friday evening meant that they were needed to settle a problem or to respond to someone's need. On Saturday evening, at the close of the Shabbes, the inexplicable actions of the preceding day would be revealed. The Besht and his disciples would try to prolong the departure of the Shabbes, for souls in torment are free during this holy time and afterward must return to Gehenna (H9).

To the ordinary Jew listening to the tales, the Shabbes is worth more than all the grosser pleasures enjoyed by the alien society (I9). Even the tannaim who reside in heaven enjoy the best of both worlds by returning to earth for the Shabbes (H8). On the other hand, desecration of the Shabbes results in punishment and destruction (H63, N10).

Learning

The preconditions for status in the hasidic community are piety and talmudic learning. All values are subordinated to the fulfillment of the laws and the study of the legal discussions, aphorisms, and tales which constitute the scriptural commentaries, the Talmud, and the Code of Laws. A pious man who is learned in the intricate byways of the talmudic writings has the highest status in the community. Scholars sit next to the Rebbe at the meals; one always walks on the left side of a scholar. On the High Holidays the seats by the eastern wall are reserved for the court's elderly scholars; fledgling scholars, the yeshiveh students, who do not pay for seats, have the advantage of standing beside the Rebbe. With few exceptions, hasidic men spend one to three hours a day studying the talmudic writings, often meeting daily at the besmedresh with a friend to study together. Men take pleasure in listening to two scholars discuss the Torah with acumen and wisdom (H1). Learning, however, means something more than mere rote or an exercise in logic. Penetrating the meanings of talmudic and kabbalistic writings is closely associated with the imaginative life. The texts have the key not only to one's conduct, but also to the powers that grant special control over events. The hasidim are certain that all the inventions of the modern age were anticipated in the Talmud and that their own studies can uplift them into a splendor enjoyed only by their great sages. As is well known, the student of the Talmud, despite all his concentration on minute details of conduct, is often remote and otherworldly.

We believe that in the Torah you find everything in the world. If you want to know the hardest geometry problems, you can take out a Gemoreh and you can learn the hardest geometry problems. There's a story that the Vilna Gaon once met in Germany one of the greatest mathematicians in the world. He was both an astronomer and a mathematician. And the Vilna Gaon never went to college and never read any books except the Talmud, and he knew more of astronomy and mathematics. There's a saying of one of the great rabbis that if it didn't say in the Torah that one and one is two, he wouldn't know how to add. Why? He says he would believe that maybe one and one is three, but he says the Torah it says first that there was the first day, and then there was another day, the second day, so he knows one and one makes two.*

The concern with talmudic learning is a prominent value in the tales.[7] The desire to learn among the hasidim of Rabbi Shneur Zalman was so great that they climbed trees to hear their master instruct his daughter (H25). Study continues even in seemingly incongruous situations in the tales, as when two yeshiveh students captured by pirates arrange to meet every day to learn (I12), or when the hasid sent by the Rebbe to a strange city immediately sits down upon his arrival and begins to study (H23). One tale relates how a hasid who returned home after a trip immediately fell to his neglected studies; it was not for several hours that he looked up to find that his family had moved away and strangers occupied his flat (WH9). Just as interesting is the reaction of the family into whose apartment he had settled: since the stranger was studying they left him undisturbed. One tale notes the possible supernatural rewards for learning: a scholar who had studied the works of Moses Al-Sheikh was visited by the ancient master in a dream at a time of danger and shown a secret exit from the city (H33).

Despite the respect accorded them, true scholars of the Torah must be humble as well as learned. The man who fails to balance his learning by his modesty falls short of the true wisdom granted by the Torah. A hasid who attended a non-hasidic yeshiveh in another city told how the rabbi fell into a fury if the students failed to honor him by standing when he entered the room:

I said to another student: "We have to give him honor as a scholar, but does he have the right to *demand* honor?"
He said: "It's his knowledge of the Torah that you must honor."
So I said: "Would he get so infuriated if he saw someone not stand up for another rabbi?" Then I left the yeshiveh to come here.*

In the hasidic world, even learning must take a lesser place than piety. Once, Moshe of Stolin, about to respond to a point of law, caught himself and said, "I almost forgot." Pressed to continue, he added, "I got so involved in my own wisdom that I almost forgot there's a God in heaven" (T63).

---

[7] In *In Praise of the Besht*, no. 4, concern over the activities of a werewolf is intensified because the children are unable to study.

Yihus

Piety and learning are not the only guides to status. One's yihus (lineage) is of vital importance, and the most highly regarded members of the community belong to branches of the Rebbe's family and to descendants of famous scholars. Yihus is an important determinant of acceptance at the Rebbe's table; it also helps decide the group with whom one learns, and how often one is called to read the Torah at the prayer services. It also plays an important part in selecting a marriage partner.

Success and Charity

Financial success too brings higher status, but only if it is accompanied by religious devotion and increased charitable works. The members of the court have common responsibilities and all must share in their support according to their means. Usually the hasidim give ten per cent of their income to maintain their community. The hasid who is financially successful must turn back a greater amount to support the yeshiveh, the besmedresh, the Rebbe and his family, and the charities designated by the Rebbe if he is to gain respect, added authority, and a closer relationship with the Rebbe. Indeed, the wealthy sink in the general estimation if their financial good luck is not balanced by good works. In some courts, each person is informed of how much money he is expected to give to support the yeshiveh. Should someone be ignored, or have the amount required of him reduced, he would consider it as a sign that he has fallen from the Rebbe's favor.

At a meeting in 1960 of the Satmarer hasidim to raise funds for their yeshiveh, Mr. Gotlieb, one of those taking pledges, approached one of the wealthiest men in the court, who had pledged five hundred dollars.

"You must give more," Mr. Gotlieb said.
"How much?"
"Double, at least, if not more."
"Then I'll give double."
"*At least* double," concluded Mr. Gotlieb. *

While speaking to another reticent donor, Mr. Gotlieb was called aside by a yeshiveh functionary: "Don't work too hard on him. He's tight. If he won't come up with his quota then we'll tell him the Rebbe wants to see him. He'll give whatever the Rebbe tells him." *

Charity is a religious as well as a social necessity, an obligation to God as well as to man, and this accounts in part for the special zeal in doing charitable works. In one tale the Berdichever Rov toasts Reb Haim for having won three cases in his rabbinical court, in each case showing how Reb Haim refused to be repaid because his service had been to God rather than to man (W5). To fulfill the mitsves one must give charity, even if as with the Lemberger Rov it means going into debt (N13). Traditions assume that when a Jew has to sacrifice to fulfill the mitsveh of giving charity he is often rewarded tenfold (H5).

The tales cut a warning edge for those reluctant to give charity: the Sandzer Rov, who would distribute his last penny, rebuked his gabai for shouting at a poor woman (H48); the rich man who refused to follow the Premishlaner Rebbe's wishes to give charity saw his wealth redistributed (H36). On the other hand, charity can save an otherwise unredeemed soul: a rich man who welcomed the Tchernobler Rebbe but not his mud-caked followers relented after learning that his own soul was perilously balanced on the heavenly scale only by the mud scraped from the shoes of a poor family he had aided in a previous incarnation (H30).

Charity is conducted on an individual as well as on an organizational basis. At almost every daily prayer service, wedding, or other gathering, a few men may thread through the gathering and receive coins from each worshipper or celebrant. A woman will wait outside the besmedresh or someone inside may collect for her (at a wedding she may enter and mingle more freely). Collections are often made on behalf of other individuals. When a poor hasid falls ill and cannot work, other members of the court collect funds for him. Indeed, some people spend almost all their time collecting charity. One well-known charity collector in Brooklyn customarily takes a taxi from one besmedresh to another to lighten as many pockets as possible at prayer time. Funds are solicited in the same way for groups, for yeshiveh students, and for building funds. It is not unusual to encounter a traveler, perhaps from Israel, making his way from one besmedresh to another throughout the city and even throughout the United States and Canada. In the previous century, such wanderers often collected funds in order to redeem recruits from the army or a poor person from debt, and one tale recalls the adventures of a zealous charity collector who accepted drinks on Yom Kippur eve to win alms and in his inebriated state later interrupted the prayer services (H19).

Despite its apparent lack of organization the institution of collecting charity is so effective that hasidim rarely become recipients of welfare, and when such applications are made, it is difficult to satisfy the welfare authorities that the petitioners have not worked for years, surviving solely on the system of charity just outlined. Any attempt to alter the old ways would meet with stiff opposition, and hasidic tradition emphasizes that ethical and charitable behavior must follow these established forms. It is told that in the time of the Baal Shem Tov there was a rabbi who promoted a general charity fund to which everyone would donate once a year. This system, however, deprived a hidden saint of his livelihood, since he did not take from the fund and people no longer gave in the customary way. This result so aroused the Heavenly Court that the rabbi was punished by being seized with the desire to convert to Christianity (H3).

If riches may be seen as a boon, poverty need not be taken as a token of inferiority or as a sign of divine displeasure. In the tales centered on village life in eastern Europe, it is taken for granted that the Jew is poverty stricken and at the mercy of the nobleman. Some courts, such as Kotsk, considered poverty to be a blessing (W12), while the Strelisker hasidim, who could become rich if they but held on to their Rebbe's prayer shawl, prayed so fervently that they completely forgot their hopes for wealth (W11). A man may be luckier being poor rather than rich, for hardship may be the magical balance needed to prolong one's life (H95). Poverty, too, is a temporary condition, not related to character or heredity, and it can be quickly reversed by the Rebbe or the will of God (H5, H23).

Yiddishkait

When the hasidim speak of Yiddishkait, they refer both to the philosophical values of Judaism and to the external rituals—the ethical and ritual laws receive the same sanction and the same merit. It is, however, by outward signs rather than by inner deeds that one can judge orthodoxy, and the most apparent concerns of the community are ritualistic. The minimum criteria by which orthodoxy can be recognized consist of observing the mitsves (commandments) of keeping the Shabbes and the holidays, attending the prayer services at the besmedresh, putting on tefillin, eating only kosher food, and maintaining the purity of the home (by this is meant the attendance of women at the mikveh and the careful observance of the accompanying sexual regulations).[8] The other key outward signs by which one is recognized and accepted as an orthodox Jew consist of wearing a head covering at all times, wearing a talis koten (a fringed undershirt), and the nailing of mezuzeh (holy amulet) on the doorpost.[9] The appearance of the hasidim is also especially marked by their peyes and beards (although a few hasidim shave with an electric razor or a depilatory, the beard is regarded as a special symbol of piety). Hasidic men wear black kaftans, or at the very least a somber colored suit, and large black hats which are often worn with the brim turned up. Hasidic women wear long-sleeved though fashionable dresses, and married women wear wigs or other head coverings.

The concerns of Yiddishkait, which are threatened by the social changes and material comforts of the modern world, are honed for contemporary listeners in a parable. The hasidic narrator tells of the Jew who decided to remove the wheels of his overloaded wagon in order to make it lighter. "A person has responsibilities. Cut down his car? No, he can't do it. He cuts down on Shabbes, charity, education. He forgets these are the wheels" (W23).

Occupations

As with all other activities in the courts, employment too is balanced on the scale of religious values. A hasid does not have a "career"; he is concerned simply with earning a living in a way which will not interfere with his religious duties.[10] Most hasidim in New York belong to the ranks of skilled workers. They are employed in the diamond center as cutters, polishers, and dealers; they hold jobs as sewing machine operators, pattern cutters, watch-

[8] See *Code of Jewish Law*, chaps. 153, 157.
[9] See Kranzler, *Williamsburg*, pp. 110–15.
[10] In *In Praise of the Besht*, the Besht is said to have worked at various occupations such as school-teacher's assistant, quarry worker, and innkeeper.

makers, linotype operators, electricians, carpenters, and upholsterers, among other skilled trades.[11]

Like most immigrant groups, many of the hasidim have shifted from one occupation to another depending on the circumstances of the particular industry. They are usually aided in making the transition from one industry to another by hasidic friends already employed and well trained. For example, Saul is a hasid in his middle thirties who has had a varied career. A man of intelligence and ingenuity, he has been able to adapt quickly to the demands of a new trade, but just as quickly the market for his services has shrunk and he has been forced to look for other work. In the summer of 1958 Saul and his brother Moshe bought a small grocery in a middle-class neighborhood in Brooklyn which had a rising number of orthodox residents. They had gone to the Rebbe for advice, but the Rebbe had said simply, "God will help." They bought the store. The previous owner had scraped along in the same spot for twenty years, but the two brothers did not last there more than twelve months. Moshe knew little English. He was lethargic and did not know what was expected of him. Saul found that he could not bring all his attention to bear on the problems of the business. The store demanded fourteen hours of his time every working day. Saul preferred to have an eight-hour job so that he could be free the remainder of the time. They soon abandoned the store at a financial loss that carried away all of Saul's savings. Subsequently, Saul was taken in by some friends to learn the diamond cutter's trade. In a short time Saul learned how to cut diamonds and was steadily employed; in 1960, however, the diamond business faltered and he was out of work. In the interim he had been married and his wife was expecting a child. Some of Saul's friends brought him to their sweater factories. They worked the night shift: no one was around, and they taught him how to set the yarn and run the machines. Then Saul was taken into a non-union shop run by an orthodox Jew. When I next talked with Saul it was during the night shift in the loft of a sweater factory. The factory was deserted and dark except for two workers in a distant corner of the factory. Saul did not speak to them because they were paid for piecework and so had no time to waste. Saul was kept busy maintaining yarn for half a dozen machines. He had a long scar on his thumb from an injury caused by his inexperience in adjusting

[11] See Kranzler, *Williamsburg*, pp. 66–77. For extended discussion of the economic structure of the hasidic community, see Poll, *Hasidic Community*, chaps. 9, 10, and 11.

the machines. He worked swiftly, setting up the spools of yarn, arranging the threads, and then gathering the fabric in boxes below. Part of the night he was on the telephone, talking with friends who had similar all-night jobs. Some of his calls were for advice on how to adjust the machinery.

Saul might have had more success had he initiated a business or found work related directly to the functioning of the community. While the hasidic community in New York lacks the economic unity of the European village, in many ways the hasidim are still economically interdependent. A small but ever increasing number have established small packaging and wholesale businesses, often in response to the particular needs of the hasidic community. Because of their disdain for what they consider inadequate precautions in fulfilling the ritual law, a number of hasidim have succeeded in establishing enterprises concerned with matseh, meat, milk, cheese, bread, noodles, salt, sugar, mayonnaise, and vitamins. Hasidic manufacturers and wholesalers can assure their customers that no conditions will be permitted which might render their products impure.[12] Still other concerns supply religious books and other articles, such as tefillin, yarmelkehs, wigs, and candles. There are a few artisans who do engraving on silver cups and candlesticks. A number of hasidim have become ritual slaughterers or have opened highly successful retail butcher shops. Some have opened groceries, vegetable markets, fish stores, dry goods stores, and a variety of other retail businesses. These retail ventures are assured of a measure of success because of the customary endorsement of their Rebbe and the patronage of their own courts, providing that they remain within the immediate neighborhood.[13] Other ventures can attribute their success not only to loyalty but also to the anxiety of their customers to fulfill the law and to the social stigma attached to using a product that does not meet the most rigid standards of Kashrut.

Although the number of business enterprises is rising, the professional class remains small. Since the hasidim disapprove of secular education because it threatens belief, only in very rare cases do hasidim attend college. In the hierarchy of religious devotion spelled out in one tale, the son of the college-educated druggist

---

[12] See Poll, *ibid.*, pp. 175–91, concerning apprehensions about food products.

[13] An additional factor encouraging patronage of the butcher shop endorsed by the Rebbe is that in some instances the profit from the store is turned over to the yeshiveh (see Poll, *ibid.*, p. 179).

goes to shul only on Yom Kippur (W19). One common appraisal is:

> If somebody in my group would go to college I would consider him an outcast even though he remained religious. *

Since so few obtain a secular education the hasidim must go beyond the borders of their community for medical and legal assistance. One member of a hasidic court, who had been raised as a misnagéd, had studied to be a dentist in Europe. "I gave it up because I had to look in women's mouths." *

Because the hasidim maintain their own school system, a high percentage of yeshiveh graduates serve as teachers in their own schools or in other yeshives and Talmud Torahs. Teaching has perhaps always been the most common occupation for those who work in the community; it is a task for which almost every hasid is qualified. One tale notes in a matter-of-fact manner: "A man had to earn a living and so he ran away to a rich land and became a teacher" (H20).

Some hasidim perform other important religious services, such as circumciser (moyel), supervisor of food preparation (mashgiah), and scribe (sofer). Of course, there are some who are rabbis of congregations.

On the artistic side, the community boasts only a single known painter, who must support himself by other means; [14] a few cantors, who must sing professionally in other than hasidic shuls since the hasidim disdain such services; and a handful of musicians, who play only at scrupulously orthodox celebrations. Here again, however, the prejudice against secular training persists: despite the importance of music in their lives, few of the hasidim have any training, and there is such a demand for their services that nonreligious musicians have to be employed at weddings.

The importance of earning a satisfactory living has been recognized by the Rebbes, and many tales deal with advice that resulted in a wise investment and a sound profit (H22), or with the power held by some Rebbes in granting such boons (W11, TA22). The social and economic systems of the New World have not lessened the concern for a satisfactory income. The cost of living is higher than it was in Europe and there is a greater demand for consumer goods. Signs of affluence take a peculiarly hasidic form: the first large purchase usually consists of double kitchen units—two

[14] See Kranzler, "Chosid from the Left Bank," *Orthodox Jewish Life,* 22 (1955): 32–36.

stoves, two sinks, two refrigerators—to ensure the separation of meat and milk products. But the overwhelming majority of hasidim are not so privileged. Many assert that since living a religious life is so costly, particularly in terms of education and food, it has become more important for the hasid to earn enough to ensure his family's continued piety. The drive for higher earnings is, however, a two-edged sword, one that cuts deeply into the time required for religious devotion.

Even though we live in America here very peacefully, we still feel very uncomfortable in this country. The way of life in this country is very hard on us—even if very free. The freedom here is unbelievable. We feel the freedom and we appreciate the freedom very much. But the freedom is very hard on us. The way of making a living is very difficult for the way of life we want to lead. We religious Jews used to go pray every morning, every minheh-mairev. It's impossible to pray minheh-mairev. By the time you come home from work on the train, it's over. So you have to pray by yourself. In the morning it's the same thing. You have to rush. Time is so short. Until you go shopping and this and that, you can't get to pray. You haven't got time to meet friends. Not meeting friends, and not learning with each other—it's hurting our belief, it's hurting our customs. It hinders us. There is a great deal of freedom. But our way of life, we believe should not be tied to a materialistic way of life. And here, from the morning till night you always have to think about the dollar. Even to make a decent living you are tied twelve hours a day. A normal business man, a small business man, even a normal worker, without a college education, without some special trade, he doesn't make more than a $1.50 an hour. And our families, and we believe in bigger families, our families have six or seven kids. And Jewish life is more expensive. Food is expensive, school is expensive, the holidays are more expensive. Even living very poor, we have to work twelve hours a day only to provide the most necessary things in life. And this hurts our way of life. Because for two or three years you work so hard you don't learn, you don't pray, you fall back six years. You're not back three years only. You're thrown back six years of learning. You forget, and this is very bad. You have to continue to work spiritually. You can't work only when you're young and it keeps you your whole life. And man is never standing on the same point. Every day he is always going up, or he's going down. You can't say a man should be on the same level all his life. He's always getting better, or he's getting worse. This means that this way of life is very hard on us. We need an hour, two hours a day, a little freedom for our spiritual lives. You haven't got time to do mitsves, to do good deeds for each other. Before the war everybody had an hour or two to go for some poor people, to help some people at the hospital. Everybody had his own way. One hour a day to do good deeds. For us it is impossible. The way of life is so tense. There's only a few hours until you go home. Until you do something, the day is over.

We still feel not free. Our minds are not free. You see, I can't put my mind to work wherever I want to. I like to learn, to study a little bit Gemoreh, to talk to a friend of mine, to do a good deed. I can't because I have to be here in the shop to make a dollar. But I need the dollar. Not to buy myself a car. A dollar to buy bread and butter and milk, which in our way of life costs more than normal. Normal people haven't got so much will to say, "Children, go in bad shoes." No normal father of children can say, "Don't eat butter." Here in America people should eat only bread and water? In Europe if the people don't eat butter, it's okay. Here, in America, in this country you shouldn't eat butter? You shouldn't eat meat at least three times a week? How could you? And there are people among us who don't eat because they can't afford it. And nobody believes it. Nobody will believe it because, because comes Passover matses are very expensive. Comes Sukkes, the sukkeh is expensive. You have to support the yeshives. We feel our children's lives depend on the yeshiveh and you have to help them. If you pay twenty dollars for each child, and you have four or five children in the yeshiveh, it's quite a lot. It costs me a hundred dollars a month for the yeshiveh alone—besides supplies. You have to give charity also. You can't refuse anybody. You're a normal human being. You want to give, you have to give, you like to give. And the way of life is not set up for these expenses. Usually a worker who has a trade, he makes $2.00 an hour to $10.00. So he has for his food, for A & P, and schooling is free. So they have enough. He could even buy a car. He could even go out whenever he wants to. He doesn't have to learn. It doesn't bother him if he stays an hour longer in the shop. Just the opposite. He's happy to be there an hour longer. He feels that he does something worthwhile, he creates something, he makes another dollar. For us this is not creating, it's hindering. This is a very big point.

We know there's more freedom in America than any place in this world. We don't complain about the freedom. But still, for our way of life, our type of people, we are not set up for this kind of life. Maybe other people are also unhappy. They don't know what's missing. But we, we felt, already a different, a better way of life. So we know it's not right for us.*

In eastern Europe hasidic customs were tied to an economic system which permitted women to substitute for men in business while the men attended to religious affairs. The social and economic systems of the New World have shifted the hasidic pattern by making the men the main support of the family and by demanding that they spend more time attending to family affairs. These factors have reduced the number of devotional and study hours available during the week and have curtailed as well the hours spent at the Rebbe's table on the weekend. As we have seen, many hasidim feel that the factors undermining religious life are not only the temptations of the city but are also the New World's demand for continual effort and for a higher standard of living. They are concerned about the subtle changes in their lives that have resulted in the loss of time previously devoted to prayer and study.

IV YOUTH AND MARRIAGE

The religious education of the young is one of the most important considerations of the hasidic community. The essential concerns are learning to sanctify one's actions and one's person; training to achieve this end begins within the first two years of life. Immediately after a hasidic child awakens in the morning his mother spills water three times alternately over his hands and recites a prayer in Hebrew with him. Later, in his second or third year, a glass of water will be kept by the bed and the child will say the prayers himself. As he learns to speak he is encouraged to recite Hebrew blessings over food that he eats; he is warned against committing sins on the Shabbes or holidays, such as carrying objects, cutting paper, snapping on lights, and scribbling; he is encouraged to evacuate his bowels before prayer. At first fulfilling his ritual obligations by rote, the child learns to include almost all of his activities in the realm of the sacrosanct. All that he does will have a bearing on his soul, on the welfare of his family and on all Israel.

Religious training is particularly intense for boys, since they will ultimately carry the major religious responsibilities. The religious roles begin to be more sharply delineated at the age of three. Until this time the young boy's hair has been uncut, and he has worn it in long flowing style. Now, at a party, his hair is clipped short and only the distinctive peyes (side curls) are left. At approximately this age also the boy receives his tsitses, a four-cornered undershirt with fringes which he will bless each day and wear to remind him to keep the Commandments. In his third year as well the young boy begins to attend all-day religious school. By the age of four he is reading letters in unison with his class, and by four and a half he is reading single words. At home he may be seen practicing his reading, emphasizing letters and words by pounding his fist on the table, much as his teacher in school does. The din that he may raise in learning never troubles his parents. He learns to translate from Hebrew into Yiddish, his mother tongue. For a long time his English is halting: many hasidic parents speak English poorly, but even if his parents are native speakers of English they will probably feel it their duty to steep him in Yiddish at home.

The world outside receives great attention. When he plays out-of-doors, the hasidic child may be cautioned not to play with other children who are not religious, or at the very least to recognize the strict borders of their relationship. He is warned not to eat anything in an irreligious or non-Jewish home. There is a range of parental attitudes on the question of relating to nonhasidic children depending on individual belief, court pressures, neighborhood and block makeup, the age of the child, and whether or not the children are Jewish or gentile.

Of course it's a risk to let your kids play with kids whose parents are not Shabbes observers. They see on Shabbes the father gets in a car, the kids get in, and maybe they all go to the beach. They're Jewish. To tell him he's a goy is not right. But they're not observant Jews. My kid said himself they must all be goyim. When children are older they have to have an explanation. We tell them they were not brought up to be observant, it's not their fault, we hope one day they will learn more, they will become religious. And my kids influence other kids. In the house they know when other kids come to visit they must wear a yarmelkeh; if they have candy they should say a blessing. I say try to teach him, try to influence him. He brought in a little colored kid, he didn't know, and had him make a blessing. I just say don't let them teach you.*

Even when there is little actual contact with the nonreligious world, the child's attitudes may be more carefully set toward outsiders:

I tell him he must wash or he is a goy. That's the worst thing in the world. His worst fear is he's going to be a goy. His worst fear in the yeshiveh is that he'll be sent to a public school. If a store is open on Shabbes he knows it is a goy. He knows he has nothing in common with a man without a hat. When I speak in English my oldest child said, "Redt nisht in der goyishe sprache." When I was a child I thought a person who did not keep the Shabbes is not a human being.*

As the boy grows older he attends English classes part of the day, but he does not consider them to be as important as his religious studies, nor does he regard his English teacher with the same esteem as he does his Hebrew teacher.[1] Nevertheless, fearful that he may absorb the more subtle values of the secular world, his English textbooks are screened to prevent him from seeing illustrations of boys and girls playing together, a fairy tale prince carrying off a princess, or a sketch of a prehistoric man. He is effectively barred from all intellectual intrusions from the outside, including the public library:

If I would see fire, would I allow my son to go into the house? There is danger, even if only a small part is burning. As his father I have to protect him.*

To provide the number of secular subjects that the law requires the hasidic boy will eventually study mathematics and chemistry rather than biology and geology. These subjects will not disturb his world view: he accepts the fact that the world was created less than 6,000 years ago and he expects the Meshiah to come on a white horse to take all the Jews to Israel.

Hasidic parents try to suffuse their children's religious activities with pleasure. At holiday time the child stays up late at night with his friends to watch the activities in the besmedresh. He is encouraged but not forced to join in the prayers. Learning is often presented first in the form of pleasant stories. As noted in a tale of the Baal Shem Tov, when the Besht is anxious for the children to have pleasant associations with religious practice he tells the parents to serve them a sweet pudding when relating the wonders of God (H1).

The tales that the boy hears set models for his behavior and help to establish his attitudes. The high adventure of the stories is not that of the youthful squire being trained in the arts of war but rather that of the novitiate being inducted into the secrets of Yiddishkait. He hears of the king's son who took delight in learning how to put on tefillin and in becoming a Jew (H10), how the Besht and other great rabbis bent all their efforts in studying in secret, and of the special pleasures and pains of being a Jew (I9). He listens to tales of the childhood of the Baal Shem Tov, but he probably does not note the striking difference between the tales of the Besht's early life and his own activities, for while it is told that the Baal Shem Tov skipped school and spent his days learning the

---

[1] In a suit decided by the New York State Appellate Court in September, 1950, the wife of a M'lochim hasid won the custody of her son on the grounds that he was being denied a secular education. See Sobel, "The M'lochim," p. 32, n. 12.

secrets of the forest, the hasidic boy has little to do with play out-of-doors, with trees, flowers, or animals. The natural world remains a mystery to him. He attends school six days a week until five o'clock. During the long school day, no attention is paid to athletics or supervised games of any sort. As he grows older, he may study additional hours in the evening with a friend. On the Shabbes he will spend most of the day at the besmedresh.

But if adults compel him to study most of the day, they also indulge him at other times. He has his moments of freedom, and then there are few restraints. Spare moments away from his lessons are spent in frenetic outbursts of accumulated energy. He bobs up and down the stairs of the yeshiveh, and with his fellows shoves his way past the unwary into school offices, probing in closets and desks. Outside the school as well as inside the halls, he plays tag and skipping, jumping, and wrestling games. Without being aware of it, he has adopted many Brooklyn street games as his own. ("We play a game, I don't know how you call it in English, but in Jewish we call it ring-a-levio." *) His play is carried over into the time he spends in the besmedresh as well: he plays tag in the aisles and drags wood on the floor as a scooter. Adults are ignored, even though they may be milling in the same area preparing for prayers. For their part the adults make no effort to hinder the games. A hasidic boy will clamber on the windows, on the Ark of the Law itself, without reprimand. When the hasidic men sing in unison, he will be encouraged rather than chastised if he should shout at the top of his lungs, his voice wailing above the singing of the congregation. The hasidim want their sons to think of the besmedresh as a home, and they are willing to have it used in the meantime as a playground.

Let him turn over the shul, let him break the benches, let him tear the books, let him turn over the talisim—as long as he's in the shul. He isn't outside on the street, he isn't with the bums in the playground, or he isn't sitting there in the park and watching a baseball game. When I pass and see a Jewish child Shabbes afternoon standing near a baseball court, watching outside the gate, it hurts me much, much more than when I come into a shul. It's actually just the opposite. There [outside] it hurts. When I come into a shul on Saturday afternoon and there's hundreds of kids, and they're turning over the place, I know that this boy, when he gets older, will always know that "my place is the shul." *

At home the hasidic child acts with great respect for his father. His father's chair is at the head of the table and the children do not sit in it. According to the law, the father is not to be contradicted on any matter.[2] In obedience to that law, reverence of the words of one's father is sometimes carried to extremes: in one tale, when the Shinyaver was told by his father not to cross his threshold he left the house through the window (T52).

In general, the father commands by his presence and his insistence on adherence to law and custom rather than by harsh punitive measures. The image of the European father is that of a reserved but intensely involved parent.

My father very seldom spanked us, very, very seldom. And I respected my father very, very much. I wouldn't sit on his chair, and his word was the most important in the house. He would not praise either—not in front of me, anyway. He wasn't openly too affectionate, but as a father was. I felt very close to him, I mean. He took a lot of care of us. He told us stories, you know in this way. He took care in a different way. My father learned with me every night. Usually every night between davening, between minheh and mairev.*

My father was a man who his main object in life was that he himself should be afraid to do something wrong. As far as he would be concerned, he would like that he should be able to sit all his life and learn and daven, and not to have anything to do with things like looking for parnosseh, making a living. This would be his main outlook. That God should be good to him, that he should be able to sit day and night and just worship by learning his Torah and by observing his mitsves. This is one thing. And there is the other main thing that he should be able to bring up his children in the right hasidic way. This I can swear, that if somebody would ask him what would you prefer, to make a nice living to be able to give your family all their needs, or to have children and not to be able to make a living, to be poor but you should have children who are going to be following the way you want them to follow, the Torah and mitsves, I'm quite sure that he would choose the second way—that is children should be followers of the Torah and followers of hasides and everything.

I happened to meet a man, he is now a Rabbi in Canada, Rabbi Morris. I remember him also from our town. He davened in the same shtibl. And I happened to meet him once and I asked him, "Rabbi Morris, what do you remember of my father? I would like to hear it from somebody." Because, like I told you before, I left home I was about ten years, not even ten. So I was away from home already, learning in different cities. So I wanted to know for myself what kind of man my father was in the eyes of his friends. So I asked him. They were about the same age.

So he told me that, "I want to tell you that your father was

[2] See *Code of Jewish Law*, chap. 142, no. 2.

considered one of the smartest men in shtibl." If anybody had something to discuss, something—a problem—he used to come to [my] father to talk it over and hear the opinion about it. "He was a very smart man," he said. And besides, I mean, that was a hasidesher Yid. There is no question about it. I mean he was a talmid hokhem [learned man]; he knew how to learn. Looking upon him, the way he conducted himself and the way he conducted the whole house, I mean, this itself showed what's important in life and how to be.*

There does appear to be some shifting in the attitudes of parents toward their offspring. In general, the postwar generation are more conscious of the effect their actions and attitudes will have on their children.

It was a mistake to be too strict. More could be done with kindness. I'm not criticizing the older generation—they brought up a religious generation. We can see what they did. With Lubavitch in general, toward children, toward the outer world, there is more kindness.

On another occasion, the same informant said:

My father used to beat me if I played ball. When I came here I went to a camp and saw religious boys in tsitses playing ball, divided into teams, I thought, what a crazy world. I play sometimes myself, handball.*

Another hasid echoed a common rationale for the change in attitude—the need to meet the threat of fresh ideas presented in the American environment:

The old European school of religious people—their way was to punish when the child was bad and to give very little praise when the child was good. When a child is being good it is natural that he be good; he is not doing anything out of the ordinary. But when he is bad, he is bad and should be punished. And most European parents were that way.

Oh, we punish our children. I hit my children, but I kiss them too. And when they do something good, I praise them. Because if I don't praise them, somebody else will praise them when they do something wrong, and they'll go looking for that praise.

Today we are in competition, and then my parents were not in competition. There was law and order like a dictatorship. Then there was only one way and now there are two ways, but the other is so strong that they have to be educated completely differently.*

The father's most profound obligations are to instruct his son in the mitsves, in the commentaries, and to induct him into the life of the besmedresh and the community. But the commanding position of the father in the family does not necessarily end with childhood.

He remains always an influential, at times dominating, power in later life.

My father still has to this day some control over me. I mean I am independent, I'm married, I have my own family, but I have to reckon many times in business and in my private life with what my father will say if I want to do something. When I was first married, well, I sort of revolted—you know I didn't like it. Then I got used to it and I like it. I wanted to go into business for myself. My father tried every trick in the trade to not have me go into business for myself. Now I appreciate it. When I got a little older, I appreciated it. At the time I revolted, but still his word was law. He showed me how it's not good and it isn't good, and without saying the word "no" he made it clear that he doesn't want me to. He did this for me. He did everything in the world so that I should stay with him. You know they say in America "just to breathe the air of liberty"—you know, it will make you hale. It is an environment that you want to be independent. At that time I wanted very much to be independent. Now it doesn't bother me. I got older a little bit. You know you get settled down a little bit and it doesn't bother me. We're all in the business; my father is the boss. The business belongs to my father. We all get wages. I mean very, very nice wages. I mean we get wages whether we work or we don't work, but still it's a family business. I mean I'm independent too. Just like I work for my father, I manufacture for myself, too.*

The hasidic mother is revered for quite different reasons. If the father makes the sharpest intellectual and moral demands on the boy, it is often the mother who defends him. "What do you want from him?" challenged the mother of the future Lubavitcher Rebbe when her husband berated their son for his concern with trivia (T61). The mother is likely to be more tolerant of her son's misdeeds, more openly affectionate, and more concerned about his health and welfare than about problems relating to the community or to spiritual matters.

My mother—in the first place she was a very beautiful woman, a real beautiful woman. If she would be in America, I mean, she was really a beautiful woman. She was tall and she had natural red cheeks and blue eyes and the whole figure. When I remember my mother she was already a grandmother. When I left home I would say she must have been in her forties, or maybe close to fifty—not more. And after going through so much suffering, daily suffering, how to feed a family, which takes away a lot of you, she was still beautiful. And she was extremely good-natured. As far as bringing up the children, she was more liberal. Maybe I'm not using the right word, liberal. I mean she was easier to the children. It was easier to be with mother.

Father a little stricter with the children. He was always after the children not to play around, always to go to the shtibl, always asked for more and more—to study more, to daven more, to be more observant and more observant. I had plenty spankings. Just a couple of smacks I guess. For example, I used to love to play football. I see they call it here in America soccer. Soccer I used to love. If he found out it was just too bad for me. Well, he did find out. You couldn't hide too much.

Mother also didn't let me. She didn't tell me to play. In fact just the opposite, she told me not to. But if she did find out she just would say, "Moshe, don't. You know your father will come home and you're going to get it from your father and you shouldn't play. And go to the shtibl." But she used to say it in an easier going way, like a mother, I guess. . . .

With father it was kind of respect. I can't recall that my father should kiss any of the children. Mother did. If father was happy I got good marks he showed his happiness not by kissing but he would take the children for a walk and talk to the children: "That's the way it should be, you are making me happy by having a good report from you and God is happy, and just keep on doing it." That's all. Mother was pleased if she saw my father is happy that I got a good report from my teacher.*

In the tales mothers are likely to act as Milev's mother, who journeyed to the strange city where her son was studying in order to cook for him and who later plagued the Kozhenitser Rebbe to perform a miracle to free her son when he was taken by Cossacks (H28). Like the mothers who protested the Rimanover's kabbalistic sacrifice of Russian troops in the Napoleonic war, given a clear choice between bringing the Meshiah or saving her son, the Jewish mother will choose the latter course (N4).

Bar Mitsveh

Until the age of thirteen the hasidic boy is not expected to adhere to all the demands of his religion and his society. At a Shabbes meal a Rebbe fired a riddle at me: "How can you be a good hasid if you don't fast on Yom Kippur and don't put on tefillin?" The answer: "If you're not bar mitsveh."

When the hasidic boy reaches the age of thirteen he goes to the besmedresh and puts on his newly purchased tefillin. From then on he is expected to fulfill all of the ritual obligations of a man of Israel.

It was an important occasion. Before I was bar mitsveh and I was davening, if I decided to skip half of the davening, I would skip it. I wouldn't skip a davening—but if I got tired, I'd finish and "God would forgive me." That was my psychology. But when I got to the age of bar mitsveh, I felt, "Now there's no more joking around—this is the time that I'm responsible for everything that I do." That was the very big change that happened when I was bar mitsveh. I would quit fooling myself that I was fooling God in a certain way. I'm just going to stand there and I'm not going to daven? I knew I had a responsibility.*

In eastern Europe little attention was paid to the bar mitsveh ceremony.

When I became bar mitsveh I wasn't even home. And what I remember is that my father sent me a pair of tefillin with a nice letter, and I was called to the Torah in the middle of the week. And this was bar mitsveh. Even if I would have been home there wouldn't have been much more. I would just have been called to the Torah.*

Most hasidim try to preserve the same attitude that existed in the past. The chief expense borne usually stems from the purchase of the tefillin, which, to ensure that care went into keeping their accuracy and purity, may cost anywhere from fifty to three hundred dollars. There may be a party for the boy at which he may give a lengthy legalistic discourse on some minor point of law, but usually these occasions are less elaborate than similar parties held by less orthodox Jews.

There are some who are starting big parties now. They get caught in certain modern concepts. Their wives demanded it, the family demanded it, the children demanded it. We think it's very wrong. First of all we think it's a waste of money; and to make a whole ceremony out of a mitsveh—the mitsveh doesn't stand for that—it stands for the purpose of putting on tefillin and to start having responsibility. This is something we never saw by our grandfathers. And in fact, if any of my friends makes a bar mitsveh in a hall and he spends money, even though he's my closest friend, I say, "I'm sorry but I don't go." I believe this—that it's the right thing—that's not what bar mitsveh stands for.*

After the bar mitsveh, the boy's life scarcely changes. Rooted in hasidic life, he has no friends outside his circle in the yeshiveh; long before he has been warned against eating in neighbors' homes; he probably has never seen a movie. He continues to attend the yeshiveh, although he is now more serious and he usually leaves the games in the besmedresh for younger children. He takes a place at prayers with the men.

In general, the boy finds easy acceptance into the adult world. All his parents expect of him is that he be a pious Jew. Of course, that encompasses a great deal, but there is little concern about his future job or his prospective income. He usually has a close relationship with his grandparents, for whom he has always tendered respect. Because young and old bear common responsibilities, there is a sense of equality between himself and other adults.

Conduct

Ideally, neither men nor women have any sexual experience before marriage; because this area is rarely ever discussed, however, little information on the subject exists. On the Shabbes some Rebbes often obliquely caution parents to guard their children from committing the sin of masturbation. When the young man matures, he himself will entrust his soul to God at night so that he may avoid having erotic dreams, and on occasion he may perform some act of penitence (H64b). In general, the sexes are governed by a host of laws guarding their contacts, and it is therefore not surprising to note the lack of discussion of sexual matters as well as the absence of ribald jokes and tales.[3]

The energy piloting less religious boys into sports, sexual adventures, and dating is usually channeled into religious devotion and a sense of brotherhood with his comrades. At times the hasidic boy may amaze his family by his religious zeal, testing himself with ritual purification and with long bouts of study.

I remember that I must have been about ten years old and a group of my friends, my age, made up to learn together early in the morning in wintertime, about 5 o'clock in the morning, or 5:30, when it was pitch dark outside and snow was coming down and there was snow up to here. And we made up that each day a different boy used to come to the other friends and knock on the door and wake him up. And we used to walk to the shtibl and sit down and learn, early in the morning. And I also remember that I once had an arrangement to study together with an older fellow than me. He used to study with me. And I had to go

---

[3] See *Code of Jewish Law*, chap. 151. There are a number of tales in *In Praise of the Besht* concerning accidental emissions and other sexual references which have no counterparts in the tales in the present collection. See *In Praise of the Besht*, nos. 209, 221, 239, 246. For the use of a sexual metaphor, see *ibid.*, no. 51.

wake him up in the morning. I used to come in the morning when it was pitch dark and knock on his door and he used to get dressed and we walked together to shtibl and we studied.*

But generally this intensity does not last long and the youthful zealot begins to follow a more temperate pattern of worship.

I snapped out of it fast. Who am I going to fool? Am I at that stage? Am I that serious? I didn't want to fool myself and I said that's it. I don't want to fool myself and walk around all day never forgetting about God one second when I'm actually not doing it.*

There is one strict standard of conduct in the yeshiveh and at home: he must keep the commandments. If he deviates, purposefully and consistently breaks a commandment or crucial custom, he is in danger of being cast out of the life of the community lest he influence others. Yet, even if he errs in this critical area, he knows that he will always be welcomed back if he expresses his willingness to conform (HA43).

I was just discussing this with a friend of mine—we were driving out to the country and discussing many subjects, so we were discussing college. He asked me what if one of my children gets to be eighteen and he says, "Father, I want to go to college. I want to become an engineer." What would happen? So I said, "The way I see things today, I would try with easy ways. He would still be just as religious as me, but he wants to go to college, he wants to be an engineer or he wants to be a mathematician. I would try talking to him. You can't punish a child of eighteen. You can't hit a child—you're not allowed to. According to Jewish law, if you hit a child even at age fourteen or fifteen, it's a sin. But I would try in every other way to stop him. But if I couldn't stop him I'd join him. Why? Because then he would become irreligious altogether. If he should feel that he lost my love, then he wouldn't care for anything. I always hope to God that I don't have to go through that. But I'm trying to look at it from a very practical point of view; I don't want to lose a child just because he went to college, and many fine religious young men are educated and are extremely fine. I probably would have to join him." *

The Match

When a young man reaches marriageable age, the Rebbe or the boy's father may suggest that it is time for him to marry, or he may decide to seek a wife without any outside encouragement.

Boys usually marry in their early twenties; the girls are often in
their late teens. (Because no children were born in Europe during
the war, couples are often close to the same age.) There is a
tendency to prefer marriages within the same court or at least
within courts having a similar outlook, although even marriages
between children of hasidim and misnagdim are no longer uncommon. The ways of meeting a prospective wife are infinitely varied
and anyone can be the shadkhen (matchmaker). The young man's
father may recommend a match with the daughter of a friend or a
first or second cousin whom the young man has known all his life
but never considered as a potential mate. Usually a friend, relative,
or rabbi will suggest a suitable person for him to consider.

In my father-in-law's house there was open house. For example,
Shabbes morning, a lot of people used to come up to have coffee. It was
not far from the Rebbe, and before they went to the Rebbe, after the
mikveh, they used to come up. My mother-in-law, she should rest in
peace, always prepared a big pot of water and coffee and cake. So this
house was a well-known house. And I was also among those who came
up occasionally for coffee. So my wife was a popular girl. I mean she
was popular, first, because everybody knew the house. Who didn't
know Weiss? And everybody knew that he has a daughter, a very nice
daughter. So people talked and talked, it would be good. And once I
decided to call her up. I called her up, and we went out, and we got
engaged. That night we made up between ourselves that we agreed. I
proposed, like they say, and she agreed. The next morning we let the
parents know that we decided to become engaged. I knew that her
father and mother wanted it. Look at my wife. She's a nice girl, she's
intelligent, and she has a good heart. What else do you need? *

At times the Rebbe himself may take a hand in suggesting the
match and encouraging the sometimes awkward youth.

I met my wife here. She's an American-born girl. I used to organize
my schools and I hired a teacher, and I hired my wife. And she used to
teach English and I used to teach Jewish. And being there we met each
other, and the Rebbe made a match. The Rebbe was the matchmaker.
The Rebbe said: "I think the girl is good for you," and "you still
supervise the yeshiveh, so you know her." And the Rebbe said, "Yes." I
asked him. If the Rebbe said "yes," it's *yes.* I never thought an
American girl would take a greenhorn. I knew very little English then.
We used to speak sign language to each other. She didn't speak Yiddish
either. She was American born. She was already a beys yaakov girl
[graduate of a yeshiveh for girls] but she didn't speak Yiddish at all.
The Rebbe also went to the father. He found out who the father was. A
very great man, a very big scholar. And he found out about her. He

thinks she's the right girl for me. So I knew her very very well also by working with her. Then the Rebbe said, "Start to talk to her already." So I came to her and I gave her to understand. She also felt it's the right thing and said okay. This was before I spoke to her father.*

Similarly, the hasidic girl is guided into marriage by social conventions controlled to a great extent by the father of the family and on occasion by the Rebbe himself.

My father asked the Rebbe when I was about seventeen or eighteen, "Should Sarah marry?" The Rebbe said: "Wait. There's no hurry." He knew there's no hurry in my getting married. Then when I was nineteen the Rebbe asked my father: "What about any matches for Sarah?" We didn't know that he [her husband to be] had asked the Rebbe. My father mentioned my husband and another young man. So the Rebbe ignored the other one and began praising my husband very highly. I was an independent kind of girl and so my parents didn't even tell me. No Rebbe is going to tell me whom to marry—so they didn't. My father is the kind of person, the Rebbe praised my husband, so it was finished. There was nothing else to discuss. That was *it*. That was in April. It took a long time and we weren't married till September. We planned to be married around February. Right after Sukkes my father went to the Rebbe and the Rebbe said, "When are you planning the wedding?" And my father told him and the Rebbe said, "No. It's got to be in Kislev [November-December]. Kislev is a lucky Lubavitcher month." [4] And so I had to make all the plans in about six weeks.*

The governing premise of a match is, of course, that the orthodoxy of both parties be without blemish.

I considered the family very much. It happens in America that girls or boys come from families which are not so religious. At that time, I had the feeling that if I get married, it would be with such a family that if my parents would be alive, they wouldn't hesitate to have those people as their in-laws. That's what I felt. I would not consider to take a girl, no matter how religious she would have been, if her parents, or her uncles, or the rest of the family would not fit into our family. I just felt I owe it to my parents that I should not do something which my parents would not do if they would be alive.*

The success of the proposed match may suffer if any of the closest relatives are not devout, and the pious son of negligent

[4] Rabbi Shneur Zalman and Rabbi Dov Baer, the son of Shneur Zalman, were both released from imprisonment during the month of Kislev (the former on the nineteenth of Kislev in 1798 and the latter on the fourth of Kislev in 1825). Both days are celebrated as holidays by the Lubavitcher hasidim.

parents may have a serious barrier to a hasidic marriage. On the other hand, interest may be sharpened if ancestry can be traced to a famous rabbi or if perspective in-laws are well known for their learning. A learned and ambitious rabbi proudly recounted that his wife was a direct descendant of King David, and despite her other charms, this was clearly the point that had won him over.

The importance of family background is clear in the tales. In one account of a hasidic marriage, the soul of the Baal Shem Tov reprimanded his daughter, Edel, for not examining the family of a new groom more carefully. When he tried to invite other deceased relatives to the wedding, he found it necessary to descend to Gehenna to locate them (WH1). In familial conflict, one's yihus takes its share of blame. Attempting to excuse himself, an erring husband says, among other things, "She wasn't from the nicest people" (WH10). The existing status system is pointed up in one tale when Reb Motel's coachman, using the Rebbe's pronouncements on equality to suggest a match between their children, is quickly reminded that a social hierarchy exists among those whom the Rebbe calls righteous (W2).

Attitudes vary in the search for a wife: for some, beauty is a significant factor; for others, intelligence; still others are drawn to a distinguished family lineage. Regardless of the qualities sought, courtship is brief and very much to the point. The meetings between the couple often consist simply of conversations in the living room of the girl's family, although some couples might take a stroll unescorted. Although a generation ago, before the latest influx of immigrants, courting hasidic couples in New York might go to a movie or a play, it is now considered too daring. At present, after a few meetings between a prospective bride and groom, a decision is reached which is voluntary on both sides. The meetings between the couple are very purposeful.

The most I ever went out with a girl was once. That was all. If she would have interested me further for marriage purposes, I would have gone out with her again. Every girl I went to see once, I went to see with my parents. I never went to see a girl by myself. And usually I never went to see her again. Because I saw right away she was too old or she wasn't pretty, or something. I never went out with a girl twice till I met my wife. We went out four or five times till we were engaged. We were engaged for eight weeks.*

Before receiving his father-in-law's approval, however, the groom may be examined with regard to his talmudic learning and his orthodox appearance. At this point the hasidic man who has accommodated himself to western ways by being clean-shaven or by wearing modern dress must decide whether he should now take steps in the other direction to please his prospective father-in-law.

When a couple decides to wed, an agreement is made stipulating the financial obligations of both families. As early marriages are encouraged, provision is often made by the families for the couple to be supported until the husband has completed his talmudic studies.

Marriage

The orthodox marriage ceremony is held under the hupeh (marriage canopy). The white-gowned bride is led in and circles the groom seven times. The rabbi begins the service over a silver goblet of wine. Bridegroom and bride sip from the goblet. The bride's veil is lifted from her eyes. The groom places the ring on the index finger of the bride's right hand while reciting the traditional wedding formula and then smashes a wine glass against the ground. Shortly after the ceremony the bride and groom dine in private, breaking the fast they have kept all day and legally consummating the marriage. They then part to join the separate festivities, for, as with all social functions of the court, the women celebrate in a different room or in a separate half of the same room. The affair is usually a catered dinner at a hall. When the groom enters the room where the men are gathered, he is hoisted aloft on a chair, and the festivities begin with the groom's friends dancing and singing beneath him. With their comrade wed, the young men enthusiastically pitch in with all the pyrotechnical footwork at their command, but the highlights of the dancing are the exuberant energies of the white bearded patriarchs. The excitement keeps up all evening. As soon as the guests finish each course of the dinner they are out of their seats to return to the dancing on the floor. In many courts, the evening heads toward its conclusion with the mitsveh tentzl, a dance in which some of the close male relatives dance with the bride while holding the opposite ends of a handkerchief (since a hasid is not permitted to touch a woman other than his wife).

The sexual act that comes only with marriage also is suffused by religious law. In conformity with the orthodox strictures, the sexual act is never performed in the light, nor is it permissible to look at the sexual organs of a woman. The hasidim impart to their natural desire a kind of holy awe—and concern for their offspring. During sexual intercourse one is advised to think of the Torah or of a tsaddik.

Sex is amongst the holiest things in religion. Sex cannot be without pleasure. I don't care what anybody would say. Without a person having any pleasure about sex, it's impossible. But sex can be so holy if it is done according to the Jewish way of life, and the religious way of life, and the hasidic way of life. Actually, we believe—not we believe, we know it for a fact—that the thoughts the parents have during their sexual relations have the most effect on the child that is being born. That means on the character and on the religion, on everything, on the whole child. The Gemoreh says in fact that, let's say, that if a person hates his wife, he's angry at his wife, and he has relations with her at that time, that child will have certain characteristics of hate. The more they love each other, the smarter the child will be. They should actually pray during relations that the children should be smart, and they should put in mind some very great person, that you want to have your child be like that great person. The thing is not that he's laying with his wife like a cat, like a dog, or like a cow, or like an ox, or they lay for the purely sexual—I mean they have no other thought behind it. A human is something higher than an animal.*

While the young couple customarily establishes their own apartment immediately after marriage, the life of the young man may not change appreciably; often he continues his studies and is supported by his in-laws and his family or by a stipend from the court (I13). But from the moment of marriage, the wife's life centers around the home. The chief religious duties of women consist of the preparation of the food, the bearing of children, the religious training of the young, and the maintenance of the purity of the home by careful attendance at the mikveh and observation of the attendant sexual regulations. The tales illustrate the consequences to women who ignore the rituals. One tale notes that neglect in attending the mikveh may result in harm to one's offspring (H52). Punishment can be even more direct for those who despise their obligations, as one tale of a terrible fiery bath indicates (H55). Other customs too must be followed. At marriage, the bride's hair should be clipped and thereafter she is to wear a wig or tight-fitting kerchief; in one tale, failure to bear children is directly attributed to ignoring this custom (HA46).

Both law and custom emphasize the importance of bearing children. The law requires that each man propagate at least one son and one daughter.[5] If a marriage is childless for ten years, the law enjoins the man to seek a divorce, although this is not often done in practice (TA25).[6] Children are highly prized and a childless couple must endure the pity and curiosity of the community as well as their own sense of frustration and despair.[7] Not have children? "Do not even think of it" notes one narrator in describing someone's plight (H37). In the tales the childless woman may travel long distances to throw herself before the Rebbe: "You must help me. I don't have any children" (HA30).[8] Some tales are introduced by the tsaddik blessing a barren marriage so that a couple could conceive (H12, H35). In the hope that his wife would emulate the story, the elder Stoliner Rebbe told how Rabbi Yaakov Emden's clever young wife kept the aged scholar alive into very old age by making him promise first that they would have a child and then that he would attend his son's wedding (W7). But petitions are not necessary too often. Families are usually large, particularly since prophylactic devices are forbidden for men and can be used for women only to prevent serious illness; in addition, sexual relations are resumed seven days after the menstrual period when women approach their most fertile time. Being a parent is a secure reward. Offered his choice of treasures by a king, the Jew says: "I have children, and I make a nice living. What else do I want?" (I14). For those whose sins prevent them from entering Paradise, the greatest reward is to wander the earth saving children's lives (H35).

While there is a great deal of family devotion, and parents may be demonstrably affectionate to their young children, there are few public displays of affection between husband and wife. As with all orthodox Jews, the hasidic couple must exercise restraint even in private. No sexual contact is permitted during the time of the wife's menstrual flow or for seven days after it has ceased and until she has immersed herself in the mikveh. During this period of time no physical contact of any sort is permitted: husband and wife cannot even pass an object directly from one to the other without first putting it down. For this reason in all orthodox homes hus-

---

[5] See *Code of Jewish Law*, chap. 145, no. 2.
[6] *Ibid.*, chap. 145, no. 4.
[7] See Babylonian Talmud, *Yebamot* 64a.
[8] In a similar beginning of a tale, an innkeeper who never had children runs toward the Besht seeking his help (*In Praise of the Besht*, no. 212). The Besht helps petitioners have sons in *ibid.*, nos. 222, 223, 224; see also no. 107, in which the Besht aids a wealthy man in having a son, although it means he will lose all his riches.

band and wife sleep in separate beds. The laws concerning conduct during the monthly cycle are clearly spelled out in the Shulhan Arukh.[9] Not cited by the law are the strains experienced by the young couple who, despite an often unromantic engagement, come swiftly to regard each other with affection, love, and a strong physical need.

Prophylactic devices are forbidden for men; however, confronted with a serious health problem related to child bearing, a hasidic woman might seek out an understanding orthodox rabbi who would permit her (not her husband) to use a prophylactic device on the grounds that the law may bend when there is a clear danger to life. (There are, to be sure, some rabbis who would not make this recommendation.) Another method that a woman might use to avoid pregnancy is to wait until her fertile period is past before going to the mikveh to cleanse herself in preparation for conjugal relations. But in general husband and wife prefer to consult an understanding rabbi.

The only way of practicing birth control is when the woman practices it. The only way is if the doctor were to tell me that she is not allowed to, that she is sick, that it would endanger her health; that she must wait two years or three years, or five years, or ten years, or whatever. I would go to a rabbi to ask him, but I know what the answer would be. I know the answer would be yes. I don't say that all the rabbis would agree, but ninety-nine per cent of them would agree. And there is no doubt in my mind that I would ask if the question should come up. I have to continue a family as long as the doctor doesn't tell me, "Listen, your wife is pregnant, she can hemorrhage, she can rupture, or who knows what," or he would say that her mental health would be very strained. If she's extremely nervous and her mental health were to be strained—then I would say yes.[*]

While there are powerful social pressures for maintaining marriage, and divorces are consequently rare, it is possible to obtain a religious divorce even on the relatively simple grounds of incompatibility. The avowed source of discord in two cases of divorce, obviously statistically insignificant, concerned the wife's charge of her husband's rigidity and aloofness, matched in turn by wife's demand for greater rapport, sympathy, and understanding. One wife reportedly complained: "He would eat, get up, and go out without a word—like I was a slave." For his part, the husband told his fellows that his wife always wanted to go out dancing, a

[9] *Code of Jewish Law* chap. 153.

common reference to cover a variety of nonreligious behavior. In the other instance, strikingly similar, the wife's father blamed himself for arranging a marriage with a rigid misnaged instead of a more sympathetic hasidic youth. In both situations the Rebbe of each court was consulted: in the first situation the Rebbe agreed that the attitudes of the couple were irreconcilable; in the second instance the Rebbe considered the wife's complaints to be childish. (In neither case, however, did the Rebbe have anything to do with the divorce itself since the act of divorce can be performed only by a court of ordained rabbis and the Rebbe is in this regard a private person.)

For those who remain within the hasidic fold, marital infidelity is rare. All relationships between the sexes are rigidly controlled, and the law prevents a man and woman (other than father and daughter or husband and wife) from being alone together. There are, of course, situations in the New World against which one must be on guard, but the hasidim have learned to accommodate themselves to them.

The right thing is not to sit next to a woman. But it has become unfortunate because we travel every day in the subway and you're tired, and you can't stand up and it has become in America the sort of thing people don't even notice anymore. In Israel you never would find an orthodox man sitting next to a woman in a bus. The women know more, the men know more, and they try to keep away. But in New York, you come home tired from a day's work, and I have a seat—I wouldn't even know who is sitting next to me. It's the very truth I wouldn't know because I take out my *New York Times* or whatever I'm reading and within three minutes I'm asleep anyway, so I don't know who is sitting next to me. I'll be very truthful, I don't even know whether it's a woman sitting next to me. I wouldn't jump up even though the right thing would be to jump up. But still I wouldn't. *

The Upbringing of Women

The social division between the sexes begins early in childhood and lasts throughout life. The modesty of the hasidic girl is protected from the age of three (or six, depending on the custom of the court) by long stockings, long sleeves, and high-necked blouses.

You have to walk a middle road. Some will say to a three-year-old girl: "Why do you shake hands with a man? Why don't you wear long stockings?" You have to protect them in this sex-saturated atmosphere, but it doesn't have to have a morbid emphasis. The Lubavitchers don't make a fuss about sleeves below the elbow and stockings to the knee. My friends criticize me for being so lenient. When we went to the country my little girl wanted to put on long stockings, and I said, "No," and made her wear shorts. I said, "She's going to get the sun. I don't care what the other children say." The other mothers criticized me, saying, "If the child wants to be religious, why do you prevent her?" *

In the hasidic hierarchy of values, women are accorded less importance than men.[10] As a result education is considerably different for hasidic girls than for boys. As the hasidim do not regard the intellect of girls to be equal to that of the boys, it is considered sufficient if they learn about the Bible, the religious holidays, and the dietary laws. Girls begin school later than the boys and their studies do not venture into the Talmud; instead, they learn more about Hebrew grammar, science, and languages, subjects thought to be of slight significance.

The hasidic girl has greater opportunity to go to college than the male yeshiveh student; however, advanced education is not particularly encouraged and the hasidic girl generally follows the approved guidelines.

I was a pretty good student. I was ashamed to go back to school and say I hadn't gone to college. We went in to the Rebbe and he suggested that I go on to study for a Hebrew teacher. Then my father told me years later, after I went out he remained and the Rebbe said, "If she really wants to go very badly, let her." But my father, of course, never told me, because he was very anxious that I shouldn't go. That's one thing I never regretted. *

The hasidic girl is carefully shielded from boys from her early years until her marriage. Matters relating to sex are never discussed. There is no preparation for the bodily changes that take place at puberty, nor is there much exchange between mother and daughter concerning marital relations. Women are even secretive about their attendance at the mikveh at the end of their menstrual cycle, for the bath is not only a purificatory rite, it is also a prelude to the sexual act.

You're not supposed to tell anyone you're going to the mikveh. Some women don't even tell their husbands. It's very embarrassing if you

[10] See Maimon's *Autobiography*, p. 176, where the hasidim threaten to whip one of their fellows whose wife had given birth to a girl. In *In Praise of the Besht*, no. 107, a hasid would go to the Besht for an amulet and give him money *even* when his wife gave birth to a girl.

meet friends there. I'd die if I'd meet my mother there, although my
mother would be more embarrassed than me. A girl friend of mine met
her mother-in-law at the mikveh and was very embarrassed.*

Theoretically, sex is as seldom discussed among hasidic women
as among the men, but while both men and women draw back from
this topic, women do have more opportunity and fewer restrictions
concerning such talk.

About those women who talk too much or are too curious we say:
"She would like to be the woman at the mikveh." [There is one woman
at the mikveh to see that the bather's body is completely submerged.]*

Hasidic women follow a curious course dictated by religion and
style. Most hasidic women have abandoned eastern European dress
for more fashionable western clothing; the dresses, however, are
always worn with long sleeves and high necklines. All married
hasidic women today wear wigs, although the wigs are set in the
latest hair styles. Hasidic women do not practice birth control;
most, however, prefer not to breast-feed their babies.

With no ritual role to play in the religious prayers, women
usually attend services only on the holidays and then they sit in a
balcony or in an adjacent room carefully screened from the men.
On the Shabbes morning, while the men begin a long day of prayer
in the besmedresh, the women remain at home where they take
care of the younger children and read the prayers when it is
possible. Women are usually not consulted by their husbands on
religious matters in which the family may be involved, such as
which yeshiveh to send their son; nor is their consent required
when activities of the court keep husbands away from the home for
periods of time. They may not even be asked to discuss the family's
move to a new neighborhood, or, for that matter, to a new country.

When we were in Paris, David wrote to the previous Rebbe asking for
permission to come to the United States. He didn't tell me. I was
annoyed because I wanted to go to Israel where the rest of my family is
living. He wanted to come to the United States. The Rebbe said, "Come
here." If he had written we should go to Israel we would have gone
there.*

The social life of hasidic women revolves around weddings,
circumcisions, bar mitsves, and holidays, although even on these
occasions they are carefully segregated from the men. In contrast
to eastern European life of a generation ago, however, hasidic
women are more exposed to the influence of the outside culture.

Unlike the men, many hasidic women go to movies and read secular books, and many listen to the radio and watch television. Although some courts have a ban on television, some of the women watch television in a neighbor's home (and some husbands may at times join them to watch the news or some special event).[11] Their education extends at least through high school and a few may even attend college; some may take jobs in business concerns or factories before marriage or later in life. There are no career women, but after marriage a woman may work until pregnancy ends her outside remunerative activities. The eastern European pattern of women tending small shops while the men study or journey on a pilgrimage to their Rebbe has been all but abandoned. Men rather than women are expected to provide for the family, although those hasidim who own small shops may continue to depend on their wives for assistance.

Although the women are loyal to the Rebbe and to the court, they do not share to the same degree the sense of camaraderie and zeal as their husbands since they take part in few of the rituals centering around the Rebbe. The choice of the men would be to study and ignore women's work and women's ways (which concern, according to the men, gossip and household affairs), but women are coming to demand a larger role in hasidic life. It also seems that an increasing number of hasidic women are able to express their resentment of the time the men spend away from the home fulfilling their obligations to the court and to the Rebbe.

An American-born hasid explains his wife's feelings and his own accommodations:

She used to resent it. She did not like it. It took about a year. It came gradually. She saw I made up my mind about it and that's it. In fact when the Rebbe was here, I went away a couple of times for the whole Shabbes. And then it was natural. It took a long time till it became natural for her, though. At first she resented it. I don't blame her. She was home alone; she had it hard with the children. The first year she didn't resent it. She didn't care till we had the baby. You know, she went out and I went out wherever we went. But after the baby— naturally she had to stay home with the children and she had a hard time. And maybe she was right, even though I never would have admitted it to her, but she was right. I tried my best. Many times I would come home and I wouldn't go to the Rebbe because my wife was also important. On Friday nights I gave in to her. I used to daven with

<hr>

[11] The Satmarer hasidim are forbidden to watch television. Reading English language newspapers is also reported to be eschewed by some hasidim. See Sobel, "The M'lochim," pp. 47–48.

her every Friday night [after the court's prayers]. But it happened that we came home very late Friday night, so I stopped davening with her every Friday night. I think she was tired. Friday was a hard day's work getting prepared for Shabbes and then I'd come home from davening [around] ten-thirty, especially summer days, and she would be tired. And I didn't blame her. So where else am I supposed to daven just to be home early? *

A hasidic magazine for women published by the Lubavitcher hasidim reflects the shifting tides in the community: in one issue a rabbi cautioned women not to have their husbands help them with the dishes too often as this would result in neglect of the study of the Torah.[12] Of course, the existence of such a problem would be inconceivable in a hasidic home in Europe. (In the same issue a letter to the editor expressed the wish that proper bathing suits be designed so that there could be mixed attendance at the beach, a suggestion promptly vetoed by the responding woman editor as contrary to the law.) [13] The publication of the magazine itself is a remarkable innovation.

There are other changes wrought by American-oriented wives who find more attractive a social life that calls for social intercourse between couples in place of the sharp division between men and women.

There were certain ways that my wife changed me—not in religious things, but until I got married I didn't know what visiting was. I didn't know that it was a thing that you could get any enjoyment from. And then my wife said she wanted to go out visiting. And I said, "What's that?" It looked as if it was crazy. "I just have to go out and sit and see the people and talk? Why do I have to visit? What do I gain out of it?" But after a while, naturally, I got used to it, and I go out with her and I enjoy it and it became a natural part of our lives. So she changed me a bit away from my parents. *

The tales, however, generally reflect the European image of relationships in marriage. Since the tales are told by men rather than by women, they contain the accepted male attitudes. Their general import is that marriage is a commandment of the Torah and the need of our nature, but that talmudic learning, pious dedication to prayer, and the relationship of the tsaddik and his followers are higher callings. Relationships between husbands and

[12] Rabbi M. Hadacov, "Spiritual Maladies of Our Age," *Di Yiddishe Heim*, 1 (1959): 18.
[13] *Ibid.*, p. 11.

wives have to be accommodated to meet the demands of learning and brotherhood.

One tale tells of a hasid who accompanied his wife to his father's house for her first visit, left her there, and returned to the Rebbe's court (WH8). In a similar tale, when the youthful Reb Mikhel left his wife with her family so that he could retire into solitude, his father placated the disturbed father-in-law: "I knew that he would want this, but not so soon. But since it's his wish, blessed be he for wanting such a thing" (T11). And the storyteller adds that three years later the zealous student became a Rebbe.

The older printed tales, such as those in *In Praise of the Besht*, depict the wife as a passive, unquestioning creature, content to toil long years for her pious husband who is immersed in his studies.[14] There are as well tender thoughts of husbands preserved in later tales, as when the Rizhyner declined to go to Israel after his wife's death since he could not leave half his soul behind (WH5), or when a hasid decided not to go to heaven because it would mean leaving his wife a grass widow (H8). But not all wives are so patient nor are all men so pious and considerate.

Marriage is trying, and some of the tales point a wry and mischievous finger at man's fate. The angel who reprimands the Jew who had little time for his religious duties because of a nagging wife is himself thoroughly rebuked. "How do you know? You're an angel." The angel so angers the Heavenly Court that he is sent to earth to see if he can fare better under such difficult circumstances. Needless to say, he fails (T1).

For the pious, one woman may be as much a burden as another. In one tale the hasid who comes to his Rebbe to appeal for a divorce dreams of marriage to a succession of wives each more shrewish than the preceding one. He remains married to his first wife— under such circumstances divorce is a waste of time (WH13). The problems of one harassed husband are solved when the Rebbe points out that his punishment at her hands saves him from being reborn countless times; learning of her inadvertent kindness, however, the farseeing wife ceases her nagging (WH12). Even the tsaddikim are not immune from nagging wives. Distressed over the peculiar ethics of her pious spouse, Rabbi Zev Wolf's wife complained bitterly to the Ropchitser Rov that she wanted her husband

[14] See *In Praise of the Besht*, no. 8. The wife of Rabbi Akiba may be considered to be the paragon of such virtue. After waiting while her husband completed twelve years of study, it was her wish that he go off for an additional twelve years. See *Ma'aseh Book*, trans. Moses Gaster, 1: 68.

to act like an ordinary man and to speak like everyone else (T33). The Maharash's wife nagged him until he settled a relative's difficulty in locating her husband—"You take care of the whole world and for a relative you don't do anything" (WH10).

Sometimes the Rebbes take pity on a henpecked male, as did the Stoliner Rebbe when he sent his foolish gabai, Moshe Gendarme, to eat a potful of horos (a dish of potatoes, barley, and beans) every Shabbes so that the poor husband would not have to face that tasteless dish for the remaining days of the week (S24).

While divorce may have been rare, the older tales indicate that desertion was not unknown (WH10, WH11). The cause of desertion was sometimes the result of long separations brought about when the husband was taken into the army. In such instances it was the Rebbe's task to locate the husband or to establish that he was dead. In order to remarry, a wife needed a divorce or a death certificate. Other sources of strife are often seen to lie in the kitchen or in an insufficient allowance granted to a wife (WH10). At such times a simple solution such as increasing the wife's allowance is said to result in a proportionate increase in the love in the house (WH3). In general, in a world of arranged marriages and no romantic illusions, the Rebbes accept few excuses from errant husbands. When an absentee husband complained bitterly to the Maharash—"Whenever I asked her for cream, she gave me sour milk. So I ran away"—he was challenged: "What do you want? A noblewoman? She's a Jewish girl and that's enough for you" (WH10).

THE REBBE

The Role of the Rebbe

The Rebbe occupies a unique position in the hasidic court and in the belief structure of the community.[1] On the one hand he directs the affairs of the court, designating the gabai, the leaders of the besmedresh and the yeshiveh. In this aspect of his duties the Rebbe may function at times as an enterprising executive.[2] But the Rebbe's role has another side, for he also serves as a mediator between his followers and God. His long hours at prayer, his special piety and concentration, and his private and public talks are directed toward that end.

In the source and nature of his authority in his court the Rebbe is quite unlike a rabbi, who, ordained in a rabbinical seminary or by a great talmudic scholar, decides on questions of ritual law. While the Rebbe may be ordained also as a rabbi, his power and authority have their roots in his intense piety, in his special relationship to God, and in his yihus (lineage). The Rebbe's position is an inherited one, usually transmitted through several generations. And, as the oral tradition makes clear, in his relationship to his followers the Rebbe functions in the uncertain areas of life rather than in the clearly defined domain of the law.

[1] For a discussion of the Rebbe's role in the eastern European community, see Zborowski and Herzog, *Life Is with People*, pp. 166–88.

[2] Some Rebbes enjoy reputations as administrators. The Klausenberger Rebbe worked in the DP camps immediately after the war and organized yeshives and built mikves; in the United States he founded schools and an old age home, while in Israel he has organized a village. The Lubavitcher Rebbe is the head of a far-reaching network of hasidim who found schools and preach to congregations. The Bobover Rebbe, who prefers that his followers be workers and businessmen rather than serve as rabbis, established a watchmaker's school after the war to train young immigrants.

The Piety of the Rebbe

The Rebbe spends a great part of each day in preparation for prayer and then in prayer itself. Each Rebbe's way of prayer, however, is somewhat different, depending on his point of view and the traditions of his court. The Lubavitcher Rebbe, for example, prays together with his court, while the Boyaner, in keeping with the regal traditions of Rizhyn, prays in a room apart from his followers. But regardless of form, the essence of *being* a Rebbe, as one hasid said, is that "he worships God every second of the day with all his heart and soul."

In his attempt to be the perfect righteous man and to protect himself from the Evil Urge, the Rebbe fulfills the precepts of the Torah with extraordinary zeal and insight. There are accounts of earlier Rebbes who separated themselves from the world (T11), who purged themselves of sin by rolling in the snow (S17), who felt the world was not worth a sigh (W6), or who caused themselves physical discomfort so that they would not partake of pleasure (T43, T45, T59). It is said that the Baal Shem Tov regarded Rabbi Haim ben Atar, a contemporary who died in the Holy Land, as greater than himself in one respect: while the Besht always purified himself in the mikveh after moving his bowels, Rabbi Haim ben Atar always went to the mikveh after urinating (T4).

Contemporary Rebbes, no less than Rebbes of the past, are said to assume additional obligations to purify themselves: The Satmarer Rebbe is said to put on three pairs of tefillin during the day.[3] The followers of the Squarer Rebbe say that their Rebbe wears his tefillin until late afternoon, and that he seasons his food so that it is unpalatable and gives him no pleasure. One Rebbe is said to abstain from conjugal intercourse, having propagated the number of children required by law. While no pious Jew would begin his prayers while feeling the need to relieve himself, one aged Rebbe delays

---

[3] The tefillin contain parchment on which are inscribed Exod. 3: 1–10, 11–16, and Deut. 6: 4–9, 11: 13–21. In the twelfth century a dispute arose between the great scholar Rashi and his grandson, R. Tam, as to the proper order of the passages; therefore, many pietists put on two pairs of tefillin during the course of the morning service—one according to the order stipulated by Rashi, and the other according to the order stated by his grandson. The third pair represents the point of view of "Shimusha Rabba." While many of the pious might put on two pairs of phylacteries during the day, it is rare that anyone puts on a third pair. See Lehrman, *Jewish Customs*, pp. 96–97.

saying the morning prayer until noon to be certain that his bowels are evacuated.[4]

The Rebbe's concerns are to be measured by a completely different scale than that of ordinary men. The Rebbe is thought to be devoid of vanity and idle concerns. The Besht was said never to look into a mirror (H9). A hasid recalled that each day as the Tchortkover Rebbe walked from his bedroom, he passed two huge mirrors on the wall, but so oblivious was he to earthly things that it was several years before he noticed them (T55). The father of the present Lubavitcher Rebbe lectured his son because the boy was too concerned about little things, such as his new shoes (T61). One account tells that Israel of Stolin practiced greeting himself in front of a mirror to teach himself the pointlessness of public honors (T56a). There are other examples of special piety in a variety of circumstances. It is said of Israel's son, the late Stoliner Rebbe, that he kept various denominations of money separated in different pockets so that he could handle his daily affairs without having to look at money (TA5); and like so many others of the pious, while out walking he is said to have kept his eyes down to avoid impure sights (TA6).[5] Even during the terrible internment in the concentration camps, the Rebbes managed to maintain their piety by extraordinary courage and guile. The Satmarer Rebbe declined to shave off his beard (N18). The Klausenberger told how on Yom Kippur he risked his life when, after being ordered to carry a blanket, he turned it into a garment so that he would not commit the sin of carrying anything on that holy day (N24).

The Rebbe too embodies all the orthodox virtues. When he gives charity he keeps nothing back, even though his own family might be in want. In one account the Sandzer Rov had to be tricked into providing for his own family by having a recipient of his charity turn over the money to the Rebbe's wife (W4); in exasperation, the Sandzer's son protested that he was no less worthy than the shoemaker's son (S10). It is said that the Lemberger Rov went into debt in giving charity (N13). Since hasidic teachings stress other qualities of character, such as temperance, humility, and modesty, the Rebbe may be expected to personify the attainment of these virtues as well. The humility of the Dinover Rov led him to place the simple recital of psalms above his own erudition and insight (W15). The pious and philosophical Rabbi Motke Nesh-

---

[4] See *Code of Jewish Law*, chap. 12, no. 3.

[5] It is said of the Belzer that he even turned his eyes away from his wife. See Langer, *Nine Gates*, pp. 11–12.

khizer, upon finding that an excited follower had mistakenly cut two holes in the Rebbe's talis koten instead of one, remarked that the talis required two holes—one for his head and one to test his ability to avoid anger (W4).

In their common intercourse with others, the Rebbes may combine their piety with subtle insights often enigmatic to observers. It is told that Reb Zev Wolf never identified the contents of his bedding since there was a dispute as to the quality of the feathers and he feared defaming the woman who had sold them to him (T33); in another instance he denied having permitted a robber to steal his silver candlesticks, asserting that he had mentally relinquished ownership of them so that the robber would not commit a sin (T32). More recently, Rabbi Halberstamm told that his father never permitted potentially dangerous words like "knife" and "evil" to pass his lips.

Even the actions of Rebbes who appeared to have left the community are reported to have been the guise for secret piety of a still higher order. Rabbi Dov Baer of Leovo, the son of the Rizhyner, left the hasidic fold for a time, and in fact joined the followers of the haskala. The tales, however, tell that he only pretended to abandon the hasidic faith in order to trick the Yetser Hora into revealing his secret to him (H50). The Rizhyner Rebbe was often criticized for the material splendor of his court, but one well-known tale relates that the golden boots of the Rizhyner concealed a secret penance in that the soles of his feet were bare and bleeding (T43). When Rabbi Israel succeeded his father and became the Stoliner Rebbe, he dressed and acted in modern fashion; but when he took a horseback ride on the morning of his daughter's wedding, it was said that rather than to enjoy the excursion the Rebbe rode to cause himself pain and to discourage his partaking of pleasure (T59).

Traditionally, the Rebbe is said to mask his piety—much as when the youthful Baal Shem Tov dressed in simple garb and studied at night to conceal his virtues. The Sassover similarly was said to have disguised himself as a peasant to cloak his good deeds (T14). In like manner, since one must not use the Torah as a stepping stone or as a source of honor, many Rebbes are reported to have cultivated reputations as ignorant men, so that only the Rebbe's faithful followers, who see him at unguarded moments, know his true dedication to learning. Today, Bobover hasidim tell how their Rebbe was seen studying in secret late into the night (TA24). The Stoliner hasidim say that their Rebbe studied secretly at night even in the concentration camp (N27), and similar

reports continued to be told of the Stoliner when he lived in the
United States:

> I had the privilege of serving him when he was unable to do things for
> himself, and many times when he was studying and he would hear a
> knock at the door, he would close his book so that people shouldn't see
> he was studying.*

The Rebbe's Role in History

The leadership of some hasidic Rebbes is further substantiated by
knowledge of their having lived as sainted leaders in previous
reincarnations. The revelation of the hidden lineage of the Rebbe's
soul adds the grandeur of a sainted past and emphasizes the per-
vading presence of the past within the Rebbe himself. The Berdichever Rebbe was said to be the reincarnation of Rabbi Akiba; Reb
Israel of Stolin was said to have the soul of the scholar Rashi, while
his father, Reb Asher, was said to have been heir to David's soul
(T60). During the Yom Kippur prayers the Apter Rov referred to
himself as the High Priest in ancient Jerusalem (T25). Awed
hasidim heard Rabbi Moshe Teitelbaum recall that in previous
lives he had been one of the sheep in Jacob's flock when Jacob had
labored for Laban, and that he had been present when Moses led
the Jews from Egypt and later when the tablets were destroyed.
Although he was reluctant to speak of his last reincarnation, which
was at the time of the destruction of the First Temple, it was
subsequently shown that Rabbi Moshe Teitelbaum had been the
prophet Jeremiah (T39).

To the Rebbe falls the guardianship of all Israel. More conscious of the destiny of the Jews, and with greater spiritual powers
because of their piety and yihus, the Rebbes are believed to take an
active part in the historic process. A righteous man can overturn
history, and tradition records how Rebbes, such as the Rizhyner,
who set aside the tsar's decree (H34), and the Sandzer, who
stopped an invading army (N6), could reverse decrees made by
the highest human as well as heavenly authorities. Faced with
impending disaster, the hasidim inevitably turn to the leading
tsaddik of the generation (T12).

The great task on which all religious Jews labor is to hasten the
appearance of the Meshiah and to bring an end to the exile, and the
devotion of the Rebbes to this work surpasses that of ordinary men.

Rabbi Moshe Teitelbaum always kept his walking stick near at hand so that he would be prepared to accompany the Meshiah. So intent was he upon the Meshiah's arrival that he would startle at a surprise entrance thinking it was *he* (T36). The Ropchitser Rov concealed his prayers for the return of Meshiah in seemingly innocuous words (T30). The Lelever and Szigetter Rebbes swore they would refuse to enter the Garden of Eden until the Meshiah appeared, although tradition reports that they were beguiled into entering and the gates shut behind them (T37).

These two ideas—the power exercised over events by the Rebbes and their desire to hasten the coming of the Meshiah—are clearly seen in 1812 when the outcome of Napoleon's campaign into Russia was said to hinge on the powers exercised by the Rebbes, while the ultimate disposition of the war would bring the Meshiah. The hasidic Rebbes were divided among themselves as to whom they should support, and in legendary tradition the tide of battle swayed back and forth in response to their efforts. Storytellers relate that Napoleon saw the face of the Lubliner Rebbe on the front lines planning the strategy to halt his advance (N2). The Lubliner feared that a French victory would bring intellectual enlightenment in the wake of sweeping social and political reform, and this posed a greater threat than the oppressive decrees of Tsar Alexander I. The Rimanover Rebbe, on the other hand, favored Napoleon. Like others, he viewed Napoleon as the warrior who would herald the final battles before the coming of the Meshiah, and he sought through kabbalistic means to ensure his victory. He is said to have magically likened his baking of matses to the destruction of Russian troops, and not even the pleas of Jewish mothers whose sons were in the Russian army could move him from his plan to force the Meshiah to come (N3, N4). It is told that Napoleon called the Rimanover his strategist, and he gave him a mantle for the Torah (N2). The Rimanover joined with the Lubliner Rebbe and the Mezhibezher Rebbe to try to force the Meshiah to appear, but the Mezhibezher Rebbe died before the appointed hour (T21). The forces that fear messianic redemption had temporarily triumphed. Napoleon, however, was doomed when at the Shabbes prayer the Rebbe of Kozhenits read Exodus 18:18, *novol tibol* (thou will surely wear away—or Esther 6:13, *nofol tipol*, thou shalt surely fall) as *Nopol tipol* (Napoleon will fall) (N1).[6]

[6] See Pipe, "Napoleon in Jewish Folklore," *YIVO Annual of Jewish Social Science*, I (1946): 294–304.

The power of the Rebbes to intervene in history did not end with the destruction of village life in eastern Europe. The prayers of the Hushatener Rebbe, who escaped to Israel, are given credit for stopping Rommel's advance in Africa during World War II (N23), and the Belzer is said to have assured victory for the Israeli forces during the Sinai campaign (N37). The pleas of the Stoliner Rebbe before the Heavenly Court are said to have succeeded in delaying the Arab-Israel war for three years (N34). Others say that he delayed World War II (N2). Before the war, the Stoliner believed that his prayers at the graves of the great tsaddikim in Israel assured the safety of the land of Israel, but he was anguished at the feeble efforts of the tsaddikim in Europe. "Why are they so quiet?" he had asked. "Why don't they try to save Europe?" (N8).

In recent times, the horrifying events and the Rebbes' works had seemed certain to herald the end of the exile. When the Lubavitcher Rebbe died in Brooklyn, New York, in 1950, four years after a stroke, his followers were stunned. The catastrophic times and the Rebbes unending efforts to redeem the Jews had seemed certain to bring success. It was inconceivable to many of his followers that the Rebbe had died without bringing about the Golden Age. Imbued with equal ardor and conviction, the Stoliner hasidim say that their Rebbe, who wore two watches—one kept the standard time and the other was wound according to time in the Holy Land (TA7)—possessed the soul of the Meshiah, but that, unfortunately, the Almighty did not grant him permission to reveal himself (T60).

The Rebbe and the Shabbes

In America today, as previously in eastern Europe, there are four ritual occasions during the Shabbes at which the court and the Rebbe meet for communal meals and food, drink, and learning are shared. The first meal (seudeh rishona) is held on Friday evening, the second meal (seudeh shenia) around noon on Saturday immediately after prayer services, and the third meal (seudeh shelishit, or shalehseudes) at dusk after the afternoon prayer. The fourth meal, the melaveh malkeh, when the wonders of the tsaddikim are recounted, is held late Saturday night. The meals are designated for Abraham, Isaac, Jacob, and David.[7] They serve to symbolize the

[7] See Minkin, *Romance of Hassidism*, pp. 326–30.

bond between the community and the historic events of the past, and between the community and God.

Seated at the Rebbe's table for the meals are the outstanding rabbis of the community, visiting scholars, and close relatives. When a young man is married, he has the honor to sit by the Rebbe's side during that Shabbes. The followers of the Rebbe crowd around his table several rows deep, often standing on benches to see and hear the Rebbe better.

The meals are always enlivened by song and often by dance as well. The hasidim have no salaried cantor, nor are there any musical instruments used, so the Rebbe will simply point to a hasid or call his name to sing. At once everyone joins in. The texts are drawn from the Psalms or were composed by mystics of later centuries, and the melodies stem from the folk tradition of eastern Europe. Often as not the melody is sung without words. In the past, some Rebbes composed songs for their followers and the custom is still carried on in some courts.[8]

During the Shabbes meals when the hasidim drink a glass of beer or brandy they wait to catch the eye of the Rebbe, then toast to his health (lehaim), and receive in return his blessing for a good and peaceful life (lehaim tovim ulesholem).[9] The Rebbe is always served extra large portions from which he eats only a small amount. (On Friday night the Rebbe is served fish, soup, chicken, and later fruit; on Saturday afternoon at the third meal, fish is the principal dish.) After the Rebbe has finished eating each portion, the shiraim (remains) of the fish, haleh, chicken, and even soup from which the Rebbe has eaten are passed out among the hasidim. The Rebbe cuts the remains into small portions, designates for whom each piece is meant (or else the gabai indicates the proper person), and the portion is then passed from hand to hand down the line of hasidim seated at the table or standing in the surrounding crowd (S7).[10] This continues until the last hasid has received at least a taste of the Rebbe's fish or until the food is exhausted. Circumstances, however, are not always so well organized and polite, and the hasidim often struggle vehemently to snatch a piece of the Rebbe's food or to sip from his bowl. (The urgency of the competition is evident in the tale concerning the

[8] See *ibid.*, pp. 306–9. The Moditzer and Bobover hasidim are especially known for their musical tradition. The Lubavitcher Rebbe also teaches his hasidim a new song every year. These "new" songs are often eastern European folk songs which are given new significance and meaning.

[9] See the description in *ibid.*, pp. 326–28.

[10] See the description in Poll, *Hasidic Community*, p. 80.

pudding snatched from the Ropchitser Rov [S7].) The origin of this custom is not known and interpretations of its meaning vary. Many hasidim see the remains as an opportunity to partake of something which the Rebbe has made holy and potent. Others hold the subtle view that the Rebbe takes from the food that aspect of it on which he subsists—its spiritual content (it is apparent to the hasidim that the Rebbe scarcely touches the food and takes little interest in savoring its taste). What the Rebbe leaves intact in the food is its material content. This material element represents the promise of material benefits to the hasidim, and to share it with the Rebbe means to partake of those benefits.

The most important moment of the meal arrives when the Rebbe gives his toyreh, interpreting the portion of the Scriptures for the week or speaking about events close to the hearts of the hasidim.

On Friday evening the Rebbe speaks twice, at what are considered two meals. At the first meal the Rebbe discusses the reading in the Torah for the week in a fairly straightforward manner. After the meal songs are sung, and then the Rebbe begins a more mystical discourse, perhaps by putting his finger down at random on a line in the portion of the week. Slowly chanting, he weaves his exigesis about the phrase (T12). Afterward, a bowl of assorted fruit is brought in and the Rebbe, beginning with the grapes, samples the fruit and passes the remainder to his followers. The atmosphere is now more relaxed and, depending on the situation, there is more general conversation and discussion at the Rebbe's table. A variety of subjects may be considered, ranging from contemporary world affairs to questions in the Talmud. When the second meal ends, the hasidim dance in a circle and sing.[11] After watching for a half hour or more, at about one in the morning, the Rebbe says "Gut Shabbes," and leaves.

On the following afternoon, those moments at the end of the third meal, when they are seeking to lengthen the Shabbes, are especially precious to the hasidim (H9).[12] In Europe the candles lit before dark on Friday would have long burned out; in New York

---

[11] On certain holidays, such as Sukkes, the Rebbe may join the circle of dancers. The festive point of the year is reached on Simhes Toyreh when the scriptural readings for the year fulfill their cycle, and at that time the Rebbe customarily dances in ecstasy with the Torah cradled in his arms. The Satmarer Rebbe has a special lightweight Torah for that occasion.

[12] It is said that the souls in Gehenna are at liberty during the Shabbes but they must return to Gehenna when the day is ended. See Ginzberg, *Legends of the Jews*, 4: 201; 6: 22. See also Buber, *Tales*, 2: 148; Newman and Spitz, *Hasidic Anthology*, p. 2, no. 9; Langer, *Nine Gates*, p. 186.

electric lights burn throughout the Shabbes. At some courts the third meal is held in a dark room to recapture the mood of the past. The hasidim stand quietly in the dark, huddled in a circle around the Rebbe's table, straining to catch his quiet words. The Rebbe weaves an intricate pattern of thoughts which unites the sayings of the past with the problems of the present. He explains apparent contradictions in the text, often presenting a rush of ideas in a semi-trance. He strengthens the resolve of his followers to keep the mitsves, points up the unique value of the Jewish soul, demonstrates the need to keep their community separate, or perhaps stresses some commandment or prohibition—the need to continue learning, the love of God, being honest in business, or avoiding sexual temptation experienced at beaches or in the movies. The argument usually doubles back and forth as illustration, allusion, proverb, and saying intertwine in the argument. The particular stress in the talks varies, of course, according to the individual views of the Rebbes. The toyreh often ends with the fervent prayer for the Meshiah to come. (The fourth meal, the melaveh malkeh, which takes place long after dark on Saturday night, has been discussed in the Introduction.)

Since the Shabbes prohibitions forbid writing or making a tape recording, the hasidim try to memorize their Rebbe's words so that they can ponder them later together with their fellows. Quite often there is someone with a remarkable memory who is particularly entrusted with the task of memorizing the Rebbe's toyreh so that he may repeat it at a later time. The substance of the Rebbe's thoughts are discussed during the following weeks and his message, the metaphors, and the exempla that he used become indelibly engraved in tradition (H87).

Often each hasid present at the Rebbe's toyreh feels that the Rebbe is speaking directly to him. There are innumerable accounts of how during their toyreh Rebbes directed remarks to one of their followers who was secretly troubled (HA45).

I had a friend in yeshiveh. He came from a hasidic house, an American fellow, and all his brothers and sisters were religious. He was the black sheep of the family. His father was still trying to save him at that time. And so his father put him into our yeshiveh. He said, "I want to live ten years and then I'll come back again religious." The first time the Rebbe was at shalehseudes [the third meal], he's sitting there and afterward he comes over to me and says: "You know, Haim. . . ."

"What?"

"I felt like the Rebbe was speaking to me: 'Moshe, why are you doing this? Why are you so bad? Why do you have such bad thoughts?' "

So that was the way—when the Rebbe spoke to two hundred people, three-quarters of those two hundred people felt that he was talking directly to them. And that was because he understood the people.*

Shabbes customs vary from court to court. The Satmarer Rebbe, for example, because of his advanced age, no longer keeps the second meal nor the melaveh malkeh with his followers. Instead of speaking on the Shabbes, the Lubavitcher Rebbe expresses his toyreh at Lubavitcher celebrations called farbrengen, which are held on days held sacred by the Lubavitcher hasidim—for example, the day the former Rebbe was released from a Russian prison. The Lubavitcher Rebbe rarely attends a melaveh malkeh, although one is usually held every week. The Stoliner Rebbe attended the Shabbes meals but he never said toyreh at those times, preferring to talk briefly, and often privately, to his followers. Rather than frighten his followers away with a toyreh calling attention to their misdeeds and demanding greater effort, the Stoliner said: "I just give you a piece of cake and you should understand what's wrong" (HA21a). On occasion he appeared at a melaveh malkeh and related a story. The Bobover Rebbe and the Klausenberger Rebbe, however, almost always attend all of the Shabbes meals as well as the melaveh malkeh. The Bobover hasidim say that before the war the Rebbe never used to share the melaveh malkeh with his followers, but in the concentration camp on Saturday evenings they would try to wash and then they would sit together while the Rebbe told tales to give the people strength and hope. On one occasion, after a dangerous ordeal, the Rebbe said: "From now on, if I live, every Saturday night we'll eat together."

Rebbe and Hasid

Often the hasid simply follows the Rebbe that his father followed. As a child he hears tales of the Rebbe, or, if he lives in the same community, he is part of a pack of boys following the Rebbe's footsteps as he enters and leaves the besmedresh at prayer time.

When I was a little boy I had great reverence for him. When I looked at him I felt that I was not in the usual way of life. I didn't know what it was. I saw it's holy. I didn't know how to act. I felt I was in a holy place. Later on I compared him to great men in our history. In my imagination I compared him to the Baal Shem Tov, to Ari ha-Kodesh, to Reb Shimon ben Yohai.*

Circumstances, however, sometimes necessitate that the hasid search for a tsaddik:

I decided I wanted to go and see for myself. So the first time I heard him, it drew me. I felt like going again. And gradually till I got close to him. When we were brought up as children, we were brought up without a reason why. We had to be this way. When you get older and reach a certain turning point, you begin to think: "Why do I do this? Should I do this? Should I do that?" And mostly what happened was that I probably started thinking just about the time I came to the Rebbe. And I would say he formed my way of thinking.*

The intimacy existing between Rebbe and hasid draws many youthful zealots to Hasidism. A young man who left his studies with a rabbi to seek out a Rebbe explains:

I was in a yeshiveh and I complained to the rabbi that there was no communication between the rabbi and the boys. He said that the distance was not great enough—when one is more familiar there is less respect. I told him I would like to follow someone [that] the closer I got to him the more I feared him.*

While the Rebbe is continually buoying the spirits of his followers, at times he uses the special powers he possesses to point out moral deficiencies. In the past it is said that Rebbe Elimelekh and the Premishlaner Rebbe could discern the secret sins of those who stood before them (H37). In the contemporary community as well Rebbes are said to be able to penetrate the deceptions of their followers.

Once the Rebbe said to Shimon: "You dance nicely on the outside, but what's on the inside?" Another time Shimon was ashamed to face the Rebbe and he was sitting by the table with his hat covering his forehead. And the Rebbe said: "Do you think that we can't see through the hat?" *

The bond existing between Rebbe and hasid is supported by deeply rooted supernatural concepts. Kabbalistic thought had propagated the idea that at the time of the giving of the Law there were six hundred thousand Jewish souls. These souls served as the source for all the Jewish souls which have been created in the succeeding generations, for the multiplication of the Jewish population resulted in the splitting of souls. The attraction that the

Rebbe's followers have for the Rebbe can be explained in the yearning of these fragmented souls to reunite with the major and more magnetic portion. This magnetic connection to his followers' souls helps to explain to the hasidim their Rebbe's ability to spot their shortcomings, to know their thoughts and needs, and to advise them on their future.

> The brain knows if there's no food in the stomach. If the soul is lacking it also sends out signals. You can't feel it. You're a soul on a lower level. But the Rebbe is more sensitive to this. *

The financial standing of the Rebbe's followers is also to be explained at times by the doctrine of souls—wealth belongs to the major bearer of the soul, the Rebbe, and he distributes it to his followers so that they may use it to maintain their religion and to support charitable causes. The doctrine also underlines the Rebbe's obligation to provide for his followers. In one tale, a rabbinic court upholds the Rebbe's right to redistribute the wealth held by a niggardly follower: "But they added that still it is a pity on that Jew and he should support him for his lifetime" (H36).

In the older tradition the Rebbe is often seen as a shepherd protecting his flock. Some, like the Berdichever, beseeched God to reward His people and found countless excuses for their misdeeds (H17). The Szigetter is said to have moved miraculously between heaven and earth to defend his followers before the Heavenly Court (H5). None of the Rebbe's hasidim are lost sight of, no matter how numerous. The memory of the Gerer Rebbe was considered so encompassing that he could tell who was missing from amongst the thousands of his followers (H60).

It must be said that these chains of attachment bind both hasid and Rebbe. The hasidim feel no less a sense of responsibility to care for their Rebbe. During the last years of his life the Stoliner Rebbe was severely ill and finally was incapacitated. His followers served him faithfully as attendants and ultimately as nurses, keeping a vigil at the hospital all night to change the Rebbe's position in bed (TA16, HA26, HA27).

The intimacy and devotion of the Rebbe to his followers is particularly sharp in accounts centering around World War II. Because of their standing, the Rebbes were at times in a position to save themselves; the legends, however, tell of their self-sacrifices. When Rabbi Abraham Elimelekh of Stolin was in Israel before the war, he foretold the destruction of Europe, and his followers tried to prevent him from returning. The Rebbe, however, insisted on trying to help his people even though he knew he would be killed (N14). The followers of the Lemberger Rebbe wanted to pay the Nazis to have him released, but he refused to be raised above his people and he went to his death with them (N12). It is said that the Gerer Rebbe paid ten thousand dollars to have his brother removed from the train carrying Jews to a death camp, but when they opened the doors of the train, he refused to leave the car, preferring to share the fate of his fellow Jews (N21).

Accounts based in the United States continue to express the interconnectedness of Rebbe and hasid. The Klausenberger often expressed his followers' inner thoughts in his talks (HA44, HA45). The Satmarer warned a follower of a future accident (HA35). The Stoliner could tell his hasidim whom they would marry (HA20), he perceived their sacred deeds (HA18), and he knew when they were absent from daily prayers while he was away (HA10). The Stoliner could also predict what would prove dangerous for his followers (HA16) and when they could travel safely (HA21).

Able to transcend mortal limitations, the Rebbe is reported to have the power to predict the content of dreams and even to appear in his followers' dreams. The Lubavitcher knew that a Jew who had left the orthodox path would shortly have a dream urging him to return to his faith (HA54). Since his death, the Belzer is also said to have appeared to one of his hasidim in dreams and to have healed him (H86b).

Although dreaming is a universal phenomenon, the symbols in dreams follow distinct cultural forms.[13] It is not unexpected, therefore, that accounts of the dreams of hasidim treat such common concerns as conversion (HA54), reincarnation (H96), redemption (HA19), and sickness (HA22, H86b) in connection with the powers of the Rebbe. Since many of the themes in dreams correspond to circumstances in daily life, the hasidim have a clear conception of some of the symbols in the dreams. The Stoliners, for example, are known for the vocal power of their prayers. The hasid who sees in a dream the deceased Stoliner Rebbe davening in a loud voice knows it to be a sign that the Rebbe is happy. He is

[13] Eggan, "The Manifest Content of Dreams," *American Anthropologist*, 54 (1949): 471–85; "The Significance of Dreams for Anthropological Research," *American Anthropologist*, 51 (1949): 117–97; "The Personal Use of Myth in Dreams," *Journal of American Folklore*, 68 (1965): 445–53. Morgan, "Navaho Dreams," *American Anthropologist*, 34 (1932): 390–406. Wallace, "The Dream in Mohave Life," *Journal of American Folklore*, 60 (1947), 252–58.

pleased by the dream since the Rebbe was ill for a long time before his death and his davening had been subdued (HA23). In a second dream, the Rebbe hands his follower a piece of haleh. In accordance with the ideas surrounding the custom of giving shiraim (remains) at the Shabbes meals, the hasid believes his dream to be an indication that he will have parnosseh (livelihood). In a third dream, the Rebbe is seen telling his follower to go into the circle and dance with the other men. The dream is interpreted as an invitation for the hasid to put aside his troubles and rejoin his fellow hasidim.

Personal Contact with the Rebbe

In Europe it was customary for the hasidim to travel before the holidays to see the Rebbe. At those times feelings ran high.

I went to Ger a few times. Whoever came in touch with the Gerer Rebbe had the feeling that he was standing before a very, very great man, a very holy man. There's no question about it, whether you are a Ger hasid, or whether you are any other kind of hasid, or whether you are a misnaged. You had to have this feeling, because he was really a great, great gaon, and a great tsaddik, and a holy man, and I say it now when I'm not quite as young as I was at the time when I went to Ger to see the Gerer Rebbe.

I was studying in Warsaw, and from Warsaw to Ger was not far at all. You had to go on a little train. In Polish *kolejka* means a small train. And this one was famous. Whoever you asked knew the Gerer *kolejka*. It was a famous little train. And it only took about an hour, or maybe less than an hour, to go from Warsaw to Ger. And I went to Ger. And I had a lot of relatives in Ger, so it was no problem for me as far as having where to stay. In Ger I met my friends from my home town—all the boys. When you came to the station, the station was full of Gerer hasidim in the thousands. So you felt among friends. Wherever you went, the same hasidim, the same people, whether they were from this town or a different town. Usually, let's say, from our town about twenty boys came. So they rented a place, a boarding place for eating and sleeping. And they ate together and slept together, of course three, four in a bed, because the people in Ger didn't have a six-room apartment or seven-room apartment. They also had one room, two rooms. They used to put up beds in every place you could possibly find a mattress, a bed. Of course the little town could not accept ten thousand people. There weren't so many houses. So a lot of people slept in the besmedresh.

In Ger it was the custom that whoever came went in to the Rebbe to say sholem. And before they left Ger, they went in to say goodbye. Whoever had something to ask, or ask a brokheh [blessing], used to give in a little note. The room was like his study. This was not only every holiday. If somebody came in on a plain Shabbes or in the middle of the week, he also went in. But on a holiday there were lines and lines of people—thousands upon thousands.

I had very, very, very high feelings. As much as a fellow of this age could understand. But you became elevated in spirit. You felt like you should do more studying and more learning, become better. The whole atmosphere was a holy atmosphere.

The Gerer Rebbe had a meal. They would sit down and eat together. And a certain group was called to sit at the table, and all the rest who also wanted to be present at this table had to stay up a whole night to have a place near the table to hear. Then the Rebbe of course said toyreh. Those guys memorized the toyreh and they said it over for the rest of the people. All of them were learned men at the table. Rabbis, and when I say rabbis it's not like a rabbi here. It was a rabbi from a whole town, not from a shul. In Poland it wasn't like a rabbi of this shul. It was a rabbi of the town. Like in our town where we had a population of twenty thousand Jews, there was one rabbi. He was the rabbi of the town. Those people who sat there were the one rov, the rabbi of the city. And then probably more important people.*

At times the Rebbe would leave his court and visit his followers in the towns where they lived.

The only time I saw the [Bobover] Rebbe was when he came to our town. It was like a holiday. We kids used to dress up in special clothes. I remember he came like a king with special horses—white horses. He had a big drawn carriage. He had special people on the horses dressed like soldiers, right in front of him and in back of him.

People lit candles in the windows. He used to come into town and it was like a holiday. People shut up their shops. Everyone went out to greet him at the station, and then went together to his house. Business stopped. Everything stopped. Everybody bought candles for the windows, for luck. And sayings. We used big signs, "Welcome." It was like a holiday. Everything in town was closed. Businesses were closed. The gentiles knew already when the Rebbe comes to town there's no more business. Everybody closes down. Everybody goes to the Rebbe and it's a holiday. The children enjoyed it very much. We stopped a half a day in school. The school was closed, and all the children went to greet him. There was great happiness. Everybody felt it was something special for the town to greet the Rebbe. Every town to which the Rebbe came used to try to do more than the other towns.*

These patterns have been continued in America. The holidays are the times when the full population of the court comes together to celebrate with the Rebbe. Followers who may reside in New Jersey, or as far away as Detroit or Montreal, stay with family or friends during this period. In addition, the Rebbe continues to make trips to visit his followers in other cities. The Squarer Rebbe returns to Williamsburg from New Square for two to three weeks each year. The Bobover Rebbe visits his followers in Montreal each year and goes frequently to London and to Israel. The Satmarer Rebbe too travels to London and to Israel.

The excitement at having daily contact with the Rebbe has not ebbed. Whenever the Rebbe appears at the besmedresh or on the street his appearance creates excitement. There is an overflow of awe and affection each time the Rebbe enters the besmedresh or steps from his office or home. A hushed silence customarily greets the appearance of the Rebbe at prayers. The hasidim stand to honor him and fall back to clear a path. Yeshiveh students may become especially flustered when the Rebbe appears, shyly darting to one side and then craning their necks to observe him. Children flock after him. The courts often have individual ways of signaling their respect for their Rebbe: when the Lubavitcher Rebbe appears to speak at a farbrengen the students welcome him with a song that rocks the hall; among the demonstrative hasidim of Satmar it is likely that when the Rebbe passes between the rows of his adoring hasidim, someone will brush past the irritated gabai to kiss the Rebbe's hand or to help the Rebbe adjust his boots.

Anything that the Rebbe does is observed with affection and avidity by his followers. Each detail of his life is meaningful: "He eats a little. Usually you bend down to eat. He sits straight and brings the food to himself. He doesn't bend to food." * On Friday evening the Satmarer hasidim may stand in rapt attention an hour and more watching their elderly Rebbe eat his soup and then doze after his meal. The hasidim will stand closely packed in a stuffy room for hours waiting for their Rebbe, and they will wait long hours in a queue into the middle of the night in order to see their Rebbe on a personal matter or to receive his blessing.

Early in July, 1959, I waited in a queue to see Rabbi Menahem Mendel Schneerson, the Lubavitcher Rebbe. Two weeks earlier I had been told that all of the appointments were filled, but that as a favor I would be permitted to see the Rebbe just before he left for a vacation. I was to be present at the Rebbe's office at 770 Eastern

Parkway at 11 P.M. It was the Rebbe's custom to meet visitors throughout the night. While the interview material gathered on that occasion is interwoven elsewhere in this work, it seems appropriate to indicate here the atmosphere existing among the Rebbe's petitioners.

I arrived promptly at 11 P.M. The office was still brightly lit and there were a number of students present. The Rebbe's assistant informed me that there were seventeen people waiting to see the Rebbe and that I was the thirteenth on the list. I went into the room which served both as besmedresh and yeshiveh and greeted Jacob, one of the students I knew. Everyone seemed expectant, and Jacob informed me that the Rebbe had not yet davened the evening prayer. The Rebbe had been closeted with a visitor from Israel for three hours and had not come out for prayers. They were waiting for him. Jacob's friend, Mendel, joined us. They were both excited at the prospect of my visiting the Rebbe. "Have you been to the mikveh? No? It's all right."

At eleven-thirty Rabbi Schneerson came out of his office to daven the evening prayers. He prayed quietly and intensely, and as soon as the davening was finished he returned to his office to meet his next appointment.

There were several people still left in the besmedresh past midnight. One student, who had been assigned to travel to South America to spread the light of the Torah in various Jewish communities, was busy copying addresses into a little notebook. Early in the morning he would be flying south, his case filled with Lubavitcher publications and phylacteries. Nearby, a student who had come from South America paced up and down. It was close to his birthday, and the Rebbe met each of the students for a short time on these occasions.

A young man came hurrying into the room and called out, "A match!" He had a cigarette trembling between his lips. He had just been in to see the Rebbe. I lit his cigarette and he rushed out. A few minutes later I saw him again as he entered the office to offer a donation to the Rebbe's assistant. His excitement had not yet died down. Outside the office he stopped for a moment by a young woman and an older woman who were accompanying him. While the young man was exuberant the young woman seemed depressed. "He just didn't understand," she said. "I couldn't reach him. At my age a woman should have children. I couldn't get him to understand."

At one-thirty the student from South America entered the

Rebbe's office. He was there for only a few minutes but when he came out he was flushed. Someone in the room started to speak with him but received no reply. Almost in a daze the boy sat down and began to write. He was trying to put down the words the Rebbe had said to him.

A young Hebrew teacher next came out of the Rebbe's office. "How long was I in there?" he asked me. When I told him five or ten minutes he seemed disappointed—not with what the Rebbe had said, but that he had qualified for only five minutes.

At 2.00 A.M. I sat down on the bench by the Rebbe's door. Ten minutes later my turn came and I entered the office. When I emerged at five-thirty in the morning, the Rebbe's next visitor was there still pacing the floor. He had been waiting all night to see the Rebbe.

Before visiting the Rebbe to receive his blessing or his counsel the hasidim go to the mikveh to purify themselves, although it may be the middle of the night (HA50). The petitioner feels nervous and anxious, even if he is the Rebbe's own brother (H59). The hasid is overwhelmed by the piety of the Rebbe, by the forces with which the Rebbe is in contact, and, in contrast, by his own naked frailty.

> The orthodox [misnaged] doesn't know how to leave his own "I." The secret is to forget about yourself, to go to the tsaddik and feel nothingness, to feel he overshadows you, that his whole life is dedicated to God.*

A hasid who went in to visit Rabbi Israel Friedman of Tchortkov remembered that "he sat there and I stood in front of him a long, long time. He looked at me and did not see me. After half an hour he asked me what I wanted. I felt like I was standing before a great man and I am nothing" (H65).

Customarily, the hasid presents a kvitl (prayer note) to the Rebbe (or he requests the gabai to write a note for him).[14] The kvitl is usually accompanied by a pidyen (donation, redemption money).[15] The pidyen may be given as a means of warding off future ills or simply in order to support the Rebbe so that he may

---

[14] See Minkin, *Romance of Hassidism*, pp. 332–33, and Langer, *Nine Gates*, pp. 10–11, 53.

[15] In its Biblical context the term refers to the amount required to redeem a condemned man or a first-born son. See Dubnow, *History*, 2: 119, n. 4. Dubnow notes: "The hasidim designate by this term the contributions made to the tsaddik, in the belief that such contributions have the power of averting from the contributor impending death or misfortune "

devote his time to prayer and to doing pious works. The amount, which varies according to the devotion and the financial abilities of the hasid, is the main source of the Rebbe's income as well as of the charity that he dispenses. The kvitl itself lists the names of the petitioner and his family and their individual requests so that the Rebbe can bless each member of the family. The kvitl must also contain the name of the petitioner's mother, for the descent of the soul is traced through the maternal line and her name is necessary to direct the prayers ("Joseph, the son of Sarah, asks for . . ."). The kvitl is, therefore, a line of supernatural communication which may lead back several generations or leap far ahead into the future. There are many accounts of the Rebbe's penetrations of the hidden content of the kvitl. It is said that the list of names alone could reveal to the Belzer whether the persons named were among the living or the dead (HA29, HA32). A glance at the kvitl was sufficient for him to ascertain whether the request was destined to be fulfilled or denied, while the hopeful petitioner could discern by the Belzer's reaction whether or not his request would be granted (H84, HA30, HA31). The Sandzer Rov is reported to have told his son, the Shinyaver Rebbe, that a Rebbe should not accept kvitlekh if he could not tell the purpose of his hasid's visit to him when the hasid first leaves his home (T49).

Problems Presented to the Rebbe

There is a wide range of subjects on which the Rebbe is asked to advise his followers: taking a new job, moving to a new apartment, opening a business, or seeing a doctor.

I was only teaching half a day, so I had time to study to become a shohet. So I asked the Rebbe whether I should, and the Rebbe agreed that I should learn how to be a shohet. Then an opportunity came when one of the slaughterhouses needed a shohet and they offered me the job to become a shohet there. I asked the Rebbe whether I should leave— that meant that I should leave the job of teaching and become a shohet. So I wouldn't decide it for myself. I asked the Rebbe and the Rebbe agreed. And so I became a shohet.*

I need more room. I asked him if I should force my tenant out downstairs and convert it into a one-family house or buy a new house. The Rebbe told me to convert the house slowly, not all at one time.*

Other personal and family problems are carried to the Rebbe. He may be called upon to solve crises in marital life, whether it be to obtain a divorce (WH12) or to locate a missing husband (WH10, WH11). At times he may be asked to settle disputes in family businesses.

I wanted to quit my father's business. I went in to ask the Rebbe also about it at that time. First I spoke with my father, and I saw my father was against it. So then I went to the Rebbe. I came to the Rebbe. The Rebbe was against it from a different point of view—a financial point of view. He said he was afraid I should take such a chance. So he told me then I should do this and this method of business. I should continue to work for my father and be independent at the same time—have an extra income. Well, I told the Rebbe it was impossible. I have to do my machine work and while I'm doing my machine work, I can't do any other kind of work. So he says that's the only way he would tell me to do it. Then about two years later I had decided already, I don't care and I'm going out independent for myself. And my father was already also going to agree to it then. He saw he had no other way out. So we went in to the Rebbe. The Rebbe listened and made us change maybe a few things and then he told us, "I'd rather have it the way I told you, but if not" . . . he would agree to the way we were planning it now. Then it happened exactly the way he had told me the first time. It just worked out that way. It just worked out exactly the way he had told me. I mean to the "T." *

As is evident, if the problem concerns the family, all of the principal parties concerned may go in to see the Rebbe together, for the Rebbe is an encompassing father figure for everyone in the court.

The Rebbe is not only a teacher but he's a father. He thinks of us as his children, every one of us, and he is devoted to our welfare as to his own children. When we're in trouble we go to him. When we have happiness we go to him. We take advice from him even above our own father. *

The Rebbe listens to his follower's hopes and his plans; he may approve or disapprove, bless his follower's course, or give pointed advice. Like the Besht's advice in one tale to buy the first thing that one sees (H8), or the Stoliner's casual appraisal of Brooklyn real estate (HA13), the Rebbe's foresight is thought to insure the most unlikely suggestion. Certain that the Rebbe's supernatural insight penetrates to the essence of every matter, the hasid searches each of the Rebbe's words for its special portent.

A significant proportion of the problems brought to the Rebbe appear to concern health—choosing a doctor or deciding whether or not to have an operation. In some instances the Rebbe may be able to name a specific doctor, and in this sense Rebbes often serve as a sort of referral service for doctors. The hasidim feel that the Rebbe's special powers ensure the proper choice. The Rebbe, for his part, is often out of touch with the realities of the surrounding culture and must depend on the most acculturated of his admirers for advice concerning doctors and specialists.[16]

At times the Rebbe's advice on choosing a doctor is practical but very general:

> We went to see the Rebbe about our son's illness. He said: "Don't spare money or time or effort. Look into it and find the biggest specialist you can. Go to him privately even if he's connected with a clinic—at least at first.*

Faced with a medical problem the Rebbe may offer either firm advice or a formula for making a decision: "In major medical problems the Rebbe says to take the advice of two doctors who concur in their diagnoses." *

Miracle Tales

The satisfactory resolution of the hasid's petition to the Rebbe is the basis for a large percentage of the miracle tales. The tales concerning the great trials in history are most widely known to the hasidim, but they are far exceeded in number by narratives which recount the lesser trials of common men. Most tales of the Rebbes concern the crucial events of life—birth, marriage, illness, and death—as well as the countless calamities of daily events. Tales of how Rebbes fructified barren marriages are among the most common miracles (HA30, HA36) and on occasion this theme serves simply to introduce the further adventures of a boy who was so miraculously conceived (H12).

Perhaps the most common tales are those describing how a Rebbe healed the sick. The Rebbe is often the last source of hope

---

[16] One hasid, Rabbi David Twersky, the son of the Squarer Rebbe and the nephew of the present Rebbe of New Square, often acts as a referral service for hasidim who need medical care. He frequently arranges for such work to be done as charity. Although he is the son of a Rebbe, he does not accept kvitlekh or act as the leader of a court. He says: "I try to accomplish by my actions what my forefathers accomplished by their blessings."

for the afflicted. "I've waited so long for a Rebbe," sings an innkeeper happily when a miracle worker arrives to attend to the ministrations of his ailing son (H61).

In some cases the Rebbe may cure with a simple prayer or with
a touch or a word. Rabbi Parakher was said to have been cured of a
fever by donning the yarmelkeh of the Tsemah Tsedek (H38). In
more recent times, when a grieved husband lamented the death of
his wife, the Stoliner Rebbe advised him to tell her to get up and
cook soup, and this simple command was enough to draw the
housewife back from the dead (H74). The present Lubavitcher
Rebbe is said to have foreseen the complications occurring at the
birth of a first child and, unknown to the parents, blessed them to
prevent harm from occurring (HA57). A Lubavitcher hasid tells
how the present Rebbe cured a man of cancer: "The Rebbe said,
S'iz gornisht' [it's nothing], put out his hand on the man's side,
and at that moment it was nothing" (HA53).

Even in the face of overwhelming evidence to the contrary, the
Rebbe may assure the recovery of the sick. The hasidim often refer
to telegrams and letters containing the crucial advice as proof of
the veracity of the tale (although the disappearance of so many
mortal illnesses may tell us as much about hasidic anxiety concerning illness as it does about the Rebbe's prowess).

There are, however, tragedies as well as triumphs in life and not
every appeal can be assured of success. On such occasions, the
Rebbe may see that his blessings will be of no avail. The son of a
Belzer hasid tells how the Rebbe, having foreseen that the hasid's
mother's first child would not live, had not wanted to give his
blessing; subsequently, the Rebbe enthusiastically blessed the second child, who thrived (H84).

At times the Rebbe will simply point out where to find a cure or
indicate which doctor will be of special help. Even the contact
between doctor and patient may be considered to be a miraculous
act. A Lubavitcher hasid, advised that he needed a doctor, was told
by the previous Lubavitcher Rebbe to return home immediately by
train on a second-class ticket. During the journey he met a stranger
who furnished him with medicine otherwise unobtainable which
made the operation unnecessary (H88).

Although the case may be placed in the hands of a doctor who
prescribes a course of treatment, the doctor still remains in a
subordinate position to the Rebbe. It is quite common for tales to
recount how a Rebbe contradicted the opinion of medical men and
had his view confirmed by subsequent events. He may urge a

patient to avoid an operation (HA4, HA56) or to have an operation (H82), and although the Rebbe's opinion runs counter to the
best medical advice, the faithful hasid follows the Rebbe's counsel
and is always rewarded. On the advice of the late Stoliner Rebbe a
hasid disobeyed the doctors and momentarily removed the bandages over his son's eyes to determine if the boy could see (HA5).
On another occasion, when the Stoliner contradicted a specialist
who insisted that an operation was necessary, he said, "If something happens to the child, shout through the streets that the
Stoliner Rebbe is a murderer" (HA4). Both tales conclude that
the child recovered. The present Boyaner Rebbe is said to have
advised a woman who had one child by Cesarean section to have her
other children naturally. In subsequent births, both mother and
child survived (HA33). So certain are the hasidim of their
Rebbe's counsel in matters of life and death that when a woman
died because of negligence on the part of her doctor it was said
regretfully, "That's because she had no Rebbe." *

Perhaps the clearest example of subordination of doctor to Rebbe
in the tales is demonstrated when Rebbe Elimelekh predicts which
doctor will effect a cure, adding that this doctor himself will then
fall ill and die (H14). In effect the tale says that doctors too are
powerless before the fateful forces which the Rebbe better understands and controls.

The counsels of lawyers receive the same short shrift as the
diagnoses of doctors, for they too possess knowledge of the secular
world which is superseded by the Rebbe's superior powers. Like
doctors, however, the special status of lawyers makes them excellent witnesses for the Rebbe's prowess. "I want to know your
Rebbe," says one awe-struck lawyer whose client won his freedom
after obeying his Rebbe rather than his attorney (N17). In this
case and others, the Rebbe's counsel matches the simple directness
of his medical advice. In one instance the hasid is told simply to
ignore the summons of the court. It is subsequently discovered that
the hasid's file is lost and he is a free man (H57). To cap the tale,
the hasid, arriving home after having written to his parents about
the favorable verdict, finds that the Rebbe had communicated the
news because he knew that the family had never received his letter.
Another tale draws a fine distinction between the various degrees
of allegiance to one's Rabbi: the fervent hasid follows the Rebbe's
legal advice no matter how far-fetched it may seem; the less-firm
believer can accept or reject the Rebbe's word as his sense dictates
(H58).

A large portion of the miracle stories deal directly with the range of powers attributed to the Rebbes. The Lubliner was called "the Seer" because his eyes could scan vast distances in space and time, seeing ahead until the day of his death (T19) and penetrating as well into the hearts of men (T20). The course of nature could be changed by those like Reb Levi Yitshok, who turned a river aside when it threatened to flood the cemetery in Berdichev (H16). The Belzer could assist a poor soul passing through a reincarnation as a dog (H96). Much as the kabbalists resorted to the secret names of angels to control events, the name of Israel of Stolin too could be relied on to ensure a safe journey (H71), and Israel's knowledge was said to extend to such secular subjects as pharmacology (H76) and musicology (H75).

The powers of these saintly men are said to extend beyond the borders of life as well. The last Stoliner Rebbe prayed by the grave of the holy men in Israel to ensure the safety of the Holy Land at the start of World War II (N8); the Hushatener prayed by the grave of Haim ben Atar in Israel to ensure Rommel's defeat (N23). Few such sites exist in the New World, but wherever they can be found there also exists belief in their potential power. The Lubavitcher Rebbe is said to visit the grave of his predecessor once a month in the hope of receiving help for the prayers he brings with him, and others testify to the peace of mind attained by visiting the previous Rebbe's grave (HA2). More direct powers may also be said to continue beyond life: the Stoliner hasidim tell that the body of their late Rebbe could not be placed aboard the plane of an airline he disliked (TA19); and that when the coffin was opened after seventeen months his body was found to be in perfect condition (TA18).

Despite the vast scope of the Rebbe's powers, in point of fact most miracles are modest, as witnessed by the two told by the Dzikover Rov about his father, the Ropchitser Rov, when he inadvertently cured a cripple by kicking him (T28) and when he kept the rain from flooding the sukkeh (T29). Similarly, solutions in life, and consequently in tales, are often quite natural; at times, however, the natural course of events is intertwined with the miraculous. A hasid considers it a miracle that the Rebbe foresaw that he would obtain a vitally needed sum of money the following day. On his part, the Rebbe regards the miracle as inevitable—God had to help the hasid since there was no other possible solution (HA39). Other problems are resolved similarly: when there is no way out of a dilemma except for the chief of police to drop dead, he conveniently does so (H42). When a recruit decided not to cripple himself nor to buy his way out of the army, the Rebbe said that only a miraculous solution was possible, and, indeed, one came to pass when the doctors chased the recruit from the office (H52).

The Nature of the Rebbe's Power

Whenever a successful resolution is achieved by supernatural means, one may say that it is the Almighty working through the Rebbe. At times, however, the Rebbe seems to accrue special power of his own. The Talmud says that "God decrees and the Righteous annuls." [17] The commandments are the sacred fibers of the universe, and the Rebbe is believed to use the secret powers they contain. If breaking a law condemns one to punishment, the tsaddik, the perfect righteous man, can prescribe a cure for the calamity.

Although power may be thought to be contained in an article of ritual, it can at times be manipulated only by the Rebbe. When bricks made by a hasid tended to crumble, the Stoliner Rebbe threw a lulev into the fire. When the hasid, regarding the perform-ance as a kind of magical procedure, tried it the next time himself and failed, the Rebbe observed: "If I say that the lulev will work, then it will work. Otherwise it's nothing" (TA9). In an earlier tale in which Reb Zusya cured a sick man by having him bathe in the mikveh, Reb Zusya was careful to join him in the bath (H14). Almost a tangible force, the Rebbe's power to bless can at times be transferred by the Rebbe to one of his hasidim (HA51).

As indicated earlier, in general the Rebbe is called on to give advice when the issue is uncertain. The Rebbe's power consists not only of foreseeing the outcome but of being able to influence future events.

It's a kind of magic. Even if it wasn't this way before, it becomes this way. The doctors prescribe one way of healing; he turns and says something else. And you see later he's right. *

The power attributed to the Rebbe is in direct proportion to his piety. Reb Yoseleh explained the wondrous powers in this way:

[17] Babylonian Talmud, *Moed Katan* 16b. "I rule man; who rules Me? [It is] the righteous: for I make a decree and he [may] annul it." Sources for this belief can be seen in Gen. 18: 20 ff.; Exod. 23: 7-14. In *In Praise of the Besht*, no. 42, God says to the Besht, "What can I do with you since I must fulfill your will?"

"One tsaddik is a tsaddik who is exalted at all times, all seven days of the week, seven times out of seven, while another tsaddik six hours out of seven is equal to his peers, and on the seventh is exalted above his peers. The tsaddik who not only makes the seventh day holy but also makes every seventh hour holy, such a tsaddik has the power that God fulfills whatever he says" (T12).

On rare occasions the power of the Rebbe may be viewed in a negative and even fearful light, for if the Rebbe has the power to bless then he also possesses the power, rarely seen, to be sure, to curse. A curse attributed to the Munkaczer Rebbe was said to have prevented the Satmarer from having a living heir (TA21). In the present community it is said that the few followers of one Rebbe, often the center of petty controversies, would leave him except that they do not want trouble from him—and they cite the death of the son of one of his critics from cancer.

> Mrs. Rothman argued with the Rebbe because she felt that he had not acted properly when he purchased his shul. Now some say: "Look what he did to that woman's son." *

Attitudes toward the Miraculous

The individual attitudes of the Rebbes have differed historically as to the stress placed on the performance of wonders. The attitudes reflect varying conceptions of the relationship of tsaddik and hasid and also of the relationship of God and man. The differences, however, are primarily of degree. Rabbi Shneur Zalman is reported to have disdained performing miracles, but he noted that there were miracles under his chair if he would but bend down and pick them up (T17). Often, the issue is not whether the Rebbe should perform miracles but whether or not the miracles should be revealed. There is virtue in keeping miracles secret much as there is virtue in studying or in doing good works solely with the knowledge of God. The Besht, for example, had to be convinced to reveal himself (T2). On the other hand, some Rebbes of the past and present have made public expressions of their powers. In the past the Strelisker could advise his followers who wished wealth to hold on to his talis (W11); in the contemporary community the Klausenberger told his followers: "I have the keys to parnosseh. Whoever wants them must catch on" (TA22). In the last years of his life, the Stoliner Rebbe too was quite open about revealing his

miraculous powers to his followers. "They don't realize they're
playing with fire," he is reported to have said (TA10). He indicated his ability to perceive the activities of the living and the dead.
Asked about a deceased hasid, he replied: "We knew him very
well, and if we didn't we can know him from the other world"
(TA13). He also believed that he had appeared before the Heavenly Court and that he had delayed the 1956 Arab-Israeli war
(N34).

Because Hasidism has oftentimes been identified solely with
wonders performed by the Rebbes and not with their profound
piety, some hasidim try to reduce the importance of wonders; what
is significant, they say, is the way of life and prayer of the Rebbe.
At times a hasid may assert that miracles no longer exist, although
immediately afterward a "true" miracle may be recalled:

> I never went to look for miracles from the Rebbe. They never made
> such an impression on my mind because I believe in greatness more
> than a miracle. The world takes the hasidim as mystics and miracles
> and souls. That was the only way they were able to attract the ignorant
> people—the people who didn't know anything years back. They wanted
> to attract these people, they showed them a miracle. But actually—I've
> just come across one now but I'd rather not talk about it. I mean
> somebody needed an operation and all the doctors said he needed an
> operation, and he wrote to the Rebbe. And the Rebbe answered this
> person, "Go to a third doctor, and you wouldn't need an operation." And
> it looks like this person wouldn't need an operation. I mean it just
> happened last week, but I didn't think of it until a minute ago because
> it just came to my mind—it's a natural thing by me.*

Miracles are, after all, a common part of life, scarcely to be
noticed. In the everyday world of miracles, wonders can be performed before the Rebbe's coffee gets cold (H28). One narrator
who had forgotten the ending of a tale about the Baal Shem Tov
simply supposes that the Jew in question was cured by the Besht
(H2). "If the Rebbe says it will be good, it will be good,"
concludes another narrator (HA48). To support this view there is
the tale of the hasid whose faith in the Rebbe's counsel led him to
pour medicine into a spoon and then dump it into the sink (H79).
In another tale a druggist fills a prescription for colored water for
a Stoliner hasid in the belief that since the hasid was sent by the
Rebbe the prescription would work regardless of the contents
(H73).

For their part, in the tales the Rebbes often reveal their human
sensibilities as well as their prowess. Rebbes often initially search

for a practical solution to a hasid's problem. The Maharash told how his father had miraculously located missing husbands, but he advised making inquiries to the government (WH10). Faced with the same problem, the previous Lubavitcher Rebbe suggested looking through the newspapers (WH11). Asked to help keep a hasid out of the army, the Maharash suggested that the recruit either buy himself out or that he cripple himself (H52). (Confronted with a personal ethical dilemma, the Rebbe can also be expected to be realistic. When the Tsemah Tsedek himself was threatened with being sent to Siberia for being a hasid, he asked one of his followers to lie for him. When the pious follower found lying unthinkable, the Rebbe asked him: "Is it better I should be arrested and sent to Siberia?" [H38].)

While the Rebbes of the past generations are all believed to have been invested with miraculous power, it must not be supposed that all hasidim regard every contemporary Rebbe as possessing similar strength. Court tensions are too sharp to permit this. Generally, wonder tales are recounted concerning one's own Rebbe, Rebbes belonging to the same dynasty, and such other Rebbes from the past and present whose prowess has come to be generally acknowledged.

The Foibles of Hasid and Rebbe

Secure in their faith, the hasidim can smile at the relationship of hasid and Rebbe. The Rebbe's preoccupation with purity may prevent him from facing reality, and in one well-known tale it prompts him to give optimistic but faulty advice to an unattractive grass widow who asks if her husband will return. "The Rebbe looks at the kvitl" (instead of the woman) is proverbial (S34, S35). The concern of some Rebbes with receiving monetary donations is the subject for humorous treatment, although unlike the versions told by the misnagdim, a pious rather than an avaricious motive is attributed to such demands (S2, S3). Mocked too is the naïveté of the hasid who would infuse the simplest action of the Rebbe, even his cutting his toenails, with symbolic significance (S5).

There are other established forms of humorous tales. Every king must have his fool, and so the Rebbe has his gabai. In reality often a shrewd practitioner of power and politics, in tradition the gabai serves as a foil for the Rebbe's wisdom. In his misunderstanding of the obvious, the gabai's roundabout reasoning is unshakeable. Acting in a kind of parody of the Rebbe's powers, the unmarried gabai decides not to marry, declaring that if he needs children he will go to see the Rebbe (S20); he finds ridiculous reasons for the Rebbe's pious acts (S16, S17); and he thinks the movement of the heavens revolves around his little village and his Rebbe (S22). The gabai is also the subject of speculation: "Some say that these people are great also, but give up their greatness helping the Rebbes. Some say that the Rebbes need them to bring them down to earth" (S25).

The Rebbe is also treated as a mere mortal man in the home, and he is not beyond the demands of his family. When the Sandzer Rov's son saw his father dispensing family funds for charity he complained, "Am I worse than the shoemaker?" (S10). The wife of the pious Reb Wolf, bemoaning the piety that made her husband seem eccentric, complained to the Ropchitser Rov (T33): "You know he listens to everything that you tell him. Tell him to talk like a human being." When the Tsemah Tsedek failed to help his relative locate her missing husband the Rebbetsn berated him: "Why don't you have any pity on her? For everyone else you take care of the whole world and for a relative you don't do anything." And when the Rebbe pointed to everyone waiting for him and complained that she too was bothering him, the Rebbetsn cut him short: "If you can't do anything, you should tell the people and they wouldn't bother you" (WH10).

The Dynasty

The dynastic reign of the Rebbes ensures the continuation of the hasidic courts. When a Rebbe dies, one of his sons usually succeeds him as leader of the court. There are often signs indicating which son will inherit his father's mantle, as when the sons of the Tsemah Tsedek tried on their father's shtraiml much as princes test the king's crown to see whom it will fit (T48). The hasidim may sometimes tease the children of the Rebbe, as they do now the Klausenberger's young sons, as to which will be the future Rebbe. The Klausenberger and the Satmarer both are younger brothers who eventually outshone their elder brothers.

In past generations several sons often succeeded to leadership in

different communities and so multiplied the number of courts and
Rebbes. But deaths among the sons may be attributed to signs that
only one at a time was destined to be Rebbe (TA2). On rare
occasions, the son may have followers of his own during his father's lifetime, as was the case with Reb Mikhel of Zlochev and
Reb Yoseleh Yampoler (T12), and Aaron of Karlin and Asher of
Stolin, the Alter Rebbe and the Yunger Rebbe (H45).

There are some circumstances favoring the inauguration of a
Rebbe not directly descended from the previous Rebbe. The Besht
himself was succeeded by Rabbi Dov Baer; and Rabbi Menahem
Mendel, the Rimanover, was followed by his disciple, Rabbi Zev
Hirsch. If a Rebbe should die without a son to accept his mantle, or
if the son declines to become Rebbe, a leader may be chosen by
acclamation from among those closest to the Rebbe. The essential
dictum of the choice is the closeness of the successor to the Rebbe,
for their intimacy in life ensures the transfer of piety and power
and the maintenance of traditional patterns. Often a son-in-law, a
nephew, or a close disciple of the deceased Rebbe is named. At
those times the elders of the court with authority and prominence
extend support to their candidates, and intensive meetings and
discussions are undertaken. When the Lubavitcher Rebbe died in
1950, the two candidates were the Rebbe's sons-in-law. Rabbi
Menahem Mendel Schneerson had the strongest supporters and
was asked to become the Rebbe, while his brother-in-law remained
head of the yeshiveh. The present Tchortkover Rebbe, Reb Hershel, now in Israel, is the son-in-law of Rabbi Israel Friedman (d.
1933), the second Rebbe of the Tchortkov dynasty; he was
preceded as Rebbe by Israel's own son and grandson, but he has
outlived them both.

Sometimes the change from one Rebbe to another, even if only
from father to son, marks a change in the court's tradition. The
new Rebbe may abandon some customs and adopt others. Sometimes the changes can be too sharp for the hasidim of the older
generation, who slowly drift away from the court or perhaps switch
their allegiance to another Rebbe who is closer to their generation
or to their viewpoint. But others put aside such questions. When
Israel of Stolin succeeded his father, the hasidim had to reconcile
his comparatively modern ways with the older traditions set by his
father, and one hasid was led to say: "I say to myself that I don't
understand anything. Then there are no problems for me, no room
for hesitation" (H69). But if the hasidim find it hard to adjust to
the change, it is equally difficult for the new Rebbe to be con-

fronted with the demands of his followers. Rabbi Moshe Mate-vicher, who became Rebbe with great reluctance, refused to maintain the custom of having a meal with his hasidim on the advent of the new moon even though they had made elaborate preparations: "You should know, my brothers, I am beginning to swim on the great sea, and if someone is going to tell me this, and someone else is going to tell me that, I could become, God forbid, withered. So I beg of you, let me alone, and let me swim in the sea. I do not keep this meal on Rosh Hoydesh" (T53).

On occasion, when a Rebbe dies some members of his court continue to revere his memory and manage to function as a court without a living Rebbe. The Bratslaver hasidim, whose Rebbe died in 1810,[18] constitute such a group, as do the M'lochim, whose Rebbe died in 1939. (The Bratslaver hasidim have a nominal leader, Rabbi Rosen, to whom they come for advice; the Rabbi does not, however, take kvitlekh.) It is regarded as portentous that some of the most important hasidic Rebbes, such as the Satmarer and Lubavitcher, have no apparent heirs. Many hasidim see in this the fulfillment of the Sandzer Rov's prophecy that when the Rebbes die out it is a sign that the Meshiah will come.

However, even when there is no immediate successor to the Rebbe and there is a time lag between the death of a Rebbe and the acceptance of an heir, most courts are too vital to languish indefinitely. In 1966, nine years after the death of the Belzer Rebbe, Aaron Rokeah, the young nephew of the former Rebbe became the leader of the court. The process of accepting the successor to the Stoliner Rebbe is now under way.

When the Stoliner Rebbe died in 1955, his grandson, Borukh Meir Yaakov Shochet, so named by the Rebbe at the boy's circumcision, was one year old. Since that time the continuance of the Stolin dynasty has remained a steady but distant hope. In 1967, as Borukh Shochet continues his studies in Israel and approaches his bar mitsveh, the court is in conflict. Many of the older hasidim in Israel have already accepted the Lelever Rebbe (Rabbi Moshe Biederman), while the younger hasidim there have remained loyal to the direct heir of Stolin. The conflicting loyalties have initiated a series of lawsuits in Israel in both the civil and religious courts concerning ownership of the yeshiveh and the collection of funds for the yeshiveh under the name of Stolin. The dispute has not only divided the court but has split families as well.

[18] Rabbi Nahman of Bratslav, the great-grandson of the Baal Shem Tov.

The Stoliner hasidim in the United States, however, do not suffer from divided loyalties. Some of the hasidim are not waiting for Borukh Shochet to attain his maturity and have already accepted the thirteen-year-old boy as their Rebbe. The new Rebbe's Brooklyn followers have made a firm commitment to him by officially giving him the Stoliner shul on Sixteenth Avenue, and they are in the process of turning over the yeshiveh as well.

Every year since the Rebbe died we have elections for the gaboyim to run the shul. This year I got up and said: "I don't think we have a right to have elections any more. We should give it to him and he should do as he sees fit." We offered it to him. He accepted. He chose the gaboyim and runs the shul through them. They're his mouthpieces.*

The family of the new Stoliner Rebbe live in Boro Park, and the new Rebbe was raised in Brooklyn and returns home for the holidays. While the hasidim have observed him as a child and beginning student, this has not reduced the new Rebbe in their eyes. Ordinary virtues have become aggrandized.

We always gave him respect. He always sat up front from the age of eight or nine. When he goes to Israel he's treated like a Rebbe. He's a phenomenon. I don't think you could take any kid and put him up front and show him respect and he shouldn't show some outward sign of excitement or awe. But it's nothing. Not that he's haughty. So he comes off the plane and there's a thousand people waiting for him. It's nothing. His father is his hasid. His father obeys him. He gives his father respect, but as far as matters of the shul or yeshiveh he tells his father. We have a meeting in his house. The boy doesn't want to talk and he whispers in his father's ear and his father says it.*

As a sign of acceptance as Rebbe, the hasidim are beginning to approach Borukh Shochet with their problems and to recount later his wonderful counsel.

Haim's baby was born last summer and it had a growth behind its ear. He asked Borukh, and he [Borukh] said, "Go see another professor and wait." And he waited and it opened by itself and disappeared. They didn't know if it was an abscess or a growth. The boy [Borukh] didn't move to make an operation.*

THE MITSVES:
THE LAW IN HASIDIC
LIFE AND TRADITION

The Scope of the Law

The belief structure of the hasidic community is dominated by the 613 mitsves (commandments) found in the Old Testament [1] (composed of 365 negative commandments and 248 positive precepts) and the host of laws formulated subsequently through rabbinical interpretation. As elaborated by the talmudic writers and their successors, the geonim and the tosafists, the mitsves comprise a vast compendium of custom, ordinance, and law encompassing all the activities of life, and they represent the legal and social needs of diverse ages. When the mitsves were codified by a succession of scholars in the Middle Ages (the most successful being Joseph Caro, 1488–1575, who compiled the *Code of Laws* ["*Shulhan Arukh*"]), they were simplified and brought within reach of the common Jew. They have remained the most potent force in orthodox Jewish life.

The circumstances the mitsves cover represent the sum total of the orthodox Jew's daily existence. The areas covered by the mitsves range over marriage, business practices, property laws, charity, care of the sick, treatment of animals, sexual relations, and

[1] The laws were first designated as 613 in number by R. Simlai in a talmudic comment (Makkot 23b). The first listing of the 613 specific laws was attempted by Simeon Kahira in *Halakhot Gedolot*. Moses Maimonides criticized earlier methods of determining the exact number of laws and listed the criteria for his selections in his *Sefer ha-Mitsvot*.

a number of other subjects (including those which can no longer be fulfilled, such as laws concerning sacrifices, slavery, and punishments for breaking the commandments). An act governed by divine law may be ritual, ethical, or philosophical in nature: one *must*, for example, love and fear God (Deut. 6:7), bind tefillin on one's forehead and arm (Deut. 6:8), fix a mezuzeh on the doorpost (Deut. 6:9), keep the Day of Atonement (Lev. 16:3), keep one's vow (Deut. 23:23), honor the Shabbes (Exod. 20:8, 23:12), provide for the poor (Deut. 15:8), restore lost property (Deut. 20:1), and honor the aged (Lev. 19:32); one *must not*, for example, wear clothing made of both linen and wool (Deut. 22:11), violate an oath (Lev. 19:12), eat of unclean cattle, fish, or fowl (Lev. 11:4, 13, 42–44, Deut. 14:19), eat anything containing leaven on Passover (Exod. 12:20, Deut. 13:3, 16:3), accept a bribe (Exod. 23:8), or have intercourse with a woman who is ritually unclean through menstruation (Lev. 18:19). To orthodox Jewry the commandments and their exegesis represent the complete code of ethical and ritual conduct decreed by God and accepted by the Jews and by no other people.[2]

There is a subtle value system which structures the mitsves on the basis of their support in Scripture or in the rabbinic writings. Commenting on breaking a law while interred in a concentration camp, one narrator says, "that is a thing that at certain times you can make it easier. It isn't as harsh as something that is said in the Torah" (N25). The permanency of the law (as already noted, some have proved impossible to carry out because of the exile or the changing social system), the degree of punishment for breaking the law, and the rationale for the law also figure in the value system. There are mitsves, moreover, regulating conduct between man and other creatures, between man and man, and between man and God. However, since the sanction for the commandments ultimately stems not from reason nor from conscience, but rather is said to spring directly from God, both ethical and ritual laws theoretically carry the same obligation and merit.

A few critics have stressed the importance of observance in hasidic life. Lazar Gulkowitsch and Max Löhr, in particular, characterized the hasidim as having little or nothing to do with mysticism, but rather aspiring to an intense piety based on talmudic

[2] Compare the seven laws of Noah which all nations must follow (Babylonian Talmud, *Sanhedrin* 56a). See Ginzberg, *Legends of the Jews*, 1: 70–71; 5: 187, n. 51; 5: 189, n. 56. See also Scholem, *Major Trends*, p. 282.

law.[3] The pious enthusiasm of the hasidim manifests itself both in their attempt to cleave to the Almighty and also in their special concern for keeping the mitsves. Underlying the community's fulfillment of the mitsves, however, is a wide range of supernatural and social concepts that warrant careful consideration.

The Mitsves and Magic

In addition to being practical standards of conduct, the mitsves have magical, mystical, and psychological aspects. Since talmudic times the 613 mitsves have been believed to bear a living correspondence to both the solar system and the human body (the 365 prohibitive commandments corresponding to the days of the solar year and the 248 positive precepts to the parts of the body). Others say the mitsves correspond to the parts of the body and the veins, while according to Rabbi Isaac Luria's kabbalistic system they are linked as well to divisions in the human soul.[4] Therefore, the performance of a commandment, or the failure to perform a commandment, has an effect on that part of the body, universe, or soul to which the commandment corresponds. In this light it is not surprising to find that the mitsves and accompanying religious objects have acquired precise magical powers of their own which find repeated expression in current belief and in the legendary tradition.[5]

The potential of the mitsves for sustaining life, for healing, and for offering hope of eternal salvation are seen in countless narratives dating from the inception of Hasidism to the present. In an account of the Besht the mitsveh of washing one's hands before eating restored a possible convert to Christianity to his senses (H3). Centuries later, another tale relates, performing the same mitsveh

[3] Gulkowitsch, *Der Hasidismus*, pp. 27, 68; Löhr, *Beiträge zur Geschichte*, p. 3. For a contrasting view, see Scholem, *Major Trends*, p. 327.

[4] B. T., *Makkot* 24a. See *In Praise of the Besht*, no. 157. Yaakov Yosef of Polonne, a contemporary disciple of the Baal Shem Tov and author of *Toldot Yaakov Yosef*, indicated that the law corresponded to the 248 bones and 365 sinews in the human body, which in turn had their counterparts in the soul. See Dresner, *Zaddik*, p. 132. The total number of letters of the Torah have been said to correspond to the souls in Israel. See Buber, *Tales*, 2: 147.

[5] Scholem notes that the promise of magical procedure usurping prayer is ever present. "There is danger of imagining a magical mechanism to be operational in every sacramental action. . . ." (*Major Trends*, p. 30).

spared a Jewish soldier in Korea from a bombing attack (HA49).[6]

The negative power of the mitsves is equally apparent: the illness of a Jew is traced to his failure to observe Yom Kippur. When he finally fasts the full day he not only succeeds in killing the root of his illness but he finds that he is able to have children too! (H37).[7] A young boy's nervous disorder is thought to be directly related to his mother's failure to attend the mikveh (HA52).

The performance of the mitsves carries its protective powers beyond the boundaries of mortal life, so that hasidim tell of a deceased tsaddik whose beard, the symbol of the pious and God-fearing Jew, was found to be in perfect condition when they opened his coffin (T62). On the other hand, exhuming the body of a man who apparently had not kept the mitsves revealed that the corpse contained two deep holes—one at the center of the forehead and the other on the left arm—where the pious Jew places the tefillin each morning when he prays (H89).

The power earned by performance is also inherent in the rituals and religious objects, such as the mikveh, the gartel (the narrow belt worn during prayer), the talis koten (the fringed undershirt), the mezuzeh, and the tefillin, which acquire magical properties of their own. Bathing in a mikveh with Reb Zusya purified the past thoughts of an old man and rid him of his illness (H14). In a tale set in Napoleonic times the fragile prayer shawl spread by the Mezhibezher served as a net to catch the Lubliner (T21). Wearing a talis koten saved a Jew from being drafted into the tsar's army (H56). In more recent times, simply arranging for the Sandzer Rov's son to be buried in his talis koten in a Nazi death camp permitted another Jewish prisoner to survive the war (N22). When a mezuzeh given by the present Lubavitcher Rebbe was placed under the ear of a patient who had undergone a serious brain operation, it is said to have brought about a miraculous cure. Afterward, to add to the mystery, the mezuzeh could not be found (HA50).

As in the case of negative action, imperfections in articles of worship adversely affect one's well-being. When a hasid in Israel suffered a heart attack, the present Lubavitcher Rebbe is said to have told the man to have a scribe examine the writing within the

---

[6] Compare the tale of the talmudic student who was turned into a frog. His initial sin was his failure to observe the commandment to wash one's hands (*In Praise of the Besht*, no. 12).

[7] In a more earthy account of punishment, the Jew who fails to observe the Shabbes loses his wallet in the toilet (H63).

tefillin to see if there were any errors. It was then discovered that there was a hole where the word "heart" should be in the portion reading "serve Him with all your heart." It is said that as soon as the tefillin were repaired the man recovered his health (HA55).

The same power generated by articles associated with the law sometimes applied as well to customs which have come to assume authority akin to law. A young wife in America who could not conceive a child followed the advice of a rabbi and cut her hair and donned a wig. Within a year a child was born to her (HA46).

Purity and Contamination

One of the dominant themes in hasidic life and tradition concerns the quest for purity, which is ensured by fulfillment of the commandments, and a concomitant dread of contamination caused by accidental, instinctual, or deliberate rebellion against the laws. The reasons for failing to observe the commandments is attributed to the Yetser Hora, the Evil Urge, which leads one to commit misleading acts of passion, to have skeptical thoughts of God and His works, and to rebel against God's decrees.[8] The hasidim attempt to combat the Yetser Hora and maintain their purity by scrupulous observance of the ritual and moral commandments.

The cares of religious faith begin from one's waking moment, and even the content of dreams is to be weighed for the presence of evil urges. Washing in the morning so that one can speak the holy name with purity and cleanliness, evacuating the bowels if need be before prayer, eating only kosher food, praying, observing the Shabbes prohibitions, learning, obeying one's parents, and giving charity are all considered to be acts of spiritual importance.

With regard to their environment, the hasidim avoid social contacts with non-observant Jews and gentiles alike, who personify the instinctual excesses and impurities from which they have struggled to purge themselves. To ensure their purity the hasidim consciously segregate themselves from the rest of the community (their exotic dress being the most obvious manifestation), just as they symbolically encircle their waists with a gartel to separate the holy and profane aspects of man.

The dangers of being tainted by a misdeed span a wide range of possibilities. One becomes "unclean," for example, by committing

[8] See chaps. 9 and 14 in Schechter's *Some Aspects of Rabbinic Theology.*

what are considered instinctual acts—by letting the emotions rule and ignoring the commandments. It is told that the Apter Rov did not distinguish between certain human beings and animals: "If you use your intelligence to do simply what you feel then it's the same thing as a cow or a lion or any animal. When an animal wants to kill, he kills. If he wants to eat this, he eats this. So if a man acts without using his intelligence to control his desires, then he's an animal" (T23). To abandon one's control is contrary to the hasidic way: the hasid who saw his comrades lust after a bit of meat knew that the meat must be impure (W7).

Care must be exercised in governing thoughts as well as actions, for doubts regarding the attributes of God or lesser doubts about any of the laws may infect the entire spiritual and bodily system. In one tale, already cited, the source of a lingering illness in an elderly Jew was revealed to be his reading of a philosophical book in his youth which undertook to discuss questions concerning the nature of God. Since he was able to understand the questions, but unable to fathom the answers, these unsolved enigmas had festered within him (H14). In another tale, a hasid asks for repentance for committing the sin of answering someone's question incorrectly (H2).

Not only is failure to abide by God's rules disastrous in this life, but any error of commission or omission involving the commandments leaves an indelible mark upon the soul which can be erased only by being purged in Gehenna or by reincarnation. All Jews are reborn until they fulfill all of the mitsves or until they rectify errors they have committed. In one legend, the Besht explains the most unjustifiable of events, infant mortality, as the result of an error in fulfilling the ritual law: a rabbi who judged a goose to be treyf when it was actually kosher is reborn to reconsider the case, and while still an infant he renders a new judgment, thereby freeing his soul to return to Paradise (H11). Those who sin intentionally, particularly if it be against the community as a whole, can expect the more severe punishment of being reborn in a lower form of life. When the Belzer Rebbe was awarding a diploma to a young man who had studied the ritual laws of slaughtering, one of the crucial means of maintaining the purity of the community, he opened the blinds of the window and pointed to a pack of dogs roaming outside: "You see these dogs," he said, "they used to be ritual slaughterers who dishonestly declared treyf meat to be kosher" (H85). In recent times in Israel the Belzer Rebbe is said to have explained that a howling dog was a sinner evolving into another form (H96).

In relationship to the mitsves, continued life is very important, since only in life can one fulfill all the diverse laws.

Solomon the King said: "Better a live dog than a dead lion." Why? Because we say that once a person dies he cannot do any more mitsves. He is finished. He can only accept payment for what he did. But as long as a person is alive, no matter how bad he was, or how good he was, he always has his opportunity yet to do mitsves and do good.*

While maintaining one's present life is preeminently desirable, a different attitude exists among the hasidim regarding rebirth. In order for each soul to complete all of the mitsves it may be necessary for it to be reborn many times. These rebirths, however, are best avoided since each new rebirth presents additional hazards and increases the possibility of committing chance errors (H10). The concern with earthly perils is focused in the legend of the hasid found guilty in the Heavenly Court of a single sin and forced to choose between a reincarnation to correct the error or being scourged for half an hour in Gehenna. It is actually his Rebbe, Rabbi Shneur Zalman, to whom the soul of his dead disciple appears, who makes the safest choice—Gehenna. There is the fearsome forecast of what is to come in the hasid's cry of dismay and the scorched imprint of his hand, but the temptations and pitfalls of our earthly existence make rebirth the greater risk (H26).

Forgiveness for the sin of not keeping the mitsves is never offered by means of immediate surrender to God or by faith alone. One is what one does; one becomes what one takes into oneself. A lifetime of neglectful behavior toward the commandments of the Lord cannot be tossed aside in a moment, for the body and the soul become contaminated. Yet so great is the power of the mitsves and so potent is the word of a great tsaddik who fulfills their every essence that sinners can be redeemed. In one tale a druggist who ignored the mitsves all his life was defended before the Heavenly Court by the Szigetter Rov, who argued that the man had never known what the mitsves meant. The druggist received renewed life so that he might have the opportunity to fulfill God's wishes (H54).

The redemption promised sinners serves to intensify the promise of what awaits the truly pious: when a man who performed but the single mitsveh of washing his hands is sent to Paradise after his death, the Belzer Rov told his followers: "And if for one mitsveh this impious man was sent to Paradise, what will be the rewards

for you who struggle each moment to perform all the mitsves?"
(H83).

The Mitsves and the Community

The stakes in fulfilling the mitsves are, however, greater than the
fate of a single soul. The least of the laws is proclaimed a vital fiber
in the web of community destiny. In his introductory remarks on
Jewish mysticism, Gershom Scholem notes that through the in-
tensification of the belief in the sacred power of the law "every
mitswah became an event of cosmic importance, an act which had a
bearing upon the dynamics of the universe. The religious Jew
became a protagonist in the dynamics of the world; he manipulated
the strings behind the scene." [9] Neglect of the commandments
resulted in exile for the community; continued denial of the tenets
by the Jews means additional punishment, delay in the appearance
of the Meshiah and prolongation of the exile.

Every Jew has to feel as if everything depends on him. That means,
as it says in *Pirke Avot* ["*Sayings of the Fathers*"], a person has to think
this way: He is on the scale and the whole world is on the scale. And if
he does one mitsveh he draws the whole world onto the good side of the
scale—himself and the whole world. If he does a bad thing, he has to
consider as if he were drawing himself bad and the whole world in
bad.*

Using the same reasoning a great number of the hasidim attribute the cause of World War II directly to the failure of the Jewish
community as a whole to keep the mitsves.

In much the same way as the soul of an erring individual is not
kept pure, the Yiddishkait of the European community, repre-
sented by the active implementation of the community's educational and charitable programs, was not kept free of contamination.
The participation of those not truly religious spelled ruin. In the
days just prior to World War II, a Polish sage said to his student:
"Do you see all the yeshives? They are run on money contributed
by people who earned it on Shabbes. They cannot last, they cannot
last" (N10).[10]

[9] Scholem, *Major Trends*, pp. 29–30.
[10] Despite these forebodings, and perhaps because of the enormous cost of
their educational system and their own meagre resources, hasidic courts in
the United States accept donations from persons who are not orthodox. In

As in the ancient past, the problems besetting the Jews can be regarded as a purgative rather than as a punishment. Seen in this perspective, the deaths due to World War II are a terrible cure for offenses committed against the law.

Nobody in the world has trouble like the Jews because they carry the responsibility for all the world. We have been exiled from Israel, the Temple destroyed. We have lost, not only in a material sense in that we are not in our own land, we have lost our highest standard of life, knowledge of God, and the highest observance of worship that was in the Temple. But, on the other hand, it is not a punishment. It is a clearing, a curing. And this cure we are supposed to take because we did not observe exactly as we are supposed to observe all the mitsves. *

Today, for the most part, the political, economic, and psychological factors giving rise to Nazism are ignored, considered meaningless by most hasidim.[11] Hitler is regarded simply as one of a succession of evil geniuses used by God to chastise the Jews for not keeping the mitsves. God is pictured as a concerned father anxious that his children follow His commandments, and Hitler is regarded as a stick used by the father to punish His children for their failure. Confronted with the problem of why the ultra-religious Jews of eastern Europe were so terribly decimated, the previous Lubavitcher Rebbe's answer points to the unique relationship existing between the righteous of Israel and God. "When you wish to chastise a child, where do you slap him? In the face!" (N31).

The hasidim say that the disobedient Jewish community in Europe possessed the power to save itself by mending its ways. During the war the Lubavitcher Rebbe echoed the plea made at other critical moments in Jewish history: if all Israel would but keep two Sabbaths holy they would be redeemed. To explain the safety of the relatively impious Jews of the United States, it is said that they were saved because of their charitable works (N8).

ADDITIONAL EXPLANATIONS

There is a danger that in this brief description hasidic belief seems too easily to dissolve into a simple structure of magical

---

one court, the Rebbe accepted a wealthy donor's gifts for the boys' yeshiveh and the girls' yeshiveh but declined to accept the donor's gift for the besmedresh.

[11] For evidence concerning the activities of the pious during the war see Ringelblum, *Notes from the Warsaw Ghetto*, pp. 21, 53, 55, 61, 83, 125, 264. See also Rabinowicz, *Guide to Hasidism*, pp. 145–49; Unger, *Sefer Kedoshim*.

power based on performance of the mitsves. Hasidic belief and tradition are multifaceted and there are countless explanatory avenues. While we have noted, for example, dominant themes concerning the cause of World War II, it is impossible to state a single cause for the war upon which every hasid would wholeheartedly agree. There are a great number of seemingly contradictory notions existing side by side which attempt to explain the overwhelming tragedy. It is difficult, for example, for some hasidim, as well as for Jews in general, to accept an explanation of the war which condemns the dead of Europe as being impious and as having been the cause of their own destruction. Some say that the true causes are unknown and can never be known. Some note that Hitler, far from being an agent of the Almighty, had free will to do his evil deeds and he is now being punished for his atrocities in the afterlife. In addition to other explanations, most hasidim also assert that the world is simply following the path already prophesied and that terrible destruction precedes the coming of the Meshiah. This necessary destruction would affect both guilty and innocent alike. As when the Angel of Death was loosed in pharoah's time, forces of evil are sometimes unleashed without any restraint.

These six million Jews had to be killed. Why? We don't know. We have no idea. We can't know. It's something we can't know because the finest of the Jewry were killed. The best—the greatest rabbis, the greatest tsaddikim were killed. We don't know why they had to be killed. All we know is that these people were killed. And we do know, you see it in the books from thousands of years ago, that before the Meshiah is going to come, in the area of the last thousand years, the closer it will be, more and more Jews will be killed.*

VII SUPERNATURAL

BEINGS AND MAGIC

Dybbuks

There is an area of belief and custom which in former times played a significant part in hasidic society and in oral tradition. In earlier times, hasidic life in Europe was pervaded by a host of malevolent spirits and demons.[1] Mystifying occurrences as well as personal idiosyncrasies were often attributed to the work of spirits and dybbuks (wandering spirits of the dead who possess the bodies of the living).

The religious rationale offered for the existence of such creatures is that they, like the miracles of the Rebbes, serve as proof of the powers of God. (One is reminded of the argument put forth in the seventeenth century by Joseph Glanvill in *Saducismus Triumphatus* concerning the existence of witches.) The dybbuk is regarded as once having been a bulwark to faith:

Why does He put him [a dybbuk] in and take him out? It is because He wants to show the people that there is a God. That gives people fear of God, and love of God and belief in God—that it should be easier for the person to believe in God. As every generation moves along there is more of a hiding of God's face, and it's harder and harder to be religious and to have real faith and belief in God. I think that Reb Meirl Premishlaner said "one day will come that it will be so hard to believe in God, it will be like climbing up a straight wall with nothing to hold on to." *

[1] See *In Praise of the Besht*, no. 162, in which a demon inhabits a house after an emasculated cock has been put under the threshold. In tale no. 84 demons are seen sitting in the woman's section of the synagogue; they are the result of the cantor's unholy thoughts. See also *ibid.*, no. 18.

Although there has been a pronounced shift in belief in such phenomena, many hasidim believe that in previous generations dybbuks existed simply because their sages said that they did. At present, too, the religious often feel obliged to defend ideas held important by their forefathers but now suffering disrepute. "There is no evidence that they did not exist," the Lubavitcher Rebbe has said, "and therefore it is more scientific to believe reliable witnesses." * It might even be possible, assert some hasidim, to be able to find a person with a dybbuk who has been placed in a mental institution. The fact, however, is that the tide of modern ideas has washed away belief in supernatural creatures.

Dybbuk? Superstition. There was a woman in the old country who thought she had a frog inside. She went to my uncle, a doctor, and he gave her something to make her throw up. She threw up. He showed her the frog. Smart doctor. The dybbuk is like that. People in crazy houses today too are like that. A woman loses the man she loves. He dies. She thinks about him, then she dreams about him, and then she thinks she has a dybbuk. Superstition. *

In addition, the change in environment from Europe to America has cut off certain sources for belief in supernatural creatures. For example, it was believed in Europe that souls returned to the Beit ha-Kneset, the synagogue of the misnagdim, which was used solely for prayer. The besmedresh and shtibl, which by contrast were used by the common folk for study, eating, and social and religious activities as well as for prayer, lacked the sanctified atmosphere of the Beit ha-Kneset and do not appear to have attracted the souls of the dead. Since there is no Beit ha-Kneset in the United States, there is no haven for wandering souls. The number of other places where such creatures could be found (especially uninhabited places) has shrunk considerably.[2]

The oral tradition reflects the situation existing today concerning belief in dybbuks. While belief in such supernatural creatures has largely evaporated, there are still some rare references (H86). On the other hand, there is sufficient sophistication on the subject to have a tale of the Satmarer Rebbe in which he refers a dybbuk-haunted victim to a psychiatrist (S36). (To be sure, the story probably owes more to the antagonism between the courts of Belz and Satmar rather than to the acceptance of modern belief.)

As supernatural creatures once served to satisfy many unanswered questions, the reason for their disappearance in the past fifty

[2] See Trachtenberg, *Jewish Magic and Superstition,* pp. 32, 67.

years is explained in accordance with traditional perspectives. The great rabbis, it is said, may have driven away the demons so that they no longer plague mankind.[3] The disapppearance of such creatures is said to be tied to the decline of miraculous power in general. This generation, some suggest, is not ready to see such things as the raising of the dead. Others assert that God is concealing Himself from us as a punishment.

Other Supernatural Forces

While spirits and dybbuks seem to have vanished, danger from other unknown supernatural forces exists and precautions must be taken. Some contemporary Rebbes continue to pass out coins as a kind of blessing and good luck charm, and some advise adding a new name to protect the sick as a deceptive and protective device (HA34).[4]

My brother once was very sick when he was a child. My father went in to the Rebbe. He told him then to change his name—not changing—but adding a name. And he promised him he'd be better. He started getting better then. It was actually a miracle. I've seen it by my Rebbe. I've seen it many times with friends.*

Another source of supernatural power faced particularly by children is the evil eye (einhora). The evil eye is attributed to people who direct envious or spiteful feelings toward those who are enjoying good fortune. When such envious visitors leave a home, the children may be noted to experience symptoms of yawning and nausea and may fall sick.[5] There remain in the community a few knowledgeable persons who possess the "good eye" and who can uncharm the victim of the evil eye. It is, in addition, customary when delivering a compliment to say immediately afterward "keinhora" (no evil eye), to prevent these words from reaching the ears of those whose jealousy might be stirred. Adults may also be

---

[3] Banishing demons to places uninhabited by man is well known in Jewish tradition. See *In Praise of the Besht*, no. 84. See also Dubnow, *History*, 1: 203.

[4] See *In Praise of the Besht*, no. 59, in which the Besht does not receive any response to his prayers for a sick girl because she had been given a new name but he had not yet been informed of it.

[5] See Trachtenberg, *Jewish Magic*, pp. 54–56.

cautioned not to buy too many things lest they arouse the envy of others (HA12).

The hasidim also continue the eastern European custom of hanging a childbirth amulet for protection against supernatural danger.[6] On the amulet, which is simply a single sheet of paper, is printed Psalm 121, the names of protective angels, and a warning against practicing sorcery. The protective measures are directed against Lilith, the chief female demon; belief in Lilith is generalized, however, and one hears only of vague dangers which surround the newborn child. This concern is particularly evident on the eve before the circumcision (wakhnakht) when malevolent forces seem to abound and special protective psalms are read.[7] In the tales it is at this time that a Rebbe's counsel may be sought to help ease the child past this dangerous barrier to life (H91, H92).

Sympathetic Magic

Jewish magic has been said to be distinguished by its association of magical power with supernatural aid from God. One invokes the Almighty for aid in one way or another rather than performing a mysterious but mechanical rite which has efficacious power.[8] In fact, however, it is often difficult to distinguish between magic and mysticism. Magical and spiritual forces often seem to come together in hasidic life and tradition, and even at those times when dedication to the omnipotence of God is clearly demonstrated a shaft of light will reveal a curious mélange of magic and piety. A key point in one narrative occurs when the Rebbe holds a piece of fish in his hand while relating a story to a hasid who has asked for help in having children. The powers of fertility believed inherent in fish are set in sympathetic correspondence with the request of the childless hasid, and, interestingly enough, in conjunction with belief in the powers and mercy of God (H61).[9]

[6] See Gaster, *The Holy and the Profane*, pp. 21–28.

[7] See Trachtenberg, *Jewish Magic*, pp. 42, 106, 157, 170–72.

[8] See Trachtenberg, "Folk Element in Judaism," *The Journal of Religion*, 22 (1942): 183, and *Jewish Magic*, pp. 19–22.

[9] In medieval Jewish communities fish was eaten by the bride and groom the day after the marriage ceremony to ensure fruitfulness. See Trachtenberg, *Jewish Magic*, p. 188; Schauss, *Lifetime of a Jew*, p. 218 and n.; Thompson, *Motif-Index*, vol. 6, T511.51. See Babylonian Talmud, *Ketubot* 5a. See also Isidor Scheftelowitz, "Das Fischsymbol im Judentum und Christentum," *Archiv für Religiouswissenschaft*, 14 (1911): 376–85.

It is, however, often difficult to fix the source of power with certainty. In tales of the tsaddikim supernatural power may reside not only in the Almighty but also in a righteous man, in his way of prayer, in the prayer itself, in a formula using the prayer, or in any combination of these. Prayer itself is a kind of preternatural power and, when under control, can be conceived of as a form of action. For example, so potent were the Eighteen Benedictions when said by the Besht that the congregation ran away in fear (T1). On one occasion, when a distraught father rushed to the Stoliner Rebbe because his child was near death, the Rebbe bid him stay up the whole night to say psalms and promised that he would do the same (HA3). To prevent Rommel from taking Palestine, the hasidim begged the Hushatener to do something—to pray (N23). The combination of these varied forces at work is especially clear in the tale of Reb Naftali of Ropchits, who from his hiding place watched the great Rebbe Elimelekh slowly encircle himself with the gartel. At the first circle the room became filled with light, but at the second turn Reb Naftali found himself gasping for air and he was forced to call out. "It's a miracle that you yelled out," admonished Rebbe Elimelekh, "because if I had put the gartel around myself another time the light and air would have become so strong that you wouldn't have been able to endure it" (T10). It is the marvelous combination of the tsaddik, the act of santification, and the religious object associated with the rite that results in such stunning force.

In the instances just cited the act of propitiating God falls into the realm of the religious. However, when one uses elements of the prayers as a formula, despite their association with the Almighty, the act tends more toward being mechanically magical rather than religious. For example, it is told that Reb Zusya forced a criminal to confess by reciting a line from the prayers said at Rosh Hashoneh: "He fills the world with his fear" (H15). Linking both prayer and magic, it is said that a Stoliner hasid was repaid a large debt after he followed the late Rebbe's advice and prayed loudly at a specified point in the prayers (H11). Another sympathetic correspondence was established by reference to the Scriptures when the Rizhyner Rebbe ordered music to be sounded three times in order to have a decree set aside (H34). The calendar and the prescribed Torah readings for the year provide a set of established correspondences: the Lubliner Rebbe could forecast the day of his death since the readings of the first four days of Nisan correspond to the first four months of the year (TA20).

Other wonders in the tales, less tied to prayer, are clearly in tune with the principles of sympathetic magic. In a tale reflecting the supernatural conflict in the Napoleonic war, the Rimanover Rebbe likened the Russian troops opposing Napoleon to the matses being shoveled into an oven—the effect of his incantation being the devastation of the troops (N3). The recruit about to be inducted into the Russian army found that the sentence ultimately written on his papers was the very one the Rebbe had written earlier on a pane of glass (H72). One tale acknowledges that talking about some event may in effect serve to bring it about (N7); similarly, in another tale, a Rebbe advises a hasid who is expecting a tragedy to "think good and it will be good" (HA48). The psychological influence of objects is seen in the tale of the rabbi who, though he made the correct decision, unconsciously had moments of doubt during a trial because unknown to him one of the litigants had slipped money into his pocket (HA47).

In general, hasidic custom and ritual are filled with symbolic language and practice which find expression in the tales. Gematria, awarding letters of the alphabet numerical values, encourages implanting cryptographic meanings in the tales, which often are prayers for the Meshiah (T30). A magical paronomastic device of striking the hapless gabai is used to encourage the appearance of the new moon (S23); similarly, a carrot dish is served at a meal because the name of the dish also means "to multiply" (WH13). In a world filled with magical correspondences, even seemingly chance actions are under supernatural direction: when the Stoliner Rebbe died, his hasidim drew lots to determine if they should take his body to Jerusalem or bury him in Brooklyn (TA18). While the community has by and large rejected belief in supernatural creatures, it has not cast aside belief in a universe whose parts are interrelated and which to some extent can be interpreted and controlled.

VIII ATTITUDES AND RELATIONSHIPS

Gentile and Jew

The hasidim take pride in the difficult path they choose to follow, which their tradition says other nations despised,[1] and in their resulting social behavior—their bent toward study and the absence in their community of crimes of violence, drunkenness, divorce, and sex deviation. They take pride as well in their intelligence and ingenuity, in their learned men, and in their ability to survive as a culture despite the terrible hardships they have undergone.

The exotic customs of the hasidim are used in part as a protective fence around their community. By distinguishing themselves from the gentiles and nonreligious Jews, the hasidim believe that they can best preserve their identity, keep their children from becoming acculturated, and prevent possible infractions of the religious law. Even when the hasidim adopt contemporary garb they try to distort the manner and style in which it is customarily worn: beaver and fedora hats are usually black, and often the brim is turned upward; coats are buttoned on the opposite side; most hasidim do not wear neckties, or if they do they may wear them folded rather than knotted; those who relinquish the long kaftan during the week usually replace it with an old-fashioned dark, double-breasted suit.

This need to maintain their insularity is a recurrent theme in hasidic tradition. One tale relates how in the time of the Second Temple a number of the pious traveled to an island where no alien philosophies were permitted (H8). The more practical considerations of such insularity also warrant attention in tradition: in a par-

[1] See p. 123, n. 2.

able which considers the possibility of compromising their laws, the hasidim assert that it is the external environment which must be altered rather than the body of laws of the Torah (W25). Another parable notes the terms for joining forces with the outside world: since the Jews are already circumcised and cannot change, it is up to others to make the necessary accommodation (W24).

The sharp division between the hasidim and the outside world finds support in a long, painful social history. The tales bear the stamp of social antagonisms. There were contests of faith (I8, H3) as well as petty and serious conflicts (H33, H64, H81). The question of conversion plays a part in parables (I14) and jests (WH12, H6), and there are stories, some humorous, concerning debates between priests and rabbis (S12).

Today as well the hasidim find ready evidence of antagonisms among outside groups which they construe as indications of organized anti-Semitism. Indeed, it would be difficult for a hasid to understand the workings of a world without anti-Semites (H15). During a crisis in race relations in the South a hasid asked to have the situation explained: "I can understand they hate the Jews— that's natural. But what have they got against the Negroes?" *

As the hasidim do not have any social relations beyond their religious circle, their knowledge of the mores of the outside community has always been limited. Because they often find housing in New York in depressed areas, compete for jobs with low-scale wage earners from ethnic groups poorly integrated into the urban scene, and hire such workers to tend menial tasks in their businesses and in their houses of worship, they continue to find evidence for the stereotype of the gentile who is thought to be morally and culturally inferior to the Jew. While the hasid represents the utmost attainment in piety and restraint, the gentile is considered the reverse side of the coin. Concerned with his appetites, the gentile is thought to act without thinking of his duties to the Almighty. Jew and gentile are both heir to the delights of brandy, but in tradition the Jew tempers his desire with divine observance (H18). The deepest familial values—the relationship of parents and children—are also seen to suffer in the gentile home. One tale relates how a gentile father was dispossessed by his children—an incredible impiety by hasidic standards (H5).[2]

It is not only impossible to think of a gentile acting in a pious

---

[2] A Jew who committed the crime of hitting his father was told by the Besht that he must stand in the mourner's place for a year. He failed to do so and died within the year. *In Praise of the Besht,* no. 233.

manner, but tradition records somewhat parenthetically the pain of thinking of a gentile performing a deed for which he would accrue credit in the other world. In a famous tale of the Sassover Rebbe, the Rebbe disguises himself as a peasant, chops wood, and kindles a fire for a sick widow. The widow records her astonishment at the good deed of the Polish peasant in a not uncommon expression: "Please, God, this is such a big mitsveh, don't count it for a goy" (T14).[3]

Similarly, following a long-established custom, the only day the hasidim forgo studying is Christmas day. Some say that this is because Jesus was a talmudic scholar and would accrue from their works further benefits for himself and for his cause.

We believe that Jesus was taken away from the Jews. He was a great power, he could have been a great talmudic scholar or a tsaddik, and he was drawn to the other side of the fence. And so in effect he becomes an inverted magnet. On a tsaddik's *day*, the day he is brought up for discussion in heaven, one would study and do mitsves in his honor. Whenever we do something our main hope is that it should be accepted in heaven. He on this day pulls this action toward him, toward his honor. If we would learn, and if we would not learn with complete purity, it would go to his merit and he would take it on his side of the fence. Rather than to the credit of the Jews, it would go to the unclean side. There is always a war between light and darkness. *

Another explanation suggests that on the night of the birth of Jesus the air is filled with unclean spirits, and that by studying the Torah on that night he might be helped to come out of the realm of the unclean. Clearly these explanations antedate the rise of Hasidism, but the hasidim continue to perpetuate them. Russian courts follow the Old Calendar and so abstain from study on January 6; courts from areas where the calendar change was accepted do not study on December 25. Some courts, now confronted with the differing customs of hasidim who once lived far apart, with typical hasidic zeal follow both calendars in this regard and forgo study on both December 25 and January 6.

But if it is a problem for the hasidim to acknowledge a gentile's mitsves, it is equally difficult for them to recognize their own

---

[3] Compare Peretz's version, *In This World and the Next*, p. 79, which does not contain this ending. The narrator heard the ending from his Rebbe. In *In Praise of the Besht*, no. 53, the victim of a near drowning urges a reward for the sailor who saved him so that he would not be the cause of the sailor's inheriting the next world.

questionable actions. In one tale, when a Jew keeps the inheritance which would fall to a gentile family, it is seen as a gift from God rather than as a deception (H5a).[4]

The family, however, is the focal point of fear and resistance to the gentile. The maintenance of family purity is a vital thread in hasidic thinking. Upon entering marriage, family relationships are given careful scrutiny. A hasidic rabbi of a congregation of hasidim and more Americanized orthodox Jews explained:

> I do weddings for my congregation or for people with whom I'm acquainted. Otherwise I don't do it. For people [in general], I don't do it. I don't know if what I would be saying is true. There are lots of adopted children and I don't know. It would affect the whole wedding. *

The hasidic view of historical events is sometimes colored by this central concern for establishing family purity. One Saturday night at a melaveh malkeh a hasid explained: "During the stay of the Jews in Egypt only one woman was forced by an Egyptian man. It's written that that's what happened. It's amazing that in all that time there was only one." *

In tradition, the dangers resulting from marriage or intimate contact with gentiles are clear: it promises the dilution of the religion and beyond that punishment to the soul as well. A tsaddik was expelled from the Heavenly Court because thirteen generations later one of his descendants would become a Christian convert (T24). Reb Aaron, the first Karliner Rebbe, was denied access to the innermost Court of Heaven because he was nursed by a gentile woman. He had to be reborn so that he could be suckled by a Jewess (H12). Similarly, to attain the heights in heaven, it is necessary for a Jewish convert to be reborn of Jewish parents (H10). In this light, it is easier to understand the actions of Graf Potocki, a convert to Judaism, who allegedly welcomed the purification that came with being burned at the stake (I9).

The tales illustrate that the identity of the Jewish soul is maintained even when one's origin is not consciously known; the actual source of one's soul often reveals itself when threatened by absorption into a gentile family. Because Jewish souls are thought to enjoy a particular integrity, in one tale the Besht is

---

[4] See *In Praise of the Besht*, no. 236, concerning an accusation brought in heaven against the Jews who deceive gentiles in the villages. See also *ibid.*, no. 90, in which Satan accuses a Jew of robbing gentiles. The tale concludes: "From this one can see that one should refrain from robbing the gentiles, since, as it is written in the books, Satan collects it back from one's holy merits, God forbid."

able to reveal to a priest that his mother had run off with a gentile while she was pregnant, but that his father's Jewish name was imprinted on his forehead (H9). In another tale of the past, when a Jewish army officer who had been stolen as a child and raised as a gentile is about to enter the bed of his new bride, the daughter of a general, he is visited by a vision of a Rebbe who reveals his heritage to him and sends him on a pilgrimage back to his own village (H45, H46).

On the basis of this long-standing social division, a contemporary storyteller can complete his narrative even when he himself never learned the final solution, or when he has forgotten the ending. To explain the disappearance of an American Jew in a suburban community, the storyteller says he thinks that he abandoned his non-Jewish second wife and family in order to return to his Jewish first wife and family. But when questioned, the narrator did not actually know what had happened to the man, nor even if he had been married before. The perspective of his culture supplied the ending for him (HA1 and note).

Nonreligious Jews

Less religious Jews are regarded with scorn by most hasidim for having spurned their legacy. Their diluted prayer services, and their temples with men and women seated together are a scandal to the hasidim. In general, the hasidim consider such Jews to be overly concerned with their cars, their comforts, and their appetites. They believe that materialism is the basis for their refusal to take the hard road of orthodoxy. The most sympathetic reaction is that of simple incomprehension.

In certain ways I don't see what his object for life is and what he is living for. I have no idea. I can't understand it. Just like he can't understand me, I can't understand him. I'm living because God created me. God made me. He gave me certain tasks to do. I have to do my utmost to keep them and that's the reason I'm living: to be religious; to follow the mitsves; to study the Torah; and the most important task for me is to bring up a religious generation. I wonder why he kills himself for his children. What are his children for? *

The hasidim make small acknowledgment of other philosophical points of view, and it usually comes as a shock to the minority who venture outside the intellectual confines of the community to find that others may hold strict ethical and spiritual values and that their conduct may be motivated by other than base impulses. Nevertheless, despite the low status of less religious and nonreligious Jews, the hasidim believe that there is something special about the Jewish soul regardless of how it is treated. In tradition, to endanger one's self and redeem a fellow Jew is a deed of the greatest piety and for it one may justly be called hasid (H28). Another tale notes that he who saves a fellow Jew may be said to save the world (H35). In contrast, to inform to government authorities on a fellow Jew is a contemptible act that cuts one off from the community (H49, HA37). The seemingly miraculous prediction that the Sandzer Rov makes concerning the death of an informer is simply predicated on his empathy for a fellow Jew. He knows when danger has passed for his brethren (H49).

Any excuse is accepted for past failure to observe the laws if one wishes to return to the orthodox faith (H54). Under special circumstances, those who have neglected the commandments through no fault of their own may have a second opportunity to rectify their errors. The negligent Jew who falls into a coma envisions himself before the Court of Heaven. There he is defended by the Szigetter Rov, who argues that he is not to be blamed because he has grown up in an improper atmosphere. The sinner wins the opportunity to return to life and prove that he will follow the tenets of the Torah (H54).

Throughout the tales there is the implicit desire to assist other Jews to fulfill their task of obeying the laws. Therefore, in contemporary life many hasidim, particularly Lubavitchers, often treat other Jews with solicitous concern, and there is widespread delight and pride in helping one who in their eyes has sinned to recognize both his special value and his special obligations (HA1, HA54).

The hasidim, on the other hand, generally fare badly in the eyes of the irreligious, and this does little to improve relations. At best, the hasidim are considered objects of curiosity, reminders of a dead past; at worst they are regarded as crude, ignorant, and filthy, an embarrassment to all Jews. The hasidim must endure stares on the street and in the subways. On the high holidays less religious Jews often take excursions into sections inhabited by hasidim to see how the pious rejoice. But the fervency of the hasidim on these occasions is catching, and one concerned tourist warned his young son, "Remember. I'm only taking you to *see* them."

Misnagdim

To a great extent the hasidim have become reconciled with their orthodox opponents, the misnagdim, who must now look to the hasidim as the bulwark rather than as the despoilers of orthodoxy. Hasidic zeal, however, has helped to renew tensions between themselves and other orthodox Jews. The ancient dispute concerning talmudic scholarship, an attribute the misnagdim say was mocked by the hasidim, has taken a new turn and at present hasidic yeshives are regarded as the most rigorous and true to the eastern European ideal. The hasidim today regard the orthodox yeshives that have incorporated secular studies, accommodated their dress to western standards, and introduced athletics as having pandered to modern society. The misnagdim resent the fact that their orthodox customs and precautions are deemed insufficient; and they feel slighted by hasidic insularity. Non-hasidic orthodox Jews of Williamsburg feel it is a direct slap to hear Hungarian rather than Yiddish spoken in the markets and on the streets. Some who are concerned to appear in touch with modern life dislike the attention that the hasidim direct to orthodoxy by their old-fashioned dress and customs. However, the older orthodox communities have to a large extent been forced to fall into step for fear of being deemed lax. Preferred meat now is not only kosher, it is *glatt* kosher— unquestionably without blemish.[5] Older customs once generally disregarded, such as wearing wigs and testing clothing to see if linen and wool are mixed (shatnes),[6] have been adopted again.

At times the line between the varying groups becomes slack, since many of the children of misnagdim have joined the ranks of the hasidim, while some of the offspring of hasidic parents are content to slip from the ranks of the zealots into the more modern orthodox fold. However, the division between the groups is being maintained. One young man, the son of hasidic parents who immigrated here thirty years ago and who now considers himself as "modern orthodox," felt rebuffed when he was to be married into a stricter hasidic family:

My future father-in-law asked me if I would wear a kapote [long coat] at the wedding, indicating I would wear it other times as well. I said I

[5] For a discussion of glatt kosher and its economic ramifications, see Poll, *Hasidic Community*, pp. 178–86.
[6] Concerning shatnes, see *ibid.*, pp. 104–7.

would have to think about it. My fiance's brother is not here. We were planning a trip to Israel, but now we're hesitating. It's good they're not here. They showed me a picture of him with a beard and peyes. We sent them a picture of me [without beard and peyes and in a modern suit] but they didn't respond that they'd seen it.*

In the oral traditions of both groups past encounters between hasid and misnaged have often been sharp, as when the misnaged called Iron Head promised to give a party when the Lubliner died (T20). In hasidic tales the misnaged is generally pictured as a skeptic who is ultimately awed by hasidic wit and wisdom (H2, H14, T14). The hasidim mock the misnaged's restraint in prayer, calling their worship a "dead davening" (S30). For his part, the misnaged, even in hasidic tales, mocks the hasid's lack of scholarship: "What place have they among learned people? They have a Rebbe. Go to him" (H2). The naïveté of the hasidic believer also presents a broad target. The misnaged tells of the rabbi who tried to command a deaf and dumb boy to speak. The exasperated Rebbe finally sentenced him to be deaf and dumb (M2). "And so it was," slyly concludes the narrator.

Treatment of the same theme—the lack of fish for Shabbes— reveals opposing attitudes. In a hasidic tale a Rebbe's faith that he would be provided with fish by the Almighty is rewarded when the fish falls through the chimney into the pot of water boiling on the fire (H62). Faced with a similar problem in a tale told by a misnaged, the Rebbe's gabai stocks a well with a fish which is then "miraculously" caught (M3).

Hasidic Courts

On an individual level, relationships between hasidim of different courts and between religious Jews in general are governed by the same tenets and similar social controls. There is an established code of law and ethics, and in the event of disputes there are rabbinical courts, which may consist of one or more rabbis, to render decisions. Often simply the threat of being brought before a rabbinical court is sufficient to settle a case. For example, when the hasidic owner of a very small shoe store moved to a new location a little further down the street to accommodate the hasidic owners of a dress store who wanted to expand, he discovered that there was insufficient heat in his new location and customers complained of the cold. After his complaints were ignored he threatened to take the owners of the dress store to a rabbinical court. The embarrassment, as well as the trouble and expense, encouraged them to buy him a small electric heater. Hasidim rarely if ever turn to the secular courts for justice, even in cases of blatant dishonesty (HA37).[7]

There is no judiciary, however, to resolve accumulated frictions that develop between hasidim of varying courts and national identities. Differences between groups encourage slighting attitudes; modified western dress or a court's reputation for ignorance and naïveté may be the targets for ridicule.

Even the respective qualities of the women come in for their share of criticism. Such discussion usually concerns the Hungarian hasidic women, if for no other reason than that they are more numerous. One rabbi who stands on the borderline between the orthodox and hasidic communities advised me:

> You will be disappointed with the Hungarian women. They were in camps during their adolescence. They never had the chance to learn. They're ignorant. All the Hungarian women know is cooking. My wife went to a gathering—she said she couldn't [stand it]. They don't know anything. All they know is how to keep house.*

A Lubavitcher hasid also criticized them:

> Hungarian women are more brazen, more demanding, more interested in clothing, comforts, pleasures. They're much less educated. The women in Lubavitch are much more learned.*

An unmarried hasid of Polish parents offered the following thoughts:

> I'd never marry a Hungarian woman. Because everybody speaks against them. Why should I have a wife and when they speak against Hungarians she should hear? The Hungarians are more fanatic. It's the land that makes them different. Like the women cut their hair so close. It's right, it's the religious way, but Polish and Russian women don't do it. With us the kids put on stockings at the age of six. With them it's earlier. It's because of the different lands. Like it says in the *Shulhan Arukh* there should be six hours between eating milk and meat. In Germany, the greatest people wait two hours. The digestion is different. With us we have to wait six hours before the food is digested. With them they digest it after two hours.*

[7] See *ibid.*, p. 71, where a hasidic Jew who sued a fellow hasid in civil court for damages resulting from an automobile accident was regarded as a traitor.

But after reconsidering his view, he added:

Look, I repeat what others say. The Hungarians are all right. I know a lot of them. They're all right. We say they're ignorant; they say we're ignorant.*

In point of fact, there is a great deal of intermarriage with Hungarian women. Many older men who had lost their wives and children in the camps married younger Hungarian women in America. When a Polish hasid kidded a Hungarian hasid, saying: "You Hungarians are all alike," the Hungarian's reply was to the point: "You curse us and marry our women."

In the past there have been deep rifts between hasidic courts for philosophical as well as for more practical reasons. At the inception of Hasidism, Rebbe Elimelekh and the Seer of Lublin parted when the latter became independent and gathered his own followers. In the mid-nineteenth century, Rabbi Mordekhai Yosef left the court of Rabbi Menahem Mendel of Kotsk because of Menahem Mendel's extreme asceticism.[8] The courts of Sadeger and Sandzer too split over the Sadegerer's display of riches and more lenient attitude toward religiosity. It is clear that the present hasidic community also has its rivalries, disputes, and differing points of view.[9]

SATMAR

The court of Satmar, numerically the largest group of hasidim in New York, is a chief source of strife in the hasidic community because of its extremist attitudes, its propagandistic energies, and its intolerant attitude toward other courts. A hasid of Polish origin complained of the unnecessary zealousness of the hasidim of Satmar:

One makes salt and he comes out that all other salt isn't kosher. Now whoever heard that other salt isn't kosher? What's salt that it shouldn't be kosher? *

The Satmarer hasidim adhere closely to the eastern Europe model, and their dress is much the same as it was in Hungary at the turn of the century. The men's peyes are usually worn so that they are clearly visible. Very few of the men have adopted western

[8] See Buber, *Tales*, 2: 39–44.
[9] On the division between the M'lochim and the court of Lubavitch, see Sobel, "The M'lochim," pp. 50–54.

dress of any sort, even neckties. The women clip their hair very close to the scalp. The toyreh of the Satmarer Rebbe often includes his plea to keep every iota of the Torah. In that he says, lies their future welfare; otherwise, all will be lost. If they cut a snippet from their children's peyes then their children will cut them shorter, and their grandchildren will cut them off altogether. They must not start to give in.

Satmarer children are not, by comparison with some other hasidic children, well oriented to the general American environment. They learn to speak English at a later age, and in general speak English badly. They are for the most part innocent of the surrounding culture. Their educational aspirations are sharply limited, and most young boys plan simply to fill factory jobs similar to those held by their fathers. The school system in which they study makes few concessions to western norms.[10] On occasion Catholic textbooks are preferred to those used in secular schools. They are far less concerned with the children's contact with Christian ideas than with their exposure to the offenses of secularism.

The goal of the Satmar court is to maintain as much as possible the court's social and intellectual isolation. Intrusions of modern life such as television and movies are banned. Even modern Hebrew is scorned, since use of the holy language in profane activities detracts from its religious significance, and the Satmarer Rebbe is reported to have said that he would rather see a Jew convert than learn a word of modern Hebrew. At present the court is located in Williamsburg, but future plans for the court may include their moving to a settlement in New Jersey where they will be better able to guard against secular inroads.

A particularly tense issue that sets the court of Satmar at odds with all others concerns their campaign against the State of Israel. There are several aspects to the argument presented by the Satmarer Rebbe and his hasidim: first, according to their view one is not permitted to restore the nation and the Temple before the Meshiah

---

[10] After an outbreak of infectious hepatitis occurred among the pupils at the United Talmudical Academy Torah Vyirah, 95 Boerum Street, a sanitary inspection at the school "revealed that the school was overcrowded; it had some 1,800 to 2,000 pupils in a building designed for 800. There were inadequate toilet facilities, sinks and drinking fountains, and in general, the sanitation facilities were grossly inadequate. What was even worse was that housekeeping was deplorable; personal hygiene practices of both students and those who handled food, were still worse" (letter from Dr. Leona Bamgartner, Commissioner of Health, to Mayor Robert F. Wagner of New York, Feb. 15, 1961). See also "Hepatitis Strikes Thirty-four Students; City Closes Academy Kitchens," *New York Times*, Feb. 10, 1961.

comes; [11] second, Jews living in Israel should follow the orthodox
rules of observance and conduct. In keeping with the first argument, the Satmarer hasidim are prohibited from voting or taking
part in the Israeli government, and they now are forbidden to visit
the recaptured Wailing Wall. The Satmarer hasidim maintain that
were it not for the establishment of the State of Israel in 1948 the
Meshiah would have appeared. In keeping with their second argument they have made public demonstrations and have carried on a
propaganda campaign against the Israeli government both in the
United States and in Israel.[12] The Satmarer Rebbe often refers to
Israel in his toyreh although he may not mention it by name.
Instead he may refer to the danger that atheists pose for Jewish
life, and how they want to destroy the Torah that has kept the Jews
together. His hasidim understand his reference.

The tensions between Satmar and other hasidic courts have
increased since the war in June, 1967. Unlike most religious Jews,
the Satmarer Rebbe fails to see the victory as evidence that
the hand of God was present. He sees only the military might
and skill of the Zionists. He believes that the war was unnecessary

[11] The talmudic source for this reasoning may be seen in Babylonian
Talmud, *Ketubot* 111a. The Satmarer Rebbe has spelled out his argument
in his work *Vayoel Moshe* (*"Moshe Begins"*), (New York: Jerusalem
Publishing Co., 1960). His most recent polemic concerning the six-day war
in 1967 may be found in *Al ha-Geuloh ve al ha-Temuroh* (*"Redemption and
Change"*), (New York: Jerusalem Publishing Company, 1967).

[12] See Martin Gansberg, "One Thousand Hasidic Jews Picket Israeli
Consulate Here," *New York Times*, Nov. 5, 1963. "In Defense of Freedom
of Religion," advertisement by the National Committee for Freedom of
Religion in Israel, *New York Times*, April 25, 1958. The campaigns of the
most zealous hasidim have centered on various issues. A handbill circulated
by the National Committee For the Defense of Religion in Eretz Israel (150
Nassau St., N.Y.C.) reads in part: "Mass Meeting. Hotel Roosevelt. 45 East
45th Street and Madison Ave., N.Y. To Protect The Holy Sabbath in the
Holy Land, July 28th, 7:00 P.M. The tragedy of Chilul Shabbos in Haifa
has aroused the anger of worldwide religious Jewry. No other city in the
Holy Land allows municipal buses to run on the Sabbath. Haifa has added to
its scandal of Shabbos buses a Shabbos Subway which is nearing completion.
Every thinking Jew can appreciate how this desecration affects the entire
concept of Shabbos-Holiness in Eretz Israel." A handbill circulated by the
World Union of Orthodox Jewish Communities, 465 W. 51 St., N.Y.C., in
the summer of 1958, cited cases of police brutality in Israel. It demanded:
"1. Stop the systematic anti-religious oppression aimed at total extermination
of religion in Israel. 2. Stop the desecration of the City of Jerusalem, holy to
all mankind, through deliberate defiling its sacred moral character. 3.
Release at once all the Rabbis and religious scholars who are now being held
in prison in inhuman conditions. 4. Stop once and for all the brutal atrocities
of the Israeli Police through which a few individuals have already been
murdered, and lots of innocent blood shed."

and that a compromise could have been accomplished. Zealously pursuing the Rebbe's arguments, the newspaper *Der Yid*, an organ of the Satmar court, has attacked the State of Israel with a ferocity that has stunned the orthodox community. In contrast, the vast majority of the hasidic community continues to feel strong tides of loyalty and faith concerning Israel, and they lend strong support to the State. The tales related since the war, tying religious practices to the victory, are an expression of the emotional envolvement and active participation of the religious community (N38–43).

In times of peace, while all hasidim oppose the nonreligious practices of the Israeli government, and none will ride on an Israeli boat because the Jewish seamen must work on the Shabbes (TA26), few support Satmar propaganda and their public demonstrations. Such activities often embarrass other hasidim, who have mixed feelings about attacking the Israeli nation in this way. A Klausenberger hasid complained:

If he [the unbeliever] wants to put in a swimming pool in Jerusalem, I'll go to war with him in Jerusalem. I wouldn't go to war with him here on Bedford Avenue in New York.*

Of special concern is the fact that anyone who opposes the Satmarer Rebbe's views is likely to find himself the target of resentment by the Rebbe's zealous followers, and as a result bitter disputes have erupted between the courts of Satmar and Square, and between Satmar and Klausenberg.[13] A pre-war antagonism between Munkacz and Satmar is the basis of the story that the Rebbe of Munkacz cursed the Satmarer Rebbe with the result that the latter has no living children (TA21). Similarly, there was a split between Belz and Satmar that came about when the Satmarer Rebbe accused the Belzer Rebbe of being a Zionist. It is said that the mild-mannered Rebbe of Belz tried to talk to the Satmarer, but to his astonishment the Satmarer walked out on him. As a result of taking opposing positions on the 1967 Arab-Israeli war, a new dispute is brewing between the courts of Satmar and Lubavitch.

The Satmarer hasidim pay more than lip service to the belief that the generations have become weaker since the giving of the law. Contemporary Rebbes are mocked, as in the tale of the dybbuk-possessed child who is taken first to the Belzer who tries but fails to exorcise the dybbuk and then to the Satmarer who scorns exorcism and suggests a psychiatrist—obviously a quite modern solution

[13] See Gersh and Miller, "Satmar in Brooklyn," *Commentary*, 28 (1959): 389–99.

Satmar besmedresh. The women's section in the balcony at the upper right is covered by a wooden screen. The men's section of the balcony is shielded from the women's section by white curtains

Morning prayer

Bedford Avenue in Williamsburg on the afternoon of the death of the Squarer Rebbe. The Square besmedresh is the building immediately adjacent to the YMHA

Yeshiveh. Klausenberg

Street scene. Williamsburg

Shopping. Williamsburg

Proprietor and son in a silver shop. Williamsburg

Fruit and vegetable market. Crown Heights

Sewing machine operator

Sewing machine operator

Diamond cutter

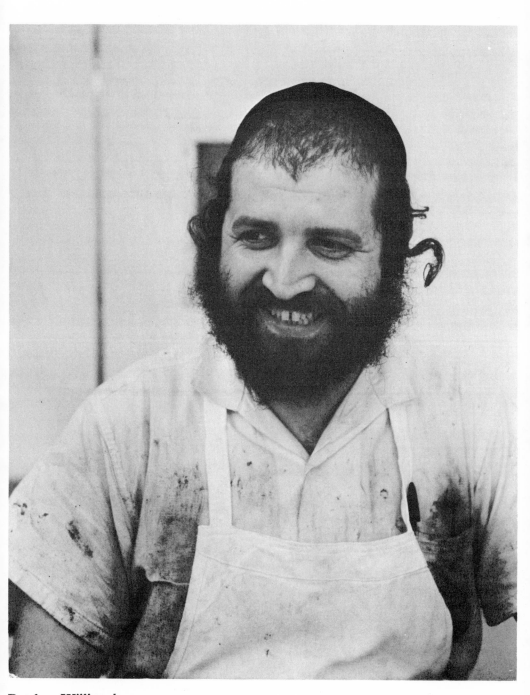

Butcher. Williamsburg

Butcher. Williamsburg

School-bus driver. Williamsburg

Father and son at a melaveh malkeh. Lubavitch

Recent immigrant and American-born hasid. Lubavitch

(S36). Similarly, a Satmarer hasid laughingly reports that the Klausenberger Rebbe claims to possess the power to offer material reward (TA22). In both cases, straightforward accounts exist—in the former case it is said that the Belzer exorcised a dybbuk (H86), and in the latter that the Klausenberger did indeed claim such power (TA22). Rather than intellectual enlightenment, however, the accounts related by Satmarer hasidim reflect the Satmarer Rebbe's skepticism concerning the miraculous powers of various Rebbes as well as Satmar hostility toward other courts. Such accounts give the erroneous impression that the Satmarer hasidim do not tell miracle tales. They do tell such tales (H54, HA35, for example)—but not about contemporary Rebbes who oppose their leader. A Klausenberger hasid explained:

> What he [the Satmarer] believes is that there is no such thing as Hasidism today. And it is not what we have accepted and will accept. He is a very radical man. And he is not accepted. He is actually not universally accepted—like I would say the Klausenberger, the Belzer, the Vizhnitser, the Lubavitcher. I'm a Klausenberger hasid. Still I believe in Lubavitch and I believe in Vizhnits, and I believe in Stolin. Satmar is more separate—they are more of a ghetto. It's completely different. It's their point of Hasidism that he says there is no such a thing as miracles any more, and there's no this and there's no that. And that's it. They believe that he's different. They believe what he says he means in regard to other Rebbes, but not to himself.

Despite this portrait of an inflammatory and demogogic court impelled by excessive zeal, the Satmarer hasidim are also among the most demonstrably affectionate of the hasidim. Their love for their children, their sense of brotherhood, and their deep reverence for their Rebbe are markedly clear. And, despite their reputation for polemic argument, most members of the court are extremely friendly and hospitable.

LUBAVITCH

In contrast to the Satmar court, the hasidim of Lubavitch are known for their greater adaptability to western customs, at least in an external sense (it should be very clear, however, that the Lubavitchers share the world view of all other hasidim). Lubavitcher hasidim wear hats of varying colors instead of mere black, and the brim is usually down; the Rebbe rarely wears a kaftan; and while the Lubavitchers wear beards, their peyes are kept to a minimum or are tucked out of sight behind their ears or tied over the top of the head. The Lubavitcher women wear wigs, but their hair is not cut particularly close to the scalp. Lubavitcher children speak English quite well and are more familiar than are Satmarer children with the secular culture and with science and technology. Their school system is carefully organized and administered, and they often write and publish their own textbooks. While the Rebbe opposes a college education for his followers, he himself was trained in college as an engineer, and his wife, the daughter of the previous Rebbe, is considered to be somewhat avant-garde.

Interestingly enough, the Lubavitch court maintains the only hasidic yeshiveh that teaches the philosophy of Hasidism, or more particularly the teachings of Rabbi Shneur Zalman of Ladi, the founder of the Lubavitch dynasty. The Lubavitchers have the reputation among the courts of having the greatest intellectual bent. This aura of intelligence extends to the women as well as to the men (although not on the same scale), since some Lubavitcher women attend a class of their own in hasides (hasidic philosophy) and in addition publish their own magazine.

Rabbi Menahem Mendel Schneerson, the Lubavitcher Rebbe, is the seventh Rebbe in the line of Habad Hasidism founded by Rabbi Shneur Zalman. He is a quiet, intense man with a kindly expression. The Rebbe gives the impression of a man restraining a well of emotion. At a farbrengen he encourages the students' singing with a short gesture, tightening his fist and arm, and the students' responses are immediate and long-lasting. Lubavitcher hasidim say that for the last few years the Rebbe has withheld his feelings. It is said that his thoughts concern the Jews remaining in the Soviet Union, whom he has given "tremendous blessings." In the past, on occasion, he has been said to weep when speaking of them. The Rebbe talks of the future with hope. Urging more responsibility and the strengthening of the mitsves, he argues that mitsves performed here are to the credit of those still in the Soviet Union. For the past two years, when the Rebbe blows the ram's horn on Rosh Hashoneh, he has called upon those who have recently left the Soviet Union to come and stand beside him. In 1967, thirty Lubavitcher hasidim, who had recently emigrated from the Soviet Union to Israel and were flown to New York for the High Holidays, stood beside the Rebbe.

The court of Lubavitch is unique in that it attempts to establish channels of communication between the hasidim and Jews of varying degrees of religiosity.

We don't push away the person because he's not frum [pious]. We talk to other Jews and try to bring them to us.*

Their aim is to preserve orthodox precepts and at the same time to draw less religious Jews into the orthodox fold (HA54). To further that end the Lubavitcher Rebbe sends rabbis to synagogues that need leaders, readers to congregations where there is a lack of learned men, and shohtim to communities where there is a need to maintain orthodox standards for the slaughtering of cattle. They publish numerous pamphlets and books, including those intended to initiate new brides into the ritual obligations of women. They have also prepared books for the children of less orthodox parents who are released one afternoon from the public schools in order to receive religious instruction.[14] They attempt to contact college groups as well, even arranging for busloads of students from out of town to spend the Shabbes at the court. At times the Rebbe, responding to a letter of thanks, may again encourage the student toward the orthodox faith:

I was gratified to learn that this experience gave you an insight into orthodox Judaism; that is, the Jewish way of life which our people adhered to throughout the generations. . . . The whole essence of man is different from the rest of the animal kingdom, for man has the ability to think and act in accordance with his better judgment and the dictates of his intellect. It is surely unnecessary to point out that the fact that Jews are a minority among the peoples of the world is not an argument for giving up their traditions and following the majority, and assimilating themselves—anymore than it would be an argument to say that the human being should follow the life of the animals who outnumber him greatly. No one will suggest, therefore, that a man should behave like an animal.[15]

In addition to working with American students, representatives are sent to remote Jewish congregations in the United States, Latin America, and North Africa in an effort to convince Jews in isolated communities to keep the Shabbes holy, to refrain from marrying out of their faith, and to return to orthodox ways. On occasion, they return from these trips with young men eager for a chance to study at the Lubavitch yeshiveh.

[14] See for example, *Curriculum of Instructions for the Religious Release Hour*, ed. Rabbi Jacob J. Hecht, vol. 1, 2d ed., 1952.
[15] Letter from Rabbi M. Schneerson, n.d. For a discussion of how one becomes a Lubavitcher hasid see Schachter, "How to Become a Modern Hasid," *Jewish Heritage*, 2 (1960): 33–40.

One rabbi who had been to Argentina and Brazil described his talk in a synagogue in a town near the equator in Brazil, where some two thousand Jews live in a city with a population of forty thousand. The rabbi addressed them in Hebrew which was then translated into Portuguese. One hundred and five Jews came to hear his talk.

I spoke to them of family purity. The people were bawling. It was more a feeling than my speech—seeing an orthodox man with a beard before them. I was there four days—Tuesday through Saturday—and during that time there was an awakening. Fifteen children sat up talking with me all Friday night and all day Saturday. I brought two of the boys back with me to study here. I did the hasidic dance with this boy. The Jews there are wealthy. There is a furniture factory and they grow coffee. They have a beautiful synagogue, but they can't get kosher meat. But I found out that the people were interested in keeping the Torah.*

Avowed attitudes toward outsiders vary greatly in the hasidic community, with Satmar and Lubavitch occupying the polar positions. A Klausenberger hasid explained:

I'll tell you an example. There's a storm at the water, a gale. Anybody who goes near the water drowns. Someone is drowning. Here are the thoughts of three people: One says, "I don't care. I'll jump in even if I drown. I'll give up my whole body." Another says, "I'll run away. Look at the terrible storm. He's lost but I can save myself if I run away." The third person answers—he gets himself down to the water and he sets himself strong. He throws a rope and calls out, "Catch it and I'll pull you out."
Lubavitch is like the first. Their way is to give out everything to pull in. They'll live in the worst community in the world, even though the person could get spoiled himself, even though something could go wrong with his children. Satmar is like the second: "If I see a person not religious, not only will I not have anything to do with him, but I'll chase him away." We [at Klausenberg] put down a yeshiveh, make it as orthodox as we want. If a man who is not religious sends us his son, we take him in. If he wants to grab on to us, we take him in. We don't chase after him. If nobody wants us, we would close the yeshiveh rather than make it modern.*

There are hasidim in other courts who have reservations about the value of the Lubavitcher program of proselytism—some because they believe that Hasidism is meant for only a select few and fear it will be diluted, and others because they question the merit of inducting American novices into such an intense religious life:

They go too fast. You see if somebody is born religious, he does things and he doesn't understand, he doesn't know what he is doing. It's a natural part of him and that's the way he'll grow and he'll be that way all his life. And there were for generations and generations thousands and thousands of Jews that actually lived that way; they davened because the father davened and they were Jews because their fathers were Jews. They didn't realize what they were doing and they didn't know what they were doing. They just did it because their fathers did it. Now somebody that does not have that background, he jumps into it too fast. And he gets too religious all at once. Most of the time it was a sign of insecurity before he became religious. Usually he was not mentally stable before he became religious and that was the reason he became religious—because he wanted to find some security. I've seen boys that become religious and they have become upset. I don't mean only Lubavitch. With Lubavitch it would happen more because they do much more missionary work than anybody else does. Actually they're the only ones that ever do any missionary work; the others hardly ever do any missionary work. By other hasidim you can find ten boys that became religious, let's just say for instance. So maybe one of them is not completely normal. But in Lubavitch you'll find a thousand boys—and you're apt to find ten or fifteen or twenty that couldn't take it.*

The Lubavitcher movement is growing steadily, with clearly defined purposes of education and proselytism. The Lubavitcher hasidim have won the respect of those outside the hasidic world as well as those in other hasidic courts because they have maintained a moderate posture outwardly while at the same time they have strengthened their religious activities. While the other courts accept donations from non-observant Jews as a matter of necessity, the Lubavitchers maintain that it is part of their program to draw in the nonreligious—or, to put it another way, to develop what is good in the nonreligious as well as the religious for the overall good of the Jewish community. Because they are engaged with the Jewish community as a whole, the Lubavitcher hasidim have no desire to achieve any sort of physical isolation.

The ways in which the problem of the rising incidence of violence in their streets is handled is an indication of the attitude and initiative of the courts. At a melaveh malkeh of a Galician court in Crown Heights, when the hasidim suggested to the Rebbe that they ask for police protection on their way home late at night, the Rebbe responded by telling of the anti-Semite whose hand withered after he threw a rock through the window of a Jew (H81). "This is better than police protection," the Rebbe concluded. In contrast, in June, 1964, after a series of incidents in which yeshiveh students were beaten up and a rabbi's wife was attacked, the Lubavitcher hasidim formed four radio-patrol car units. Five young men in each car cruised the Crown Heights area from midnight to five in the morning to report any suspicious persons and to escort home anyone who requested it. The cars were in communication with a central office, and everyone in the community received notice of the office's telephone number. The unarmed patrols were intended to overwhelm any attacker by the weight of their number until the police arrived. (On Friday night, non-Jews in the neighborhood, both Negroes and whites, took the place of the hasidim in the patrols.) Their efforts brought them nation-wide attention, and some success in policing their area.[16]

At the time of the Arab-Israeli war in June, 1967, the Lubavitcher Rebbe captured the center of attention of the hasidic world. In contrast to the Satmarer Rebbe's scornful appraisal of the war, the Lubavitcher Rebbe urged active spiritual participation and aid.

The Saturday before the war broke out the Rebbe spoke at a farbrengen. "You will be saved and nobody will touch you. If there will be a war we will win immediately, and in order to protect our community we should, everyone should, wear tefillin." This same day, Saturday night, we sent a cable that this is the word of the Rebbe. The following day our followers went to the army. They put on tefillin. Even the generals put on tefillin. When they went to the Wall each and every one was wearing tefillin.*

In tales told both here and in Israel the Lubavitcher Rebbe is seen to have exerted an important influence (N38–41). It may be said that the Lubavitcher Rebbe now has the prestige in the hasidic world enjoyed by the Belzer Rebbe until his death in 1957. Adding to the Rebbe's increasing aura of piety and power is the fact that Shneur Zalman Shazar, the president of Israel, is attached to Habad Hasidism. Much to the dismay of secularists in Israel, on a

---

[16] Douglas Robinson, "Hasidic Jews Using Radio Cars to Foil Brooklyn Negro Toughs," the *New York Times*, May 27, 1964. The patrol system lasted from 1964 to 1966. It was abandoned when the hasidim decided that they were receiving better police protection.

The Lubavitcher hasidim are, however, planning to abandon their yeshiveh on Bedford Avenue and Dean Street in the Bedford-Stuyvesant area of Brooklyn. As a result of several incidents enrollment in the yeshiveh has dropped from approximately 500 students in 1963 to a total of 200 students in 1967 (see David Halberstam, "Two Ghetto Worlds Meet in Brooklyn," *New York Times*, April 23, 1964). A new yeshiveh is being constructed on Ocean Parkway.

trip to the United States in August, 1966, Shazar made an unexpected midnight visit to the Lubavitcher Rebbe.[17]

As might be expected, the Lubavitcher Rebbe does not enjoy universal acclaim among the courts. The Lubavitcher Rebbe and the Satmarer Rebbe are often diametrically opposed of late, particularly concerning the State of Israel. In addition, the Lubavitcher practice of putting on tefillin with Jews who are not orthodox has caused the Satmarer Rebbe to observe that one is not permitted to put on tefillin with nonreligious people and that such a gesture, unaccompanied by a full religious life, is meaningless. At a farbrengen the Lubavitcher Rebbe has responded that it is not only permissible but it is a mitsveh.

> The Rebbe said he had received a letter from someone in Israel raising this question of tefillin. The Rebbe said, "What is a foolish hasid?" In the Talmud it says that a hasid is not allowed to touch a woman, but what if she's drowning? He's not going to touch her? Such a person is a fool.[18] The Rebbe said of the letter writer: "A fool he surely is and a hasid it's still to be decided." The Satmarer hasidim got excited because they're sure he meant their Rebbe.*

The differences between courts are not easily rectified, and once started, social pressure and tradition serve to perpetuate disputes. On occasion the rancor between courts may erupt in cruel pranks reminiscent of the actions taken by the misnagdim and hasidim in previous centuries—as when some years ago the Squarer hasidim were summoned by telephone by persons unknown to attend the funeral of their Rebbe, who was very much alive.[19]

Given the nature of hasidic court life it is a fairly simple matter to start nasty rumors circulating:

> I'm skeptical about some stories since once I inadvertently started a rumor with some friends as a prank. The Klausenberger Rebbe was coming back from Israel. I was studying in the Tselemer Rebbe's yeshiveh.[20] There were others there from other Rebbes, and there was

---

[17] Shneur Zalman Shazar is the third president of Israel (1963–   ). Shazar was born in Stolpce in tsarist Russia in 1889 and received a traditional religious education. His father and grandfather were Lubavitcher hasidim. Concerning Shazar's midnight visit to the Lubavitcher Rebbe, see the *New York Times*, August 1, 1966.

[18] B. T., *Sotah* 21b. "What is a foolish pietist like?—e.g., a woman is drowning in the river, and he says, 'It is improper for me to look upon her and rescue her.' "

[19] For other examples see Gersh and Miller, "Satmar in Brooklyn," pp. 397–98.

[20] Rabbi Levi Yitshok Grunwald, the Tselemer. He is actually a rov rather than a Rebbe.

one fellow from Satmar. The one from Satmar was a fool. Two fellows
went over to him and said the Tselemer Rebbe just received a letter
from the Satmarer Rebbe that he should tell his students not to go to the
Klausenberger Rebbe's talk. He said, "It's not so! And if it is so—then
it's right!" And he got excited.

In a day or so I was walking on the street and people were telling me
that the Satmarer sent letters to the Tselemer and all the other yeshives
not to send their students to hear the Klausenberger. Nobody believed
me when I said I know it's not true.*

The strengths of the hasidim—their intensity of devotion, their
special customs, their sense of brotherhood within the court, their
pride in the prowess of the Rebbe and their fierce loyalty to
him—also serve to accentuate differences between courts and to
create an atmosphere charged with controversy.

PART TWO

THE
LEGENDS

INTRODUCTORY NOTE

The tales are arranged within each section in approximate chronological order according to the dates of the Rebbes referred to. Since a great many of the Rebbes were contemporaries there is a good deal of overlapping. On occasion the chronological order has been altered for thematic reasons. Variants of tales have been included when they contained significant differences or new information. In the headnotes each tale is marked with a letter (T = Tsaddikim, TA = Tsaddikim in America) and a number (T12) designating the order. (Some tales have been marked with a number and a letter following [e.g., H75a]; these tales were collected after the other tales had been numbered.)

Additional information is given following each tale. Each storyteller has been given a letter (A = Z). Further data about the storytellers, as well as a list of the stories each narrated, is provided in the appendix. (Since some tales were collected during ceremonial occasions when a large group was present, it was not possible to identify the source of every tale in this manner.)

Following the letter designating the storyteller is the name of the court to which the storyteller belongs (e.g., B, Stolin).

Tales are also marked at their conclusion with an "E" or "Y" to indicate whether they were told in English or in Yiddish.

Approximately one-fourth of the tales were recorded in Yiddish; the remaining three-fourths were recorded in English. Translations of the tales told in Yiddish were almost always made with the help of at least one bilingual speaker from the same court as the narrator. A question that occurred early in the collecting was whether the language employed caused significant differences in cultural detail. Therefore, texts of forty tales were obtained in both Yiddish and English from bilingual speakers. Two of the principal narrators also translated each other's Yiddish versions. Compari-

161

son of these texts indicated that the primary factor affecting detail appeared to be the personality of the narrator rather than the language he employed. The language used was found to be one variable affecting form and content; translating the tales, however, presented greater risks of altering the texts and introducing error. Clearly, using the English version simplified the problem of presenting the tales to an English speaking audience. (Some Yiddish, however, was employed in many of the tales told in English. Most often these words have been translated. Foreign terms left untranslated have been explained at least the first time they are used and thereafter may be found in the glossary.)

As few editorial changes as possible were made in the tales. If something was narrated out of order, the tale was not rearranged. Due to the intermingling of tongues, however, liberty was taken on a few occasions of shifting a word or two in a sentence. Individual styles were not tampered with, and differences in language and tone are apparent in the most casual reading of the tales. Similarly, only minor changes have been made in the texts translated by hasidim.

An effort was made to identify the major figures and the place names cited in the tales. A list of Rebbes and other historical figures may be found in the appendix. Identification was not always feasible, particularly where persons and places enjoyed only local fame. In a very small number of instances lesser known place names may have been obscured when the tapes were transcribed. The names of contemporary individuals, other than Rebbes and persons of historical interest, have often been changed to avoid identification.

THE TSADDIKIM

Three Scholars (T1)

The Holy Baal Shem served three scholars in his generation.

One was called the Tvuos Shor.[1] The Baal Shem was told that Tvuos Shor was the leading scholar of the generation, and he went to Tvuos Shor. He was there for twenty-four hours and the Tvuos Shor took out a pipe. And when he did this the Baal Shem took a hot coal and put it into the pipe of the Tvuos Shor.

The second one was the brother of the Haham Zevi.[2] There is a difference of opinion who the brother of Haham Zevi was. Some say he was Rabbi Eliezer and some say he was Rabbi Haim. And he was a great man. He was a rabbi in the city of Berliter. And the Baal Shem was told that he was also one of the greatest scholars of his generation, so he went to visit him. He went into his house, and the rabbinical court was sitting outside because of the heat, but he was lying under blankets and he was shivering from cold. When he saw the Baal Shem come in, he said, "Young man, will you do me a favor? Heat the oven, please. Make it a little warm."

So the Baal Shem went out and he carried wood, and he heated the oven so that the house became scorchingly hot. It was like a hot coal. When he felt that the room had become warm, he crept out from under the blankets, and as soon as the court saw that the rabbi came out from under the blankets, they went in right away, and a young man who was waiting for them to complete a divorce also went in with them. And they started to complete the writing of the divorce. They are sitting and writing the divorce and sweat is

[1] Tvuos Shor (Tvuat Shor; "Produce of the Shor"): Rabbi Ephraim Solomon Shor, talmudist, Rabbi in Brisk and later in Lublin. He died in 1634, sixty-six years before the birth of the Besht.
[2] Haham Zevi, Zevi Ashkenazi, Rabbi of Lemberg and Amsterdam. 1658–1718.

pouring from everyone because of the heat. The rabbi is feeling quite well. Before that he was cold. And it took as long as it should take, three hours, three and a half hours, four hours, and they finished the divorce and the court ran outside immediately to cool off.

The young man delayed departing, and the rabbi gave him a pat on the back and told him, "Young man, don't be too hasty to judge." The young man was weak physically and he was a very young man and he had a lot of trouble with his lungs, and when he departed he told him, "Young man, do not be a prosecutor any longer."

When he went out, the rabbi said to the Baal Shem Tov, "Because you have enlivened me by making the room warm, I will tell you the story of this young man," and he mentioned the town where the incident took place.

"There was once a pious Jew who prayed, learned, and fulfilled all commandments. When he died, and the Heavenly Court started to investigate in order to render judgment on him, and they asked, 'Did he learn?'

" 'Yes, he learned, but it wasn't exactly up to par.'

" 'Did he daven?'

" 'Yes, he davened, but it was also not up to par. It was like water which is disturbed—it is water, but it is not clear.' They asked him why this is so.

"He answered, 'I very much wanted it to be different, to be up to par, but I had this wife, and she used to run in and she used to start gossiping.' She would curse him and disturb him in every possible way, and it was that way even in the middle of the davening. He really wanted to serve God with clarity, but she would interfere.

"They were thinking it over at the Heavenly Court, and then they said, '[When] the words of master and the words of the pupil [are in conflict], whose are obeyed?' [3] In other words, 'What are you complaining of? Your wife didn't let you. God said you're supposed to learn and pray with clarity and you complain that your wife didn't let you.'

"So he saw that they became angry at this angel who just said that, and he said, 'How do you know? You're an angel. You have no emotions. How do you know what the world is like? Did you ever try it?'

"And the Heavenly Court became angry at that angel, and said:

[3] Babylonian Talmud, *Kiddushin* 42b.

'Because of the angel's hasty words, it is decreed that this angel be
sent down to earth to prove himself under the same circumstances.'
If he would be able to prove himself—and they will give him the
same type of a wife—if he will prove himself and demonstrate that
it could be done, that it is possible to serve God with all these
hindrances, then they will also judge this soul who has just come to
us. And if he fails, then he [the soul awaiting judgment] will go to
Paradise. And the angel was born and that was that young man
who just was divorced. When he was seventeen years old, this
young man was already spitting blood, and he had to get a divorce
because of his wife. And because of that the rabbi told him, 'Do not
be a prosecutor.' "

The third person who was said to be one of the greatest scholars
was the Pnei Yehoshua (Face of Joshua), after the book he wrote.[4]
His given name was Joshua. And in what city was he rabbi? In
Lemberg. At the time when the Pnei Yehoshua accepted the rabbinical position in Lemberg, he issued a decree that all the small
cities surrounding Lemberg should not make their own minyonim,
but should come to pray in Lemberg. He did this in order that all
the money collected should be able to be used in a proper manner to
benefit the city as a whole, because in the small towns the money
would not be spent to the advantage of the majority.[5] And the Pnei
Yehoshua heard after the high holidays that they had kept their
own minyen in one of the small villages.

So the Pnei Yehoshua sent for him and he asked him, "Didn't
you hear my decree?"

So he said, "Yes." And he gave him an excuse: "We couldn't
come. We couldn't make it." And he had a good excuse. But since
he broke the decree of the rabbi, his punishment was to be that the
next day the whole city of Lemberg would assemble and this man
who had his own minyen would have to recite all the prayers of the
High Holidays. Today people would not mind this decree. Why not
recite? Prove oneself. But in those days it was very embarrassing to
get up on a weekday and recite the whole set of prayers. But since
it was decreed, nothing could alleviate the punishment. It was to be
fulfilled.

And they let it be known in the whole city. And all the people
came and assembled in the big synagogue. Some were hanging

[4] Joshua Heshel ben Falk, author of *Pnei Yehoshua* ("*The Face of
Joshua*"), Rabbi of Lemberg. He died in 1648, fifty-two years before the
birth of the Besht.
[5] This refers only to monies collected for the holidays.

from the ceilings, some were standing on the windows, and some on the lamps. They came to see the show.

So the young man stood up and began to say "The Fathers," the first part of the Eighteen Benedictions. And when he finished saying "The Fathers" and came to "Thou sustainest the living . . ."[6] [the prayer continues, "And bringest back to life the dead in great mercy"] the court ran away out of fright, and only the Pnei Yehoshua and the court of scholars remained. And when he began saying, "And you are to receive the dead . . ." they all ran and the Pnei Yehoshua fainted.

Only the young man remained. The young man, who was the Baal Shem Tov, ran and spilled water on the Pnei Yehoshua who had fainted. This is the third service that he did for the scholars. When the Pnei Yehoshua fainted, he spilled water on him, thus serving the Pnei Yehoshua. And when he revived him—what bigger service can you do for a scholar than to give him back life?

When the Pnei Yehoshua was revived and came to himself, he said, "Young man, I did not mean to include you when I made my decree." In other words, he could continue as he was accustomed and make his own minyen.

And these were the three scholars of the generation who were revealed to be the three leading scholars whom he served in one way or another.

Another way I have heard this story told—in fact, I have seen it written in this latter version—that he was a rabbi of the city, and his wife brought bread into the house by going to market every day. What I am saying now refers to the second story, about this man who was spitting blood. And she dealt with fruit and other things, and in her home the poverty was great. What happened was that there was a big piece of wood, and every time they used to knock splinters from the wood and they used to heat the stove with it. Of course they were miserly with the wood they put in because this was the only wood they had. But when they told the Baal Shem to make warmth he took the whole piece of wood and put it into the oven. And as soon as she went into the house and saw that the piece of wood was not there, she grabbed some instrument and wanted to hit him, "What's the idea of burning a whole piece of wood at one time?"

So he said to her, "Do not touch him. If you do the world is

[6] The second part of the Eighteen Benedictions.

liable to turn over, because you don't know who he is." And she
went off to the side.

PP, Lubavitch, Y

Reb Moshe of Kitev (T2)

The Baal Shem lived in Kitev. The rabbi from Kitev, Reb Moshe,
discovered the Baal Shem for the world. He told him, "You must
go out." He was there incognito.[7]

I am the eighth generation from Reb Moshe on my mother's
side.

Q, Tchortkov, E

Come and See (T3)

Dov Baer was once a misnaged. Misnaged means to be against
Hasidism. You know why? They were very holy people, those
people who were against Hasidism. Then they had a good reason
why they should not be hasidim. In those times there was one by
the name of Sabbatai Zevi, the false meshiah. So they were very
afraid of the new way. Maybe he is also one of those kind. They
were religious people, the most scrupulous. They were afraid to
follow this way. So that's why the Rabbi Dov Baer, in the beginning—he was old like the Baal Shem Tov—he did not want to
become a hasid. The Baal Shem Tov sent for him. He told people
and then more people that he should come to him. He didn't want
to. Until at last he made up his mind that he will go.

So when the Rabbi Dov Baer, the Maggid of Mezrich, came
to the Baal Shem Tov, he didn't even talk to the Baal Shem Tov.
He doesn't know who he is and then he wanted to go away already.
He called him in and he told him, "You learned already a lot of
Kabbala, right?"

---

[7] Rabbi Moshe of Kitev, d. 1738. Compare *In Praise of the Besht*, nos.
15, 22, 31. The Besht is said to have revealed himself at the age of thirty-
six.

So he said, "Yes."

"Let me show you that you never learned." So he told him, "Tell me the meaning of this piece." He took out a book by Reb Haim Vital.[8] He never saw the meaning before. In the Gemoreh they say "shema" twice, come and hear, come and hear. What's the meaning of this? When Shimon ben Yohai writes in his book he doesn't say "shema" twice, he says "hazeh" twice, come and see. There is a difference between those two. In the Talmud you read just hear, and in the Zohar, the book that Reb Shimon wrote, when you learn you see something. Until now you learned Kabbala and you just heard with your ears, but now I'll show you how to learn. You will see."

Then he didn't go away, Rabbi Baer.[9]

X, Bobov, E

The Greater (T4)

It is said that the Baal Shem Tov said that Rabbi Haim ben Atar [10] was greater than himself in one respect—while the Besht went to the mikveh each time after moving his bowels, Haim ben Atar went each time after urinating.

DD, New Square, E

Not the Time (T5)

They say that when the Baal Shem Tov wanted to go to the Land of Israel the reason why he wanted to go was to meet with this Or ha-Haim [Haim ben Atar]. They say that if they would have met then the Meshiah would have come. And that is why they weren't able, because the time wasn't ready yet for the Meshiah to come.

W, Boyan, E

[8] Haim Vital, Safed mystic (1543–1620).
[9] Compare with the tale of how the Besht won over Rabbi Dov Baer, *In Praise of the Besht*, no. 62.
[10] Haim ben Atar: Haim ben Moses Atar (1697–1743), Italian talmudist and kabbalist, author of *Or ha-Haim* ("*Light of Life*"). He died in Jerusalem.

Love (T6)

The Besht said, "I hope I can love a tsaddik as much as God loves a wicked man."

Q, Tchortkov, E

Rashi (T7)

I never saw it printed but it's actually world-famous. In one place Rashi is trying to describe the clothes that the High Priest was wearing.[11] So the Baal Shem Tov says, "Why couldn't Rashi explain it any other way?" So he says, "Rashi was walking in the street. And naturally he did not look where he was. He was just looking where he was walking; he did not look at any of his surroundings. All of a sudden he picks up his eyes and he sees a woman riding on a horse, and he sees her wearing an apron. So Rashi thought, 'Why did I see this? There must be a reason why I saw this.' And he was just writing the Rashi then on that portion where they were talking about that apron that the High Priest was wearing. So he understood right away that he saw that apron so he should be able to describe in Rashi in the fewest words what that apron is."

S, Klausenberg, E

The Third Brother (T8)

This is the third story I heard from the Bobover Rebbe.[12]

This story is about the brother of Rebbe Elimelekh and Reb Zusya. His name was Rabbi Nosen. Reb Nosen was lost for quite a

[11] Rashi: Solomon ben Isaac, commentator on the Bible and the Talmud (1040–1105). The reference is to Rashi's textual comments.
[12] The two other tales referred to are H14 and T10.

few years. Then they found out that he is in a certain hotel. And so Rebbe Elimelekh with Reb Zusya put on different clothes—they put on clothes as working men—and they went out searching for the hotel where their lost brother was.

They finally found the hotel and they rented a room for a few nights. They didn't have any place to eat so the only place where they could eat is with their brother Reb Nosen. That of course made them very happy, because they could notice his actions in the course of eating. They noticed some queer actions of Reb Nosen. In the middle of the meal he kept jumping up every few minutes and running to a book in the bookcase and he wrote down a few words in the book. Then he quickly closed the book and put it back in the bookcase. This went on during the whole meal.

After the meal, Rebbe Elimelekh with Reb Zusya went to sleep, but in the middle of the night they got up to see how Reb Nosen conducted himself during the night, and they noticed that this went on during the night also. Every few minutes Reb Nosen would take out this book, write down a few words and put it back in the bookcase. Then Reb Nosen would take out the book, he would sit over it, and he would start crying. And he cried and he cried until all the water from his eyes was on the pages of the book. And then he closed it.

In the morning Reb Elimelekh and Reb Zusya told Reb Nosen that they are his lost brothers and Reb Nosen was very happy to see them again. And they spoke over old times and they told him all about what happened in their father's house. And then Rebbe Elimelekh with Reb Zusya said, "We have one question yet to ask you, Reb Nosen. What is the meaning of your getting up every few minutes and writing down a few words in that book? In the nighttime we noticed you also did the same thing and then you sat over the book and you cried. And we'd like to know the meaning of that."

And so Reb Nosen told them, "The meaning of that is that now there are a few days left before Rosh Hashoneh. On Rosh Hashoneh everyone has to give a record of all he has done through the period of the last year. I'm sure I have many sins in the past year, and also not only sins but many bad things that I did to my friends and bad things that were not correct to do. And so I wrote down as many as I can remember, and every time I remembered another thing, another sin, or another bad thing that I did, I quickly ran to the book and I wrote it down. And then when I couldn't remember anything more, it was right near Rosh Hashoneh, I took out the book and I cried over the book. When my tears fill the pages of the book, and it erases the words of the book, that means it has erased all my sins and all the bad deeds that I did throughout the whole year, then I know that God has forgiven me."

When Rebbe Elimelekh and Reb Zusya heard of the great standard, and what a great person their brother is, you can imagine the happiness that was among them. And they lived together the rest of their lives.

XX, Lubavitch, E

Elimelekh (T9)

Once, Rebbe Elimelekh asked God to make him Moses, our Rabbi. But he said if He has created Moses already, Moses would have to become Elimelekh—so better leave it alone.

QQ, Square, E

The Gartel (T10)

There was once a big tsaddik in the town where Rebbe Elimelekh lived. The tsaddik's name was Reb Naftali Ropchitser. He came from the town of Ropchits and he was called the Ropchitser Rov. Now Rebbe Elimelekh always davened the afternoon prayer with a minyen, but for the evening prayer he always went into the house, locked up the house, and he always prayed by himself. Now the whole town wondered what he did by himself in the house, and everyone would have liked to watch how he davened, but nobody dared to go into the house—except this Reb Naftali Ropchitser. He dared once to enter the house of Rebbe Elimelekh.

He went in a few hours before the evening service. He went upstairs and he hid himself underneath a bed. Rebbe Elimelekh came in a few hours later, he locked the front door, he went upstairs, he closed the door of the bedroom, and he made preparations for the evening service. He took out his gartel [prayer belt] and he slowly wound it around himself. After he wound it around himself one time Reb Naftali Ropchitser noticed that the room

became very, very light, extremely light, and when Rebbe Elimelekh took the gartel around himself a second time, Reb Naftali
noticed that the room became still lighter and he never saw such
brightness in his lifetime. And then he felt something inside himself. He felt that he was gasping for air. He began to feel faint and
he yelled out to Rebbe Elimelekh, "Oy . . . oy."

Rebbe Elimelekh quickly took off the gartel and he found that
Reb Naftali Ropchitser was hiding under the bed the whole time.
He said, "Reb Naftali, what are you doing underneath my bed?"
Reb Naftali answered him that he wanted to see how the great
tsaddik Rebbe Elimelekh prayed and so he hid himself underneath
the bed. Rebbe Elimelekh answered him then: "It's a miracle that
you yelled out after I put the gartel around myself only two times,
because if I had put the gartel around myself another time, the
light and the air would be so strong that you wouldn't be able to
stand it."

XX, Lubavitch, E

Reb Mikhel of Zlochev (T11)

This is about Reb Mikhel Zlochever, whose father was Reb Yitshok Drubevicher, who was a wealthy person besides being a great
tsaddik. At the age of fifteen he [Reb Mikhel] was married to a
rich man's daughter. After the ceremony he went to his father-in-
law and told him, "I want you to prepare a private room for me
and I want to be separated from my wife for a while."

The father-in-law felt very bad and he said, "I'd like to think it
over with your father," thinking that his father will convince him
otherwise.

But his father said, "I knew he would want this, although not so
soon. But since it is his wish, blessed be he for wanting such a
thing."

So for three years he was in solitude, and his food was delivered
through a window. After three years he came out and he was a
Rebbe.

His friends from the yeshiveh looked upon this scornfully. One
of the boys as a kind of jest came to him with a kvitl and said, "My
wife is ill. Could you help her?"

Reb Mikhel said, "No, I can't."

He left laughing, proving to himself that Reb Mikhel was no Rebbe. But then he heard that his wife was very sick. News was brought to him that his wife was very sick. Reb Mikhel felt very bad about this because the bad news came through him. He was the cause of the bad news. So he went away to Brody to study by a great scholar.

While in Brody the misnagdim there wanted to excommunicate the Baal Shem Tov. He felt very bad about this and left them immediately and went to the Baal Shem Tov. The Baal Shem Tov upon greeting him gave him a blessing and told him to go to the city of Zlochev and become Rebbe there.

O, Lubavitch, Y

The Son's Decree (T12)

I'm going to tell a story about Mikhel Zlochever. Mikhel had five sons, the youngest was Reb Yoseleh Yampoler. He was a sharp-witted man. None of the other children would accept any hasidim while the father was living. People used to go to both the father and to the son.

It was the time when the hasidim lived in small villages. At those times the hasidim that lived in the small villages were the most prominent hasidim. They sat day and night and they learned. That was their job, and the wives used to keep stores and support the family. The Jews rented businesses and land from the nobility. On this land they had all kinds of livestock: lambs, sheep, and so on. Each one would have his few head of cattle and supply of brandy and the gentiles would take brandy from them on credit the whole year. When it would come harvest time they used to bring in potatoes and flour, and they would usually repay their debt double-fold. They were grateful for the credit.[13] And they lived and they

---

[13] Jews leased from the nobility pasture and timber land, and the rights of distilling and selling liquor, keeping inns, milling grain, and controlling fishing rights. The arendator, as the Jewish tax farmer was called, bought and sold grain and supplied essential goods such as salt, tobacco, and tools, although accounts of the activities of the arendator usually center on the distillation and sale of liquor. In his dealings with the peasant, the arendator necessarily extended credit. In this tale the relationship of arendator and peasant is seen in a favorable light; usually, however, the ventures of the arendator, bought dearly from the absentee nobleman, to be sure, made them

were able to devote most of their time to study. They lived in a few rooms: in one room they had the older people, the father-in-law; in the other room they had the son-in-law. They also had teachers for the bigger children and the younger children, and they all sat in one big house.

There came about a decree that the Jews have to leave the villages. "What are we going to do? What are we going to do with the livestock, the sheep and lambs?" If somebody has a guest room, he could take the people in, but how were they going to make a living? There was a great panic, and they came to the conclusion they should pick out two great people and send them to the leading tsaddik of their generation to plead their case.

The one who was considered the leading tsaddik of the generation was Reb Mikhel. They went to this tsaddik. And when do you come to the tsaddik of the generation? On Shabbes eve. Came Shabbes eve they went to the tsaddik. They gave a pidyen, and they went in to see the tsaddik. They stayed over Shabbes and the conclusion of the Shabbes, and they decided they have to go home. Next week they will go to the Reb Yoseleh, his son.

They came to Reb Yoseleh Friday night. The custom used to be that you stayed by Reb Yoseleh, at his house, and the Rebbe would sing songs. He would sing one stanza and the hasidim would sing one stanza. On that Shabbes at the table the Rebbe asked questions about a festive Shabbes: "Whoever sanctifies the seventh as is proper, whoever observes the Shabbes according to law so as to avoid profaning it, his reward is very great according to his work." [14] Reb Yoseleh derived the following toyreh: "Why does he call it at times the seventh and at other times call it the Shabbes? Why does he have to repeat himself? Why could he not just say, 'Whoever sanctifies the seventh according to law,' and so on? Why does he have to use it twice? It seems from the wording of the song that he is getting more reward than the work he has done."

Reb Yoseleh explained there are two types of tsaddikim: "One tsaddik is a tsaddik who is exalted at all times, all seven days of the week, seven times out of seven, while another tsaddik six hours out of seven is equal to his peers, and on the seventh is exalted above his peers. The tsaddik who not only makes the seventh day holy but also makes every seventh hour holy, such a tsaddik has the

unpopular with the peasantry. Occupying a midpoint in the feudal system, between lord and peasant, the arendator often served as the butt of the general unrest.

[14] The first verse of Kol mekadesh.

power that God fulfills whatever he says. Therefore I decree that each man should remain living in his home."

The people were overwhelmed because they always knew that Reb Yoseleh was one of the greatest tsaddikim, but they did not realize he was one of those tsaddikim who were righteous seven out of seven.

And Reb Yoseleh concluded, "And I say each man to his camp and each man to his flag!" [15]

When they came to say goodbye to him after Shabbes, he told them, "Go back peacefully. You will remain in your villages and towns just as I decreed."

The next week they went back to his father and related what happened. So the father answered also in the language of the Gemoreh: "God says the son's strength is greater than the father's. I only gave you a blessing, but he decreed that it is so." And so it was.

O, Lubavitch, Y

To Whom Do I Owe Thanks? (T13)

Reb Yoseleh Yampoler received a letter from Moshe Leib Sassover thanking him for praying for him, and Reb Yoseleh explained: "The thanks are not coming to me."

"Why?"

"Because a while ago I received a letter from Reb Moshe Leib Sassover asking me to pray for him since he is sick. So I went up to the Heavenly Court and there I met my father. My father asked, 'Yoseleh, what are you doing here?' So I said that Moshe Leib sent me a letter that he's sick. So my father, Reb Mikhel Zlochever, took me to the Heavenly Court. I stood outside. My father went in, and I heard the court telling my father that they need this Reb Moshe Leib in heaven. So I went in and said, 'But we need him here also.' And so they asked my father, 'What do you say?' He answered, 'I agree with my son and therefore he should have a complete recovery.'

"So to whom does he owe the thanks?"

O, Lubavitch, Y

[15] Numbers 1: 52.

Mitsveh (T14)

Reb Moshe Leib Sassover, he was always helping out people, and he was always running around to do every kind of mitsveh, except when he used to sit and learn.[16] They said that on the night before Yom Kippur, when the prayers for forgiveness are said, he would disappear for a couple of hours from his house. Some of the people said he went to heaven. But one of these misnagdim, he doesn't believe a person can go to heaven and he wants to find out what's happening here. So he goes and hides underneath the bed; he gets into the room before the Rebbe goes to sleep, and he hides underneath the bed. Underneath the bed he hears him sleeping, he hears him krekhtsen, "Oy, oy," krekhtsen. He was afraid he might fall asleep but he couldn't fall asleep because of the way the Rebbe was lying on the bed.

Finally, about one o'clock the Rebbe gets up, and he sees him take a jacket that a goy wears, like plain goyim used to wear, and he puts on a hat and he puts on a pair of boots like a peasant, and he looks completely like a peasant. He sees him take out a hatchet and then jump out of a small window where nobody can see him. He makes sure he's away and he jumps out right after him. He follows him and he sees him going into the forest, and he sees how he's chopping wood. He's chopping wood? He's chopping wood. What is he chopping wood for? He sees him take a big bundle of wood and walk all the way to the end of the town.

He comes to one of the poorest houses of the town where there lived a woman whose husband had just died and she herself had a small baby. And it was freezing in the house. He starts talking in Polish and he knocks on the door and she says, "Who is it?"

He says it's this and this goy, Vassili. Who knows? The name of a peasant.

So she says, "What do you want?"

He says, "I want to sell you some wood."

She starts crying and says, "Well, I don't have any money for wood. How can I pay you for wood?"

So he says, "You silly woman." He says, "First let me come in." So she lets him and he starts telling her, "You silly woman. I'm a goy. I don't know anything. But you are a Jew and you have such a

[16] This tale was made famous by Peretz under the title "If Not Higher" (*In This World*, pp. 76–79).

great God and you're still worried about paying money?" And he comes in.

And she says, "But I'm lying here sick in bed. I can't even put the wood on the fire." And so he puts the wood on the fire. And while he puts the wood on the fire he says the prayers about the destruction of the Temple to himself. He heats up the woman's house and he goes. He takes care of whatever has to be done, this and that in the house, and he goes. The woman is left standing there and she keeps on saying, "Please, God, the goy has such a big mitsveh but don't give it to the goy. Don't figure it for the goy because a goy shouldn't have such a mitsveh like he's having." [17]

The Rebbe goes back and he jumps through the window, and he dresses himself up and he goes out to say the prayers of forgiveness.

So then the misnaged says, "That's greater yet than going up to heaven. This is something greater than being able to go up to heaven."

S, Klausenberg, E

Belief (T15)

Levi Yitshok of Berdichev told his father-in-law he was going to his Rebbe.

"Why?"

"Because I believe in God."

His father-in-law laughed, "Bring in the maid. She also believes in God."

"She believes. I know."

SS, Stolin, E

The Creator (T16)

The Berdichever once said—he always stressed the devotion of the Jews—and he said one time, "If I was the Creator, I would give men what they need. This man needs health—I would give him

---

[17] See *In Praise of the Besht*, no. 209, in which Rabbi Nahman of Kossov would not allow a gentile the mitsveh of feeding straw to the animals. See also *ibid.*, no. 53. Peretz's version does not contain this remark.

health. This man needs children—I would give him children. This man needs money—I would give him money. You, God, You have everything in your possession. You can give everybody, each person, what he needs and what he wants. Why don't You give it to him? I would if I were in Your place. I would give everyone exactly what he wanted."

Then he thought for a few minutes. Then he said, "Maybe if I was the Creator I would act the same way that You are acting."

V, Lubavitch, E

Miracle (T17)

The founder of Habad [Rabbi Shneur Zalman] said: "There are miracles under my chair, but I do not want to bend down and pick them up." [18]

V, Lubavitch, E

The Closed Door (T18)

I'm not sure if this concerns Reb Borukh Mezhibezher, the Baal Shem Tov's grandson, or a different tsaddik.

The Rebbe said that he is not going to go into Paradise. Knowing that the Jews are going to have terrible troubles, he is not going to go into Paradise unless they alleviate the troubles of the Jews. So he was standing in front of the door and they were begging him to come in and he refused. Then he saw a Torah scroll fall out of the ark onto the floor. So he rushed in and picked it up, and they closed the door behind him.

M, Stolin, E

[18] Compare Buber, *Tales*, 1: 102. See also *Tales*, 1: 50. Concerning miracles and prayers, see Newman and Spitz, *Hasidic Anthology*, p. 262, no. 12.

The Seer (T19)

They said of the Lubliner that like you wash out a cloth he was able to wash out a soul when he talked to a person. He could see things that happened from very far off. The Lubliner begged God that he should take away his vision. He didn't want to be able to see so far because in the world there were very bad things that he didn't want to see. So God helped him and he was able to see for only four hundred acres on each side.[19]

X, Bobov, E

The Ninth Day of Av (T20)

In the city where the Lubliner Rebbe was, there was a rabbi—not a Grand Rabbi but a rabbi who decides smaller questions. Is this okay to eat? He was one of the misnagdim. He was called Azerner Kop [Iron Head].[20] He had a sharp head. He said, "When the Lubliner Rebbe passes away, I'll give a large reception and eat and drink to my pleasure."

When this was told to the Lubliner Rebbe, he said, "I promise you, he wouldn't even drink a drop of water." The ninth day of Av is a fast time when you can't drink and eat—this was the time when he died.

The Ropchitser Rov was at his bedside when he passed away and he asked him, "How did you know the exact day?"

He said, "During the readings of the first twelve days of Nisan, the first four days which symbolize the first four months, I saw what was to happen. On the fifth day, which symbolizes the month of Av, I saw up to the ninth day, and so I knew that on that day I would die."

CC, Satmar, E

[19] For a version of this and other tales of the Lubliner's miraculous vision, see Langer, *Nine Gates*, pp. 180–82; Buber, *Tales*, 1: 303–10.

[20] Azerner Kop ["Iron Head"], Rabbi Azriel Horowitz of Lublin. For tales of Iron Head, see Buber, *Tales*, 1: 310–12; Langer, *Nine Gates*, pp. 182–85.

The Window (T21)

The Lubliner Rebbe, the Rimanover Rebbe, and the Mezhibezher Rebbe made a pact between them that the three force the Meshiah to come. They set a date on Simhes Toyreh, in the year 5575 [1814].

Suddenly, before Rosh Hashoneh, the Mezhibezher Rebbe took sick and passed away twenty-two days before Simhes Toyreh. I don't remember what the Rimanover Rebbe did. And the Rebbe of Lublin didn't know the first passed away. He did his part on Simhes Toyreh—he was dancing with the Torah. There was a small window on the upper floor where he met his hasidim. He went up in the room and closed the door. He was there for hours and hours. The hasidim didn't know what happened. Then they heard yelling in the courtyard. They ran out there, and he was hurt.

"While praying my part," he said, "Someone took me by the arm and pushed me through the window. I would have been killed, but the Mezhibezher Rebbe came and spread out his talis like a net and caught me so the fall was not so hard. Then I knew that he was dead. If I knew it before that, I never would have started."

After that time the Lubliner Rebbe took sick and died on the ninth day of Av, the day when the Temple was destroyed.

CC, Satmar, E

Forgiveness (T22)

"Slihes" means forgiveness. Four or five days before Rosh Hashoneh, you wake up early in the morning and say slihes, the prayers of forgiveness. You ask God to forgive you. The Apter Rov, Reb Joshua Heshel of Apt, used to say this: "The soul is yours, and the flesh is also yours. So have pity on your work and forgive us."

X, Bobov, E

Cows (*T23*)

The Apter Rov, Abraham Joshua Heshel from Apt, was a very great tsaddik. They used to call him "the man who loves the Jewish people." He loved every Jew. He was a very holy man. Once people, some nonreligious people, came up the stairs (he lived on the second floor), and he asked the man who was sitting near him, "How can cows come up? How can cows climb up to this floor?"

So the gabai of the besmedresh says, "Those are not cows."

So the Apter Rov says, "That's not true, I see cows there." They started arguing and he said again, "It's cows." The Apter Rov said, "What's the difference? A cow has four feet and this is a cow of two feet with a human face. What is the difference between a cow and a man? Only the intelligence. If you use the intelligence to do what you feel like it's the same thing as a cow or a lion or any animal. He wants to kill, he kills. He wants to eat this, he eats this. So if a man acts and he doesn't use his intelligence to go against his will he's a cow." [21]

So the Apter Rov saw those people coming up there who had done many sins and he saw them as cows. He was such a holy man his eyes couldn't see anything that wasn't holy.

X, Bobov, E

The New Tsaddik (*T24*)

This is about a student of Reb Mikhel of Zlochev, Reb Shimshen.[22] When Rebbe Mikhel died, his student went to the Apter Rov. One time he came to the Apter Rov, and he kicked him out and he told him, "I don't want you here. Go away by yourself, and learn, and do what you want to do and don't come to my table."

He explained to his hasidim: "In heaven the tsaddikim sit in court and they expelled one from the court. Why? Because they

[21] For a saying of the Sassover Rebbe, see Newman and Spitz, *Hasidic Anthology*, p. 53, no. F3.

[22] Reb Shimshen: Yaakov Shimshen Spitkover, d. 1800. He is also considered to be a disciple of the Maggid of Mezrich.

saw that thirteen generations later, one of his children is going to convert, and now that he was expelled they are looking for someone to take his place. They wanted to take this person that was chased away to replace the one that was sent away from the court. So I said like this, as long as he's sitting like this by my table and he's not doing anything for the world, so they have a right to ask for him over there. But now that I sent him away and he had to become a Rebbe on his own and he's needed in this world, they can't ask for him over there."

A, Stolin, Y

The High Priest: I (T25)

It is said that the Apter Rov was reborn many times.[23] Once he was a High Priest in the Temple. On Yom Kippur, in the Avoda,[24] the reader refers to the High Priest, "he said." But the Apter Rov stopped himself and pondered: "Why should I say '*he* said'?" And so he prayed, "*I* said." [25]

CC, Satmar, E

The High Priest: II (T26)

The Rabbi Mendel Rimanover was reborn one hundred times. He says once he was the High Priest in the Temple.

You know, on Yom Kippur when we pray, there's several pages where we say how the High Priest spoke. So we say: "And that is

[23] Among his many reincarnations the Apter was said to be the High Priest, the president of the Sanhedrin, and a prince of the Jews in Mesopotamia. See Langer, *Nine Gates*, pp. 169–70.

[24] A section of the Yom Kippur afternoon prayer portraying the Yom Kippur service of the High Priest in the ancient Temple.

[25] For other tales of reincarnation, see T26, T39, T40, T60. See also *In Praise of the Besht*, no. 228, in which a quarrel between the Besht and Rabbi Nahman is attributed to the former bearing the soul of King David and the latter that of King Saul. See also *In Praise of the Besht*, no. 108, in which R. Yudel is said to be the reincarnation of Samuel the Prophet, and no. 82, in which the Besht says that he himself is the reincarnation of the Saadia Gaon.

how the High Priest spoke." You should take the blood and do this and do this and that is how the High Priest said it.

And when Reb Mendel was praying, this was also about one hundred years ago, he was saying, "And that's how *I* spoke." He didn't say during the prayer: "And that is how *he* spoke"—"And that is how *I* spoke."

X, Bobov, E

The Soul of the Maharal (T27)

The Shpoler Zaideh had the soul of the Maharal—the one who made the Golem.[26]

U, Stolin, E

The First Miracle (T28)

This is the way of Bobov. All the rabbis were very hidden and they did not reveal anything—no great miracles. Some show what they're doing. Not that they want to show off. I wouldn't say that. But they have another way. But Bobov—it started in this way.

It started with the Ropchitser Rov. Ropchits is also a city in Poland. This Ropchitser Rov was the father of the Dzikover. He was also a very hidden person. You never saw him do anything impressive. After his death, his son, the Dzikover Rov, said, "The world tells of many miracles performed by my father, but I know only three of them." Our Rebbe told us only two of these. The third he didn't want to tell. I'll tell you the stories of the two miracles.

Once there was a very big wedding. As the Ropchitser Rov, who was the oldest of the rabbis and the grandfather of the bride, was to be there, rabbis came from all over Poland. In this city—the city was Kolbisef in Poland—there was a man who had been crippled for nine years. He couldn't move. The doctors had given up on him. They went to see all the rabbis and nothing happened. So the friends and relatives of this crippled man told him, "Now is the

[26] Rabbi Loew of Prague, d. 1609.

time for you to get help. All the rabbis in the whole world are going to be here, and the greatest and the oldest rabbi, the Ropchitser Rov, is going to be here as well. So the best thing for you to do is wait for him on his way to the wedding, fall to the earth, and beg and cry and maybe he'll help you."

In those days there weren't any closed sewers in the streets like there are now. They were like small canals. There were small bridges you could pass over from one house to another. They knew that all the rabbis would go first to the Ropchitser and from there go to the wedding. So they said, "Place your bed on the way so that he won't be able to pass, and when he comes over the bridge he'll ask what's wrong, and then you'll fall before him and cry and beg him and maybe he'll help you."

So that's what they did. They put the bed by the bridge so that it blocked the way. The Ropchitser Rov came out and he saw a person lying on the bed. He started yelling: "What's wrong with you? Are you crazy?" He gave him a kick and the man got up from the bed and ran away like he was on fire. The whole city knew he had been crippled, but the Ropchitser didn't know anything about it.

The wedding was performed and the next morning the gabai told him the whole city is talking of the rabbi's miracle.

He said, "What miracle?"

And the gabai said: "Doesn't the Rebbe know that there was a crippled man outside, and the Rebbe just gave him a kick and he ran away?" The Ropchitser was so ashamed that he didn't go outside for three days. He was ashamed that he had made a miracle.

X, Bobov, E

The Second Miracle (T29)

The second miracle he told happened on Sukkes. He [the Ropchitser] came at night and he had to go in a sukkeh. It was showering and thundering and raining. You know the law is you're not allowed to go in a sukkeh when it's raining. If it's raining you're not allowed to go in. It's the first night. In the sukkeh you have to wait a couple of hours. If it doesn't stop you're allowed to eat in the room. You're not allowed to eat when it rains because the Torah doesn't want you to have pains. You're doing a mitsveh and you'd have pains eating in a sukkeh if the rain should go on the top of your head in the soup and the meat.

So the first hour was terrible, and the Ropchitser Rov was turning back and forth, back and forth. And he was waiting—maybe it's going to stop raining. Then he took his son, the Dzikover, he was a small kid, by his hand, and he told him: "Tell the people they should have everything ready, and as soon as I come in the sukkeh they should put everything, all the food, on the table and then take everything out."

He took him by his hand, and not even one drop of rain came down in the sukkeh. They ate fast. He was very much in a hurry. He ate very fast and he took him by his hand and he said, "Let's go." He took him by his hand and they went out. As soon as they went out all the rain that was on top of the sukkeh suddenly came down and the water rose till the window. There was so much rain on the top. Understand? It didn't come down. It stayed on the top. That's all.

He heard another one but the third one he didn't tell us.

X, Bobov, E

Ninety-one (*T30*)

You see I heard a lot more things from the rabbi. You see, he [the Ropchitser Rov] was a very hidden man. He was a student of the Lubliner Rebbe. He used to crack jokes all the time. You see we believe that a very great person when he speaks with somebody even about business he could have something else in mind. He doesn't have to have in mind the same thing as he's saying. He could be thinking about higher things than we understand—even with his words. I'll give you an example.

The Ropchitser Rov used to say every time when there was a wedding, "der zivek zol oyleh yufeh zein" [the match should be successful], they should have a good life. But then his son explained what he meant: yufeh, that is a yod, a pē, and a hē; a pē is eighty, and a yod is ten, that is ninety, and a hē is five, that is ninety-five. God's name is ninety-one—when you count the letters it comes out ninety-one. After the Meshiah comes, God's name would not be yod kē vov kē; it is going to be four more. So it is going to come out four more than ninety-one. So it is going to come out four more than ninety-one, ninety-five. That's exactly like we said before—yofeh. So when he said the zivek [the match should be successful] he meant you should put together all the names, yod kē vov kē and adneh and it should come out ninety-one.[27] That means he begged the Meshiah to come and the name should be ninety-five, not ninety-one like it is now. It should be ninety-five.[28] You understand? That is what he meant. I just told you an example of how we don't know what he meant by his words. His words are very hidden. You used to weigh his words. You never heard him talk a lot.

X, Bobov, E

Tears (T31)

There was another rabbi, Zev Wolf of Zbarazh. Everybody he called tsaddik. Anybody that he saw. He couldn't see any bad thing in a person. There was once a time they were putting a lot of rabbis in jail, so all the Jews came to him. "You're a man who never says a bad thing about a man. So if once you're going to say something, God will surely do what you want. If a man never says a bad word unless he really cares about something, God will do it."

So he took them down the cellar and showed them a bag filled with tears that he cried to God he shouldn't be able to see any evil in a man, that God should help him to see only good, he should never say anything bad about a man. "So now you want me to say something bad." He said, "I'll never do it." [29]

X, Bobov, E

The Robber and the Tsaddik (T32)

The wife of Reb Zev Wolf of Zbarazh did all the business, and he sat and studied. Once he was studying and on the table were candlesticks. A robber came in. Reb Wolf saw him but he didn't

[27] To avoid pronouncing God's name, Adonoy is pronounced adneh and yod hē vov hē is pronounced yod kē vov kē.

[28] For an example of gematria, see *In Praise of the Besht*, no. 245.

[29] Regarding crying tears into a bag, see T8.

say a word and let him take the candlesticks. Then his wife came in. She saw that the candlesticks were not there. "Hey, where are the candlesticks?" She says, "A thief must have come in and stolen them."

He started shouting at her, "What are you talking about a robber? How do you know what happened? You call him a robber—maybe something else happened. Why should you call a man a robber when you don't know what he did?" Then he explained: "I saw a man come in and I saw that he wants to take something. I wanted to prevent him from doing a sin. I thought in my mind that from now on the candlesticks are not mine. Anybody who wants them can take them. So he took them. But he didn't take *my* candlesticks because I said that anybody who wants it can take it. So why do you call him a robber? He's a tsaddik. He didn't take anything from me." [30]

X, Bobov, E

The Quilt (*T33*)

I know another story about Reb Zev Wolf of Zbarazh. You know a quilt has feathers inside and sometimes the feathers gather on this side so that you have to shake them up in order to get all the places even. But Reb Zev Wolf never said "Shake up the feathers!" but he said "Shake up *what's inside!*"

His wife used to complain: "He's such a crazy man, he doesn't talk like a human being. Why doesn't he say shake up the *feathers* like everyone else does? No, he says shake up the *insides*."

Once they went to the Ropchitser Rov for a visit and his wife went in to the Ropchitser and told him: "You know he listens to everything that you tell him. Tell him to talk like a human being. Somebody robs things and he doesn't look, he doesn't care." And

[30] A like tale is found in B. T., *Ta'anit* 21b–22a. When two scholars took his mattress, Abba considered the mattresses as charity. In *In Praise of the Besht*, no. 70, the Besht tells someone not to turn around while a thief is stealing the horse's halter. Later, rather than publicize the matter, the halter is simply paid for and redeemed. Compare with Buber, *Tales*, 1: 161; Newman and Spitz, *Hasidic Anthology*, p. 92, no. 4. See Waxman, *History of Jewish Literature*, 3: 28. For tales on a similar theme see Buber, *Tales*, 1: 190; 2: 211; Newman and Spitz, *Hasidic Anthology*, p. 37, no. 19.

she told him the story about the feathers. "He never says shake up the *feathers*. 'Shake up the *insides*.' He doesn't talk like a human being. If you tell him he'll listen to you."

So the Ropchitser Rov called in Reb Wolf and said, "What are you doing? Everybody you call tsaddik. You don't talk like a person. Say, 'Shake up the *feathers*.' "

Reb Wolf said, "I'll tell you why I say that. I remember that ten years ago a woman came with the feathers to sell to my wife. The woman said, 'These are *down*'—the smaller, softer, more expensive kind—and my wife said, 'No, those are plain feathers and I'll give you the plain price.' They started arguing and arguing and the woman that sold them swears that they're down and my wife swears that they're plain feathers. What should I do? If I say shake up the *down* that means that my wife lied, she swore falsely. Should I say shake up the *feathers?* That means the woman lied, she swore falsely. So I say shake up *what's inside*. That's all. Am I not right?" [31]

X, Bobov, E

Garbed in Holiness (T34)

This is a short but deep story. The Mitteler Rebbe [Rabbi Dov Baer, the son of Shneur Zalman] told Reb Iser that after the death of the Alter Rebbe [Shneur Zalman], Freydkeh, the sister of the Mitteler Rebbe, dreamed about her father. In the dream she was looking at him very hard. The father asked, "Why are you looking at me in so penetrating a manner?"

She said, "I see you're clothed in holy and refined clothes."

The Alter Rebbe answered her, "Reb Shimon ben Yohai is garbed in holiness." [32]

When the Mitteler Rebbe told this story to Reb Iser he banged on the table, and he said: "It is a brief but penetrating story. Because from the time of the Shimon ben Yohai until the Alter Rebbe

---

[31] See Buber, *Tales*, 2: 229. For other examples of Reb Wolf's concern for others, see Buber, *Tales*, 1: 159–60; Newman and Spitz, *Hasidic Anthology*, pp. 206, 439.

[32] Shimon (Simon) ben Yohai, second century teacher, one of the Tannaim, and legendary author of the Zohar.

there were a lot of tsaddikim in heaven and from all the tsaddikim he referred to Shimon ben Yohai."

J, Lubavitch, Y

Why? (T35)

The day, according to tradition, that the Temple was destroyed, the ninth day of Av, he [Rabbi Moshe Teitelbaum] would stand by the window waiting, murmuring "Why, why, why?" He told the children, when he went to bed each night, not to hesitate to wake him up when the Meshiah appears.

CC, Satmar, E

He's Here (T36)

They would say about the Yismah Moshe [Rabbi Moshe Teitelbaum] that he was expecting his son or son-in-law, I don't know, somebody, and he was already waiting every day whether he's coming. All of a sudden somebody opens up the door and says, "He's here already." He meant the son-in-law or whoever was supposed to come. "Meshiah! Meshiah!" he starts running, "Meshiah!" It did not enter his mind. . . . It just goes to show that the only thing that was on his mind was the Meshiah.

S, Klausenberg, E

David's Fiddle (T37)

I heard from Satmarer Rebbe who heard it from his father that he [Rabbi Moshe Teitelbaum] was thinking so much about the loss of Israel and the destruction of the Temple that once he told the hasidim a story about Rebbe Mendel of Rimanov who used to say, as in the Talmud, that if everybody, while he is in this world, would think about the loss of Jerusalem, when his time comes he can help by saying that he wouldn't enter Paradise if the Meshiah does not come. Rebbe Mendel said, "I'll simply tell them that I won't enter."

The Lelever Rebbe said, "According to tradition, when the Rebbe died he wouldn't enter heaven. By a trick they honored him to give a sermon before the other tsaddikim, and after he entered Paradise they kept him talking." The Lelever Rebbe said, "I don't think there is a trick to get me into Paradise. I'll never go there unless the Meshiah enters."

So the grandson of the Lelever Rebbe, the Szigetter Rebbe, explained why the Meshiah did not come: "Because when my grandfather passed away and didn't enter Paradise, they asked David to play on his fiddle. When the Rebbe heard the beautiful music, he asked them where it was coming from, and they told him. And he followed them in, and he's still listening to the playing of David." [33]

CC, Satmar, E

The Fool (T38)

After waiting all his life for the Meshiah, when the Satmarer Rebbe's great-great-grandfather died, he said to God: "How could you fool such an old fool like me?"

UU, Satmar, E

The Three Reincarnations (T39)

I heard this from the Satmarer Rebbe.

His great-grandfather [Rabbi Moshe Teitelbaum] was born three times. The first time he was one of the sheep of Jacob when he worked for Rebecca at Laban's house.

The second time he was in the group that left Egypt with Moses. He lived during the forty years of the desert at the time when the tablets were destroyed. They asked him did he take

[33] See Newman and Spitz, *Hasidic Anthology*, p. 249, no. 10; see also p. 247, no. 3, p. 69, no. 5. See Hirsch, *Rabbinic Psychology*, p. 242.

Moses' part or Korah's part? [34] He answered that it was pretty hard to say "You think Korah was a hoodlum? He had a good purpose in mind."

The third time he was alive when the Temple was destroyed, but he wouldn't say who he was. And the fourth time he was here. As proof he showed the marks on his shoulder where Jacob had hit him when he was a sheep.

The people who heard the story went to the Kalever Rebbe and they told him the story: how he was one of the sheep of Jacob, and then among those who left Egypt, and how he lived at the time when the Temple was destroyed but wouldn't say who he was.

The Kalever Rebbe said, "I'll tell you who he was. He was Jeremiah the prophet, and as a sign he said that every night at twelve o'clock you'll hear him talking only about the destruction of the Temple. There isn't a single speech he makes that he doesn't cry that the Temple was destroyed. And he is so expectant that the Temple will be rebuilt that he always has his talis and tefillin and walking stick beside him so that he's ready when the Meshiah comes to rebuild the Temple."

When those people returned to Moshe Teitelbaum, the Oheler Rebbe, they told him they knew his secret.

"How do you know?" he asked them, and they told him what the Kalever Rebbe had said that he was Jeremiah the prophet. "If he says so," he replied, "then it must be so, but what puzzles me is how does he know it?"

CC, Satmar, E

Reincarnation (T40)

The great-grandfather of the Satmarer, Yismah Moshe, remembered where he was standing when the Torah was given.

The Apter Rebbe said he was a king at one time, and once was a high priest.

It is said of the Berdichever that he was the reincarnation of Rabbi Akiba.[35]

SS, Stolin, E

[34] See Numbers, chap. 16.
[35] Rabbi Akiba: Akiba ben Yosef (c. 50–132 A.D.), Palestinian Tanna, the subject of innumerable legends.

Without a Rebbe (T41)

Hirsch of Rimanov tells how the forces of evil, the Yetser Hora [the Evil Urge], came to God and said, "What's the good in the Jews having a Rebbe? It's another trick for Him to lead them to God."

God replies, "There will come a time when they will not have a Rebbe."

SS, Stolin, E

The Alarm Clock (T42)

There was the Bnei Isoskher—he was the Dinover Rov.[36] He was a very great man. So once he was saying toyreh. He was sitting by the table and speaking to the people. You know, lecturing as you would say. All of a sudden an alarm clock started ringing. It was Shabbes, and so they couldn't stop the alarm clock. So he gave a scream, "Shah!" and the alarm clock stopped. And after he finished the toyreh, it started ringing. It finished off the ringing.

S, Klausenberg, E

The Way of a King (T43)

The Rizhyner Rebbe, he was the first Rebbe who acted like a king. He was the Rebbe's [Rabbi Shlomo Halberstamm] great-great-grandfather. He was named Israel after the Baal Shem Tov. He was born on the same day. His name was Rabbi Israel of Rizhyn. He was a Rebbe with a gold chair and with servants. He wore golden boots. He had horses like a real king. Wherever he went, he had so much.

There are seven shepherds: Abraham, Isaac, Jacob, Joseph, Moshe, Aaron, and David, and so everyone has another way of how

[36] Bnei Isoskher (Issakhar): Rabbi Zevi Elimelekh Shapira of Dinov, d. 1841/42.

to be a servant to God. David's way was kingly. So every Rebbe could take one of the seven ways and be a servant to God. The Rizhyn took this way.

We saw sometimes the Rizhyn was standing outside—it was very cold—on ice. They were walking on the street and he was talking to somebody. He wanted to go up but he couldn't walk. He tried to move his feet and couldn't. He tried to move from the place and he couldn't. He ripped his feet off. They found out that he goes with boots of gold, but there's no sole. That's how he walked around. So his feet got frozen to the ice. That's how things are hidden. That means he followed a hidden way. It looks like a kingly path, but. . . .

X, Bobov, E

Punishment (T44)

The Rizhyner Rebbe said: "They can't punish me with anything. Because if God says to me to go to hell, I will do it. So they can't punish me with anything."

UU, Satmar, E

As Much as a Hair (T45)

They say that the Rizhyner said this on his deathbed before he passed away. The Gemoreh says that there was a certain rabbi, Rabbi Yehuda ha-Nosi,[37] who was very, very rich. He said, before he passed away, that with all his riches he didn't have any pleasure from this world—as much as his finger even. In other words, he was saying that with all his riches he never had any pleasure from this world. Whatever he did with his riches was between him and God. He did whatever he was supposed to do. He gave charity. Whatever he did was for a reason. So the Rizhyner said: "Reb Yehuda ha-Nosi he didn't have as much as a finger. I say about

[37] Yehuda ha-Nosi (Judah ha-Nasi), redactor of the Mishna (c.135–220 A.D.).

myself that I didn't have pleasure from this world as much as a hair—even less."

That is what the Rizhyner said about himself.

W, Boyan, E

The Singing (T46)

In the city of Korets there were two tsaddikim, Reb Pinhes of Korets and Reb Yoneh. And on Purim everyone went to Reb Pinhes' house, and Reb Yoneh was left alone with an empty house and with nothing to eat. And this Reb Mordekhai the Tsaddik came to Reb Yoneh and took from his suitcase a large haleh to make a meal for Purim, and he started to sing "The Rose of Jacob." [38] During the meal Reb Pinhes went outside and heard this beautiful singing, and he went back into his house and he told the people sitting there: "There's someone who is singing beautifully at Reb Yoneh's, and we must go and hear him."

So they all went to Reb Yoneh, and Reb Pinhes said, "If he is so great that Reb Mordekhai the Tsaddik comes to him, we should come to him as well."

BB, Slonin, Y

Memory (T47)

Now I'll tell you a story of the third Lubavitcher Rebbe. He was called the Tsemah Tsedek. The Tsemah Tsedek had a son, and the hasidim called the son Rabbi Maharash. The Rabbi Maharash later became the fourth Lubavitcher Rebbe. At one time when Rabbi Maharash was a small child he learned with a friend, with another boy, who later also became a great rabbi. They learned together for a while. After that they learned the toisefes [Tosafot]. [39] They both did not understand it. So the Tsemah Tsedek came into the room and noticed how the boys were trying to study the toisefes. The Tsemah Tsedek interpreted the toisefes. Afterward he said he had

---

[38] "Shoshanas Yaakov," a Purim song.

[39] Tosafot: critical and dialectical glosses on the Babylonian Talmud by medieval talmudists after the time of Rashi.

not seen this toisefes for twenty-five years. After that the Tsemah Tsedek went out.

The Tsemah Tsedek's son said, "My father has a good brain. He remembers what happened twenty-five years ago. He saw this toisefes twenty-five years ago and he remembered it on the spot."

So the other boy, the Kopuster Rov, said, "I see more than your father does.[40] I see everything that your father has, all that he has thought of, in the past twenty-five years. And I know that he did not think of this toisefes in the last twenty-five years."

X, Lubavitch, Y

The Shtraiml (T48)

The Tsemah Tsedek had three grandchildren: Zalman Aaron, Reb Mendel, and Shmuel [Sholem Dov Baer]. The two, Mendel and Zalman Aaron, came into the room and saw Tsemah Tsedek's shtraiml on the table. They began to try it on. The Tsemah Tsedek reprimanded them and stopped them from trying it on. Shmuel came in and tried it on, and he did not say anything. He was going to be the Rebbe.

YY, Lubavitch, Y

Kvitlekh (T49)

I heard this from the Klausenberger. The Sandzer Rebbe, the grandfather of the Klausenberger, said: "A Rebbe that doesn't know the time a disciple is leaving his home to go to see him and doesn't know the purpose of his coming, his needs, he should not accept kvitlekh [petitions]."

He said this in front of his son, the Shinyaver Rebbe, and he asked his son, "Do you know this?"

And the son said, "Father, I know this." [41]

Z, Klausenberg, E

[40] The Kopuster Rov, Yehuda Leib, was also the son of the Tsemah Tsedek.

[41] Rabbi Simha Bunam of Pshiska was said to know the wishes of a carriage load of hasidim coming to see him. See Buber, *Tales*, 2: 243.

Honor (T50)

The Szigetter Rov, the grandfather of the Satmarer Rebbe, wrote a book called *Yekutiel Leib* [*"Good Hearted"*]. He and the Huster Rov and the Chernigover Rov were friends—the closest friends that people ever could be. Once when they met at the unveiling of a school, the Chernigover Rov started to say to the Szigetter, "You go in first"—in order to honor him.

"No." He refused and wanted the other to go in first. Each tried to honor the other. Finally the Szigetter Rov said: "If your knowledge of Torah is greater than mine, then you must go first, and if my knowledge is greater than yours then you have to obey my commands."

CC, Satmar, E

The Three Friends (T51)

When first one of my friends married, and then Moshe was about to get married, I went over to his house to congratulate him. He said, "Well, you always have some story to tell. Can't you think of anything for this occasion?" And I told him this story:

Of the three friends, the Huster Rov died first. The second to die was Chernigover Rov. And the Szigetter Rov said, "Once we were a seghol (˙.˙), then we were a tseyre (··), then a hirik (·) [Hebrew vowels]. How will I go on and bring out things about the Torah?"

CC, Satmar, E

Father and Son (T52)

The Shinyaver was always arguing with his father. The real reason behind it was that he saw in a dream that he was going to take over his father's dynasty. He understood his father was going to die, so he decided to argue with him so he could not take over his father's dynasty—so the whole dream shouldn't be true. I don't remember the story exactly, but it was something in that order. But whenever they were together they were always arguing— always arguing.

So once he was in a place and his father said the law is this way—and he was arguing with him. So the father said to him, "Don't step over the threshold any more. I don't want you to step over my threshold any more."

So he went and jumped out the window because his father told him not to step over the threshold. He could not step over it. So he didn't step over it. He went out the window.

S, Klausenberg, E

The New Rebbe (*T53*)

This story happened with the first Rebbe from Slonim. The Rebbe's father was sick. He gave his son a prescription, and he went to Warsaw to fill it. And when he came back his father was dead already. He came in to the court and he saw that everything was pitch dark. Where are all the people of the court? Don't ask. He threw away the medicine. So they sent out to each of their shtiblekh—each shtibl should send two representatives to choose a Rebbe.

There were two candidates: the Rebbe's son and Reb Moshe Matevicher [the previous Rebbe's son-in-law]. I knew him. Eighty per cent of the hasidim were for this Reb Moshe. And he said, this Reb Moshe said, "You can't be a Rebbe in Slonim unless you know Kabbala, and I don't know any Kabbala."

So the Rebbe's son said, "I'll teach you Kabbala two hours a day."

So he said, "If you know it, be Rebbe yourself." They continued fighting like that without coming to any resolution. Each wanted the other to be Rebbe.

So they started traveling, everybody together, and they came to the city of Gornits, near Bialystok. The gaboyim came to their Rebbe. "Since tomorrow is the Blessing of the New Moon, we want to make a meal in honor of the new month."

So he said, "Make it. If you want to do it, go ahead." So this one gave twenty groshn and that one gave twenty groshn and they got together and they bought a duck. They fixed the duck and made a meal.

In the morning, after davening, they asked the Rebbe to please wash and come in to the meal. So he says, "I don't want to. I don't want to, and if I want to come in when you're ready to pray, I'll come in, and if not, then I won't. I don't want to make a meal now. I don't keep this custom."

"But you told us to make a meal."

"Sure I told you to make a meal, but not for me."

So they said, "But it was so expensive." In those days, it was expensive to buy a duck. This was seventy years ago.

"You should know, my brothers, I am beginning to swim on the great sea, and if someone is going to tell me this, and someone else is going to tell me that, I could become, God forbid, withered.[42] So I beg of you, let me alone, and let me swim in the sea," he said. "I don't keep this meal on Rosh Hoydesh." So he said, "You could make a meal."

And then they made a meal and had a farbrengen, but he didn't come in to join them.

BB, Slonim, Y

The Blessing (T54)

When he [David Moshe, the Tchortkover Rebbe] made kiddish Friday night, when he said, "In six days God created the whole world," and he was holding the wine cup in his holy hand, the wine would bubble and run over like there was a fire under it.[43]

Q, Tchortkov, E

[42] "Novol tibol," withered. Exod. 18:18. After Moses' father-in-law warned him he would wear away if he remained the only judge, Moses created the judges. Compare the use of the term in N1.

[43] When the Besht prayed, the water in the barrel trembled (*In Praise of the Besht*, no. 35).

The Mirrors (T55)

At morning and at night he [Reb Israel of Tchortkov] walked from his bedroom through a great big room. There were two mirrors on the wall. They were brought from Vienna to Tchortkov. After some years he walked by and asked his son, "When did we buy these mirrors?"

I was there when he asked his son this question. When he had special visitors he sat in this living room. He had great visitors a few times a year.

Q, Tchortkov, E

Free Will (T56)

A sick man came to the grandfather of Rabbi Halberstamm [the Bobover Rebbe]. He had bad lungs. The Rebbe said a blessing, and the man felt better.

He then returned to the doctor, who had told him he was deathly sick, to ask about his diet, and the doctor said: "Are you still alive?"

The man explained that the Rebbe had said a blessing.

"Fooey," the doctor said. "Can he replace lungs? Why is it that the Rebbe only blesses what's inside? Why doesn't he replace a foot?"

If the Rebbe could substitute limbs then man would not have a choice to do good or evil. Man has choice, therefore, only for what is inside.

G, Lubavitch, E

Song (T57)

This is about the present [Bobover] Rebbe's father. You know the song that you heard on Saturday night. He made that up. He composed all songs that you hear here. He was a great composer.

He composed thousands of songs. He was one of the few rabbis that could compose songs. In all the places where hasidim sing songs, one hasid composed the song, the rabbi heard it and said that it was good, and they all sang it. But in Bobov the Rebbe himself made the songs.

One of the biggest cantors, Joseph Rosenblatt, maybe you heard of him, he was in Bobov a couple of times, and he heard some of them.[44] And one song that the present Rebbe's father composed, he said, all his life he tried to compose a song for those words, the song should fit those words so that you should understand the meaning from the song, and he couldn't fit music to it. He was amazed how a rabbi, not a cantor, could do it.

X, Bobov, E

The Children Will Inherit (T58)

The [Stoliner] Rebbe's father died in Ger before he was married. Before he left home, he had to go for an operation. He said goodbye to the Rebbetsn, and he indicated it was the last time he would see her.

She cried, "You're leaving a boher, a young child."

The Rebbe quoted her a portion from when the Jews were in the desert rebelling against Moses: "The children that you say will be spoiled—they will inherit everything."

M, Stolin, E

The Horseback Ride (T59)

He [the Stoliner Rebbe's father] would do strange things. Once there was a wedding between the families of two Rebbes. It was probably his daughter, but I'm not sure. An hour before the wedding ceremony, he went out with a horse and went horseback riding. No one could understand.

One person never doubted. Before the wedding, the Rebbe

[44] Joseph Rosenblatt (1880–1933), famous cantor and composer of synagogue songs. He lived in both Europe and America.

went to the mikveh. He saw that the Rebbe's back was full of sores
and wounds. He saw how horseback riding would give him pain,
so that he shouldn't enjoy himself.

M, Stolin, E

Words of Praise (T59a)

The [Stoliner] Rebbe's father was at a wedding and they were
waiting for him to come out of a room. They were waiting a long
time. Finally someone peeked in and saw him standing by a mirror,
saying: "Hello, Rebbe. How are you? Sit down." He was praising
himself to the heavens with words of praise and greeting.

Later they asked him, what does this mean? He said, "I'm going
out into public and I'm going to get all this honor. I'm practicing
to myself—what does all this honor mean? It means the same as if I
were saying it myself—nothing."

M, Stolin, E

In Every Generation (T60)

The [Stoliner] Rebbe's father had the soul from Rashi. The
Rebbe's grandfather had the soul from King David. He said of
himself, somebody said of him, that he was the Meshiah, but the
Almighty did not give permission.[45]

The Baal Shem Tov said that the Meshiah is born in every
generation. The only thing is, if he isn't given permission he dies
like everyone else. He fades away and people know him like everyone else.

U, Stolin, E

[45] See an earlier Karlin-Stolin tradition of messianic expectations in Rabinovich, "Karlin Hasidism," *YIVO Annual of Jewish Social Science*, 5
(1950): 151. Rabbi Nahman of Bratslav also thought he had inherited the
soul of the Meshiah. See J. G. Weiss, "Contemplative Mysticism and 'Faith'
in Hasidic Piety," *The Journal of Jewish Studies*, 4 (1953): 28.

The New Shoes (*T61*)

When the [Lubavitcher] Rebbe was a young boy, ten, they bought him new shoes for Passover. The day before Passover, they were working before Passover, baking, and the Rebbe noticed how he was too concerned about his shoes. He was watching them too much. He called him and gave him a lecture how low it is for a Jewish boy to have in his mind such low things like nice shoes, that you shouldn't get dirty when going to observe Passover. Such small things. He gave him such a lecture till the boy started to cry and didn't stop till he vomited up every thing that he ate.

And the mother came to the father. "What do you want from him?"

"I want him to be my son, not a piece of meat. He's supposed to be my son. Don't worry, he'll be all right."

V, Lubavitch, E

The Beard (*T62*)

The [Boyaner] Rebbe's second brother was in Leipzig before the war. He was called the Leipziger Rebbe. In the late thirties he left for Israel. He left for Israel after Hitler came to power. I will tell you why. They tell a story.

The Leipziger always was wondering why he ever came to Leipzig. Leipzig is a German city. There are hardly any hasidim there. The only hasidim that were there must have been Polish Jews who happened to leave Poland and they lived in Germany. They lived in Leipzig. Otherwise, the Germans themselves were not hasidim. There were a few Boyaner hasidim and there was a mixture of some other kind of hasidim that also were there.

In Leipzig there is buried the Rizhyner's oldest son—the one who passed away right away [Reb Sholem Yosef]. He didn't have a city. His oldest son is buried in Leipzig and there are one or two others also buried there. Then the Germans decided that they wanted to destroy the cemetery. So the Leipziger asked a few of the hasidim they should dig it up and they'll relocate it. And they dug up the grave and they found that his body had disintegrated. I mean this was after quite a number of years, but that his—I think the bones and the beard—were whole. I don't know about the bones, but the beard I remember for sure. The beard was whole.

And that happened just recently. We met people who saw it. A person came over and he saw it himself.

So he said that's the reason—now he understands the reason why he was sent to Leipzig—that he should be there to be able to save this grave—to dig up this grave and to relocate it, and to put it in a good spot—to do this good deed.

W, Boyan, E

I Almost Forgot (T63)

Moshe [of Stolin] was known as a learned man. Once he was in court with two rabbis. One gave his opinion of how the law should be. Moshe interrupted and said he was wrong and gave his side. Then he said, "I almost forgot," and he refused to finish. The others said, "What? Finish." So he said, "I almost forgot that there's a God in heaven. I got so involved in my wisdom that I almost forgot there's a God."

M, Stolin, E

THE TSADDIKIM IN AMERICA

Elijah the Prophet (TA1)

The Alter Rebbe [Rabbi Joseph Isaac Schneersohn] was in Chicago. On Passover it's the custom to send a small boy to open the door for Elijah the Prophet. The Rebbe himself got up and opened the door. He said, "Should I send a small boy for Elijah the Prophet?"

D, Lubavitch, E

He Will Inherit All (TA2)

He [the Stoliner] went to Israel. His brother [Abraham Elimelekh] wrote there they should accept him as Rebbe. When he was in Israel, the Rebbe here [Yaakov] died. His father had said, "He will inherit all." It was as though two couldn't be Rebbe at the same time.

FF, Stolin, E

Truth (TA3)

They said of him [the Stoliner Rebbe] that if there was a minute bit of truth under the floor he would rip it up with his bare hands to get at it.[1]

F, Stolin, E

[1] The same was said of Aaron of Karlin. Buber, *Tales*, 1: 202.

The Golden Scale (TA4)

The [Stoliner] Rebbe said, "In my mouth I have a golden scale. Before saying a word I weigh it on that scale."

A, Stolin, E

Holy Eyes (TA5)

He [the Stoliner Rebbe] used his eyes as little as possible. One time he called them the heilige oygen [holy eyes], for use only for holy things.

If he had to give money, he would have different denominations in different pockets so he would not have to look at it.

M, Stolin, E

Impure Thoughts (TA6)

When he [the Stoliner Rebbe] walked through the streets it was a common sight to see him walking with his hands shading his eyes, looking down, that he shouldn't have impure thoughts.[2]

F, Stolin, E

Two Worlds (TA7)

The Stoliner Rebbe loved Israel. When he would be sitting at a tish he would say, "They're doing this and this in Israel."

He wore two watches, one on each hand. On one, they say, he had the time in Israel. He lived in two worlds.

F, Stolin, E

[2] For an incident concerning this theme in the life of Rabbi Shneur Zalman, see Buber, *Tales*, 1: 267–68.

Unseen (*TA8*)

There is a cave in Israel called the Ramban's cave. Ramban Nachmanides hid there. For some reason the Arabs also believe that cave to be holy, and you're not allowed to go in. So [in 1936] he [the Stoliner Rebbe] went there with a yeshiveh boy. He went into the cave. They went in, the Rebbe said psalms there, and as they wanted to go out, they saw a group of [Arab] soldiers coming in. So the boy got scared, so he says to him, "Don't get scared. Just stand over here and they won't see you." And they marched past him and they marched out, and they brushed right next to him, and they were unseen.

Then they came out and he says: "If you don't have to see, you don't see." [3]

M, Stolin, E

The Lulev (*TA9*)

A Jew had a factory to make bricks. To make bricks you had to have a very hot fire. One time the fire was not working. They couldn't fix it. The bricks would crumble. They couldn't make the fire. The factory wasn't working. So he went to the [Stoliner] Rebbe, and the Rebbe took a lulev and told him to throw it into the fire. And the factory was working.

Later on the factory was on the blink again and he went to the Rebbe's house and took the lulev and threw it in. But it didn't work. He went to the Rebbe.

The Rebbe said, "If I say that the lulev will work, then it will work. Otherwise it's nothing."

A, Stolin, E

[3] See HA14, HA27.

Fire (TA10)

The Stoliner Rebbe said, "Those who hang around us don't realize that they're playing with fire."

M, Stolin, E

Five Hundred Miles (TA11)

The [Stoliner] Rebbe said, "Any leader who can't see a distance of five hundred miles is no leader." [4]

M, Stolin, E

To See (TA11a)

The [Stoliner] Rebbe said, "When I get up in the morning and I go out into the clear air, I can see what my people are doing or thinking at home under their covers."

M, Stolin, E

Cement (TA11b)

The [Stoliner] Rebbe once said: "What is a pair of eyes that water and cement could block its vision"—meaning that a wall does not prevent the Rebbe from seeing.

M, Stolin, E

[4] Compare T19.

Simheh (*TA12*)

The Rebbe always wanted simheh [joy]. He said, when he wasn't feeling well, he said, "Go on as if I'm there."

B, Stolin, E

The Eyes of a Tsaddik (*TA13*)

This man Zelig died when the [Stoliner] Rebbe was six years old. And when he used to sit by the Rebbe's father, the Rebbe would always place him at the head of the table because he was by the Rebbe's grandfather. And the Rebbe's father would say, "Blessed are the eyes that looked at the eyes of a tsaddik." He passed away when our Rebbe was six years old.

Our Rebbe was sitting at the table, on the day commemorating the dead, and he asked, "Who knows Zelig's mother's name?"

Reb Mendel had a brother who was deaf in one ear, who leaned over and asked if the Rebbe knew Zelig.

So the Rebbe answered, "We knew him very well, and if we didn't we can know him from the other world." (The Rebbe always spoke in the plural, "we.")

M, Stolin, E

The Stranger (*TA14*)

Mendel was very close to him [the Stoliner Rebbe]. In Europe one time he was riding and he fell sick and they were looking for a doctor, and all of a sudden a man in army clothes came with a satchel, they didn't know from where. He took care of him, massaged him, brought him back to himself. They found out later this was Elijah the Prophet. He didn't mention it, but he gave a hint.[5]

[5] For another appearance of Elijah, see H28 and note.

Once, another time, this man passed by. He said, "Do you remember this man?" He wouldn't reveal a lot of things because he wasn't allowed to, but from what he said they came to that conclusion.

B, Stolin, E

The List *(TA15)*

The [Stoliner] Rebbe ruled with an iron hand. He made them send a list from Israel of those who attended the davening every day. One time the person who sent the list didn't want to say who was not there. The Rebbe wrote: "Better write the truth because we know anyway and it only makes it worse."

M, Stolin, E

Thunder *(TA16)*

When the Rebbe was sick, Israel served him day and night because he was paralyzed. One night during a severe thunderstorm, he called him up to his room and asked that he should seat him on a chair, and after each boom of the thunder, he would say "Do you hear it?"

The Rebbe's wife came into the room and saw the Rebbe listening so intently to the thunder that she asked, "Does the Rebbe fear thunder?"

The Rebbe gave a bang on the chair and said, "We are afraid of God alone." [6]

M, Stolin, E

Shabbes *(TA17)*

The last year the Rebbe was paralyzed. When Israel came in one Shabbes, he asked him, "Are they talking about the Meshiah on the streets?"

[6] Concerning the fear of God, see Buber. *Tales,* 1: 50.

Israel answered, "You know the Meshiah doesn't come on Shabbes."

The Rebbe said, "He could come on Saturday night." [7]

M, Stolin, E

The Torah Protects (TA18)

When the Stoliner Rebbe died they had no will. They didn't know if he should be taken to Israel or not. As soon as they would find out his wishes they would take him there. There were different factions. Some held that since he had purchased this cemetery the year before, he wanted to stay here. They threw lots, and it was two to one that he should remain here till they knew more information. The gabai came from Israel and they had a judgment, and it was decided that he should be taken to Israel.

Sixteen months had passed. They took him to Israel after sixteen months. The body was flown by airplane to Israel. After sixteen months the body was found uncorrupted. It was just like it was on the first day. It's like that with a great tsaddik. If you follow the Torah, the Torah will protect you.

B, Stolin, E

The Airplane (TA19)

When he [the Stoliner Rebbe] was living, he passed a remark that he didn't want to go on this and this airplane. [After his death] they couldn't understand why when they tried to get him on a plane of this company, and there was space there and everything, they couldn't do it. It was a puzzle to them. Then someone recalled what he said, that he didn't want to go on that airplane of that company.

B, Stolin, E

[7] For tales of Rabbi Moshe Teitelbaum and the Meshiah, see T35–T38.

He Knew (TA20)

He [the Stoliner Rebbe] was taken to Israel on another plane, and he was laid to rest in a place where he had asked where this man was resting when he was in Israel eight years before. I think it was Mendel Vitebsker. When they told him where he is, he shed a few tears and then he went away. He knew already.

B, Stolin, E

The Curse (TA21)

The Satmarer [Rebbe] had a daughter and she died. At that time he had an argument with the Munkaczer Hasidim and the Munkaczer [Rebbe] said to the Satmarer: "Your children won't live." It was a curse.

R, Lubavitch, E

Parnosseh: I (TA22)

The Klausenberger Rebbe said: "I have the keys to parnosseh [livelihood]. Whoever wants them must catch them."

S, Klausenberg, E

Parnosseh: II (TA23)

A Satmarer hasid told me that when the Klausenberger Rebbe went into great enthusiasm on Purim, he said: "I have the keys to parnosseh. Whoever wants them can grab them from me." He laughed because he is a Satmarer.

NN, ————, E

The Secret Scholar (*TA24*)

The first time I came here I watched him [Rabbi Halberstamm of Bobov]. He is a very hidden man. The first time I came here I found him twelve o'clock, two o'clock, staying up learning. Nobody knew about it. The whole day you never see him learning because he's got to take care of the yeshiveh.

X, Bobov, E

Divorce (*TA25*)

In accordance with the Torah you must divorce your wife if after ten years of marriage you have not had any children.[8] The Rebbe divorced and remarried his wife in the same night. That is what it is to be a Rebbe—to see *through* the Torah.

R, Lubavitch, E

Ships (*TA26*)

The question of whether Israeli ships should travel on Shabbes came to Lubavitch. The Rebbe said: "No Israeli ships should travel on Shabbes. It is a desecration of Shabbes."

They protested his decision. He wrote an eleven-page letter in Hebrew—it would be fifty pages in English—explaining in engineering terms why it could not be done, why it was a desecration of Shabbes. When it was received in Israel, they couldn't understand it. They had to call in the chief engineer. He read and said, "Schneerson is correct."[9]

That's why I have to go to Israel on a goyishe [non-Jewish] boat.

R, Lubavitch, E

[8] See Babylonian Talmud, *Yebamot* 64a; *Code of Jewish Law*, chap. 145, no. 4.

[9] Rabbi Schneerson studied engineering at the Sorbonne. He was employed as an engineer when his predecessor died and he was called on to become the Rebbe.

HASIDIM AND TSADDIKIM

The Preacher (H1)

This is a story of the Baal Shem Tov when he had not yet revealed himself. He used to travel to various cities and towns. In those times, it was right after the events of 1648, and there was not one family that was not affected by those events. Every family used to tell how at least one member of the family was a victim of those events.[1]

The preachers at that time who used to travel around preaching to the people were of two different classes. They used to speak to these people and bring out that their forefathers used to risk their lives for their own beliefs and the beliefs of their fathers and they used to strengthen their will and belief in God. That was one class. The second class had the style of scaring the people and of telling them of the punishments that come from all the sins that they do. They used to describe God as a jealous God who punishes, and the punishment is for every little thing and the punishment is strong and hard. The sentences in the Torah that tell of the punishments and the curses used to be the foundation of all their speeches, and they used to say for this and this sort of sin God would send this and this bad punishment.

The preachers used to be very religious and sincere people. And they surely meant to do good for the people of Israel so that they should better themselves in their general actions. But they did not always find the right way to approach the people and often they insulted the people and brought a bad name upon the people. They gave the impression to the simple people that God—who is actually

[1] The narrator is undoubtedly referring to the uprising of the Ukrainian Cossacks in 1648, and the consequent massacre of Jews. Although the event occurred in the century before the birth of the Besht, it had long-lasting social and psychological consequences.

a merciful God—is a God who punishes and takes vengeance. If the preacher was a good-hearted person then his words used to come out pleasantly; but if the preacher had a harsh and mean character then his words came out harshly and meanly, and every word used to bite, and even the coarse words of the preacher used to make a deep impression.

These were the years when the Baal Shem Tov was still hidden. He used to go around together with his disciples to various cities speaking to the plain people and strengthening their belief in God.

One time the Besht came to a small town. The masses of the people were very simple. Most of them were working people and many of them were farmers. But they were religious people and they used to daven three times a day with a minyen and they used to say the daily psalms.[2] On Shabbes they used to say the entire book of Psalms twice, once before daylight and once in the middle of the day. The ones who knew a little bit more used to say for everyone a few sentences from the Bible or from a portion of the *Ethics of Our Fathers*. When the Besht used to come to that town he would take great pleasure in seeing these simple people, their plain manner of praying, and their simple saying of the Psalms.

It was in the times when the Besht was dressed as a plain Jew, as a tailor or a shoemaker, and he was wearing his famous coat, a pelts [fur coat], and he used to be able to enjoy himself among the plain Jewish people and their families. The Besht used to enjoy himself by spending time with the small children and teaching them the prayers, *I Thank the Lord*, *Hear O Israel*, and *The Torah Moses Taught Us*.

It was in the summertime when the Besht reached the town and he noticed how the people of that town were worried and in low spirits because of the hardship they were having in business. It was a very warm and sharp and bitter summer, and the fields which were not very good in the beginning were spoiled and became in even worse condition. It was a real pity on the town, and although the Besht was ready to leave, because of the pity he felt for the town he decided to bring some more holy men to pray for the welfare of the town.

The next day there were more of the Besht's holy colleagues and together they tried to redeem the town and they prayed for the town. And God, who listens to his tsaddikim, made fall a heavy

---

[2] There are certain psalms designated for every day of the month. The practice of saying these psalms is intended particularly for those unable to study the Talmud.

rain, and the fields and the grass, which looked like they were in a state of faint, livened up, and there was great happiness in the town. All the faces lit up and everyone said thanks to He who lives forever, "Blessed be He who lives forever."

Everyone went around telling about the miracle of God, about how their vegetables which were dried out and half-dead came to life after the heavy rain. Men, women, children were continually speaking of the great miracle—that God brought the rain and God had pity on them and had sent his good messenger, the blessed rain. And it was Thursday night and the heads of the community decided they will call it the Great Shabbes, and they will say the Psalms three times, and the added third time everyone must attend—men, women and children—everyone except the sick people. And in honor of the great kindness God showed to the village, everyone should make a sweet pudding. In every house they should give it to the children and tell them about the kindness that God did for them and their village. And when the Besht and his holy colleagues saw the great happiness of the village and saw what would happen that Shabbes, they decided to stay around that Shabbes to see and to share the happiness of the village.

That Friday morning there came a maggid [preacher] to the village and he came to the head of the village and asked permission to speak to the village that Shabbes. From the letters of introduction that the maggid had, he seemed to be from the elite of the maggidim, inasmuch as in the letters of introduction it said that after a few minutes of speaking tears would pour from the eyes of the audience and he would make everyone feel like repenting. The head of the community was a sincere and very religious man and he told the preacher that this Shabbes, when the maggid wants to preach to the community, had already been set aside to say Psalms.

As soon as this maggid heard the words of the head of the community, he told him off angrily, saying, "How dare you insult the Torah by insulting me in such a manner? How dare you insult me by not wanting to listen to my preaching? You have time to eat the pudding, but you don't have time to hear a few holy words from a great scholar like me. Hell itself will be too easy a punishment for those who insult in such a manner."

The head of the community became afraid, and with tears in his eyes, he begged the maggid for forgiveness and he begged him to speak and to go immediately to the rabbi of the community to set the time for his speech.

So he told the head of the community, "According to protocol the maggid isn't even supposed to go to the head of the community, but he has to go to the rabbi." He told him, "Actually, when a preacher comes to a community, the rabbi sends his most honored messengers to see the preacher."

Hearing this, the head of the community ran quickly to the rabbi and repeated the words of the preacher. And so when the rabbi heard it, the rabbi himself was a great Torah scholar and a deeply religious man, and the rabbi and the head of the community came back to the preacher and the rabbi and the preacher immediately began to speak of learning. The rabbi found out that the preacher was a true Torah scholar. The head of the community was standing on the side and he had great pleasure from the conversation that the rabbi was having with the preacher. They decided that the time that the preacher was going to speak was after the third meal until the time of *Song of Ascents*.[3] The rabbi invited the preacher to his house for a meal, and during the entire meal the discussions were only of the Torah, and they discussed the deep portions with great acuteness.

It was immediately known in the town that a great Torah scholar had come to town and was a guest of the rabbi and would speak after the third meal on Shabbes. They knew that this Shabbes was different from every Shabbes in the whole year in that on each Shabbes they would bring one candle to shul, and this Shabbes they would bring an extra candle to the shul. There was great happiness at the lighting of the candles Friday night, and great happiness with the songs sung Friday night, and the saying of the Psalms Shabbes morning, and the special saying of the Psalms giving thanks to God, and at presenting the sweet pudding and at the telling to the children of the kindness of God. And the Besht and his holy colleagues were overjoyed seeing the great happiness of the town on that Shabbes, and they were very happy that they stayed over Shabbes in that town and saw this happiness with their own eyes.

When it came time for the preacher to give his talk, he stood up and started out by declaring that in the *Ethics of the Fathers* there are seven types of punishment that God brings upon the Jewish people, and he translated this into Yiddish so that he was sure everyone would understand what was going on, and everyone cried bitterly. The preacher spoke very loudly in a coarse and angry tone, and he told the town the punishments they were going

[3] That is, until they held the evening prayer.

to get for not being religious. God will punish them first with hunger so that the crops of the field will dry up and the crops will be burnt, and then God will punish them in their own homes. The listeners were constantly crying, and tears continuously poured from their eyes. The preacher continued on listing punishments, that God will punish with blood, first with small children and then after that with older people, and it will be a town with widows and orphans. A bitter cry came from the people and many fell faint on the ground.

The Besht entered, and seeing the great cry among the people and realizing that it was because of the great maggid's talk, the Besht rose up on one of the stands and he shouted at the preacher, saying to him, "Why do you yell at the Jewish people? God has been good to the Jewish people and bestowed upon them many blessings and kindnesses." After the preacher's exposition, the people said the mourner's prayer for the rabbis.[4] They said the *Song of Ascents* with great happiness. That means that you have to make spiritual things from material things, as when the Jewish people coming back from visiting the holy Temple in Jerusalem used to bring with them the spiritual things they saw and heard in the holy Temple and they used to make spiritual things from the material things. The holiness that they saw in the Temple during the holidays of Simhes Toyreh and the Assembly of the Eighth Day was to bring light in the homes and lighten it for a full year. And God shall enlighten the Jewish people materially and spiritually, that everyone should recognize the truth, the revealed portions of the Torah and the hidden portions of the Torah, that the truth is the real religious way of life and the true religious way of learning and education, and He shall send us our redeemer and He shall gather us from all corners of the world in our days and bring us to our holy land in our days.

WW, Lubavitch, Y

The Brothers (H2)

There was a town near Kiev where there were three brothers. They all were very educated. They knew how to learn, and two of them

---

[4] After parts of the prayer dealing with learning a special prayer is said.

became followers of the Baal Shem Tov. One of them was a
misnaged. All of them lived in one large house, and they all learned
together. They had two different ideas, and the misnaged sometimes spoke about things that were below their level. One time in
the middle of learning, the misnaged asked his brothers a very
hard question and they did not have an answer for it. They
searched and searched until one of them found an answer.[5]

Later one of the brothers who answered the question was with
the Baal Shem Tov and he asked the Baal Shem to teach him a way
of praying and learning. So the Baal Shem Tov told him, "Once
somebody asked you a question and you gave him the rule incorrectly." He did not remember when someone asked him a question
he did not answer correctly, and the Baal Shem reminded him of
the time that his brother asked him a difficult question. So he asked
the Baal Shem Tov for repentance for the sin of answering incorrectly. The Baal Shem told him, "It's a hard question, even harder
than you think it is. Before you'll be able to understand the question, I'll have to repeat the whole thing from the beginning." The
Baal Shem Tov told him the question three times and he answered
it three times until the brother understood it. Though he was a
great scholar, he could not grasp it until the Baal Shem had told
him three times.

He came home and told his brother who was a hasid what the
Baal Shem said, and it took a few days to learn, together with
the brother who was a misnaged, what he had learned. He asked
the question again. You could learn it deeper and deeper before you
came to the answer. You must learn the question well and repeat
the question over and over. He saw that it was a terribly difficult
question. He repeated the answer of the Baal Shem, and he saw
that the answer of the Baal Shem was filled with heavenly wisdom.
He learned with one brother and then with the other.

In the same region they had an uncle who did not live too far
away, about six hours walking distance from the house. The uncle
also was a great scholar. He learned many hours a day and he was
also a businessman. They wanted to ask the uncle this question. So
the misnaged and a few misnaged friends learned the whole portion thoroughly and agreed to go to the uncle to ask him, because
everyone saw it was such a good question. The other two brothers,
since they were hasidim, prayed longer hours than the misnaged,
and the misnaged and his friends went to the uncle a few hours

[5] Compare *In Praise of the Besht*, no. 225.

before them. When the two brothers arrived at the home of the uncle, they saw that everyone had already told the question to their uncle and everyone was enthused by the good question. Everyone tried to laugh at the two brothers, the hasidim. "What business have they among learned people? They have a Rebbe. Go to him. They have no place among learned people."

The brothers laughed it off and waited a bit of time while the others searched for the answer. But they could not find it. And so finally, one of the brothers who was a hasid said, "Before I go further, I'll have to explain the question again." He repeated the whole question. "I have the answer as I heard it from a great scholar." Nobody knew where he had heard the answer, including the misnaged brother. And so he told them the answer and the people became amazed at such a heavenly answer containing such wisdom. They all agreed that this was an answer from heaven, and the old man, the uncle, concluded from the answer that, "This was a tremendous scholar who told you this, and I agree to leave my business to go to hear this great scholar."

So the brothers said, "Maybe you say you'll go now because you're enthusiastic about the question, but after a time your enthusiasm will die down."

"No," the uncle said, "I'm ready to go to this great scholar to hear his toyreh."

So he finally told that he heard it from our Rebbe, the Baal Shem Tov. He told him the whole story: how he told him the question and the answer, that he came to him to learn a way of davening and learning, and how the Baal Shem had been asked a question. He told him the question and the answer, and so the uncle said, "I agree to go to this person since he's nearby." All the friends went too, but the brother who was a misnaged, even after he heard the whole story, he was so stubborn he still did not want to go to him. Not only did he not refuse to go to the Baal Shem Tov, but he made jokes, and when they came home to the big house the brother set aside his quarters from the others and would not have anything to do with them. When they came back, all the friends became followers of the Baal Shem, and he in stubbornness refused to have anything to do with anyone.

A little while later the misnaged became ill, and at the same time the Baal Shem came to the same village where he was living. Even though he had heard of the greatness of the Baal Shem, he lay sick in bed and still spoke in anger of the Baal Shem Tov. Two or three days passed and the Baal Shem accomplished what he had to do in the village, and when he was ready to go away he told the two brothers he wanted to see their misnaged brother. Since he was sick in bed he could not run away. The Baal Shem came to the house. There was happiness in the house of the two brothers. The Baal Shem went over to the sick person, placed his hand on the sick person and said, "In the Gemoreh it says a needle in the lungs makes an animal treyf."

Mahet (מחט) means needle; lungs are called *re'eh*. Sin is hidden in the word needle. The root of the word *mahet* (מחט) *het* (חט) which means sin. *re'eh* (lungs) means to see a sin. Sin comes through things that are seen. He interpreted the whole argument. The Gemoreh discussed *mahet* and *re'eh* and it is interpreted that if sin comes it is because of vision. There are six scholars who argue about it. Three say it is kosher; three say it is not kosher. They say it is not kosher because if a needle perforated the lung the animal would not live twelve months. The souls of the three rabbis who said it was kosher are rooted in the criterion (*mideh*) of kindness rather than the criterion of severity.

He told this to the misnaged. I know it up to this point. The story is left off in the middle. What the Baal Shem said further, I don't know, but most likely the man became well.

LL, Lubavitch, Y

Charity (H3)

One of the students of the Baal Shem Tov went to a city and became the rabbi there. And he wanted to change the custom of the city. Instead of the poor people going around begging, he thought they should have a fund to which everyone should donate once a year and they would distribute it among the needy. But in the town there was a tsaddik nistor who did not take from the fund, and since his source of income was cut off—people did not donate privately anymore—he was left penniless. This aroused a judgment in heaven against the rabbi, and as a punishment they decreed that he should want to convert to Christianity.

So it was Shabbes afternoon, and the rabbi got this desire to convert. And he ran to the priest and he told him to convert him. The priest was busy at the time, and so he put him in a room and he gave him brandy to drink and he let him stay there for a few hours.

Meanwhile, while he was getting drunk, the Baal Shem Tov, during the third meal, saw what was happening, and he tried to intervene for his student. The only merit that he could find for the rabbi was that all during his life he never missed melaveh malkeh, and they told him that if he eats at the melaveh malkeh tonight, he will be saved. So the Baal Shem Tov tore off a piece of the haleh from the third meal and gave it to one of his students and told him to pray the evening prayer and go.

The student set off blindly along the road and he felt that there was something out of the ordinary, because at times he was flying along the road without any hindrance and at times every step felt as though something was holding him back. Finally he came to a big church and he entered it and started wandering through it blindly until he came to a room where he saw the rabbi lying there drunk. He understood his mission and he persuaded the rabbi to eat some bread. "And since you're eating the bread you might as well wash before it."

Once the rabbi ate the bread he came to his senses and started to cry, "What have I done to myself?" And they immediately left the church and the rabbi was saved.

BB, Slonim, Y

Sabbatai Zevi (H4)

The Besht was in Bomla for Shabbes. A lot of tsaddikim went to Bomla. The Alter Rebbe [Rabbi Shneur Zalman] was there, and the Mitteler Rebbe, the Tsemah Tsedek, was there. But this is about the Baal Shem Tov. He came on Friday. He came to the rabbi and he came late, toward evening. The rabbi was a distinguished rabbi and the house was already clean for Shabbes. There was fresh sand on the floor—there were dirt floors. The rabbi went to greet the Baal Shem Tov, but the Besht said that he smelled a foul odor from the house and he cannot go in. So the rabbi goes into the house and he sees that the house is clean. He feared that maybe he smelled something wrong with himself. The Besht said, "No, I don't mean you, I mean the house. Go look by the bookcase."

He looked in the bookcase and someone had put in a book concerning Sabbatai Zevi. After he took the book out, the Baal Shem Tov went into the house.[6]

YY, Lubavitch, Y

The Sack of Money: (I) (H5)

The Besht sent two people to go to a small village and they came to a Jew living there and they said, "We want to be here for Shabbes." The Jew was a very poor man but still he did not refuse them, and he took them in and he borrowed food and money from all the goyim, and they stayed from Friday through Thursday night. Thursday night they left him with an empty house and in debt from their being there a week.

So a week later a goy bangs on his door, and calls out, "Let me in."

"What do you want?"

"I want to drink."

"I don't have anything. I have an empty house."

He says, "If you have a bottle of brandy let me smell the bottle."

So he lets him in, he squeezed out a drink for him, and the goy shows him he has coins with the surface rubbed off and he does not know if they are good or not. "I can't get rid of them, but maybe we can do business." The goy explained to him he was kicked out of his house by his own children, and this is all he has, and he is not sure if the money is good or not. He found a sack of money hidden in a tree. So he gave him one of these coins.

He went into town to see if it was good and slowly built back his business again. The Jew figures that if two Jews brought him such luck that a goy came in with money, he will go to the Baal Shem Tov himself.

While he was at the Besht's the goyim had a holiday and the goyim decided that they should make peace with the goy who was kicked out of his house. They went to him and said, "It's not right to live at a Jew's." They tried to entice him to come back home. So the goyim made a big party and they took the goy back home and

---

[6] Compare *In Praise of the Besht,* no. 64.

the wife was left alone at home. In the middle of the night they banged on her door, and they said that the goy died. She was afraid that while he had been there he had told them about the money he left with them. The end was that the goy did not say anything about the money, and even the cows and other things also belonged to the Jew.

So the Besht said, "We wanted to do this Jew a favor. He was a poor man, and I wanted to help him. Whatever was missing, he did not moan, he did not sigh. He accepted his plight. That is why I sent him two people to eat him out of his home."

GG, Stolin, Y

The Sack of Money: (II) (H5a)

As we're speaking about divine providence, there was another story which I heard in reference to the Baal Shem Tov.

It once happened that there was a very poor man, and he came repeatedly to the Baal Shem Tov for a blessing that he might have a livelihood, that he might be able to get out of the plight of poverty in which he found himself. But the Baal Shem said nothing to him. Till finally the man was in such dire circumstances that he pleaded with the Almighty for help. And after this had happened there came a knock at his door and a gentile, a farmer, knocked at his door and told him that he would like some brandy. He must have a glass of brandy. The Jew said that he had no brandy in his house, but the gentile said, "I'll give you money. Go into town and buy brandy."

And so the Jew went into town and he bought brandy, and he brought it back to his house and he gave it to the gentile. And the gentile drank it. Now the gentile kept doing this repeatedly, and pretty soon the Jew had made a bit of money and he always kept on hand in his house a bottle of brandy for the gentile. Now one day the gentile came to him and said, "Why do I have to give you money every time? Every month I'll give you a lump sum for the brandy that I drink, and you'll be able to have a little livelihood from that and I won't have to keep running back to where I keep my money hidden."

Now the Jew heard this and he decided it would be a good idea. After a few months the gentile said, "Why do I have to keep running back? I have a large treasure hidden. Now I'll tell you where this treasure is and you take whenever you want money from this treasure."

And the Jew said, "Fine." He was agreeable to this. And a short while later the gentile died. When the Jew heard this, he realized that the gentile, who had been at odds with his children because they had thrown him out of his house and farm, realized that he had probably not told his children about the treasure. But he waited a while and finally found that the gentile had actually not told his children about the treasure and the Jew took the money for himself.

And the Baal Shem told this story and said: "It was because that this Jew finally came to asking the Almighty for help that he was given help."

D, Lubavitch, E

The Inspired Convert (H6)

Near Bomla there is a forest where they say that the Besht dug a well so that he could have water to wash his hands in order to pray the afternoon prayer. As he was leaving some ruffians came and they laughed at the Besht. Someone said that his beard is like a goat's beard. So the Besht mentioned that this person will become a Jew.

As they were traveling they came to the next village and this fellow came running after them. And he said he wants to become a Jew. So they circumcised him right there on the spot, and they asked him, "What happened to you?"

He said that when he heard the words from the Besht he felt so inspired that if he had not found a moyel he would have circumcised himself.

YY, Lubavitch, Y

You Can (H7)

There once came a rabbi to the Baal Shem Tov. I don't think he was a hasid. So the Baal Shem Tov told him to do this and this.

He said, "I can't do this."

The Baal Shem Tov said, "You can, but you don't want to."

So he said, "I really can't!"

The Baal Shem says, "You don't want to!"

They couldn't agree. He said, "I can't." The Baal Shem Tov said, "You could only you don't want to."

So the Baal Shem Tov says, "Go home and you'll see you can but you don't want to." So he went home.

On the way he went past a king and one of the wheels of the king's wagon was broken. So the king saw a Jewish man walking, so he called him, "Zydzie." (That's how they say a Jewish man in Polish.) "Come over here!" He saw that a king called him so he went over. "Help me pick up this wagon! I have to put on the wheel."

So he says, "I can't."

He says, "You could, but you don't want to!"

He says, "I really can't."

So he told him, "You could!" Then the king told the servant to give him a slap. So he slapped him. Then he picked up the wagon. "You see you could."

Then he knew what the Baal Shem Tov meant when he said he will come home and he will know, "You could but you don't want to." But this king did not know that he was doing something for this man by saying, "You could but you don't want to."

See, when some people talk you don't know what they mean.

X, Bobov, E

The Charm for Swift Travel (H8)

This story is called "How the Baal Shem Tov Received the Charm for Swift Travel."

There were several Jews who surrounded the Baal Shem Tov who were called batlonim. They were not like men we think of now who wander around and have nothing and do not have steady jobs. These were unworldly people. Their whole job was to learn the holy Torah. They looked into its hidden meaning and they prayed and did mitsves—good deeds. One of the Jews, who we will call Reb Yaakov, was one of these batlonim. The Baal Shem Tov used to support them with money. Every Friday night he sent them

money. One time the Baal Shem Tov did not send any money to
Reb Yaakov, and so his wife thought that the holy one had forgotten to send it. They waited a second week and he still thought he
forgot to send it. So they went hungry. They waited a third week
and they did not know what to do. Her husband was sitting and
learning and he thought of food and still there was no money in the
house. It was a terrible thing. So she went to the Baal Shem
Tov.

The Baal Shem Tov received her and said: "Now I will give you
money. But don't ever come to me for money anymore. Buy the
first thing that you see. But don't ask any more money from
me."

She went out and saw a goy with a goose. So she thought she
will buy the goose. So she bargained with the goy and she bought
the goose, despite the fact that the goy wanted more money. And
she bought the goose. The goose laid eggs, and from the eggs there
were little geese. Everything went well and she sold the geese. She
kept on selling the eggs until she bought a small farm. The farm
did well and so they bought a bigger farm and still a bigger farm
and everything went well. Then, he thought, why does he need a
farm? He'll open a business. He opened a business and it went very
well. Then he thought, "I have so much money, why should I
handle it? I'll deal in diamonds. They're more valuable than gold
and worth a great deal. Despite the fact that they're very small,
they always keep their value." The Jew went to Leipzig. Then he
went to Bristol to trade. He thought he might as well go to Africa
and earn more money by buying the diamonds there. That was the
advice that the Baal Shem Tov gave him.

He went on a ship and in the middle of the ocean there was a big
storm and the ship sank. This Jew held on to a board, and he was
saved. He came to an island. There he saw a great big town. He
went into the first house and he saw cooked food on the oven. There
was tea, and on the table there was bread, and he looked around
and saw there were holy books and other things that were necessary. There were tefillin and prayer books as there should be.
There were talisim and fringes as there should be and the Jew was
very satisfied. So he prayed and he ate something and he went
further. He walked in the city and he did not meet anybody. Days
passed. It was a beautiful city but he did not see anybody.

On Friday morning he got up and he discovered that the whole
town was filled with Jews. They were buying food for Shabbes and
buying haleh, baked goods, everything for Shabbes. The Jew

asked, "What's going on here?" but nobody answered. At night he went into the shul and he prayed there and they did the services very nicely. At night somebody asked him to come in to eat, and say the blessing over the wines, but not a word did anybody tell him about what was going on in the town. The Jew noticed that right after havdoleh—when it is the law and custom of Israel to put your finger in the wine of havdoleh, and you put out the havdoleh candle, and you smear it on your eyes—that as they smeared it on their eyes they disappeared.

One week passed, two weeks, three weeks, and the Jew did not know what to do with himself. So he thought he would go over the hill to the house of the rabbi of the town and hear his havdoleh. And just as the rabbi was going to dip his finger into the wine he grabbed the wine away quickly and said he would not return the wine to him until he tells him the secret of what was happening in this town. He did this and the rabbi said, "All right, I'll tell you. It was in the time of the Second Temple. There were a great number of Jews in Israel, religious Jews, and it was not like it should be. So they thought that the religious Jews would go to an island and support themselves and in that island they won't allow any others to mix with them nor permit any strange philosophy. They came to this island and they were all learned in Talmud, tannaim. And they had several charms among them, and one of the charms was for swift travel. And because of this, every holiday they would send messengers with money for different sacrifices for the Temple. The messengers would offer the sacrifices on their behalf. After that, one time the messengers came back. Their clothes were torn and they carried sacks on their backs, and there were ashes on their heads. They were very miserable. They said that the Temple was destroyed, and the Jewish people were driven into exile. They did not know what to do and so they remained there. And that was how it was. They approached the Heavenly Court. They decided that for them the prize of Paradise is insufficient. God said that the best thing He gave to the people on earth was the holy Shabbes, so that the Jews would have a reward because they are such great tsaddikim. So Paradise will be their home every day of the week, and they will be able to celebrate the holy Shabbes on earth. And so it was."

And when the rabbi ended his story he said, "And now that you know the secret, I give you a choice: either you can come with us to heaven, because I see that you are a great tsaddik, or I will give you the charm for swift travel and you will be able to go right back to where you came from. As soon as you arrive there open your hand and the charm will depart. I warn you that if you do not release the charm for swift travel you will belong neither to this world nor to the other world. You will remain forever in Gehenna and nothing will help you."

The Jew thought very hard and said that he cannot leave his wife a grass widow and his children to be orphans. "I'd better go back to them."

He wrote the charm on a piece of paper and he placed it in the hand of the Jew. As soon as he did it, a second later, he was in his town. When he wanted to open his hand to release the charm for rapid travel to fly back to the island, he saw and felt that on his hand was another hand that would not let him. It was the holy Baal Shem Tov standing there. He said, "It does not matter. You can give me the charm. Everything will be all right!"

And this is how the Baal Shem Tov received the charm for swift travel. He used the charm to save Jews and to save souls and there are many stories that all of us tell.[7]

D, Lubavitch, Y

The Priest (H9)

I heard this story from my uncle.

The Baal Shem Tov was always seeking to lengthen the Shabbes, as did all of the tsaddikim. The purpose of this was to do a favor for the wicked souls in Gehenna. Every Shabbes the wicked are released from Gehenna and the longer the Shabbes the more time they have out of Gehenna. But one Shabbes, as soon as the time was passed, he did not lengthen the Shabbes any longer and he told his students that he must go away. And he told the coachman to prepare the coach and wagon. As usual the coachman did not know where he was going; instead, the horses simply went by themselves. They started on their way, and though the journey was very far, with the Besht's power the way was miraculously shortened and in a short time they arrived at a certain town. There they told the people that a wonder man had arrived who heals the sick

[7] Concerning miraculous speed ("hastening of the way") see *In Praise of the Besht*, no. 211. For references to earlier Jewish and Christian accounts, see Ginzberg, *Legends*, 1: 294; 5: 260, n. 287.

for whom even doctors cast away their hope. No one knew the purpose of the Baal Shem's visit, but he called over two of his favorite students and told them to accompany him wherever he would go, and he told them to fetch a mirror for him. This caused considerable wonderment in itself as it is known the Baal Shem Tov never looked in a mirror. But as the Baal Shem Tov told them to do it, they followed his instructions although they wondered what would happen next.

Suddenly, the priest of the town became very sick. This priest had caused a great deal of trouble for the Jews. The doctors did not know what to do. The priest had a servant, and this servant informed the priest that there was a holy man in the town who undertook to cure people who could not be helped by doctors. Since the priest was an anti-Semite and the holy man was a Jew, the priest was very reluctant to see him. But since his life was at stake he relented and decided that they could bring the holy man to him. And so they called the Baal Shem Tov, and he came with the two students and with the mirror which was in his briefcase. When they arrived at the house of the priest he told the two students to wait outside and he entered the room where the priest was lying on his deathbed. He had the mirror with him and he was alone with the priest. When he put his hand on the priest the priest woke up and asked him: "What are you doing here?"

The Baal Shem answered him: "Do you know that you are on your deathbed and the doctors have given up hope for you? I want to surprise you. Do you know that you originate from Jews? It happened in this way. There was once a pious man who married into a very nice and fine family; but Satan mixed in and a goy took the woman away from the man while she was pregnant. The man died from the misfortune and in the other world he came to the Baal Shem Tov and complained he could not have any rest. After his child had been born the goy did not want to keep the child since it was Jewish, and so he gave him to a monastery. There the child grew up to be a priest and a hater of all Jews and had caused a great deal of trouble to the Jewish people. The father could not have any peace in the other world knowing that his son was causing trouble for the Jewish people." And the Baal Shem Tov told him: "You are the son of the Jewish father. You were sent to the monastery to learn." And he said, "I'll prove it to you. When you look into this mirror that I am holding you will see letters on your forehead and the letters will spell out the name of your father." And he told him, "You should know that the maid that you have in your house is really your mother. The goy threw her away. After she married the goy she could not return to the Jews again and so she found a job in the house of the priest—not knowing it was her own son. I will prove to you that she was your mother. I will call her in and ask her to identify a birthmark and she will tell you where it is."

And so it was that they called her in and the Baal Shem Tov told her that they knew who she was and that she should know she was Jewish and that the priest was her son. She told them of the birthmark and when they found it she felt like fainting. "What can we do now?" she asked.

And the Baal Shem Tov told her, "You must still stay by the priest because I will make him better. You remain with him until all the harsh decrees against the Jews are corrected." And he said to the priest, "When you get better you will annul all of the decrees you have made and you will take your mother and go to a certain town where you will find a little shul. There you will be well known."

And so it was that he annulled all of the decrees that he had made. And he took his mother and went to that town and he converted back to being a Jew. There they found a tsaddik nistor [one of the hidden righteous] and that tsaddik nistor was one of thirty-six of the world. Some people say that this tsaddik nistor's name was Um Tsaddik Nistor and people used to come from all parts of the world to ask a blessing from him.[8]

VV, Lubavitch, Y

The Tutor and the Nobleman's Son (H10)

This is a story of the Baal Shem Tov. I heard it on Saturday night from Rabbi Halberstamm [the Bobover Rebbe].

Usually the Baal Shem Tov took his students on a wagon and they went from one city to the other. When something religious was wrong they fixed it, and they went far places and it took a half an hour and they were there at the place. You do not see how you

[8] Um Tsaddik Nistor: "Um" is probably an abbreviation of Orenu u-morenu, "our light and teacher," or adonenu u-morenu, "our master and teacher."

got there. You just look on the side and you are there in a flash. They did not know the reason but that was how it was.

Once the Baal Shem Tov told his students that he wanted to go to this and this place. So the students knew it was before Shabbes and he would not ride on Shabbes. If you really would go by wagon it would take you a week or more to come to this place. So they knew if the Rabbi [the Besht] told them he wants to go he probably knows what he is talking about. So they went on the wagon. They just started talking to each other and the man who drove the wagon said, "All right, here you are." They went half an hour, an hour, and they were at the place.

Then the Baal Shem Tov told the hasidim they should go knock at the door of this and this place and ask if they could come in. So they did it. There was a woman there. She did not have any husband. She had a boy. The Baal Shem Tov went in. Nobody knew what he was talking about with the woman. Afterward they found out that he asked the woman to give him the boy to study with him. Then when 'he will be older, when it will be the time when he should get married, he will send him back. Then they thought they are going home already. After they had the boy they thought it was all the Baal Shem wanted. But the Baal Shem Tov said, "Now we have to go in the other direction, in the opposite direction, about a thousand miles away. We have to go in another direction."

So they came to some other place, and again the same thing, they were there very fast. So the Baal Shem Tov told the students they should ask at this and this place that he wants to go in there. So they asked and he went in there. And there was a girl, also the same age. So the Baal Shem Tov went to the woman there also and asked if she could give him the girl for a year. She said yes.

Then a few years passed. The Baal Shem Tov arranged that both the boy and the girl should marry. And then he sent them off. And it was like a riddle, you know. The students did not know what had happened. He went and took a boy; then he went over there and took a girl. They did not know what happened. The Baal Shem Tov saw that his students are wondering—they did not know what was going on. And he told them, "You want to know what's going on? I'll tell you a story," he said.

"Long ago there was a king of Constantinople, and not far from the palace there lived a Jew, a teacher. He taught small children. And the teacher had a child, a small child, and the king had a small child, and those children lived near each other and so they played together. When the Jewish teacher's child became five years old, he started to learn the Bible. So the king's son said, 'I want to learn too.' He wanted it and so he taught him too. Even though he was a Christian, he taught him. Then they became older, and the teacher's child, the Jewish boy, put on a talis koten. He wanted to put one on too. So he said, 'Your father's going to kill me.'

"He said, 'My father lets me do anything that I want.' He had only one son, the king, so he gave him whatever he wanted.

"So then a couple of years passed and the time came when the Jewish kid should be bar mitsveh. So he made a big ceremony. When he went to put on his tefillin, the king's son, who was also the same age, also came. He saw they were putting tefillin on him. So he went over to the teacher, 'I want this too.'

" 'You're crazy. How could I put this on you? A Christian is not allowed to put this on.'

" 'I'm very sorry, you have to put it on.'

"So he said, 'If I put this on you, your father is surely going to kill me for that.'

"So he said, 'I don't care. You have to put it on. I'm going to tell my father.'

"So he said, 'If you're going to tell your father, your father's going to hit you for it because you want to put it on.' But that kid didn't care. He heard something inside pulling him to Jewish things. What the Jews did he wanted to do too. So the teacher saw that he couldn't get rid of him. So he told him like this: 'Listen, a Christian can't put this on. If you want to put this on you have to become a Jew. But I can't make you a Jew.'

" 'What do you mean you can't? I want to be a Jew,' he said.

" 'Listen, if I'll make you a Jew, you surely know your father will kill me for that. I'll give you a good idea. You know you're the only son that the king has. So anything that you want he'll give to you. So tell him you want to go out and see the whole land of the king, your father. You don't need a lot of servants, and he should give you only one servant. And I'll give you a letter. You'll come to this and this city, to a rabbi, and he'll read the letter and he's going to make you a Jew. But I can't do it. When you're halfway with the wagon, you'll tell the servant that you want to learn how to drive by yourself. He'll go down and you'll take the horses and you'll run away. Nobody's going to know about you and that's all.'

"The son was very happy with this idea. It's a good idea. He really wanted to become a Jew. So the same day he went to his father and told him, 'Listen, every day I'm in your palace, but I don't see anything—only this city. I would like to see all the cities in your land.'

"So the father became very happy. 'Why not? I'll arrange it for you any time.' So he told him, 'Tomorrow morning, I'll give you a lot of servants and you'll go where you want to.'

"He says, 'No, I don't need them. I don't like too many servants. I have arguments with them. I just need one.'

" 'All right.' He gave him one servant and the next day they went in the wagon. They started out. In the middle of the way, like the teacher told him, he told the servant, 'I want to learn how to drive the horses alone. You take a rest over there. I'll come back. I'll just go around and come back.' The servant went down. He went to the tree, and you know he was tired and so he started sleeping. And this boy, the king's son, took the horses and started going faster and faster. The servant was asleep for hours and he was very far away. Nobody could have seen him.

"I forgot to tell you before, he told him to take clothing, and change into clothes so he should not look like the king's son. So he changed the clothes right away, so that nobody should know who is riding in this wagon. People would think that a poor man is riding, a poor boy. So he drove till he came to the city where the rabbi lived. He came in, he introduced himself, who he is, and who sent him, and he showed the letter.

"So the rabbi said, 'First, the law is that you're not allowed to convert so fast.' First, you have to tell them, 'No, we don't want you, we don't need you.' If you see that he really wants to—so then. The rabbi started talking with him, talking with him. They talked a lot, and he saw that he really wanted to become a Jew. So he converted him, and he became a Jew.

"That kid had a very smart head. He became one of the students of the rabbi. He had a big yeshiveh, and he started studying there. He became one of the best students. The whole yeshiveh knew this boy. They gave him the name Abraham. He was the best student.

"So time passed. The boy was already about eighteen years old. Years passed. And in this city where the rabbi lived, they had a custom that once a year the priest of this whole city made a speech. Everybody had to come, Christians and Jews, to hear him. And at the place where the priest was talking, there was a big pulpit. The pulpit was made with nice things. All around it were nice pictures so that the people should like to look at it. And on one place they put a diamond, a very expensive diamond. The priest thought that the simple people who did not know anything about good things would look at the nice flowers and the nice pictures; but the man who came from a great home, a rich man, he would not look at those flowers. He just would look at the diamond, at how beautiful the diamond is.

"Before, I forgot to tell you that after a couple of days passed and the king saw that the boy was not there, he sent posters every place. 'Who is going to find my son?' And he would give him this. And all they knew about it is that the king's son is lost.

"The priest thought that maybe this is how he is going to find out if the king's son is there. He is going to see who looks at only the diamond. You understand? Because it was a diamond that nobody had. Because the plain people thought it was a piece of glass or something. They did not understand the value of it. So the priest started talking to everybody, and everybody came, the rabbi with his students, and everybody was looking, usually at the nice flowers, at the nice pictures, but one boy he saw, one student, he didn't take his eyes from this diamond. All the time his eyes were on this diamond. So after he finished the speech he sent somebody to tell the rabbi that he wants to see this and this student. He wants to see him. So the rabbi heard that he wanted to see him. Maybe he wanted to talk to him. Well, he has to send him because everybody has to listen to the priest. He was the boss of the city. So he came over. The priest took him in a room, he locked them in, and he said, 'Listen, I knew that you're the king's son.'

"So he said, 'You're crazy. I'm the king's son?' You know, he started lying. 'I'm not the king's son.'

"So the priest said, 'I saw you. You were looking at this diamond the whole time and this proves it. Why should you look at this diamond? Nobody else was looking at it.'

" 'Because I saw it before some place.'

" 'Where did you see it? You couldn't have seen it any place except in the king's palace.'

"So the priest started arguing with him, talking with him, till he had to say, 'I am the king's son.'

"Then the priest started talking, 'Listen, if I just go and tell your father that I have found the king's son, he's going to make me rich, and maybe he's going to kill you. Because you're converted, because you became a Jew. But listen, I'll give you a good idea,' the priest said. 'If you'll marry my daughter, I wouldn't tell anybody and you could still be a Jew too.' So the priest said, 'Maybe you're going to ask what will I have if you marry my daughter and nobody's going to know that you're the king's son?'

So he said, 'I don't care. It's good enough that I know about it. I'll know that I have the king's son for a son-in-law. That's enough.'

"So he said, 'Listen, maybe yes, but first I have to ask the rabbi. If he says it's all right.'

"So he went over to the rabbi, and the rabbi said, 'If the priest's daughter becomes a Jew too, if she converts, then you could be married. Like this she's a Christian. You can't marry her now.'

"So the student went back and told this to the priest. The priest said, 'Okay. I'll let her convert. Just marry her.'

"Years and years passed, and this boy, this student, Abraham, he was a very holy man. He started studying all the books, all the Jewish books, and higher things and higher things, till his mind was not even on this world. His mind was on higher things than we understand. And all that time, he was sitting and thinking, and you could not even tell that he was alive, he was concentrating so hard. He could not even see one thing. His eyes were closed. When he came back he was like a different man.

"Once it happened that he started sitting like that and thinking, and his eyes were closed. An hour passed—two, three. She started to go over to him and shake him and nothing happened. He doesn't move. She thought something happened. So she called doctors. Doctors came over. They couldn't make him alive. They said, 'We don't think he died, but we don't know what happened.'

"After about six hours passed, he came back to himself. He said, 'Listen, I really came to tell you something.' So he told her like this: 'When I was just thinking like that, it came the time that I really should die. Only if I would die now, there would be one thing wrong: I did everything that I had to do in this world.' Hasidim hold that the person comes to this world to do something. If he finishes all his good deeds, God doesn't want that maybe he should make a mistake, and so he takes him away from the world. So he said, 'I did everything good, but one thing was wrong—that I was born by a Christian. So I can't go to the really good place as if I was born from Jewish people. So I have to die now and then be born again, and so then everything is going to be all right. Then I'll be born by Jewish people and so I'll be a pure man—everything is going to be all right.' So he said, 'I was thinking that first I should go and tell you. If you say all right.' Because it depended on him. If he wanted to live, he could have lived. You understand? Give him a chance, maybe he wants to live longer. So he said, 'I'll ask you what you say. That's why I came back. If not I would not have come back. I would stay already. I ask you if you say all right.'

"So his wife says, 'All right, but I want to die with you too. And then I want to be born with you together.' A couple of days later both of them died."

That's where the Baal Shem Tov ended. "See now, this boy is the same boy that I took. He's the one that died and now is reborn, and this is the same girl. That's why I had to take them both together and get them married again. That's why I had to take the boy from over there and the girl from there and nobody understood why." [9]

X, Bobov, E

The Goose (H11)

One time the Baal Shem Tov took his students and they traveled to an inn. When they arrived at the inn the Baal Shem Tov said that he would prepare a feast, and as he was a shohet he asked the innkeeper, who was a Jew, to bring him some geese that he might be able to slaughter them according to the Jewish law. After he had slaughtered the first goose and opened it to inspect it, he found a question. He asked the innkeeper if he had a child. The innkeeper then told the Baal Shem Tov that he had a child who for many years had been in perfect health, but lately the child had done nothing more than lie in its bed unable to move or speak. The Baal Shem Tov then instructed the innkeeper to bring the child to him. He showed the child the goose and asked the question as to whether or not it was kosher. The child then said, "Kosher." And with this the child died. The innkeeper and his wife were very upset, and they asked the Baal Shem Tov why this had happened to them. The Baal Shem Tov told them the following story:

"In the previous generation there had been a very great rabbi who had written various rabbinic responses in reference to this particular question as to whether or not a goose having these certain physical defects is kosher or not. He said that it was

[9] There are numerous similar stories of the conversion of emperors and popes (see Gaster, *Ma'aseh Book*, 1, nos. 33, 95; 2, no. 188; compare H12, I9; see also Gaster, *Exempla of the Rabbis*, no. 149). The tale may be a Jewish form of the frame-story of Barlaam and Joasaph, a legend widely known in India and Europe. Most elements other than the frame, including the accompanying parables, are missing. Other points, such as the gem offered by the prince's tutor which can be seen only by one who is pure, seem to have been retained in a radically altered form (see Budge, *Baralam and Yewasef*).

treyf—it was not permissible to be eaten by a Jew. This was not accepted by the higher court, the Heavenly Court, and the only way that the soul of this great rabbi could reenter heaven was to correct this wrong which he had done."

So the Baal Shem Tov in his desire to help this soul had come to the inn for the specific purpose of having this act rectified.[10]

D, Lubavitch, E

Aaron of Karlin (H12)

The father of the first Karliner Rebbe was a tsaddik nistor, and he did not have any children.[11] They went to the Baal Shem Tov and he gave a blessing to have a child. And the child grew, and as soon as he finished nursing he died. So they came back to the Baal Shem Tov crying, and the Baal Shem Tov told them a story:

"A king had no children and he kidnapped a Jewish child from birth and raised him as his own." Then follows a portion like the previous tale I told of Graf Potocki [see I9]. "He had a teacher who put on tefillin. The boy was also caught and killed. So when the soul came back into heaven, it was a very holy soul; it could not take the place where it belonged because it had been nursed by a goy. They wanted a parent to take the soul back as a child to nurse. So that is why it was born to you. Since you went through so much we will give you another child that will live for generations." This was Reb Aaron Karliner.

M, Stolin, E

The Bandit (H13)

Reb Aaron Karliner was traveling and he stopped over at an inn with one or two hasidim. They tied the horse and wagon outside, and a while later a few hasidim traveling to meet him passed by and saw the Rebbe's wagon and said, "The Rebbe must be in

[10] For examples of how reincarnations were ended, see *In Praise of the Besht*, no. 12; Buber, *Tales*, 1: 310–11.
[11] Rabbi Aaron's father was Rabbi Yaakov from Yanov. He made a meagre living as the shammes in the Karlin besmedresh. It is told that Rabbi Aaron came from a whole line of hidden tsaddikim.

trouble." He said, "The owner of this inn is a masquerader." He wore a long beard, and fooled people who came in the inn. He would steal their money, and once he went in you did not get out. He started to think, "If we go in, we're lost too. But the Rebbe is there so we must stay with the Rebbe." They went in.

The Rebbe was not downstairs in the dining room, but the gabai was sitting there and they whispered, "You don't know what kind of a hole you fell into." Just then the Alter Rebbe came out. He did not say anything. The owner came out with a big fat gartel [prayer belt]. The gabai said, "I've got yohrtsait [anniversary of day of death] tonight and want to pray with a minyen for the Amen." This man was a Jew but a bandit. So they had a minyen and prayed the evening prayer.

So how do we know the story? The Rebbe used to make a meal and tell this story. He filled up a glass of brandy and the bandit drank it and fell asleep. And he is still sleeping today.

I heard this from Mendel and the Rebbe too.

A, Stolin, E

The Unknown Illness (H14)

In the town where Rebbe Elimelekh lived there also lived a great rabbi by the name of Rabbi Rappaport.[12] Even though Rabbi Rappaport was a great scholar he never went to any hasidic Rebbe. There came a time that Rabbi Rappaport became very sick and the doctors did not know what to do for him. He was close to death. Now Rabbi Rappaport had a daughter who was acquainted with all of the miracles that Rebbe Elimelekh did, and she knew about all the other tsaddikim and what miracles they performed. And Rabbi Rappaport's daughter asked her father for permission to go to Rebbe Elimelekh for a blessing for him. At first Rabbi Rappaport did not want to give permission for his daughter to go to Rebbe Elimelekh because he did not exactly believe wholeheartedly that such miracles could be performed by men; but when he saw that all other hopes of a cure had vanished he finally gave permission to his daughter. He figured it could not be of any harm, and so his daughter went to the famous Rebbe Elimelekh.[13]

[12] Probably Rabbi Haim Rappaport, the Lemberger Rov, d. 1771.
[13] Compare Zevin, *Sipurei Hasidim*, Torah, pp. 445–46.

When she entered the house of Rebbe Elimelekh she told him that her father was very sick and the doctors had given up hope. Rebbe Elimelekh told her that she should return immediately to the house, and when she arrives home she will find three doctors there. Two of the doctors will go away saying that they can do nothing more for her father. The third doctor will also begin to leave, but then he will return with a cure. He will think of a means to cure her father. He will write it down and give it to her father, but as soon as the third doctor returns to his own house, this doctor will die. And Rebbe Elimelekh told Rabbi Rappaport's daughter one more thing. "I'm only giving you a blessing now on the condition that your father returns to see me after he is cured." And so Rabbi Rappaport's daughter returned home.

As she entered her house she found three doctors there just as Rebbe Elimelekh had said. Two of the doctors went away saying that there is nothing else they can do. The third doctor started to leave saying there is nothing to do, and then he thought of something. He returned, wrote down a cure, and gave it to the great rabbi, Rabbi Rappaport. Then he left. A few minutes later the whole town was buzzing. The doctor had just passed away. It happened exactly as Rebbe Elimelekh had said.[14]

Now Rabbi Rappaport's daughter told this to her father. After her father became well she told him, "Rebbe Elimelekh only gave me this blessing for you on the condition that you must see him." At first Rabbi Rappaport was not in favor of seeing Rebbe Elimelekh because he never went to see a big Rebbe before, but then after seeing such a miracle and realizing the greatness of Rebbe Elimelekh, he decided that he would pay a visit to Rebbe Elimelekh.

Rebbe Elimelekh told him, "Even though you think you're cured now, you are not completely cured. There's still one thing missing and that only my brother Reb Zusya can cure for you." And he gave him directions in which town to go. Rabbi Rappaport took a horse and wagon and went to the town where Reb Zusya was.

When he came to the town he did not know where to go and so he went to the first house that had a mezuzeh on the door. He

[14] For other tales concerning Rebbes and doctors, see H82, HA4, HA5, HA7, HA8, HA9, HA33, and HA42 (in which three doctors are consulted). See *In Praise of the Besht*, no. 26, for an argument between the Besht and a doctor; in no. 95, the Besht prays for a sick doctor; in no. 245, the doctor turns out to be a thief.

knocked and a man with a great beard opened the door. Rabbi Rappaport asked him, "Could you please tell me where Reb Zusya lives?"

And the man with the big beard answered him, "You've come to the right place, Rabbi. I am Reb Zusya. I've heard about you and I've heard how my brother Rebbe Elimelekh cured you, but that you are still missing one thing and that only I can cure you. You must do exactly as I tell you." And so Reb Zusya took Rabbi Rappaport down into the mikveh [ritual bath]. He dipped himself in the mikveh first and then he told Rabbi Rappaport to dip himself in the mikveh. As Rabbi Rappaport came out of the mikveh he felt that he was a different sort of a person.[15] And then Reb Zusya told him, "This thing that was left over in you was due to the fact that when you were a child, a young boy, you read certain books called hakireh sforim. Of course they are deeply discussed questions by highly righteous people and no child should be reading those books. However, since you have read some of those books in your younger days, something made an impression on your brain. And since every spiritual thing is connected with material things it was the cause of your sickness. Now since you dipped yourself in the mikveh you have forgotten entirely what you read in those books in your younger days. Now you are completely cured." [16]

XX, Lubavitch, E

The Silver Casket (H15)

In Annopol, in the Ukraine, a casket of silver was stolen from the king. He naturally accused the Jews and threatened them with expulsion. So they went to Reb Zusya of Annopol, the brother of

[15] On the power of the mikveh see H55, HA52. See also *In Praise of the Besht*, no. 101. Compare Buber, *Tales*, 1: 52, 75–77, 82–83.
[16] The Jewish Council of Four Lands in ancient Poland attributed the Frankist heresy to the incautious study of mystical writings; therefore, they forbid the study of the Zohar before the age of thirty and the writings of Isaac Luria before the age of forty. See Dubnow, *History*, 1: 214. See Newman and Spitz, *Hasidic Anthology*, p. 24, no. 8; p. 315, no. 1, where special care is required for the reading of Maimonides' *Guide to the Perplexed*, lest it raise doubts. See *In Praise of the Besht*, no. 129, in which a tiny foreign thought—that he will soon conclude the prayer—enters a student's mind.

Rebbe Elimelekh, and he told them to tell the king that in three to four months he guarantees he will have the money back.

The time came closer and closer and he did not bother to raise the necessary money. So finally when it was only a few days before the end of the term, he sent a message to the king that he is coming, and he wants the king to greet him with all his army and servants lined up.

The king complied and he came to greet Reb Zusya. Reb Zusya came and looked over the army and he said, "Someone is missing. The garbage collector is missing." So they found him and put him in line. And Reb Zusya said a sentence from the prayers of Rosh Hashoneh. The sentence is: "We are asking God to spread His fear throughout the world. Make the world fear You."

The garbage collector heard this and started screaming, "Please don't repeat that again. If you do I'll drop dead." And he immediately confessed and showed the king that he had stolen the silver and he had placed it in the garbage barrel so that no one could find it and he could take it later.

GG, Stolin, Y

Old Man (H16)

There's a famous tsaddik from Berdichev—Reb Levi Yitshok. There is a river running through the town. Once it overflowed and it threatened to sweep away the graves in the Jewish cemetery. Reb Levi Yitshok was an old man. He came and tapped with his cane and said, "River, go away! *Otstup!*" [withdraw] in the dialect there.

My brother went there to visit and he told me that the river is like a dalet,[17] like an elbow. Today the Jews call the river Otstup and the Christians call it Old Man because Reb Levi Yitshok was an old man when he did this.[18]

EE, Lubavitch, E

[17] Fourth letter of the Hebrew alphabet (ד).

[18] When a pious woman was drowned crossing a swollen river, it was said that the Baal Shem Tov caused the river to be dried up (see Buber, *Tales*, 1: 84–85). Similar legends were told of the saints (see Loomis, *White Magic*, p. 40).

God-Fearing (H17)

Levi Yitshok of Berdichev had great love for his brethren and he used this when praying to God. He would show God that the Jews are God-fearing.

After Passover eve when leaven is prohibited, he went over to a Jew and asked for contraband silk, and he was told, "All you want, Rebbe." Then he said, "I want a piece of bread," and he was told, "God forbid, Rebbe."

And he said, "God in heaven, look at Your children. Silk that the tsar forbids, that soldiers search for and with guards at every post, can be obtained in unmeasurable quantity, but bread which is forbidden by Your commandments alone cannot be obtained." [19]

F, Stolin, E

Shnapps (H18)

The Rebbe of Berdichev said: "If you wake a goy up in the morning and you say, 'Here, John, there is a glass of shnapps,' he takes it. If you wake a Jew and offer him, he says, 'I didn't wash my hands yet.' " [20]

F, Stolin, E

Ransom Money (H19)

Once there was a hasid of the Berdichever Rebbe who used to go around collecting for redemption money.[21] One time the Berdichever told him he has to collect five hundred rubles. So he collected for almost a whole year, and the whole amount he collected was only two hundred rubles. So when he was on his way home to

[19] See Newman and Spitz, *Hasidic Anthology*, p. 310, no. 3.
[20] That is, he has not yet purified himself.
[21] For other tales concerning the redemption of prisoners, see *In Praise of the Besht*, nos. 123, 124.

Berdichev, it was Yom Kippur eve. He stopped off at an inn and saw three young men spending their time as one spends time before Yom Kippur. So when the men saw him they said, "Sholem alei-khem. Where do you come from? What do you do?"

He told them, "I'm collecting redemption money. I still need to collect three hundred rubles."

So one of the men said, "I'll tell you what. Drink down a glass of ninety-six proof brandy and I'll give you a hundred rubles."

So he figured to himself, "On Yom Kippur eve he is going to fill himself up with brandy?" But he figured that the Rebbe considers the money to be very valuable, so he figured he will drink the glass of ninety-six proof brandy. So he drank it up.

And the man told him, "Drink another one, and I'll give you another one hundred rubles." And he finished that one also, and then still a third drink for another hundred rubles. Then he took the money, and he started out on his way to the Rebbe to give him the money.

When he came into the village he thought he did not want to come in drunk to the Rebbe. He will lie down for a while in the shul, and after he takes a nap, he will go and bring in the money. So he went to sleep. After he got up it was already in the middle of the night. He got up, he sees it is light in the shul, talesim all over the place. They are in the middle of davening. And he wakes up and he walks up to the top of the pulpit and he starts saying, "Thou hast shown. . . ." [22]

There was a great commotion in shul. Here he comes back drunk. So the Berdichever said, "He lived through Yom Kippur and Sukkes and now he is up to Simhes Toyreh."

YY, Lubavitch, Y

The Good Precepts (H20)

A man had to earn a living, and so he went away to a rich land and became a teacher. And he was in that land for twelve years. After he made enough money, after twelve years, he went back to his wife and children. And he decided since he is going by the hamlet where the Berdichever Rebbe lived he would visit him. When he

---

[22] A prominent prayer said on Simhes Toyreh in connection with the Torah processions.

came to the Rebbe, the Rebbe was davening. After davening the Berdichever Rebbe asked him if he would like to come into the house for a snack, and so he went in and there was a little brandy on the table. And the Berdichever told him, "If you want, I will tell you a story. But if you want me to tell a story you will have to pay me three hundred coins." [23]

So he says, "All right, I'll pay you three hundred coins."

So the Berdichever told him: "There is a talmudic saying, that if you're journeying on the road and you come to a crossroads, you should turn to the right."

He waited and waited for more, but nothing happened, and the Berdichever said, "I'll tell you another story, but it will cost you another three hundred coins."

At first he did not want to give three hundred coins for the story because he saw what kind of story it was, but since it was the Berdichever, he decided to give another three hundred.

"The second story is, an old man and a young girl is half a death." And that is the second story that he told him. And the Rebbe said, "I will tell you another story for three hundred."

He does not want to go along with it and then decides he will.

The Rebbe told him a third story: "Do not believe what you do not see with your own eyes."

After these three stories, he left and on the way home he comes to a crossroad and he hears people running, running, running. Where are they running to? After a thief. So he thought to himself, "The Rebbe told me a story. I can't remember it. Let me try to remember." He remembered: "When you come to a crossroads always go to the right." So he tells the people to go to the right and they catch the thief.

And he went further and it became night, and he had to have a place to sleep. So he saw a house, and he thought he would sleep over there. But he saw that the house was dilapidated and wind-beaten and run-down, and he looked inside and he saw that the people did not have anything to eat themselves. And he thought, "I'm going to eat here and sleep here? It's not for me." And he went further till he came to a second house.

Finally he came home to his own town, and as he came close to his own house he saw a young boy go to his house, knock on the window, and go in through the window. He stayed a few hours and came out. Every night this young boy used to come home. After he

[23] See tale type 910B, Aarne and Thompson, *Types of the Folktale.*

went into his own house and saw his wife and children, it was a few years since he had last seen them, his wife explained that they had not had any money to pay the rent, and so the nobleman had taken one of their children as security. He was teaching him to be a soldier, but his mother told him that every night he should come home and she would teach him how to daven. And when he came home he paid up the rent and got back the child.[24]

YY, Lubavitch, Y

The Polish General's Letter (H21)

A lady had a sum of money hidden in the house. A troop of soldiers went by, and when she left the house they went into her house and one of them took the money. And she went to the Shpoler Zaideh, a student of the Maggid [of Mezrich], and he told her to go to the general of this army and tell him to line up his soldiers. "You will pass in front of the soldiers. The soldier who will say, 'Yid!' and spit, you will know he's the thief."

So she went to the general and he agreed to do it, "But on the condition that there can be no mistake; otherwise, it will be on your head."

She did it and one soldier said "Yid!" and spit as they passed, but he denied taking the money. So the general ordered him to be whipped. After one lash he confessed. So the general said, "You're a soldier who's not scared of lashes. How come you confess so soon?"

So he said, "As soon as you gave me the first lash I saw a man with a beard, holding a sword beneath me, saying, 'If you don't confess, I'll run you through.' " So he confessed and gave it back.

The general told this woman, "I suppose that your rabbi is a magic-maker. I order him to come to me to prove that he did it out of godliness and not out of magic."

So she went back to the Rebbe and told the Rebbe, "The general wants to see you. He's not satisfied."

The Rebbe answered, "I'm not going to the general. You go back to him and tell him this." This was the time when Russia was

---

[24] The situation described in the third incident had its real life parallels. See Dubnow, *History*, 1: 266.

fighting with Poland. "Yesterday you wrote two letters—one letter to the tsar telling him that all is well on the front, that you are winning the war; another letter you wrote to the Polish general agreeing to sell out your army to him. But you mixed up the envelopes, and you have already mailed the letter written to the Polish general to the tsar, but the letter addressed to the Polish general is still in your pocket."

She went back and told him, and he took out the envelope written to the Polish general but the tsar's letter was inside. So he understood that he mailed the letter to the tsar which was written to the Polish general. So he took out his gun and shot himself.[25]

M, Stolin, E

Handkerchiefs (H22)

The Shpoler Zaideh came into someone's store as if he had the intention of doing business. It was a dry goods store, and he went through the whole store, and said, "This isn't merchandise. Nothing is worth anything here." He saw a few handkerchiefs. He said, "This is merchandise," and he left.

A short time later there was a war. And when soldiers came into the city, they looted it. They came into his store, and they didn't take anything except the handkerchiefs and left.

B, Stolin, E

Ten Thousand Rubles (H23)

A hasid came to the Lubliner. He had no money. He had to make a marriage dowry for his daughter and he was down and out. The Lubliner sent him to a certain city and said, "Stay there and God will help you."

So he listened and he went. He went to an inn there. He found there the cheapest inn, sat there, and was learning. The innkeeper

[25] This tale is also told of the Rebbe of Kozhenits during the Napoleonic war. See Pipe, "Napoleon in Jewish Folklore," *YIVO Annual of Jewish Social Science*, 1 (1946): pp. 297–99.

saw that he was learning and became very friendly. He saw he was not doing any business. He said, "I don't understand it myself. The Rebbe sent me here—so here I am."

The innkeeper said, "Once I was very rich. I had ten thousand rubles in cash. But once I had to move. I had the ten thousand rubles in ten bundles, and I was ready to pack it into a trunk. But when I came back it wasn't there. I tried to find out who took it. It was no help."

While he was there, he saw that this innkeeper kept a teacher there for his children. He was a poor man but he supported him so that he could teach his children. The hasid became friendly with the teacher also. The teacher said, "I have to confide something very personal to you. I've always been poor. I worked for the innkeeper. He treated me very well. One day while moving he left out ten thousand rubles. I couldn't contain myself, and I took it. He came back and thought the servant took it. I should confess. As soon as I took it I was sorry, but I was ashamed. I couldn't give it back. I've been carrying it on my conscience. I don't know what to do. Maybe you could give it back to my employer."

"Okay." He took it. The next day he went back to the innkeeper, and he said, "Tell me the story again. What would happen if the money were found? Years have gone by. If I give it to you, would you ask any questions?"

"It's insane. It's past. The money's gone."

"Here. No questions."

"It's the same belt, the same money."

"You promised not to ask any questions."

But out of gratitude he gave him one of the packages. He went back to the Lubliner and was happy.

A, Stolin, E

Approval (H24)

This story is called "How the Alter Rebbe [Rabbi Shneur Zalman] Received the Approval for the *Tanya* from a Tsaddik Nistor." There lived in the city of Liozno a poor Jew who was a teacher. And every day his wife baked cakes, and on his way to teach the children, this Jew used to bring the cakes that his wife baked to the various households to sell them. You should remember that this was a very poor Jew and that he lived on the outskirts of the city.

Once, at night, a nobleman came to him, and he was frozen. The nobleman asked the Jew to let him in and the Jew let him in. He asked the children who were sleeping on the oven to get off and to let the nobleman sleep there.

Early in the morning when it became light, the nobleman got off the oven and went away. The Jew's children climbed on the oven and cried, "Papa, Papa, the nobleman has left his moneybelt."

The teacher went up there and he saw that the pocketbook was full of money. He didn't know what to do. It is a mitsveh to return what someone loses. He did not know what to do. So he thought he would go to the holy Baal ha-Tanya, Rabbi Shneur Zalman, and he would ask him what to do.

Rabbi Shneur Zalman told him, "You don't have to be afraid. It was a righteous gift that you found and the goy surely won't come back. You shouldn't feel any alarm. Enjoy the year." His wife could stop making cakes and after a year he should return to him.

After the year the Jew came back to the Baal ha-Tanya and asked him what to do, and the Baal ha-Tanya said it would be a good idea to open a store. The Jew opened the store, and as soon as he opened it he made out very well. He went back to the Rebbe again and asked what to do, and the Alter Rebbe said, "Why do you have to buy from the various tradesmen? You're better off to ride to Vitebsk and buy there." He listened and he rode to Vitebsk. But the Alter Rebbe warned him that every few months he should come to him. After a few months he went again to the Alter Rebbe and he told him, "Why should you go to Vitebsk? Go to Moscow and you can buy there." He went to Moscow, there was a bigger place, and he got more money and he bought goods cheaper. After a few months he became richer and richer—all from the money that he found. He went to the Alter Rebbe and the Alter Rebbe said, "Why do you have to go to Moscow, when you could go to Leipzig? There is a great market there a few times a year and you can travel there." The Jew went there and bought the merchandise he needed and he came back to Liozno and there he made a lot of money. Before he went the second time to Leipzig he went to the Alter Rebbe and the Alter Rebbe said, "When you come back this time bring me back a gift."

He went to Leipzig and looked for a present for the Alter Rebbe. While he was there he thought he would buy him a snuffbox. He bought him a beautiful silver snuffbox and he went back to Liozno to the Alter Rebbe. He gave him the gift and the Alter

Rebbe told him, "That's a beautiful present, but that isn't what I meant."

The Jew felt a little crestfallen. So he thought—the next time he goes he will buy him a golden snuffbox, and the Alter Rebbe will surely be satisfied. The next time he went he bought him a very beautiful snuffbox. It was so shiny that the Baal ha-Tanya used to look into it and see whether the tefillin were placed on the right spot on his forehead. (This is another story which I will not tell now—how beautiful it was.) He came back and gave the Alter Rebbe the box.

The Alter Rebbe said, "It's very beautiful, but it's still not what I meant. When you'll be in Leipzig the next time, go into a theater."

The Jew heard this and he said, "Whoever heard of going into a theater with so many bums? A religious Jew and especially a hasid?" But since the Alter Rebbe tells him to, he will go.

After a while he went to the city. He went to the theater and bought himself a good seat—a box seat. As soon as he came in he closed his eyes and fell asleep. The Jew fell asleep and he did not know the drama ended and the janitor was clearing the theater. The janitor saw him and woke him up and he said, "My fellow Jew, fellow Jew, please, please get up." And he saw that the janitor was also a Jew. The janitor gave him a greeting and said, "Where do you come from?"

And he gave him a greeting back. "I'm from Russia. I'm from Liozno."

"Oh, do you know Rabbi Zalman?"

"Reb Zalman? Who is Reb Zalman? I don't know a Reb Zalman."

"I think he's a Rabbi there."

"Oh, you mean the Alter Rebbe?"

So he said, "Yes."

He wondered how does a janitor come to know Reb Zalman?

He said, "When you see Reb Zalman again, tell him Carl sends regards."

Well, the Jew heard this, he put on his coat and left. When he came home he went to the Baal ha-Tanya. He asked him how he passed his time and he said, "I went to the theater."

And the Alter Rebbe said, "Did you meet anyone there?"

He said, "Yes, who knows, I met a Jewish man by the name of Carl who sends his regards.

The Alter Rebbe was very pleased. The next time he goes he should take the package that he will give him.

Well, it is understandable that this Jew went again. As soon as he came he went to the theater. It is understandable that traveling so far he was exhausted and so he fell asleep, and the same thing happened again. Everybody went out and the janitor came. The janitor woke him up and gave him a greeting again and the Jew said, "I have something for you. I didn't have your address so I had to come here. The Alter Rebbe gave me this package to give to you."

What was in the package? The Jew did not know. The janitor took the package. He told him, "Do whatever business you have to do, and before you go back in two weeks let us meet again."

He came back to the theater because he did not know Carl's address. He fell asleep again, and the janitor woke him up again, and he said, "Now I have a package for you, and now I'm going to give you my approval on this." He should come again. He gave him the package. And the Jew noticed that inside the packages were pages from the book of the Tanya, the book the Baal ha-Tanya had written for every Jew so that wherever he had to go he should serve Almighty God the way God ordained. It is for every-body—not only tsaddikim but for every Jew. So Carl looked on every sheet and said, "The Holy Spirit shines from every letter. I give my approval on this." With that Carl went away.

The Jew took the package and went to the Baal ha-Tanya and gave him the package and he said to him, "What does it mean that Carl has given his approval on this?"

The Baal ha-Tanya indicated that Carl is one of the thirty-six tsaddikim that are in every generation and can do great and right-eous deeds for the Lord of Israel. The Baal ha-Tanya had to go to that tsaddik nistor, that Carl, to receive his approval.

The only way to know if a story is true is if it has testimony from witnesses—that is, true witnesses. This story has been passed by hundreds of people. I heard this story from Rabbi Bernstein from Montreal and from other people also.

D, Lubavitch, Y

Hasides (H25)

Reb Iser Homler was by the Alter Rebbe [Rabbi Shneur Zalman]. The Rebbe used to say hasides to his daughter Freydkeh quite frequently. One time, it was either on a Shabbes or a holiday, he was there when the Rebbe said hasides to his daughter Freydkeh. The daughter Freydkeh was a weak little girl, and around her house there were many gardens. So the hasidim thought that when the Rebbe would say hasides to his daughter, they would stand on the trees and the bushes and listen through the window to the hasides that the Alter Rebbe was going to say.

When the Alter Rebbe heard that he was afraid they were going to break something. He said, "Why don't hasidim learn *Tanya* better?" And he grabbed the Mitteler Rebbe by the collar and asked, "Why don't you learn *Tanya* better? From *Tanya* the hasidim can become like our father Abraham."

N, Lubavitch, Y

Gehenna (H26)

This story is about Reb Noah. He was a student of Lubavitch. He died and he came to the Court of Heaven. They looked into his case and they found out that all his life he had observed everything that he should in the highest way. Angels came who were born from his good deeds and they were witnesses for him: "I was born from this good deed." [26] Thousands of angels came who had been born from the good deeds of this tsaddik. And the Court was going to decide that he should go immediately to Paradise.

All of a sudden an angel appeared and he said, "Wait a second! I have to tell something about him." And he said, "I was created from one bad deed that this tsaddik did in his lifetime." And he brought out what he did.

The Court of Heaven deliberated and they said he should have either one half hour in Gehenna or he should be reborn on earth to fix what he had failed to do the first time. Reb Noah answered the court that all his life everything that he had to decide he asked his Rebbe. He never did anything without asking the Rebbe; therefore, he wanted to ask the Rebbe to tell now what he should decide. They looked over his records in the Court of Heaven and they

[26] According to Jewish tradition, after death one's good and bad deeds take the roles of defenders and accusers (see Ginzberg, *Legends*, 5: 70; Newman and Spitz, *Hasidic Anthology*, p. 261, no. 16). There are said to be angels for each blessing (see Buber, *Tales*, 1: 62, 194).

found out that he was right. Everything he did he asked the Rebbe's permission.

The Rebbe, Rabbi Shneur Zalman, was sitting with his hasidim and he said to them, "Reb Noah is asking now what he should select: either Gehenna, a half hour of hell, or be reborn in this world a second time." They had nothing to say. They were waiting. And the Rebbe put his holy hand on his forehead and he rested his head on the table a short time. Then he said: "Gehenna . . . Gehenna." [27] In the second when the Rebbe said the word Gehenna, they heard a voice, "Oy, Rebbe!" And they saw on the wall by the door, the mark of a burned hand—the fingers of a hand burned into the wall.[28]

And do you know that I know the family of this Reb Noah? [29]

V, Lubavitch, E

The Curse (H27)

This was in the time after the separation of the hasidim and misnagdim. One day a person called Reb Areleh wanted to go to the grave of the Alter Rebbe [Rabbi Shneur Zalman], and the caretakers of the grave did not want to let him in. So he crept up on top of the window, and he fell downstairs where the grave was. When he fell by the grave he yelled: "Oy, Rebbe." After that the caretakers would not let him out. They wanted to get back at him. He went on the side, somebody broke open the lock and he went out of the grave. As he went out, he cursed the town and since then the whole town has suffered as a result.

LL, Lubavitch, Y

Milev the Hasid (H28)

There was once a man named Milev Hasid. Hasid is a name. You know, around here everybody who dresses like a religious person, with peyes, they call him Hasid. In olden times Hasid was a

[27] See *In Praise of the Besht*, no. 137, in which a martyr decides not to be reincarnated since it could jeopardize his chance of entering heaven.

[28] Compare M6.

[29] Reb Noah's son married the daughter of Rabbi Shneur Zalman. The son born of their union was the Tsemah Tsedek.

big, big title. Today you don't find a great Rebbe like that. In the
olden times it wasn't a shame to be called Hasid. It was a big title.
Reb Milev they called Reb Milev Hasid. Why did they call him
Reb Milev Hasid? He was sitting by the Kozhenitser Maggid, a
very great Rebbe. He was sitting day and night by the Kozhenitser
Maggid, just learning.

He had a mother. She said, "Having such a son I'll live where he
is living." His mother lived in another city but she came to Kozhenits and she just stayed there. When this Reb Milev would come
home she would be able to cook for him a piece of chicken, he
should eat, he should be healthy. This was her whole life—her only
son.

In those times the Cossacks would go around catching people
and put them in the army. So Milev was going in the morning to
daven and those Cossacks went by. They just grabbed him and put
him in the army. His mother found out what happened, her only
son, Milev, and she ran to the Kozhenitser, "Milev, my Milev, they
took him into the army. Milev, my Milev."

So the Rebbe said, "Don't be afraid. Milev is not going to the
army."

So she understood what the Rebbe meant. Milev would not be a
soldier. He will come back.

But she said, "My Milev, my Milev if he's even one minute with
the Cossacks, they'll hit him, they'll kill him, and he's so noble, so
sensitive. No, I want my Milev."

"Look, I told you Milev is not going to be a soldier."

She just fell to the floor and begged him, "No, I want to see him
right now. I want to see Milev back right now."

So the shammes brought the Rebbe coffee before davening. So
the Rebbe said, "What do you want? I'm not going to drink the
coffee until Milev is going to come back. What else do you want?
I'm not going to drink the coffee until Milev is going to come
back."

So she knew that for the Rebbe to drink the coffee is a very big
sin. So they sent out people very far to see if Milev is coming back.
If the Rebbe said so. . . .

Well, the wagon went away. So they are looking. You know
they sent one person ten feet, another twenty feet, one should
report to the other one. One was looking at the other—Milev might
come in. One, two, about five minutes pass: "Yeah. Hey, Milev is
coming!" So they told the Rebbe, the Kozhenitser Maggid, "Thank
God, Milev is here." You can imagine his mother, how she was.

Then all the hasidim went over to Milev. "What happened? Tell us the story. What happened? How did you get off?" So he told them:

"When the Cossacks went with the wagon and horses, I saw just after the wagon a man is walking. The wagon is moving at a fast speed. You know, they had about twenty horses tied to the wagon, and this man just walks by the wagon, and he says, 'Milev, come down. Milev, come down.' "

And this man who was walking by the wagon, most probably Elijah the Prophet [30] or who knows who, screamed to Milev, "Come down."

So Milev said, "I'm not going to go down. There's another Jew on this wagon. If you take him down too, I'll go."

So the man said, "No, I don't want him. I want you. Come down."

"I'm not going to go down. If you take him, I'll go. If not, I'm staying." That is what Milev said.

This Jew just disappeared. Five more minutes went by and he comes again. "Milev, come down," he says.

"No, I'm not going to come down unless you take this Jew."

So he says, "Take him. Take him. You come on. Come out."

So Milev said, "I took this Jew and we went down and the Cossacks didn't hear. We just went down from the wagon. Nobody heard. I don't know what happened, and this Jew disappeared. And that's what happened."

So the Kozhenitser Maggid said, "Obstinate. Because of your refusing, my coffee got cold," he says.

Then they called him Milev Hasid. Because this is a high degree of holiness. He had said, "No I'm not going down. I don't want it should be a favor for me alone." The Kozhenitser Maggid prayed to God, He should help him. "No, I'm not going to go down till you take him." That's why they called him Hasid: he didn't care about himself.

X, Bobov, E

[30] Elijah is the saint who appears most often to help Jews in trouble. The greatest number of hero tales in the Ethnological Museum and Folklore Archives in Haifa concern Elijah (Noy, "Archiving and Presenting Folk Literature in an Ethnological Museum," *Journal of American Folklore*, 75 [1962]: 24). See *In Praise of the Besht*, no. 53, and TA14; see also Beatrice S. Weinreich, "Genres and Types of Yiddish Folk Tales about the Prophet Elijah," *The Field of Yiddish*, pp. 202–31.

The Opposition (H29)

This story I heard from the previous [Lubavitcher] Rebbe, in Leningrad. It was during Lag Baomer [31] in the city of Leningrad, in the year of 1925 or 1926.

This took place in the town of Veneh. The rabbi of that town was a relative of the Rebbe. He had opposition from two rich men and a rich woman. So he sent a letter to the Mitteler Rebbe [Rabbi Dov Baer, the second Lubavitcher Rebbe] who was at that time in Karlsbad, in Russia. He sent a letter telling him the whole story and the Rebbe sent him back a letter. The Rebbe wrote back like this: The first rich man should have deep regret immediately and God will forgive him. To the other rich man he said he should "be careful, lest we come out and meet you with a sword." [32] To the rich woman he wrote back that "the only wisdom of a woman is from her sewing." [33]

So the letter came to the shul and after the prayers he showed the letter to everyone. The first rich man, who the Rebbe said if he has deep regret immediately God will forgive him, answered, "What good do I have actually from bothering them?"

The second rich man said sarcastically, "A new general has sprung up overnight."

The woman wasn't in shul.

When they were going home from shul, the second rich man noticed that there were Cossacks in town and he said, "How do Cossacks come to the town of Veneh?" And one of the Cossacks took out his sword and cut off his head.

The rich woman had a liquor business. She sold liquor. You had to pay certain taxes to the government and in a short time the government investigated her. They found she didn't pay her taxes, and they took away her whole business. [34]

---

[31] The thirty-third day in the time of Omer, i.e., the counting of the days between Passover and the Feast of Weeks.

[32] See Numbers 20: 18.

[33] See Babylonian Talmud, *Yoma* 66b; Exod. 35:25.

[34] Compare *In Praise of the Besht*, no. 67, in which the Maggid Yitshok Drabizner accused a woman of confiscating goods. Her baby dies. Those who try to revenge themselves on the Maggid also die (see *In Praise of the Besht*, no. 20, concerning the man who became a spirit because he had mocked the hasidim).

Then the news came back to the Mitteler Rebbe what had happened.

J, Lubavitch, Y

Mud (H30)

Reb Motel of Tchernobl went with his students one night. It was a very cold night. They went into a town and they rested there. One of his students told him that in the town there was a very rich man, and other wealthy people used to spend the night at his house. This rich person had a nice house, but he was very stingy, and he did not invite poor people to spend the night with him. But they thought that since Reb Motel of Tchernobl was there he would invite him in because he was such a great man. They went to the house of this rich person and knocked at the door. As was his custom, he did not open the door, but Reb Motel of Tchernobl went himself and knocked at the door, and they noticed somebody looking through the window. When he saw it was Reb Motel Tchernobl, he opened the door and he said hello and he bestowed many honors on him. Reb Motel Tchernobl told him that he was not there alone, but that he had a whole group of students with him, and he will have to take them in the house also. So the rich man looked at the students and saw that they had dirt and dust on their feet and he asked, "How can I take them in? They'll dirty the whole house."

So Reb Motel Tchernobl said: "I will tell you a story. Once upon a time there was a rich man who was also very stingy. He also did not allow anyone in his house. Once on a journey he saw another family traveling, and the family got stuck in the mud. Their wagon had turned over, and he had pity on another Jewish family and he went out from his wagon to help them. He took the family with the children in his wagon and went further on his way.

"After many years he died and came into the next world and made an account of what he did in this world. He had many things against him on his record: that he was a rich man and he did not take people into his house. Then one angel came and said, 'Once this man helped a Jewish soul. And not only one soul, but many souls!' They saw this good thing that he did and this thing was very weighty. This is one of the big mitsves, and this thing that he did made the balance even. Then there came a small, thin angel and he said that this man had another good merit—that if you take the mud from those people and put it on the other side of the scale it will outweigh all the other things. This was the mud from helping those Jewish people. So he said, 'Even though he still does not have enough things to outweigh the bad deeds he had done, send him down to this world once again and see if he holds this Jewish mud very dear to him. Then he can win his case.' "

So when Motel of Tchernobl told this rich man the story, fear fell upon him and he said, "Come in, Yiden. The more the merrier. The more mud you bring in, the better to save me." [35]

LL, Lubavitch, Y

The Little Horse (H31)

Reb Motel of Tchernobl was once in a place, and he was sitting and talking with a man. So he told the man, "Let me see your books for your business—who owes you money, who you owe money. I want to look them over."

"No, I'm afraid I would not like that."

First he showed him around the whole place. He showed him all his farm, his cows, his horses. There was a small horse. You know he had a big load but he kept up with seven other horses.

So Reb Motel told the man, "Maybe you want to give me this small horse as a donation."

So he said, "I would give you three other horses except this small one. This small one does more work than ten other horses. I can't give you this small one."

He started begging, "Give it to me, give it to me."

He didn't want to give it. "I'll give you everything that you want except this horse."

"All right." Then he went in the room. He said, "Let me see your books in which you figure the business." So he showed him the books. "And who is this?"

"This man he owes me so much and so much."

"Who is this?" He asked about everybody. Then he came to one. There was three hundred dollars. "Who is this?"

[35] This tale is also told of the Rizhyner. Newman and Spitz, *Hasidic Anthology*, p. 169, no. 9. Mud is used to save the soul of a driver who pushed the wheels of a tsaddik's wagon from the mud, thereby enabling him to reach shul before sundown on the Shabbes (Gross, *Maaselech un Mesholim*, pp. 152–54).

"Oh, that three hundred dollars I'll never get back any more. He died and he was a poor man. His children haven't got any money. I won't get paid back this money."

So he said, "Maybe you want to give me those three hundred dollars. Give me a donation. You say you wouldn't get it any more. Give it to me. That means that this man doesn't owe you no more."

He said, "Why not? All right."

"That means that this man doesn't owe you no more."

So he said, "That's right." So he crossed it out.

As he was crossing it out a man came running in from the farm. He said, "The small horse fell down and he died." The small horse fell down and he was dead.

So the man got so excited. He ran here and there. He started moving the horse, "Hey!" It wasn't alive. So he came in after that. "Oh Rebbe, you know what happened? The small horse that the Rebbe wanted before died."

"So what do you want? The man doesn't owe you any more—no more horse." He didn't understand what he was saying to him. "You see this man owed you three hundred dollars. He came up to the other world and he didn't pay you. He didn't finish what he was supposed to. So God decreed he should work for you. His soul was born in a horse and he worked for you. You forgave him what he owed you, and so the horse died. So why do you want the horse?" That's what he said.[36]

X, Bobov, E

The Cloak (H32)

The Hasam Soyfer lived about a hundred years ago.[37] Officially he was not a hasid. He was an Ashkenazi. But, actually, one of his Rebbes [the Frankfurter] was a big hasid and he had many things from hasidim. He actually was accepted very widely by the hasidim too.[38]

One day a religious person did something very nasty; in fact, it was something very nasty business-wise. It was really something

[36] See *In Praise of the Besht*, no. 215, for a tale of a man reincarnated as a horse to redeem a debt. Sholem Asch used the tale in his novel *A Passage in the Night* (see especially pp. 14–15, 37–38).

[37] Hasam Soyfer (Hatam Sopher), d. 1839.

[38] The teacher of the Hasam Soyfer was Rabbi Nossen Adler, d. 1800.

that would be nasty even if you would not be religious, but it was especially so if you were religious. So a man came in to him, probably it was a government official or something, and told him, "All religious people are crooks."

So he says, "Well, you just contradicted yourself, and I'll prove it to you with a parable." He said: "There was once a very wealthy man who lived out of the town a couple of miles, and he was quite wealthy and he had a lot of gold and jewelry. One night about three o'clock at night he hears a knock at the door. He says, 'Who is it?'

" 'The Police Department.'

"He sees a whole bunch of policemen come in and he asks them, 'What do you want?'

"So he says, 'Well, you didn't pay taxes and we've come to seize all your belongings.'

"This fellow is screaming, 'What are you telling me stories I didn't pay taxes? I know I paid all my taxes.'

"So he said, 'Don't tell it to us. Tell it to the judge. We have an order to take your goods. We will take your goods. We'll give you a receipt for it and tomorrow go and tell the judge.'

"So he says, 'Okay, take it. What do I care? I know I'll prove it. I'll show him my receipts.' So they took all his valuables, all his insurance and they left.

"The next morning he wasn't even in a hurry. He comes into town and he walks into the police station and says, 'Oh yes,' and shows them the receipt. 'Last night you sent policemen to grab all my valuables because I didn't pay taxes. Here are my receipts. I paid taxes.'

"So the police chief says, 'Well I never sent any police. We never sent anybody for you. It's some kind of mistake. There were some impostors. They pretended that they were police.'

"So he started screaming, 'The policemen, they're crooks and they're robbers,' and this and that.

"So the police chief said, 'No, it just proves that policemen are honest. When policemen came to the door—what happened? You knew a policeman was honest, and so you gave him the goods. So what does an impostor do? Because he knows policemen are honest, he went and he dressed up as a policeman, put on a police badge to show you that he's honest so that you should give him all your belongings. But actually policemen are honest. It was just a bunch of crooks that dressed up in police uniforms.' "

So the Hasam Soyfer said, "The same thing is true for religious people. Religious people are honest. But if somebody who is dishonest wants to fool the people, he dresses himself in the cloak of religious people and he pretends that he is religious."

S, Klausenberg, E

The Pogrom (H33)

This is a story concerning Moshe Al-Sheikh.[39] He lived about 500 years ago, but this happened later in Russia. This happened during the times of the pogroms. The goyim had surrounded the Jewish community and they were going to slaughter the Jews. The rabbi knew that there was nothing to do and he felt very bad, and from weakness, from sorrow and despair, he fell asleep. He dreamed that a man came to him and said he was Moshe Al-Sheikh, and he said, "Since you learned my works so well, I am able to tell you of a secret way out of the city that no one knows about." And the rabbi was able to save the people.

BB, Slonim, Y

The Trumpet (H34)

During a hard time for Jews all the rabbis declared a day of fasting. The Rizhyner went out, and in his court he had a gate of real gold. He stood there and called three times for music. He told the musicians to play three times. Three times he stood behind the gate.

When they told the Apter Rov how the Rizhyner conducted himself on that day, he told them, "This is the meaning of what is written in the Bible, 'If your enemies will come upon you [meaning Israel] you shall blow a trumpet and God will help you.' " [40]

After he did this, all the restraints the tsar had ordered were abolished. I don't know if he fasted that day or not.

Q, Tchortkov, E

[39] Moshe Al-Sheikh: a talmudic rabbi (approximate dates 1507–1600) who was a pupil of Joseph Caro of Safed.
[40] For the warlike use of trumpets see Num. 10:1–10, 31:6; II Chron. 13:12–15.

The Soldier (H35)

I heard the story several times from different people. The story is
as follows: There was a little village in Europe by the name of
Rizhyn, and there lived Rabbi Israel Rizhyn. What does it mean to
be a great tsaddik? A great tsaddik is a Jew who learns a great deal
and who becomes a holy man. And a great many Jews become his
hasidim.

One time there came to him a couple, a man and a woman. They
were married a long time but did not have any children. They
asked that the Rebbe pray for them that they should have a child.
The Rebbe heard the tale of their broken heart and sympathized
with them. And he prayed that after a year they should have a son.
If a tsaddik prays for you, as the Gemoreh says, then God hears his
prayers. And after a year the couple had a child.

The child developed miraculously, very beautiful and well behaved. This child of a year old behaved miraculously, not like
children of his age. Time passed and the child was three to four
years old and he became ill. And doctors gave him up. They could
not help him at all. Naturally the mother went to the Rebbe again,
as he had prayed for the child before, and she poured out her
aching heart again, saying that the child is not well and that the
doctors gave up the child for lost.

The holy tsaddik, Rabbi Israel Rizhyn, told her again, "Go
home and your child with God's help will surely get well again."

The mother, having great faith in the tsaddik, went home with
great hope that her child will get well again. When she got home
she found the child in the same condition as before. She sat down
near the child's cradle, and when she discovered the child in the
same condition as before she began to cry. As she was crying she
fell asleep by the cradle. She woke up from sleep and saw a soldier
holding a bottle in one hand and a spoon in the other hand. And she
saw how the soldier was pouring from the bottle into the spoon,
and giving the child to drink. She knew that the door was closed
and no one could come in. But here a soldier is standing. She
became very frightened and began to scream. And as she began to
scream the soldier fled. From that time on the child began to get
better and better. Out of thankfulness she went back to the Rebbe
to thank him for the great wonder that he showed her.

So Rabbi Israel Rizhyn said, "I'll tell you who the soldier was."
And Rabbi Israel began to tell a marvelous story. "Years ago there

was a child, an orphan, who nobody wanted. He lost his parents. And he was brought up among goyim. Naturally he did not have an orthodox upbringing, nor even a general Jewish upbringing. He did not know that he was a Jew. By a coincidence when he grew up he realized that he was a Jew. When he was older he joined the Army. Naturally they took him in the Army and he stayed there a few years. Once, all the soldiers, about a hundred soldiers, were sent by their General to a certain village. And as they were soldiers their behavior was not of the best. They attacked the people in the village and killed seventy people. On the way back they met a Jew who seemed to be poor. As they were afraid of his informing on them, they hung him on a tree, and if he had not been saved he would have died. This soldier," said Rabbi Israel Rizhyn, "who was by the bedside of your child was among the hundred soldiers, and when he saw that they were hanging the man he resolved to save this man. He must save this Jew. He was also afraid that if they saw him saving this man he would probably be hung also. He went a short distance and he slipped away from the company and he went to save this Jew. The other ninety-nine soldiers did not notice that he was missing and they went further. Coming to their camp their officer counted them to see if they were all there, and they discovered that one of their number was missing. And he began to inquire about that soldier. They said they did not know his whereabouts nor when he ran away. So he sent a few soldiers looking for him. Going back they saw that he was walking with this Jew and they realized that he had saved this man. Not only that but he had returned the money that was taken from him. The man escaped and the soldier was hung.

"When he came to the Heavenly Court, in the bosom of his fathers, they did not know what to do with him. They decided that a Jew who saves another saves the world. But to send him to Paradise? He was a plain man and not worthy of what is received in Paradise.

"So the Court decided that as long as he saved a Jew his work should be to save children's lives." And Rabbi Israel explained that this was the soldier who also saved the child. And the bottle that he held in his hand was a healing medicine. And so the child was saved. The woman was very thankful and went home.

And that is the end of the story. What can we learn from this story? Many things. Firstly, we can learn the strength that resides within a holy man which makes him more spiritual and holy. Just as in those times it is the same in these times: if you pray to God you will be saved. From this story one should learn that one does not live for one's self but must help others and be religious and serve the Almighty.[41]

YY, Lubavitch, Y

Wealth (H36)

Now I will tell you a story of Reb Meirl of Premishlan. It once happened that a hasid came to Reb Meirl and the hasid said, "I need three hundred rubles. I have a daughter who I have to marry off, and a few children for whom I haven't paid the teacher for some time."

So Reb Meirl wrote a note on a piece of paper, and he gave it to him and he said: "Go to this particular wealthy person and tell him to give you three hundred rubles on my account."

"Why should the Rebbe send you to me? Do I owe the Rebbe three hundred rubles? What business do I have with the Rebbe?" The wealthy man said, "I'll give you fifty."

So the man replied, "What do you mean fifty? The Rebbe said three hundred."

He bargained, and finally offered to give one hundred.

So he told him, "I don't want to do any business with you. Either give the whole amount or not."

He took the note back to the Rebbe and told him the story. The Rebbe says, "Okay."

"What can I do?"

"Go to a different wealthy man."

And he took the note and went to the second man. This wealthy person also did not have too much money on hand, but as soon as he saw the note from the Rebbe, he said, "Sit down. I'll go out and get you some money." And he went and pawned all his valuables—whatever he could lay his hands on. It took a whole day till he got the money together. Finally, by night he raised the money and brought him the three hundred rubles, and he gave him extra money for the journey too.

After a few months there came to the Rebbe a poverty-stricken young man with torn shoes. "Why did you do it to me? I offered one hundred. A fire had to strike my house and burn everything down?"

---

[41] In a variant bereft of the supernatural, a soldier explains how he became a doctor (Newman and Spitz, *Hasidic Anthology*, p. 318:4).

So the Rebbe said, "I'll tell you a story. Listen, when Reb Meirl was supposed to come down to this world, he was asked, 'Meirl, what do you want?'

"He said, 'I want twenty-five thousand rubles.'

"He was asked, 'Meirl, what do you need twenty-five thousand rubles for?'

"So he answered, 'I'll take the money and give it away to five balebatim [householders], and whenever a poor man will come to me I'll tell one of my balebatim who is holding my money in trust to give him a few hundred rubles.' And I picked out a few balebatim and you were one of those. But when I ask you for my three hundred rubles, you say, 'What kind of business do I have with you?' You don't want to give it up. In other words you're dishonest. So I took away the money that I put in your trust and I gave it to somebody else. What can I do? The only thing I can do is invite you to stay in my house and I'll give you food and support you because you're a poor man."

I heard it was a court case and Reb Meirl held a trial to see whether they should take away the money from that Jew or not, and it was decided that Reb Meirl had a right to take away the money that belonged to him and give it to somebody else. But they added that still it is a pity on that Jew and he should support him for his lifetime.

YY, Lubavitch, Y

All His Sins (H37)

In the time of Reb Meirl of Premishlan there was in a village a couple, and she was a pious and honest Jewish woman. He was a boy from the streets. And, do not even think of it, they did not have children. The woman heard of the wonderful stories of Meirl of Premishlan, and she pleaded with her husband that he should go with her to the Rebbe. The man laughed at her. He did not believe in any Rebbes. She went alone. She came to the Rebbe and asked the Rebbe to help her.

Reb Meirl replied, "I can't help you unless your husband comes."

She cried, "My man will not come to a Rebbe."

"Go home and tell your husband that Reb Meirl said that he

should come, and as a sign he should appear, tell him that in the market on such and such day, in this street, in this hour, he committed a sin." He told exactly what he did.

She came home and told it to her husband. The husband realized that this is no ordinary thing. He decided that he would go to the Rebbe. But how can he tell his friends from the street that he is going to the Rebbe. They will laugh at him. He told them that he is going to Leipzig for business. He came to the Rebbe and he wanted to greet him.

The Rebbe said, "When one comes to Reb Meirl one says one is going to Reb Meirl. One does not say that one is going to Leipzig. Go home and tell your friends that you are coming to the Rebbe and then you can come."

He now saw that the Rebbe knew everything that happened to him. He went home and told his friends that he is going to travel to the Rebbe.

When he came to the Rebbe it was the eve of Yom Kippur. The Rebbe greeted him and he said to the Rebbe, "I am a very sick Jew. Doctors don't permit me to fast on Yom Kippur."

The Rebbe said, "Good, but you should not eat before I tell you to eat."

The eve after Kol Nidrei came and then it was after the evening prayer. The Rebbe says, "It's not so terrible. You can wait until the morning." In the morning the Rebbe said, "You can wait a little while longer." And then after the morning prayer he did not have any strength. When it came to the additional prayer,[42] however, the Rebbe pressed him on just a little further. "You will soon eat." Then when it came to the concluding prayer, just before it came to nileh, the concluding prayer, the Jew felt renewed vigor. He did not feel weak and he fasted a whole day.

After the fasting Reb Meirl said, "You were ill and did not have children because you did not fast. Fasting on Yom Kippur is medicine for you."

Later he came home and he was blessed with children and he remained firmly tied to Reb Meirl.

In the meantime, being one of his hasidim, Reb Meirl told this Jew who had become a hasid, "As you live on the border between Poland and Russia, there will come a time that a tsaddik will have to run away from Poland and you will be the one who will have to save him."

[42] The additional prayer (musaf) is usually said some time between twelve and three in the afternoon.

Years later when he was a little older he heard that the Russian Rebbe [Israel of Rizhyn] had to flee from Russia.[43] He went to Russia and he met the escaping Russian Rebbe. He spoke to him and he put him on his shoulders, and he carried him through the woods. Going through the woods he saw from afar that there was a hut containing the border guards. He told the Rebbe, "You remain here and I will go to them." He came to the guards and they were playing cards. He asked if he could play with them.

They said, "Yes."

"So we'll play." He knew how to play cards. When he started to play he realized that he should lose and so they won everything. They became good friends with him. Talking in this way he brought up the question and said to them, "You know I have a Russian rabbi there in the woods, and I want to take him across the border."

They said to him, "You can. You can take him."

While carrying the Rebbe, he said, "Rebbe, I have saved you. What will I receive for this?"

The Rebbe said, "I tell you that you will have the world to come only if you inform your children that as soon as you die they should let me know."

Time passed by. The Jew became old and he died. And the children remembered what he had said, and they immediately ran to the Russian Rebbe and told him that their father is dead. The Russian Rebbe went to the window and began to recite all the sins that the Jew had committed. He did not keep Shabbes, he ate treyf, he did not put on tefillin. He started to recall all the sins that he had committed.

The hasidim said to him, "Rebbe, have pity for a Jew who saved your life. How do you repay him with such an account?"

The Rebbe answered, "Every Jew must repent of his sins before he dies. Sometimes a Jew dies before he has the opportunity to repent. It is good that someone else can repent for him. I recounted all his sins as a favor to him. I promised him the world to come and I am keeping my word."

M, Stolin, Y

[43] In 1838 Rabbi Israel of Rizhyn was arrested by the Russian authorities and sent to prison for twenty-two months. After his release, he fled to Jassy, Romania, and then moved to Sadeger in Austria, where he reestablished his court. See Horodezky, *Religiöse Strömungen im Judentum*, pp. 208–11.

The Unsigned Letter (H38)

Reb Hillel Parakher was a big hasid of the Tsemah Tsedek.[44] At that time the Russian government began to persecute the Tsemah Tsedek. It was against the law to have a farbrengen. They were going to arrest him and send him to jail. He had to send off a letter and have it signed by three rabbis that he was not breaking the law.

The shammes wrote the letter. In it he said things that were not true—that the Rebbe didn't follow hasides. The Rebbe wanted Reb Hillel to sign it because he was an important hasid. He gave him the letter and Reb Hillel said, "I raised the pen and put the point of the pen on the paper and stopped. How can I sign it if it isn't true?"

The Tsemah Tsedek said, "Is it better I should be arrested and sent to Siberia?"

He put his pen to the paper and stopped again. "I can't." He could not do it. It was impossible.

He became sick. He had a fever from worry and being upset. He could not do what the Rebbe asked.

The Tsemah Tsedek came to see him and he told him that he had a fever. The Tsemah Tsedek said, "If your head is so hot take off your hat and wear a second yarmelkeh." It was his custom to wear two hats.

Reb Hillel said, "Rebbe, give me your yarmelkeh." The Rebbe did and he became well.[45]

OO, Lubavitch, Y

The Letter (H39)

Reb Hillel Parakher had a custom, never to mail a letter after noon on Friday. He did not want to send a letter on Shabbes.

[44] Rabbi Hillel Parakher, d. 1864.
[45] See *In Praise of the Besht*, no. 212. After the Besht had a sick man hold his stick and wear his hat, the man walked to a minyen for the first time in ten years.

Once the Tsemah Tsedek told him to send a letter in the afternoon. He did it because the Rebbe said so. But on Monday the Rebbe said, "You see, though all the letters were taken away, the letter that Reb Hillel Parakher mailed Friday afternoon was left in the box."

OO, Lubavitch, Y

The Winter Way (H40)

Haim's grandfather came from Dubrovna. The Tsemah Tsedek sent him to Nechenka, a Polish city, to be a rabbi. He was there three-fourths of a year and he had fights because it was Polish and he was Russian. So he wanted to leave. The Tsemah Tsedek sent him money and told him which route to take. You have to come from this town to Lubavitch and there he would give him money. Haim's mother was still a girl at the time. They went to Lubavitch and from Lubavitch they had to go some place further and the Rebbe told them to go the summer route on the road rather than the winter route on the ice. To go on ice is easier but he told them to go on the summer route and not the winter way.

The mother fell asleep (Haim's mother was yet a girl) and while she was asleep the coachman went on the ice. The girl noticed it and awoke her mother, and the mother told him to go back to the right road. So he obeyed and he went back. As they went they heard the sound of a big wagon traveling on the ice and it fell into the water. They were going on the summer route and they heard another wagon going on the winter route fall through the ice. Then they understood why the Rebbe said they should travel on the summer route.

YY, Lubavitch, Y

The Well (H41)

A certain youth came to the Tsemah Tsedek, and as he was approaching the home of the Tsemah Tsedek in Lubavitch he heard a lot of noise coming from behind the Tsemah Tsedek's house. He went over to see what was happening. He saw a group of children around a well. The well had a wheel on top and a bucket attached to that wheel, and a small boy, who later on turned out to be the Maharash, was lowering children in the bucket into the well and taking them up. Sometimes they paid him and sometimes they did not. So he said to the Maharash, "Could you lower me into the well and then take me out?"

"Yes," he answered.

"I don't think that a small boy like you could lift me up."

So the Maharash answered, "I can take you down and lift you up."

Time passed and this youth got married, had children, and became a wealthy and successful businessman. For one reason or another he had trouble with the government, and the government wanted to confiscate his property and arrest him. So he came running to Lubavitch. The Tsemah Tsedek was no longer alive, and the Maharash was now Rebbe. He wrote a note to the Rebbe explaining the circumstances and asking the Rebbe to help him.

The Rebbe said, "I can't help you."

So he became angry and he said, "You once promised me that you could pull me up."

So the Rebbe said, "If I promised you, I will fulfill my obligations. Go home and everything will be all right."

When he came home he found out that the papers and all the evidence had burned and so he escaped.

YY, Lubavitch, Y

The Chief of Police (H42)

A man sold wood across the border. This way he avoided taxes. The police were after him. He was expecting a big order. It was on its way and he heard there was a trap set for him. The wood would be confiscated and he would be arrested. He went to the Rebbe— Rabbi Menahem Mendel.

"What should I do?"

The Rebbe said, "Take counsel with three other Jews and see what they say."

He spoke together with three friends. They looked at one another, and they did not know what to do. Finally, one said, "The only thing that will save you is if the chief of police drops dead."

He went back to the Lubavitcher Rebbe.

"What did they say?"

"They said I will be saved only if the police chief drops dead."

"Okay. I say so too." That was all.

The night the shipment came that was due. The chief of police and his men were on the river bank waiting. It was due at midnight. The police chief took out his gold watch to look at the time and he dropped it in the river. It was a valuable watch. He dove into the river after it and was drowned.

See? The Rebbe knows what he wants to say, but he prefers to have three Jews to work it out themselves and then agree with them.

LL, Lubavitch, Y

The Grave (H43)

There was a woman in Paris who was not so well, and a Mr. C. wrote to Rabbi M. that a woman was very sick in Paris. So Rabbi M. wrote to the Rebbe one time. Then he got a letter from Paris that she was not well, and so he wrote him a second time. The day after he wrote to the Rebbe he received a letter from Paris saying that the woman died. So he wrote to the Rebbe that she died, and he also wrote to the Rebbe that in the time of the Tsemah Tsedek one of his hasidim became very sick so his son went to the Rebbe to ask him for a blessing. And the son told the Tsemah Tsedek that his father asked him if the Tsemah Tsedek would answer the father in a letter. So the Tsemah Tsedek wrote a letter and the son brought it home.

When he came home he found that his father had already passed away. They opened up the letter from the Rebbe and it said in it: "The Almighty should send you *refuoh shlemoh bekever* [you should recover completely in the grave]. The correct saying is *refuoh shlemoh bekorov* [you should recover completely in a short time]."

MM, Lubavitch, Y

We Small Fish (H44)

A hasid of the Tsemah Tsedek saw that the Tsemah used a pitcher with three handles to wash his hands. He thought to do the same thing.

The Tsemah said, "For you, two handles are sufficient." [46]

The hasid said, "No, heaven protects great men like you, but we small fish have to look after ourselves."

OO, Lubavitch, Y

The Officer: (I) (H45)

During the reign of the Stoliner Rebbe, Reb Aaron Karliner—who is also called the Beis Aaron or the Alter Rebbe because during his period, his son, Reb Asher, was also Rebbe, and he was called the Yunger Rebbe—during their time, in tsarist Russia they would at times kidnap very young children from their homes and raise them in military schools for the tsar's army. So it happened that one of the hasidim who was attached to the Yunger Rebbe—his son was kidnapped and taken away into the tsar's service.

---

[46] There are customarily just two handles on the pitcher. The ritual of hand washing is described by Langer. "We perform this duty [washing of hands] as follows: First we pour some clean water into a pot, but before doing so we must make sure that the pot is intact. It would never do to pour the water into a flower-pot—which has a hole in the bottom. Next, there must be no notches on the rim of the pot. The edge must be as even as the knife we use for killing animals. We take the pot of water in the right hand; from the right hand we put it into the left hand, and from the left hand we tip half the water over the right hand. We then take the pot into the right hand and with the right hand we pour the rest of the water over the left hand. We rub our hands together and bless God 'that He has sanctified us with His commandments and ordered us to wash our hands,' after which we wipe our hands thoroughly. Throughout the entire holy ceremony we carry a towel over the left arm. A proper Chassid always carries a towel in addition to a handkerchief. When wiping our hands we must keep the left hand continuously covered by the towel. Not everybody knows this, but it is very important. Only when we have washed our hands in this way and wiped them really thoroughly and conscientiously can we finally bless the bread and eat." Langer, *Nine Gates*, pp. 47–48.

The son grew up not even knowing where he came from or that he is Jewish. He grew up knowing that he is the tsar's Cossack and that the tsar's wish is his command. He excelled in his studies and he excelled in his military achievements, and finally he caught the eye of his general who admired him very much and he presented the hand of his daughter to him in marriage. The soldier accepted the proposition and a date for the wedding was set.

The wedding was with all military pomp and procession, and after the celebration the bride and bridegroom retired to their quarters. However, as he came into the room, he saw there a Jewish rabbi, a hasidic rabbi, with a long beard, warning him not to approach his bride. He didn't know what this meant—maybe he's tired, maybe he drank too much, maybe he had too much excitement, and so he figured maybe he'll let it go one night.

Came the second night and the rabbi is there. This time he tried to push it out of his mind, and the rabbi came to him and said, "Should you go near her, I'll choke you." And he grabbed him by the throat and he saw that this was no monkey business.

Came the third night and the rabbi was there again and he threatened him not to do anything. So he asked the rabbi, "What should I do?"

He said: "You are the son of a Stoliner hasid. I want you to jump out the window, escape from the army camp, travel till you hear the name of the city of Stolin, and there you will ask for the Rebbe."

He obeyed. He jumped out of the window and left the camp.

The end of the story is repeated by the hasidim who were then in the besmedresh of Stolin and were surprised by the appearance of a Cossack in tattered army clothes who did not even have the resemblance of a Jew. He came into the besmedresh and asked, "Where is the Rebbe? Where is the Rebbe?"

Assuming that he meant the Alter Rebbe, they brought him into the Alter Rebbe, "Here is the Rebbe."

He looked at him and shook his head no. "There must be a different one here." So they brought him to the Yunger Rebbe, the son. As soon as he saw the Yunger Rebbe, he fainted dead away. Because that was the one who had come to him to prevent him from marrying the non-Jewess. Later he was brought into the shul and grew up to be one of our fervent hasidim.

M, Stolin, E

The Officer: II (H46)

This story happened one hundred years ago. The Christians, Russians, used to steal babies, and raise them as gentiles. It happened with one of our own hasidim. He was stolen as a baby and never knew he was Jewish. He was raised as a Christian. He went into the army, became an officer, and he got married.

On his wedding night, as he was lying in bed, a picture came into his mind, the face of a man admonishing him. The man said, "Go to Stolin." Stolin was in the Polish part of Russia and he was far away deep in Russia. He followed the advice and did not touch his wife. He lay down and the dream was repeated. Finally, he ran away, in uniform. It was reported in the papers that a lieutenant ran away on his wedding night.

He went to Stolin, where both father and son were Rebbes. He went in to see the father, said he wanted to see the rabbis. He made such a tumult that they let him in. He looked at the Rebbe and said, "No, this is not the man I saw."

The Alter Rebbe said, "Take him to my son." They took him to the Rebbe's son. He looked at the Rebbe and said, "That's the man," and fainted.

A. told that when he came to Stolin this man had a long white beard and they used to point him out as the man who figured in the story.

SS, Stolin, E

Our Champion (H47)

I heard this from the Satmarer Rebbe.

A man was praying at the Sandzer Rov's when they prayed slihes, prayers for asking for forgiveness. They were praying to the Almighty. "Look upon us. We have lost our champion and have no one to look after us."

When the man said the prayer he was crying. The Sandzer Rov said, "Why are you crying?"

The man answered, "How can I pray such a lie to the Almighty and say that we have lost our champion when you are our champion?"

The Sandzer Rov laughed and asked him, "How can a hasid be so foolish?"

CC, Satmar, E

Charity for the Widow (H48)

This also happened with the Sandzer Rov, the Divrei Haim. It was well known that he was a very charitable man. He never left anybody out. He was a prince. At night he used to give charity, and he was well versed in the Torah regarding charity. One time there came in a woman, a widow, and she was bargaining with him. As much as he gave her it wasn't enough. The Rov's gabai was there and it annoyed him a great deal. The gabai told her she should go. It bothered him very much: "Why are you torturing the Rebbe? You're giving him a headache. It's enough." He began to yell at the woman, "Go away and leave us alone."

Perhaps he didn't listen to him and gave the woman as much as she wanted. Then the Sandzer Rov went over to the gabai and said, "Imagine if you died and your wife came in to ask for money, and you were standing here, your soul would be standing here, and you were looking at how she was begging. And there came a gabai to her and he began to yell at her. Would that please you?"

S, Klausenberg, Y

The Informer (H49)

The Talmud says that an observer of the mitsves will never suffer evil. You should know one thing—that if a rabbi says something, he never says things from his own mind. He says what he read in holy books or studied in the Talmud. Some people look in the Talmud and they just see what's written. There's something else between the lines. In this you need a little sense. You understand?

The Rebbe's grandfather, his name was the Sandzer Rov. He

wrote a book that was called *Divrei Haim* [*"The Words of Life"*].
It's questions and answers—answers to people of the whole world
about questions in the Talmud.

The Rebbe had another grandfather—his name was Rabbi
Leyzer of Dzikov. He lived in Dzikov. They lived in cities in Poland: one lived in Sandz and the other in Dzikov. They did not call
them by their family name—the family name is Halberstamm and
the other one's name was Horowitz—but they used to call them by
the names of the cities: the Sandzer Rov and the Dzikover Rov.
They were both related by marriage. The Dzikover's daughter was
the Sandzer Rov's daughter-in-law.

In the city where the Dzikover lived there was an informer. He
was also a Jewish man. And this Reb Lezer Dzikov was a very
frightened man. He got frightened over everything. So once this
informer said that he was going to go to the government, to
Warsaw, a big city in Poland, and tell the government that he did
this and this and that he wants to gather people around him and
overthrow the king. You know—lies that they made up at that
time. And then they will take him and put him in prison—in
chains. And he got very frightened. And the Dzikover believed
very much in the Sandzer Rebbe, his in-law. So he sent a man to
the Divrei Haim [the Sandzer] he should go and he should beg God
for him that something should happen to this informer so that he
could not do what he wants to. So the Dzikover sent a man, and the
man went right away. And on the way in any place that he stopped
he told them there should be horses waiting so that he could go
fast and wouldn't have to wait until they fed the horses and changed
them. Till he came at twelve at night to the Sandzer Rov. They
heard that a man came from the Dzikover and they let him in right
away. And so he told them the story of what the Dzikover Rov
said.

So the Divrei Haim said all right and told him to go out for a
minute and he's going to write him a letter. The Sandzer Rov said
he's going to write him a letter. Then he called him in and the
Sandzer Rov started writing the letter. And you know it was a
friendly letter, and at the end of the letter he wrote: "About the
informer that you wrote me, I think that he died already. I think
so." That's what he wrote. Then he gave him back the letter and
the person came back to the Dzikover Rov.

The Dzikover Rov read the letter and he got happy. He knew
that if the Sandzer Rov said so, it's probably like that.

Then a few days later it happened that they saw in the Warsaw newspaper that this informer came to Warsaw at night. He didn't know where to go and so he went to a bakery that used to be open at night. It was cold, and he went at night. There were big ovens, and so he went on top of the oven and he lay down to take a sleep. In the middle of the night he made a bad turn and fell off the stove and died. So the Dzikover Rov was very happy.

So after a time the Dzikover Rov met with the Sandzer Rov and he told him, "What a great miracle you showed."

So he said, "What miracle? What miracle? I don't know any miracle."

"Don't you know you wrote me in the letter that he died and that's how it was." And they figured it out and it happened at the same minute when he wrote. They figured out what hour it was.

"I don't know what you're talking about. I don't know any miracle."

"So how did you know that you 'think he died'?"

"I'll tell you the truth," he said. "If somebody tells me that he's got trouble, I feel very much for him. Exactly as if it was to happen to me. I wrote the letter. Then at the end of the letter, I felt better. I don't know what happened. Why did I feel better? Why didn't I feel the trouble of my relative? So I thought probably he died already."

That's what he said.

X, Bobov, E

The Yetser Hora's Secret (H50)

The Baal Shem went to heaven and asked how to bring the Meshiah closer. They told him that there was one thing that the Yetser Hora has which if he can learn he can bring the Meshiah before the appointed time. He has it concealed and will not give it up. The Baal Shem prayed and argued for him to give it up. He could not do it.

Dov Baer tried to find out from the Yetser Hora himself and to take it from him. Reb Baer, the Rizhyner's son, did the same thing—to make some connection with the Yetser Hora to see how he could take it from him. He also failed. After he failed he left

Leovo and lived in Sadeger. He stopped being a Rebbe, although he was still religious, still a hasid.[47]

Q, Tchortkov, E

The Cripple (H51)

This is a story about the Rebbe Maharash. He came to Leningrad with a group of people. One person went to Leningrad on business—he dealt in different types of meat. He used to sell wagonloads of meat. He was not a hasid. When he came to Leningrad he went to see the Rebbe. They asked him, "What do you have to do with the Rebbe?"

He said that he was called to the army and he was an only son. Yeshiveh students were exempt from the army in those times, except when they did not have the quota. So he said that there were times when doctors would falsify papers, make some appear to be sick, and cause ruptures. Then they would also take boys from the yeshiveh. In Nebel in Lithuania at that time the doctors were bribed, and so the custom was that before going to the army board they would go to Lubavitch. So this fellow also went. He told the story to the Rebbe and he asked him, "Maybe I should cripple myself?"

The Rebbe said, "No." He was a healthy fellow and the Rebbe said not to harm himself.

So then he went to go to the draft and he used a different device to make himself appear yellowish and sick. And he saw that according to the quota he would surely be taken. So he was angry at the Rebbe, since the Rebbe told him not to harm himself. He will be taken and he did not want to serve. When it was almost his turn a specialist came to the city: he was a specialist in making cripples. He fixed him so that one foot should be thicker than the other. He used benzine so that the foot would swell up. It burnt him so much

[47] Rabbi Dov Baer of Leovo, the younger son of Israel of Rizhyn, d. 1876. In 1868 he left Hasidism and wrote an open letter attacking the movement. He was embraced by the members of the haskala, the enlightenment. As this story indicates, his followers remained faithful to him. After a period of time, Rabbi Dov Baer returned to the hasidic way, explaining that his brother's death had unbalanced him (see Horodezky, *Religiöse Strömungen*, pp. 221–24).

that he was willing to serve not only three years but thirty years to free himself from the pain. And the danger was greater because they could see it was not normal, and for this they could send him away to prison.

The next day he went to the army board. It was his turn to go into the doctors. He was ready to go in. He was the next one by the door, and they came out and said that the quota was filled. He suffered with his foot for a while.

YY, Lubavitch, Y

A Miracle (H52)

This is a story about the Rebbe Maharash. There were two twins and they both were called to the army. And the law was that twins were considered as one, and only one would have to go. So they went to the Rebbe Maharash and they asked the Rebbe what to do about the one that had to go. So the Rebbe asked, "Is there money so that he can buy himself out?"

So they said, "No."

"If he doesn't have any money," he said, "what about making himself a cripple?"

So they said, "He doesn't want to."

"So what do you want? A miracle higher than the way of nature? Let it be so."

So he came to the board. When he came in to the medical examination, the people started laughing at him. "Look who wants to join the army!" They did not even look at him. "He's sick. He's a nothing." They chased him out of the draft board.

YY, Lubavitch, Y

Students Have to Laugh (H53)

As a student, Rabbi Schneerson's great-grandfather [the Maharash] was active in Russia trying to better the lot of the Jews. There were many pogroms. Many students who were irreligious also were working. They began to work together. At one time the students felt that the times were especially bad. Anti-Semitism was rampant. The Maharash went to the cemetery to visit the grave of his father, and when he returned he said to the students that his father told him that the situation is not so bad. They all smiled. They didn't believe him.

He said, "I see you are smiling. It isn't that you don't believe. Such things are laughed at in your environment at the university. They're not up-to-date. You may believe, but when you are together, students have to laugh. Students have to laugh."

C, Lubavitch, E

Judgment (H54)

People came to the Szigetter Rov from a thousand miles away and no one knew the reason why. Suddenly after havdoleh someone--not a hasid—said, "Oh! He is the one!" and fell unconscious. Afterward the Rebbe told them to keep the fellow. Rabbi F.'s grandfather's brother, he was a smart man, and he was curious as to why this happened. He followed the man, saw him go to the railroad station. He asked him, he forced him to tell him what happened.

The man said: "I am a druggist from London. I know nothing of Shabbes or Yiddishkait. Once I became sick and the doctors gave up hope. I was in a coma and I dreamed that I came before the judges of the next world. They started to weigh my mitsves and my evil deeds. My evil deeds, my sins, weighed more. They passed sentence: 'He has to die.' Then I heard a voice—'Make way for the Grand Rabbi of Sziget!' The Szigetter Rov came in and asked, 'What has happened here?' They told him that here's a man whose bad deeds weigh more than his good ones and he's been sentenced. The Szigetter Rov argued that it's not right since the man grew up in an atmosphere that prevented him from knowing what the mitsves are. He hadn't put on tefillin because he was never told to put it on. The Szigetter Rov said, 'We have to keep him alive so that he can come to know what the mitsves are so that we can see if he will accept them. Then we can see if the sentence is wrong. If he doesn't do them then we can punish him.' "

This happened when he was in a coma and the family was around his bedside. The members of his family saw that he was starting to sweat. Right afterward he got up and started resuming his normal course. He didn't know there was such a town as Sziget in Hungary. He started to follow a religious life.

Once he was on a bus in Hungary and he heard of Sziget and wanted to see the Rabbi of Sziget. He recalled the dream and wanted to find out more about it. When he came in to the Szigetter Rov he recognized him, and that is why he fell unconscious.

Then F. said he understands why people come from thousands of miles away.[48]

CC, Satmar, E

Sulfur (H55)

I stood by the deathbed of my mother and the Slonimer opened the door of the room and came in with his talis on his shoulder and he called out, "Balebosteh [housewife]! Come here. I want to tell you a story."

"In a certain city, I forget the name, the keeper of the bathhouse was awakened in the middle of the night by three women who said, 'Please give us the key.' She gave them the key, they went into the mikveh, and she went to sleep. They did what they had to do for about a half an hour, an hour, two hours. They woke her up, gave her back the key, and paid her money.

"In the morning, the same two women came again with a third woman. She gave them the key. 'We have to go to the mikveh.' She gave them the key and she continues on. They bathe again, they give her the key, and pay her.

"On the third night she said, 'Please take the key and I will also join you.' They undressed and went into the mikveh. She put on a bathing dress and went in also. She saw two of the women ordering the other, 'Undress.' And she was standing and sobbing. It was terrible. It broke your heart.

"The keeper said, 'What's the matter with you Jewish women? What are you afraid of? The mikveh is a good mikveh and there's nothing to be afraid of.'

"She doesn't answer. She undoes a button and weeps, and from one button to another she finally undresses.

[48] References to heavenly trials are common in the tales (see H30, H31). Concerning visions of the other world, see *In Praise of the Besht*, nos. 41, 166; see also Newman and Spitz, *Hasidic Anthology*, p. 236, no. 2.

"They said, 'You're ready? Go in.'

"She began to scream so much it was frightening.

"The keeper says, 'What's the matter with you?'

"They took her on both sides and put her in the mikveh. She screamed until the whole town shook.

"The women took her from the mikveh, gave her her clothes and said, 'Get dressed.' They paid the keeper and said: 'Tell the wives of your city that this is what we do to women who neglect going to the mikveh.' And she put her finger into the water and it was scalding. It was fire—burning like sulfur."

And the Rebbe said, "Why do I tell this to you? Tell your neighbors this story." The neighbors were already modern people.

BB, Slonim, Y

Talis Koten (H56)

There was someone who was already serving in the army near the city of Rabich. There was a group of soldiers and they decided to go to the Lubavitcher Rebbe. So this soldier came in to see the Rebbe and when he saw the Rebbe he fainted. The Rebbe asked them to revive him. And he was sitting there in a faint. So the Rebbe said, "Buy him a talis koten. If you put on a talis koten they'll free you from the army."

A few days later they reviewed the soldiers, and when they came to him they said he would be discharged.

He was a religious man, but not a Lubavitcher hasid. He later moved to Poltavia and on the day when he was freed he used to have a celebration and tell the story of how the Lubavitcher Rebbe told him to buy a talis koten.

EE, Lubavitch, Y

The Army (H57)

K. went to Lubavitch in Russia. He was called to the army. It was not like here. It was terrible. He got sick and it was delayed. There were two times to be called—the first of the year and the middle. He went to the Rebbe, Rabbi Sholem Dov Baer. Usually the best time to go to be examined was in the middle of the year. They did not need so many and sometimes they rejected you. The Lubavitcher Rebbe said, "Go in the beginning of the year."

"Why the beginning? The middle is usually better." Finally he thought that the Rebbe knows Talmud best, but does he know of practical things? So he signed up for the middle of the year.

The doctor who was supposed to examine at the beginning of the year was terrible. You could not bribe him. What happened? The doctor got sick. He got sick and they had to call a Jewish doctor who was this man's own doctor. He knew his case would have been rejected, but he had to go in the middle of the year. What should he do? Run away? This time he went to the Rebbe.

The Rebbe says, "Run away."

"But then they'll give me a big fine."

"Pay the fine."

He runs away. Later he was called in and they gave him all his papers. He goes to a lawyer. The lawyer says, "They made a mistake. They gave you your papers. This is the only copy. Burn them." And he did.[49]

YY, Lubavitch, Y

Nu? (H58)

This doctor had a son-in-law who was also a Polish hasid. And he was a shohet in a town in Poland. When the Lubavitcher Rebbe came to that town in Poland, he wanted to find out what kind of a shohet he was, and so he asked him to show him how he sharpens his knife. And it pleased the Rebbe to see how he sharpened his knife, and he ate meat of the animals that he killed. Through that, the shohet became closer to the Lubavitcher Rebbe.[50]

It was the time of the First World War and they called the shohet to serve in the army. He asked the Rebbe what to do, and the Rebbe told him not to register. They were a little bit afraid but they waited.

[49] See a similar tale in *In Praise of the Besht*, no. 150, in which the Besht advises Reb Motel not to go to court until they send a cart for him.

[50] It was customary for a tsaddik to ask the shohet to show him his knife to establish the perfect sharpness of the edge and hence its fulfillment of ritual law (see *In Praise of the Besht*, no. 178).

One day a good friend of his came to his house and he told him that he knows of a doctor that will defer him from the army. So when he heard such a thing he ran after the Rebbe, because the Rebbe was not in that town, in order to ask him what to do. Should he register with a note from that doctor? So they met the Rebbe and they asked him what he should do. His wife asked him, and the Rebbe answered in these words: "I told him not to register, but if he wants to register—nu?" They told the shohet that if he was a fervent hasid of the Rebbe he would not register, but since he was not such a fervent hasid of the Rebbe he should register.

He went back to the town where they register in the army. The order of registering was that you registered at night and afterward you went to the doctor and then returned to the place where you registered in the morning. He registered in the evening and he went to the house of the doctor. When he came to the doctor's house he found out that the old doctor was not there any more and there was a new doctor in his place. He did not know what to do. Finally he decided that he was going to ask the doctor to fix up the card for him.

He went in and asked the doctor if the older doctor had left any message about him because he had spoken to the old doctor already and had been told he would fix everything up. The second doctor told him that he would try. Then the doctor told him, "You're free."

When he returned to register, the doctors saw that he was free, and they said among themselves: "If he's free, who will we take? He's a healthy Jew." They decided among themselves to send him to Charokeh to be examined by other doctors there. So he finally went to Charokeh and they examined him there, and after a lot of difficulty he got himself a blue deferment card. Then he understood what the Rebbe said when he told him not to register but if he wants to—"nu?"

YY, Lubavitch, Y

The Brother (H59)

The son [Rabbi Abraham Mordekhai, the Gerer Rebbe] of the rabbi [Rabbi Yehuda Leib] that I just told you about [H60], told something of his father's way of life. Each moment of his life was planned. He did not sleep at all—maybe two hours a day. Even the greatest man, before he came in to see the rabbi, he would tremble with respect.

The Rebbé had a brother almost the same age as himself who came in to see him almost every day to talk over some things with him. He was familiar with him. They had lived together. I saw him myself once before he came in to see the Rebbe. It was at a big house, with big gates and with maybe a few thousand people there. Out of respect they let the brother in before anyone else. I saw myself that before he went in he walked up and down, trembling, nervous.

T, Ger, Y

The One Who Is Missing (H60)

I heard this story from a man, Shimon of Kalish in Poland. He was a hasid by the grandfather [Rabbi Yehuda Leib] of the present Gerer Rebbe. Between Rosh Hashoneh and Yom Kippur maybe ten or twenty thousand people used to come to see the Rebbe. A friend of Shimon's was in to see the Rebbe that night. Maybe twenty thousand people were there that night. A hasid became sick and a number of hasidim went to see the Rebbe. A friend of Shimon was with them. The Rebbetsn said, "I can't wake up the Rebbe because he's slept only an hour. But," she said, "if you talk loudly maybe you can wake him up yourself." She went out.

They all started to talk and the Rebbe woke up. He washed his hands and asked what was the matter. They said, "A hasid is sick." He told them to take him to Warsaw where they had big doctors. The man died later.

So Shimon asked if he knows this man. Sometimes people came once every ten years. The Rebbe said that he did not know him, but he said, "Later on, when people come to say goodbye when they go back home, when everyone will pass in front of me I'll know who is missing."

He knew the ten thousand people in his mind, and remember this man was there only one time.

T, Ger, Y

The Pretender (*H61*)

There was once a Jew, a hasid of the first Bobover Rebbe, Rabbi Shlomo Halberstamm, who didn't have any children. This man came every Shabbes, every holiday to the Rebbe that the Rebbe should pray to God for him that he should have a child. It was the evening before Yom Kippur, and at the evening meal the Rebbe took a piece of fish and he called over the hasid who did not have any children. He did not give the fish to him but instead he held the piece of fish in his hand and started telling a story.

He said: "There was once a Rebbe, the Lubliner, who was called 'the Seer,' and people traveled from far and near to see him. A few hasidim wanted to go to the Lubliner for the holiday. They didn't have any money to rent horses and wagons, and so they started walking from one city to the other. They thought that perhaps they'll find somebody who'll give them a ride on the way. So they went. They were so poor that they didn't have any money for a place to eat, but they still wanted to go to the Rebbe.

"Finally some of the company said, 'Listen, we have no money, we have to walk so long, we're so tired, let's make one of us Rebbe. We'll make somebody a gabai. We'll dress him so that he'll look like a Rebbe, and everybody will push to him. People will see a Rebbe so first they'll give us to eat and they'll give us horses so that we'll be able to travel further. You know everybody will have respect for a Rebbe.'

"They were all very religious people and nobody wanted to do this. 'If I'm not a Rebbe why should they call me a Rebbe?' But they said to save somebody's life you're allowed to do anything. So they drew lots and one of the hasidim was chosen and they said, 'You have to be a Rebbe, you have to.'

"They traveled further with the new Rebbe and his gabai and they came to a city which was nearby. The people of the city heard, 'A Rebbe is coming, a Rebbe is coming.' One of the innkeepers there ran out, 'Oh, sholem aleikhem! Aleikhem sholem! I've been waiting so long to see a Rebbe. I have a child that's very sick and the doctors say they can't help him.' He started crying. But first he called in the Rebbe with the hasidim and he made a big meal for them. Then he fell to the Rebbe's feet and he begged him, 'You could help me. My child's so sick.'

"The Rebbe just looked on the other fellows, 'What does this fellow want of my life?'

"They said, 'Shush! Don't talk. Just go with him.'

"So the innkeeper showed him where the child was lying and he bent over and he blessed the baby, God should help, the child should be well. And he went out, and the innkeeper thanked him and he gave him money for their journey.

"They came to the Lubliner. They were by the Rebbe, but this Rebbe did not mention a word about the story. He kept it to himself. They stayed there over the holiday, a couple of more days, and then they started back. They still had the money that had been given to them.

"When they came near to the place where the sick child had been, the innkeeper ran out to them with happiness. He thanked them, 'Listen, as you went away the kid just got up and he asked to eat. He was healthy like any kid.' He made another big meal for them and he gave them money.

"You know the hasidim said to the Rebbe, 'Listen, us you can't fool. We know you're not a Rebbe. What happened? What did you do? Maybe you are a Rebbe and you didn't want to tell us? What's going on here?'

"And he said, 'I don't know. On my life, I didn't do anything.' They started bothering him until he had to tell them. So he told them like this: 'Listen, when the Jew called me to go over to the child and bless him I started thinking: is it this Jew's fault that he thinks that I'm a Rebbe? Why should he be punished? He thinks that I'm a Rebbe, but I'm not. And I thought of a psalm of David which asks God not to allow him to be disgraced in the eyes of those who honor him.[51] This man believed in me, and so I bent over the crib and started praying to God: This man, this hasid, is a good man. Why should he be denied your help? I know that I'm good for nothing. I'm not a Rebbe. This man thinks that I am a Rebbe. I'll go away and he'll see that the child remains ill, and he'll say that a Rebbe can't do anything. He thinks that I'm a Rebbe and so why not help this man?[52] That's the prayer that I said by the crib and it looks like God took my place and helped the child. That's all.' "

So the Bobover Rebbe was just holding the fish and telling the story, and when he came to this point, he just told the same thing over that this Rebbe had said: "He thinks that I'm a Rebbe"—the

[51] Possibly Psalm 31 or 71.

[52] The Rabbi of Kobryn made a similar plea (see Buber, *Tales*, 2: 167).

people that he spoke to knew that Rabbi Halberstamm was speaking about himself and his hasid. He repeated it as if it happened there: "He thinks that I'm a Rebbe. So why shouldn't he be helped by God? Let God help this gentleman. Even if I'm nothing." And he said it over several times. And that year it just happened that he had a boy.

It's a true story and it happened by our Rebbe too.

X, Bobov, E

Fish for Shabbes (H62)

There was a time when people didn't have any fish. People gave thousands to have fish for Shabbes, only fish. It is a very big thing to have fish on Shabbes. There are stories about fish.

There was once a Rebbe, he never missed even once eating fish on Friday. This happened to the Rebbe's grandfather Moshe Yosel [the Oheler]. Once he traveled someplace, and there was no fish at the place. "No," the fisherman said, "We can't have any fish."

This is a true story. Everybody knows about it. It was fifteen minutes before the beginning of the Shabbes and he didn't have any fish. He had such belief in God that God would help him out so he would not miss having fish: "I'll have fish for Shabbes." So he said, "First, I'll take a pot with water and I'll put it in the kitchen so if they'll bring me fish now I'll be able to cook it. The water will be boiled." Understand? And he went around the room praying that God should help him and give him a fish. And as he was going back and forth the fish came through the chimney. A fish just fell in the pot like it was cooking. An eagle went past. He had a fish in his mouth and dropped it. And the fish got cooked right away. The fish got cooked for Shabbes.[53]

X, Bobov, E

The Shoemaker (H63)

Tonight at six o'clock I met a man on the street. He gave me a "sholem aleikhem," asked where I'm from, where I'm going. I told

[53] See M3 for an opposing view of how a Rebbe obtains fish. See also Graf Potocki's attitude concerning fish for the Shabbes (I19, I20, I21).

him I'm a Bobover hasid. He's an old man and remembers the Rabbi's father. He told me, "I'll tell you something that I saw myself concerning this Bobover Rebbe."

So he told me the Rebbe's father used to go each summer to a vacation place in Austria called Krenets. All the rabbis and rich people used to come there in the summer, take baths there, like in Sharon Springs or in Saratoga. But across the street from where the Rebbe lived, window against window, was a shoemaker. And this shoemaker used to work on Shabbes. The Rebbe sent down one of his hasidim to tell him please, he does not want to see through his window a Jew working on Shabbes. He should please stop it.

So the shoemaker answered, "Nobody's my boss. I'm not his hasid. I won't do what he says. I want to make a living."

So then the Rebbe's wife, our present Rebbe's mother, used to give him her shoes to fix, but the Rebbe told her to tell the shoemaker that she can't give him the shoes to fix because he does not observe Shabbes. So she went and told it to him, but he answered the same thing—"I don't care what the Rebbe says." The Rebbe sent another hasid to tell him that the money that he is going to earn on Shabbes would not last.

Then this man who is telling me the story started to laugh. He told that at night he came into a restaurant to eat and noticed that the shoemaker who also ate there was not present. Suddenly the shoemaker came in crying. So he said to this Jew, his name was Konigsburg, he said, "What's wrong with you, Mr. Konigsburg?"

"I'll tell you what happened." You know, fifty years ago they made men's rooms with a big hole in the floor. So when he went out there the wallet in the back of his pocket fell out down into this toilet.

"This," he said, "I remember since I was a small boy."

X, Bobov, E

The Policeman (H64)

They had a case, somebody, a Polish policeman, did something wrong, and they reported him to the police station and they fired him. The policeman threatened them with their lives because of this happening. They went to Moshe from Stolin, and told him what was happening. He promised them, "With God's help nothing will happen to you."

This policeman had one single daughter. All of a sudden she took sick. Doctors came, but they could not find out what ails her. Their neighbors said he had started up with a Jewish party and God was punishing you for threatening their lives. They saw she was a healthy girl, but she was getting worse and worse. The doctors did not know why.

He liked his girl very much. He came to the Jews. They were scared. They thought he was going to hurt them. He begged them, "Don't be scared." He asked for forgiveness. They forgave him. He was glad, and soon after the girl became well again.[54]

I was told this story by the pickle man in the public market.

B, Stolin, E

A Rebbe (H64a)

Reb David Biderman, he lived in Jerusalem. He comes in the line of the Lelever Rebbe. There's a whole story of how he travelled.

He told his father he wants to go to Europe to find a Rebbe. His father told him: "You have me."

So he said: "A father can't be a Rebbe."

He answered him: "So you have the Wailing Wall."

The son answered: "I want a Rebbe that answers."

His father said: "If you would be on the highest level you'd hear the Western Wall answer."

The end was that he went to Europe and he became a hasid of Bes Aaron of Karlin.

M, Stolin, E

The Sin of the Young (H64b)

He [Rabbi David Biderman] went to Europe and he became a hasid of Bes Aaron of Karlin. By a tish the Rebbe was giving out a

[54] Compare I1.

corn cake, and this was given as a penitence for the sin of the young [nocturnal emissions]. When Reb David came to take the cake, the Rebbe refused to give it to him, saying: "You do not need it."

M, Stolin, E

I Am Nothing (H65)

I was very near to Reb Israel [of Tchortkov], although you cannot know a Rebbe. There were times when he sat on a little couch in his room where he received people. There were two leather chairs and a little sofa. One chair stood on each side of the desk and he sat on the sofa. He sat there and I stood in front of him a long, long time. He looked at me and did not see me. After a half an hour he asked me what I wanted. I felt like I was standing before a great man and I am nothing.[55]

Q, Tchortkov, E

Too High (H66)

The Rebbe [Israel of Tchortkov] spoke very quietly. When he sat down by the table he ate very little. When he said toyreh, he was very quiet the whole time. The hasidim pressed together. Nobody made a move.

The Lubliner Rov told me this: there was a rabbi who came and when the Rebbe went out my uncle asked him if he understood what the Rebbe said. He answered, "No, because the Rebbe spoke too quiet."

The Lubliner Rov, Meyer Shapiro,[56] the founder of a big yeshiveh, answered: "No, you are mistaken, the Rebbe spoke too high."

Q, Tchortkov, E

[55] Compare the reaction of Rabbi Israel of Kozhenits before the Maggid of Mezrich (Buber, *Tales*, 1: 287).
[56] Rabbi Meyer Shapiro, the Rabbi of Lublin, d. 1934.

Lemon and Sugar (H67)

This happened by Reb Israel. I was three years old. I had diphtheria. I was in Tchortkov and my father went to the Tchortkover Rebbe. The Rebbe prayed in a room on the side of the besmedresh. My father was so excited he didn't ask the gabai to let him in. He burst in and cried that his child was ill. The Rebbe said, "Don't worry. Give the boy lemon with sugar." My father gave it to me. I choked up what was stuck in my throat. My father said I recovered immediately.

Q, Tchortkov, E

Three Ways (H68)

Reb Haim Brisker [57] came to the previous [Lubavitcher] Rebbe's father [Rabbi Sholem Dov Baer] in Rostov to discuss a topic, and he had to be with the Rebbe over Shabbes. When the previous Rebbe's father heard that Reb Haim Brisker was coming, he took all the books from the table and left only the *Lekutei Torah*, the book by Shneur Zalman, with the page bent in the place that he wanted Reb Haim Brisker to see. He knew that Haim Brisker would ask a question that concerned the page that he bent.

This is what happened. Haim Brisker came in, and he looked for a book to look at. He did not find any except the one book on the table. He opened up the book to that page, and he said, "I came to ask a question on that."

The previous Rebbe's father was praying. Reb Haim was looking into the *Lekutei Torah*. The previous Rebbe prayed early in order to be able to meet Reb Haim, and as Reb Haim was looking into the *Lekutei Torah*, he asked the previous Rebbe a question concerning the *Lekutei Torah*.

The previous Rebbe said, "I could not undertake to answer the question, but ask my father when he finishes praying and he will explain it to you."

[57] Reb Haim of Brisk: Rabbi Haim Soloveitchik of Brisk (Brest-Litovsk), a leading talmudic scholar. A friend of Rabbi Joseph Schneersohn of Lubavitch, he was neither hasid nor misnaged (d. 1923).

He waited till the father finished praying, and he showed the Rebbe the *Lekutei Torah* and explained his question. He said he would like to study his hasides because the Tanya [Shneur Zalman] was such a great scholar in revealed portions of the Talmud he would like to see his Kabbala, his hasides. So after Shabbes he showed him one of the books that he had written on hasides in the year of 1906. He asked the Rebbe to give him the *Essays*,[58] the book on hasides. After a period of time Reb Haim said to the Rebbe that not only is he a gaon in the revealed source but in Kabbala, the hidden studies. Before Reb Haim left, they made an agreement that in all situations concerning communal affairs, they should confer together before they make announcements.

One time Reb Haim could not wait for the Rebbe and he started to make an announcement concerning communal affairs. The Rebbe came in just as Reb Haim was in the midst of his discussion, and he heard what Reb Haim had to say. Then when the Rebbe spoke he said: "There are three ways to interpret what Reb Haim said. It cannot be the first two because they are contrary to teachings of the Talmud. So it has to be the third way."

And Reb Haim said, "Yes, I meant the third way and not the first two."

YY, Lubavitch, Y

No Room for Hesitation (H69)

When a Rebbe dies and a son takes over, there are always people who knew the father who cannot remain with the son. When the Stoliner Rebbe's father [Israel] took over, he was completely different from his father. He even dressed differently. He went like a businessman. He wore a kaftan but he did not dress in resplendent fashion as Rebbes did. He took over when he was four.

One old hasid, killed in the war in Israel, stuck with him all the way. When they asked him how he managed to do this, he answered, "I say to myself that I don't understand anything. Then there are no problems for me, no room for hesitation."

M, Stolin, E

[58] *Maamarim* (Warsaw, 1925).

This Face (H70)

The past [Stoliner] Rebbe's father became Rebbe at three or four
years old. They say that when he was a half year old a famous
hasid spent a half year at Stolin. Then he went away. He revisited
Stolin thirty years later. When the Rebbe looked on his face the
Rebbe said, "This face I have seen already."

SS, Stolin, E

The Power of the Name (H71)

This is told about the [Stoliner] Rebbe's father. They were traveling over the ice. They were in a horse and sled. The ice was pretty
thick, but it started cracking. Someone else was there. He was
scared.

"What are we going to do?"

The Rebbe mentioned a name: "Herr Perlow is passing
by"—the Rebbe's name. "Mr. Perlow is going through here."
They went through without any damage. God helped, and they
went across. Nothing happened.[59]

He was not allowed to mention what happened while the Rebbe
was alive. If he told, nothing good would happen to him. He was
allowed to tell when the Rebbe went away from this world.

B, Stolin, E

The Writing on the Glass (H72)

F. related a story. He was going to be taken into the army in
Poland. He went to Israel, the Rebbe's father. The Stoliner took
him to the glass window. It was frosted, and he wrote on it.

[59] Concerning the power of names, see *In Praise of the Besht*, no. 231; see
also Trachtenberg, *Jewish Magic and Superstition*, pp. 78–103.

Whatever he wrote there, the recruiting army officer wrote the same thing. He was refused.[60]

B, Stolin, E

Water and Coloring (H73)

Mendel said that there was a man whose child was very sick. He went to the Rebbe's father, and the Rebbe's father had his own prescription book and told him to go to a certain store in Warsaw. He went to that street and the prescription cured the child.

His neighbor had the same problem. The man said he would go for the same prescription. He went to the drug store and the man said, "Who sent you?" Earlier he asked the first man who sent him, and the man said the Stoliner Rebbe and he said okay. Now this man said, "Who sent you?" and he said his neighbor, a friend.

So he said, "I can't give you the same prescription. For that man I gave water with coloring. When he said that the Stoliner Rebbe sent him I knew it would work."

A, Stolin, E

Make Soup (H74)

This happened with the [Stoliner] Rebbe's father. A man had a wife and she died. She was an elderly woman. They put a blanket over her and candles by her side. The man went to the Rebbe and cried, and said, "Who is going to take care of the children?"

"Go back. Tell her to make soup."

The man was going but he went to her and said, "Go and make soup." She got up and made soup.[61]

If I saw it it would mean nothing. I would say get up and make soup and I would expect the person to get up.

U, Stolin, E

[60] In a similar magical incident Rebbe Elimelekh spills his bowl of soup. Subsequently, the emperor, while trying to sign an edict against the Jews, spills the inkwell and spoils the document (Buber, *Tales*, 1: 259).

[61] The Stoliner Rebbe's son, Yohanan, was also said to have raised the dead (see H93).

The Concert (H75)

All five sons of Reb Israel of Stolin, known as the Yenuka, the
child, were excellent musicians. The Yenuka once passed an out-
door concert, went over to the conductor afterward and said, "You
know you're making a mistake."

The conductor said, "Yes, but I don't know how to correct it."

"Well," the Rebbe said, "You do this and that."

He knew everything.

F, Stolin, E

Homets (H75a)

This happened with one of the Stoliners. It was the night of
Passover. The rabbi in this city was a misnaged and the Rebbe sent
the shammes [beadle] to the rabbi: "You have homets [food unfit
for Passover] in the house." He had just searched and cleaned the
house and so he laughed and sent back the shammes. Later he
became scared. He searched the house but he didn't find anything.
Later the shammes returned: "You have homets in the house." He
searched again but he didn't find anything. The shammes returned
a third time. Finally he looked in an obvious place—the breadbox.

He went to the Rebbe. "If you were so sure there was homets,
why didn't you tell me where it was?"

"The closer someone is to me the clearer picture I get. You're
further from me so I got a hazy picture of where it was."

M, Stolin, E

The Prescription: I (H76)

A general was with the mayor in Stolin, and he said he had heard it
said there was a wise man in Stolin. The mayor said, "Yes."

"How can I get to talk to him?" the general asked.

"I'll invite him," the mayor said, "to a discussion."

While they were having a discussion, the general's wife came in and whispered something to the general.

The Rebbe said, "What's the trouble?"

The general said, "My wife is ill. The doctor gave her a prescription but the druggist can't fill it."

The Rebbe said, "Let me see it." He looked at it and said, "This prescription can be written in two ways." He rewrote it and returned it to the general's wife.

The wife went off and when she returned, she said the druggist said, "Yes, *this* we have."

The general asked him, "How do you know these things?"

The Rebbe replied in Russian, "God alone studied with me." [62]

The general smiled, and the Rebbe, insulted, rose, and went out, which was something to do to a general in Russia. But the general was simply impressed, and he asked, "How can I win the Rebbe's favor back?" The mayor invited the Rebbe again and the general apologized to him.

F, Stolin, E

The Prescription: II (H77)

In Europe, a general, nobles, could shoot a person in the street. They could make you climb a tree and shoot you down like a bird. So all the nobles when they came to Stolin asked for an audience with the Rebbe's father. They knew how great he was.

Mendel knows a fellow who was there when it happened. The fellow told him. The mayor of the town asked the Rebbe to meet a few generals. While they were there one of the dukes' wives enters and walks over to one of the dukes and whispers in his ear. It was about a prescription. The Rebbe asked what happened. She explained that the druggist could not read the prescription. The Rebbe took a look and said, "This could be written two ways. I'll write it so that he'll understand."

Sure enough, she came back with the medicine. So they asked him where he studied, and he answered: "With God alone I learned." One of the dukes thought it was a joke and smiled. The

[62] When the Besht was asked where he had learned medicine, he replied: "God, blessed be He, taught me" (see *In Praise of the Besht*, no. 245; see also no. 26).

Rebbe picked himself up and walked out. The mayor told the dukes to make another appointment and apologize. They were playing with their lives. So they made an appointment.

A, Stolin, E

The Drunkard (H78)

When he was a kid, the [Stoliner] Rebbe's father was walking on the street. He was called the Frankfurter because he died in Frankfurt on the Main. He was walking on the street, and hundreds of hasidim were with him. A goy, drunk, was trying to get past to see the Rebbe. They pushed him away.

"That's not nice," the Rebbe said. "Let the goy in." He was drunk. He told him to his face, "You'll never touch a drop of liquor again."

This man [who told the story] was a kid and he followed him. He walked down to a bar and asked for a drink. He took the drink and he started shaking. He fell on the floor and was kicking. His wife came and took him home. He never touched another drop.

U, Stolin, E

Medicine (H79)

F., who was by the [Stoliner] Rebbe's father, told how a certain man was sick and the Rebbe told him to buy medicine, fill a teaspoon up with it and pour it out into the sink.

A, Stolin, E

The Trade (H80)

A young hasid was in Karlin for the holidays. Before he left the Rebbe gave him an envelope, with instructions to give it to the Rebbe's grandfather, who was then dead.

On the way home he took sick in a strange town. The people of the town met another Stoliner hasid, and they told him of his sick friend. Consequently, he went to visit him and he saw that he was dying. He told him of the letter the Rebbe asked him to deliver. The other hasid, who was much older, suggested that they trade places and let him deliver the letter. The younger one agreed on the condition that he will return to him to relate what transpired in heaven. They traded places and the older man got into bed and became very sick and died. He was buried with the letter in his hand.

The younger hasid relates that his friend came to him in a dream and said, "As soon as I was buried, a messenger came and asked me if I have a letter for the Karliner. I said that I have, but I must deliver it personally. I was led from one gate to another and at each one they wanted to take it away from me, but I persisted that I alone must deliver it. Finally, I was brought into a great hall and the Rebbe came and took the letter from me. Then the angels wanted me to go back to stand trial, but the Rebbe said, 'Since he is here, let him remain.' " [63]

ZZ, Stolin, Y

Blood Poisoning (H81)

In my father's time [Rabbi Ben Zion Halberstamm] there was an anti-Semite who threw a rock through the window. Later he got blood poisoning and his hand had to be amputated. This is better than police protection.[64]

P, Bobov, Y

The Operation (H82)

A Polish Jew from Chuguyev came to Kharkov in order to be cured by a doctor. This doctor was a specialist and a friend of this Polish

[63] Dubnow cites a legend in which a petition is put in the hand of one recently deceased so that he could present it to the Lord (*History*, 2: 22).

[64] This tale was told at a melaveh malkeh in response to a suggestion that the hasidim ask for police protection so that they could walk in safety at night.

Jew. An uncle of mine was there also. He was a respected Jew there. He went with other Jews to the specialist to talk with him about things in general. They asked him what was new, what was he doing. He told them, and then the specialist said: "I'll tell you a story about the Stoliner Rebbe. You'll laugh, but I'll show you facts that it's true."

He said: "In the town of Chuguyev there was a rich man who had factories, and one of his workers was a hasid of the Stoliner Rebbe. And the worker's wife became sick and she had to see a big doctor in Kharkov. He couldn't afford to go but the rich man learned about it and gave him the money to go to Kharkov. When they came there the specialist found out that she had cancer. Everyone knew she had cancer, but to operate would be more of a danger. So it was left that they were not allowed to operate. They decided to write to the Stoliner Rebbe and they sent a telegram with my return address. The Rebbe answered that they should operate right away, and I told it to the husband. The husband begged the specialist to operate on her. They operated on her and they found out that she never had cancer, only the intestines were turned over, and after the operation she walked out a healthy person. And in case you don't believe me, I still have the telegram."

AA, Lubavitch, Y

One Mitsveh (H83)

At Belz they used to tell the story of a man who was not religious but who kept one mitsveh—he washed his hands before eating. He ate treyf, he did everything, but this mitsveh he kept.

Once he was on a road and he came to a forest where bandits were and he stopped to eat. He went to look for a stream to wash his hands, and as he wandered in the forest he was found by the bandits and killed.

When his soul arrived in Heaven it was thought he would immediately be sent to Gehenna. No, it was decided that since he had risked his life to perform a single mitsveh, he would go to Paradise.

And they say the Belzer Rebbe used to add, "And if for one mitsveh this impious man was sent to Paradise, what will the rewards be for you who struggle each moment to perform all of the mitsves?" [65]

J, Lubavitch, Y

The Second Child (H84)

My grandfather tells me that when my mother became pregnant, when it came close to the ninth month, grandfather took father and went to the Belzer Rebbe. It was close to the time, and it was customary that the Belzer should give a blessing. My grandfather told him of the circumstances, but the Belzer did not answer. He repeated it twice, "I want a blessing." The Rebbe said something, but he just mumbled. The child died. When my mother became pregnant the second time my grandfather and father went again. This time when they told the Rebbe he took a terrific interest, told them which hospital to go to, which doctor to take, to go at a certain time, and he assured them everything will be perfect. To them it was a miracle. It was a sign that he saw that the first child would not live and he did not want to say good luck, to give his blessing.[66]

JJ, Belz, E

Dogs (H85)

When a young fellow wanted to become a shohet [ritual slaughterer] the Belzer Rebbe gave him a diploma when he knew the laws. Then he opened the blinds and there were dogs in the back.

[65] Compare HA49 and Langer, *Nine Gates*, pp. 49–50. For a description of the court of Belz, as well as tales of the Belzer Rebbes, see *ibid.*, passim. Compare the tale of a man who kept the single mitsveh of washing his hands before eating. He was slain as a consequence of his other actions, but this single, consistent act of piety won him a reprieve before the Heavenly Court (Newman and Spitz, *Hasidic Anthology*, p. 167, no. 2).

[66] See HA25.

"You see these dogs," he said. "They used to be shohtim who abused their privileges and declared treyf meat to be kosher." [67]

C, Lubavitch, E

The Dybbuk (H86)

There is a story about the Belzer Rov in Israel. A Yemenite woman started screaming. I don't know the case exactly, but they heard a voice in her. It was talking. And they took her to the Belzer Rov. And the Belzer Rov went out into the yard and he chased the dybbuk out. That was one story that was just recently. [68]

S, Klausenberg, E

The Belzer (H86a)

I went to see him [the Belzer] twice. Once before I was bar mitsveh and once afterward. When I went to see him I was suffering with my ears, but afterward I was all right.

BBB, Belz, E

Dreams (H86b)

Some people today have been helped by the [Belzer] Rebbe in their dreams. One man in Jerusalem was lame. The Rebbe came to him and helped him up, and when he woke up he was all right.

The Rebbe has been dead for nine years. He was seventy-six. August 7 is his yohrtsait.

BBB, Belz, E

[67] Compare the tale of the dishonest butcher in Gaster, *Ma'aseh Book*, 1: 52. See *In Praise of the Besht*, no. 250, in which a sinner is transformed into a dog and then into a fish.

[68] Compare S36, a tale told by a Satmarer Hasid.

Disciples (H87)

Now I will tell a story that I told once after a few drinks. It was tasty then to hear it. [The storyteller's glass is filled.] To your health. This should be a happy month and a happy year.

I was by the previous Rebbe the last time in 1919 on Simhes Toyreh. After that we could not travel any more. There were great things revealed at that time. Since we are all his tmimim [hasidim] I will start the story as the Rebbe started it to his tmimim.

The whole discussion was about the tmimim, and before that he mentioned how he made tmimim. The Alter Rebbe was chosen from heaven, and it is known that he was chosen and his children after him. God chose the Alter Rebbe and we stem from David the King. And he started to speak about tmimim. And he reminded us of the saying, "What does God ask from you? To fear!" He asked the disciples to remember that there are always tmimim. And he continued on, "No matter where you should be, no matter what the times may bring, you should always remember you are tmimim."

So they always wondered if the Rebbe meant that he knew that there will come a time when they will be in different countries. But after they saw the written discussions that the Rebbe held, they saw it clearly written—they saw that he used the terms "in whatever countries they shall be." They realized that the Rebbe saw a time when the disciples will be in other countries. And he always stressed you should always remember you're tmimim. In good times and bad you should always remember you are tmimim and there is a very nice story connected with that.

The Rebbe appointed an overseer of the money that goes for the brandy, and Reb Hershel agreed that he would be responsible for all the money, and he wanted the Rebbe to assure him that he will have all his needs fulfilled. The Rebbe told him he will have all his needs fulfilled.

Reb Hershel said, "No, I don't mean materially, I mean spiritually." Reb Hershel thought he did not need the Rebbe's blessing: he was rich at the time; he had one factory in Krebechuk and one that he just bought in Rostov.

The Rebbe said, "You will be fulfilled spiritually also." And then the Rebbe said quietly, "You will all be fulfilled. And how do I mean fulfilled? That you will all come back to Lubavitch safely, just as you went away."

Then Reb Hershel told a story that he heard that Reb Shmuel saw the Rebbe in 1920, and the Rebbe also told him: "God will help you so that you will come back to Lubavitch."

J, Lubavitch, Y

The Train Ride (H88)

This happened to L. C. He was in the fruit business. He became sick and went to the doctor, and the doctor told him that he needs an operation. He went to the town of Vitebsk because they had a nice hospital there. Since his fruit business often took him to Leningrad he decided to go there to ask the Rebbe where he should have the operation—in Leningrad or in Shamenz. At this time the [Lubavitcher] Rebbe was on vacation and he went to the Rebbe and asked him where to have the operation. The Rebbe said, "In my view you do not have to have the operation in Leningrad but you should go home immediately." And the Rebbe told him that when he goes on the train he should travel second class.

On the train he was in pain and he was yelling, and he heard a knock on the door. A man came in and said, "I have some medicine for you that you can't get anywhere, not in a drugstore nor from a doctor. It was left over by a German who once went on this train." So he took the medicine in his hand and as soon as he did so he felt better.

And he brought the medicine back to Leningrad and until this day he feels that he does not need any operation. And now he understands why the Rebbe told him to go back on the train in second class.

YY, Lubavitch, Y

Punishment (H89)

The past Lubavitcher Rebbe told how in an old diary he read that two Jews in Paris saw a body taken from a grave. They looked at the corpse and they saw that on the forehead and on the left arm where the tefillin [phylacteries] are placed there were big holes.

EE, Lubavitch, E

The Horse (H90)

I heard Rabbi Schneersohn tell this.

This man used to go to the town of Lubavitch in Russia every once in a while to hear the great rabbi speak. And in his later years, when he was quite an old man at the time, his wife and his family, his children, asked him, "Why don't you buy a horse and wagon and that would make it easier for you to go?"

So he said: "When I come to the world to come I will get rewards for many of the things I've done. And one of the things will be my going to Lubavitch every time and hearing the toyreh of these great tsaddikim. And if I will be in heaven and I will ask reward for that and I will go with a horse, the horse will also want reward for that. And since he will definitely get rewarded for going to Lubavitch, I don't want to be together with a horse in Heaven."

Rebbe Schneersohn told it at a fabrengen in reference to the fact that misnagdim often ask questions—some in earnest, some to mock. To those who mock, don't bother to answer. And in this reference, he told the story of the hasid and horse—the misnaged being the horse.[69]

XX, Lubavitch, E

Wakhnakht: I (H91)

A hasid who was plagued by the fact that his children would always die on the night before their circumcision came to the [Stoliner] Rebbe for a blessing. The Rebbe gave him an envelope and told him that with his next child he should have the moyel and ten people in the house the whole night, and if something happens he should open the envelope. The hasid obeyed, and when it was just at dawn they heard the mother of the child screaming that the baby is choking. They tore open the envelope and the note had two words [in Russian] "Circumcise immediately." The moyel performed the circumcision and the baby lived.

GG, Stolin, Y

[69] This analogy was also drawn by Rabbi Jacob Joseph, the Maggid of Ostroh (Newman and Spitz, *Hasidic Anthology*, p. 310, no. 4).

Wakhnakht: II (H92)

A woman whose children had always died before the briss came to
the [Stoliner] Rebbe for help. The Rebbe wrote something on a
piece of paper in Russian, and told her to put it under the baby's
pillow. If the baby became sick they were to open up the kvitl and
follow out the instructions. She gave birth and eight days later, the
night before the briss, there was a wakhnakht—the father stayed
up all night with his fellows and said certain prayers. At the
wakhnakht they saw the baby getting blue in the face; they noticed
convulsions gripping it. The father remembered the kvitl. It was
just getting light. The note said to make the briss right away. The
moyel was there. They made the briss and the baby survived.

Mendel, who told the story at the last yohrtsait, said he knew
the person. He lived in Stolin till he was seventy years old. They
called him the "moyfes kind" [miracle child]. He lived till he was
seventy. He was killed by the Germans.

SS, Stolin, E

The Rebbe's Touch: I (H93)

The Rebbe raised someone from the dead. Reb Mendel saw it on a
wagon. The driver fell off and hit the concrete. He banged his head
and died. A doctor examined him and pronounced him dead.

The Rebbe was laughing. He said, "Put him in the wagon."
The Rebbe rubbed the back of his neck. The man got up and went
out of the coach.

The hasidim went back to the place where it happened and made
a blessing. We make a blessing when there is a miracle. When
they came back the Rebbe asked, "Did you make a blessing?"

U, Stolin, E

The Rebbe's Touch: II (H94)

In Europe, there is one case when a man was riding in a wagon and
he fell. He hit his head against a stone. The [Stoliner] Rebbe

touched him on the head a little bit and he came to himself. He recovered immediately.

B, Stolin, E

Poverty (H95)

Stories tell how in Europe it happened that a man because he became poor went to see the Rebbe and wanted the Rebbe to help him so that he should become rich like he was before. The Rebbe said he cannot do anything for him. But the man went to a brother of the Rebbe's, Moshe, and he wished him he should be like he was before. But the result was, he was not long in this world.

The meaning was, he was meant to be poor so that he should remain longer in this world. The Rebbe refused to help him because he would be harming him. The Gemoreh tells us that sometimes hardships can prolong one's years. He could not do anything to help him for his own good.[70]

B, Stolin, E

The Dog (H96)

In 1939, before the Karliner Rebbe came to Israel, and the hasidim did not know he was planning to come, the rabbi and the shohet of Tiberias had a dream on the same night. A soldier who was killed during the First World War came to them, and said that the Karliner Rebbe was coming to Israel and he was the only one who could help him attain peace in heaven. The dream repeated itself on the next night.

When the Rebbe came to Israel, a dog barked continuously the whole night. In the morning the Rebbe went to the Sea of Kineret to immerse in the river. The rabbi and the shohet came and told him of their dreams. He went back to the river to immerse, and asked the shohet to immerse also and repeat the dream. He then said that the dog will not bark any more, showing that the soul of

[70] See *In Praise of the Besht*, no. 107, in which a childless hasid will have a son, but will lose all his wealth.

the soldier was evolving. It was residing temporarily in the dog, and it had no rest before the Rebbe helped him.[71]

M, Stolin, E

[71] Compare *In Praise of the Besht*, no. 12, in which the Besht helps to free a sinner from the form of a frog. For other dreams see H96, HA22, HA23, HA48, HA54.

HASIDIM AND TSADDIKIM

IN AMERICA

A Mission (HA1)

Ten years ago, in the summer, the [Lubavitcher] Rebbe [Joseph I. Schneersohn] sent ten boys, students, to my farm with a mission to bring a certain M. to the melaveh malkeh. It was eleven years ago. It was the last year [1950] the Rebbe was alive. The Rebbe told the boys to tell me I should make a third meal in H., New Jersey, and see that M. should attend. And I should ask for M.'s mother's name.

We went to the village and we bought herring and some brandy. And we told the people of the town there will be a third meal, and we made a minyen Friday night. A boy, G., was the oldest of the boys who came, and he prayed and he learned. And at the third meal I asked the gabai of the shul where could I find this fellow M., because the Rebbe said I should bring this person to the third meal. The gabai said, "Here he is. As long as the shul is standing, he never came here. It's fifteen years already."

We prayed the afternoon prayer and we all washed and he washed also. And the problem arose, how could we ask his mother's name? How could you go to someone and say, "Tell me your mother's name." So I elected to ask him, and I sat down near him at the third meal. We started drinking lehaim [to your health], and I said that since tonight is my mother's yohrtsait, and it was not, I want to drink lehaim for her soul. And I mentioned her name, and I asked him, "What's your mother's name?"

So he answered, "K."

We said the after-dinner prayer and we dispersed.

He was never seen in the synagogue again. I saw him on his way to work but never in the synagogue. A few weeks later I asked the gabai: "How come we never see this M. in shul. We never see him."

The gabai answered, "The person has disappeared since the third meal and he left a wife, a goyeh with two brats. And the police are looking for him."

([At another telling the storyteller concluded:] We think that he had a Jewish wife and children. He left them and married a goyishe woman, then left her to return to his first wife. I only think—I don't know.

I don't know why the Rebbe wanted his mother's name, but you can see the powerful attraction of the Rebbe that he could draw into the synagogue on that night a man who never appears there.)[1]

EE, Lubavitch, Y

The Rebbe's Grave (HA2)

The [Lubavitcher] Rebbe visits the grave of the previous Rebbe once a month. Someone may ask help for one who is sick and the Rebbe prays. Do you want to hear a story? Two weeks ago I was standing here and two women came in. They live somewhere upstate. They wanted to know where the office was. They said every year they came here to give a donation. So I said, "If I'm not getting too personal, why do you come here every year?"

One woman explained: "A number of years ago I lost my husband. I was in terrible despair. I was depressed. I couldn't do anything. I was in the care of doctors. I didn't know what to do. Ten years passed. I thought then I would be able to stand it if I visited the grave. I thought I would feel better. It was worse. I felt terrible. There was a rabbi there who wanted to know if I wanted him to say prayers. I said no, but I asked him to explain what the little building was that was there. He said that it was by Rabbi Schneersohn's grave and it was placed by the grave of a great man for people to visit there. I just wanted to sit there. I sat there ten minutes and I felt better. I felt at peace. So now I come here every year to give a donation."

TT, Lubavitch, E

---

[1] For a similar tale set in Poland, see Newman and Spitz, *Hasidic Anthology*, p. 197, no. 1.

Psalms (HA3)

The [Stoliner] Rebbe was a very hidden person. Most of the stories about him concern the last five years of his life when he began to reveal himself.

One of the first stories that occurred concerned a fellow in Bronsville. He had a grandson who had polio. They took him to a hospital and said that he would not last through the night. He should pick up the body tomorrow for the funeral.

He called the Rebbe and begged for mercy.

The Rebbe said, "Do something!"

"What should I do?"

"Stay up the whole night and say psalms. I'll do the same."

They did so, and the next day the baby crawled out of the crib—it had been crippled—and it was completely well.

M, Stolin, E

The Operation (HA4)

There was a child that was ill. The parents were told by a specialist that he should have an operation and even then he had only a fifty-fifty chance. The boy's parents went to the [Stoliner] Rebbe and the Rebbe said, "Don't operate. He'll be all right."

The hasid was willing to listen but his wife objected. They told the specialist that they would not go through with the operation. The specialist said, "Who says you shouldn't operate? Who goes against the word of a specialist?"

They returned to the Rebbe, and the Rebbe said: "I said no! If something happens to that child shout through the streets that the Stoliner Rebbe is a murderer!"

The child recovered.

F, Stolin, E

The Bandages (HA5)

There are stories here about a person who couldn't see, a child, and so he [the Stoliner Rebbe] mentioned they should go to this hospital, to this and this doctor, and have an operation. And after the

Wedding. Williamsburg

Wedding

Dancing at the conclusion of a melaveh malkeh

Elderly hasid

Proprietor of a fabric shop. Williamsburg

School teacher. Bobov

Davening wearing talis and tefillin

Mother and child. Williamsburg

Family. Williamsburg

Mother and child. Williamsburg

Young boy. Williamsburg

Young girl. Williamsburg

Young children. New Square

Storytelling at a melaveh malkeh. Lubavitch

Children playing in besmedresh. Lubavitch

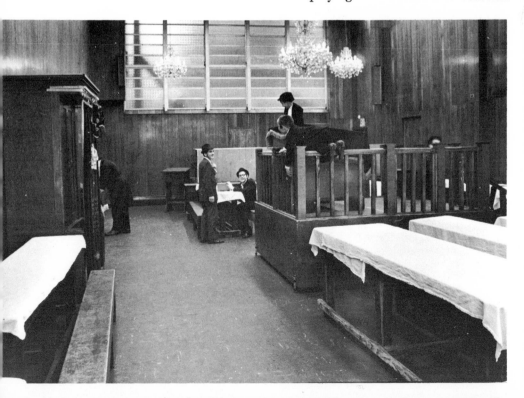

Newlyweds. Williamsburg

operation, he told him—of course his eyes were bandaged—right after the operation untie the bandages and put a candle before him. And of course the nurses would not let him. "What are you doing?" He had to put up a fight, and despite opposition he followed the orders of the Stoliner Rebbe. As soon as he unbandaged—yes, he saw that he sees, he bandaged it back again. He followed instructions, and it came true—the child regained his eyesight.

B, Stolin, E

The Well (HA6)

People in Detroit, they're not orthodox, told me when he, the [Stoliner] Rebbe's brother, went there, there was a well outside the town where they would get water for the city. It broke and then was fixed. It broke the second time. The Rebbe passed by and saw the men working. He said, "It's useless to work." They had to give up.

U, Stolin, E

The Cure (HA7)

A man in Detroit, A., was very sick. The Stoliner Rebbe, came to him, by his bed, comforted him, "Everything will be all right."

He was amazed that everything came out all right. I was in Detroit at that time and he mentioned that.

B, Stolin, E

It's Nothing (HA8)

A rabbi had a niece in Brazil, and he received a letter from her saying that she was sick and that the doctors had given up hope for her. The doctors had said that if she took such and such medicine and kept to such and such diet, it would prolong her life a little bit. The rabbi showed the letter to the Stoliner Rebbe.

"S'iz gornisht [it's nothing]," the Rebbe said.

A shock of wonder went through him, that a man should take the responsibility to say such a thing and to make his opinion public like that.

The Rebbe said, "She should not take this, but she should take this."

She is alive and well today. And to the rabbi the wonder was that he did what he did knowing his reputation was at stake.[2]

F, Stolin, E

The Letter (HA9)

There is another story from South America. Some fellow country-man sent a letter that his child has only a short time to live. He [the Stoliner Rebbe] read the letter and said, "It's not true. The child will live."

Time passed by and the doctors were surprised. They didn't know what was happening. But the Rebbe's words prevailed and the child lived.

B, Stolin, E

The List (HA10)

When the Rebbe was in America, he had organized groups in the yeshiveh in Israel and the groups would have to report weekly to the Rebbe about who missed coming to prayers, who missed coming to the different schedules of learning. And there was a time that the people who sent the lists were afraid to mention the latecomers or those that missed, and they would omit their names from the list. And the Rebbe became angry and said, "Why don't they send me a complete list? Are they trying to spare me any heartache? I know anyway who attends and who does not attend, so they might as well send me a truthful list."

M, Stolin, E

[2] See HA53.

The Debt (HA11)

Berel G., who was always a very close and a dear friend to the Rebbe, dealt with someone in business, and the man owed him $10,000. He came to the Rebbe for help that he should repay him. The Rebbe said that he should give him $200 inside of fifteen minutes. Since he did not have that amount at home he took a taxi to his store and rushed back to the Rebbe, a minute before the time was up. The Rebbe counted over the money and gave him back some, and told him, "Tomorrow at 'And David Blessed' you should daven loud." He obeyed, and right after the prayers the man came and repaid him.

The next year the same thing happened and he asked the Rebbe for help. The Rebbe refused because people would say that Berel comes to the Rebbe only for money.

M, Stolin, E

The Evil Eye (HA12)

A man on Livonia Avenue asked the Rebbe's opinion. He wanted to buy property. The Rebbe said he shouldn't do it. He said he has a house here, here another house. "Do not buy too many things." He meant to be careful of the evil eye.

B, Stolin, E

Real Estate (HA13)

Some Stoliners that the Rebbe helped wouldn't support him. A real-estate operator used to take the Rebbe for rides. He was doing himself a favor. He would go to all the houses and say, "Do you like this one? This one?" The Rebbe would say, "Yes—no." The man made himself a fortune.

FF, Stolin, E

Not to See (HA14)

Nobody knew he [the Stoliner Rebbe] went away to Israel. When he traveled from here to Israel, he had a servant, but he packed the bags himself. He put a stamp on—Cunard Lines. The servant asked where the Rebbe was going. He said he is going over on a ferry to Spring Valley. He could make a person not see things. He could make you not see a person. If you don't have to see, he would make you not see.[3]

A, Stolin, E

Frozen (HA15)

The Rebbe had to travel from Haifa to Jerusalem during the war in order to make papers to come to America. F. wanted to come along and the Rebbe said it was dangerous. However, after the liberation the Rebbe leaned his head in his arms on the doorpost and said, "You can come if you will lie on the floor of the taxi."

The whole way the Rebbe didn't say anything and the road was full of shooting. Then the Rebbe asked F. to sit up, and pointed to an Arab on a hill who was aiming directly at their car. The Rebbe said, "He wants to shoot but he can't." He stood there frozen and was unable to shoot.

M, Stolin, E

What Is Dangerous (HA16)

When the Rebbe was in Israel during the war of liberation, his home was in Haifa. And for Shabbes the boys would travel from Jerusalem to Haifa to be with the Rebbe. However, since the road was very dangerous during the war, there was a mother—a widow—who did not let her only son, Mayer, travel to Haifa.

[3] See HA27, TA8.

The Rebbe looked over the gathering on Shabbes and asked, "Where is Mayer?"

The boys answered, "His mother is afraid to let him go since it is dangerous."

So the Rebbe said sorrowfully, "It's a shame that this woman thinks that she knows what is dangerous and what is not dangerous."

After Shabbes they found out that Mayer was killed by a bomb in Jerusalem.

M, Stolin, E

The Map (HA17)

Once he [the Stoliner Rebbe] took a general on the roof of the yeshiveh in Israel. He pointed out on the map what will happen till the Meshiah will come. This soldier, he is a big man in the army now. Fellows from the yeshiveh in Israel asked him what the Rebbe said. He is afraid for his life if he would tell. And this soldier is not religious. He said that everything the Rebbe said up to this date has come about. This must be ten years ago. Eight or nine things have already happened—the war in Korea. Remember the soldier is not religious. He would not tell what will happen, but when it happens, he would say the Rebbe said that.

U, Stolin, E

The Secret Mitsveh (HA18)

L., a young American fellow, was learning in the Stolin yeshiveh. He was searching for a Rebbe, and he could not find one who he felt knew him and his shortcomings so that he should be able to follow him. L. had a custom that during Hanukeh, when his parents would leave town, he would clean his house as for Passover and prepare packages to send to Israel. No one knew about this. After doing this, he came to the table for Hanukeh by the Stoliner Rebbe.

The Stoliner Rebbe said, "I'd like to know if your face has the same shine on Passover eve as it has after doing tonight's mits-veh."

L. knew where his Rebbe was.

M, Stolin, E

Great Merit (HA19)

It was the last day of Passover, and the [Stoliner] Rebbe was conducting the memorial meal. This is a gathering of hasidim the evening after the memorial services said on the holiday. At this gathering the Rebbe used to speak and mention different members who have since departed, and their being mentioned by the table, by the gathering, was for the benefit of their souls. At the gathering on the eve of Passover, the Rebbe called David and asked him to mention a few of our hasidim who had died recently. On the spur of the moment, David thought of a few who were killed in the Israeli war of independence, and later he mentioned another couple of our hasidim. And that was it. The Rebbe drank lehaim and he said that we could benefit the souls by mentioning them here.

A few weeks later it was the second night of Shevuos, and David dreamed that a young man since departed came to him in his dream. And David asked him, "What are you doing here? What do you want from me?"

He said, "Tomorrow night is the memorial meal with the Rebbe, and since you forgot to mention me on Passover, I want you to mention me this evening."

David related this to the Rebbe at the table and the Rebbe said the soul must have had a great merit to be able to come down and remind someone that he should be mentioned at the table.

M, Stolin, E

Prediction (HA20)

People tell you things every day. The Stoliner told Y. his wife will have been born in Israel. This is everyday stuff with tsaddikim.

U, Stolin, E

The Favor (HA21)

I wanted to go home to Cleveland before Passover. Shabbes came close to Passover, and so I was going to fly before Shabbes. The [Stoliner] Rebbe said, "No. I'll turn you over with the plane."

I said I'd take the train.

He said, "Catastrophes can happen to a train too."

I said, "I'll go home Saturday night."

He said, "No, go Sunday morning."

I said, "Okay." That Saturday night, the train had a crash. No one was killed but there was a crash.

When I came back, the Rebbe said, "The idiot doesn't know what a favor we did for him."

M, Stolin, E

A Piece of Cake (HA21a)

The Stoliner never gave toyreh. He said: "The earlier Rebbes would talk hasides and the people would get insulted and run away. Then the Rebbes spoke about themselves, but the people understood and ran away. I just give you a piece of cake and you should understand what's wrong."

M, Stolin, E

The Dream (HA22)

This happened to me. My wife was very sick, and one time, when I made a blessing before the Torah, he [the Stoliner Rebbe] hollered at me, why I didn't come to him and ask him I should be granted a favor. He knew the seriousness of the case and he was angry at me. He wanted to help whoever he could, especially someone attached to him. He wanted to help on this case.

One Friday, just after the Shabbes meal, I lay down to rest. The

Rebbe came to me in a dream. He appeared to me. I saw his face, a holy face. He said he knows my bitter heart and wished my wife be well again in every way. Then I woke up.

The doctor said, "In such a case, if a person comes out a hundred per cent, it's very unusual." To his amazement everything was all right.

I hadn't asked the Rebbe because I didn't want to nag him about such a case. He came to me in a dream. I went to other Rebbes in the neighborhood, but I know that it was through the Stoliner Rebbe that my wife was helped.

B, Stolin, E

Three Dreams (HA23)

When I moved over here, the Rebbe was not in this world anymore. I bought a business. My married daughter moved here. I bought a house. I wanted to be near the yeshiveh. I wouldn't go to anybody else. After he died, he came in my dream. He was saying the Eighteen Benedictions so loudly I could not understand. When he was alive he davened very quietly. You know the Stolin way is to daven loud, but the Rebbe was sick. In the dream, he was davening so loudly, he was very happy.

The second time, he was sitting at the table, giving shiraim [remains]. He handed me a piece of haleh [sabbath bread], as if to say, I should have parnosseh [livelihood], I should not worry.

The third time, at the table, he said, "Go into the circle and dance with the other men."

He appeared other times in my dreams.

B, Stolin, E

The Telegram (HA24)

I didn't ask many times. I didn't want to nag him. He was sick. I made mistakes. I bought a house. I didn't want to nag. I had a case in court. He was in Israel. I sent him a telegram asking for his blessing. He replied, "Everything will be okay." Thank God. It was so.

B, Stolin, E

The Briss (*HA25*)

A young man was plagued with his wife having miscarriages. He was finally warned by the doctor that it was dangerous for her to try to have any more children. So when his wife was pregnant he came to the Stoliner Rebbe for a blessing. And the Rebbe said: "This one you will lose but the next one will be all right."

And on Simhes Toyreh, a year and a half or two years later, he walked from Bronsville to Williamsburg to tell the Rebbe that today was his son's briss. My brother told this to the Rebbe. The man couldn't go in to the Rebbe—he was sick then—and the Rebbe started to cry.

M, Stolin, E

Yohanan (*HA25a*)

Fourteen years ago [in 1953] our Rebbe [Yohanan of Stolin] visited Israel for the holidays and he was then in Haifa. One day a Sefardic-Italian Jewess came to the Rebbe's gabai and asked for an audience. The gabai forwarded the message to the Rebbe, realizing that the Rebbe had very little time and would not be able to receive her. Much to his surprise the Rebbe told him to have her come tomorrow morning at eight-thirty.

The next morning during davening the Rebbe asked if she is here already and toward the end of the services someone mentioned that she was waiting outside. The Rebbe removed his talis and tefillin and went with the gabai to receive her. She complained that she was childless after many years of marriage. The Rebbe gave her a diet [to follow] and asked that she keep in contact with the gabai. After the Rebbe's return to the States, the gabai wrote him that he had received a letter from her saying that she's expecting a baby and she wishes to have the baby born in Israel. (She had gone back to her family in Italy.)

The Rebbe wrote back that she should make sure to be in Italy at the time of birth. It seems that she disregarded this letter, because at a later date the gabai wrote the Rebbe that he received a letter from her from a town in Israel that she is here in Israel with her husband because she wants the baby to be born here.

The Rebbe did not answer to this. A while later the gabai forwarded this letter to the Rebbe: "You don't know who your tsaddik is. It seems that it was so important that my baby be born in Italy that my husband's father died and he had to return home to settle the estate, and then my father died and I was called back to Italy. And my son was born in Italy."

The Rebbe wrote back: "Ask her what name she gave him."

She answered: "It was strange that we did not previously pick a name for the baby. But on the day of the briss, both my husband and I thought that the name Yohanan would be a nice name." (She did not know that the Rebbe's name was Yohanan.)

M, Stolin, E

Yarmelkeh (HA26)

When the Rebbe was lying in the hospital he had no strength to move himself. One side was paralyzed and the other side lacked sufficient strength. Every hour and a half he had to get out of bed. We used to take him out of bed. It was a job to carry him out, to move him. When we would move him, his yarmelkeh used to fall off. In the middle of the night it was hard to find. So I was made gabai of the yarmelkeh.

With me in the middle of the night I'm in a trance. Once they woke me up. We moved the Rebbe. Then, "Where's the yarmelkeh?" I was like stunned. "Where's the yarmelkeh?" I knew I put it someplace, and I scratched my head and I felt two yarmelkehs. I had put it on my head.

So the Rebbe said, "Yiddel wants to become a Rebbe."

A, Stolin, E

The Hospital (HA27)

The Rebbe was due to leave the hospital Friday afternoon and did not want anyone to know of it. M. had to bring food for Shabbes. He came to the hospital in the morning to ask what the Rebbe wanted. The room was in disorder with the suitcases and clothing ready for packing, yet he didn't see anything. Only after he left, the Rebbe had someone phone M., to tell him not to come.

We asked the Rebbe how come M. didn't see the Rebbe packing. The Rebbe answered, "If we don't want him to see, he can't see."

A, Stolin, E

Uncorrupted (HA28)

After seventeen months, the Rebbe was dug up here and the coffin opened in Israel. In Israel they're not buried in coffins. The body was perfect.

M, Stolin, E

All His Children (HA29)

I'm going to tell you what happened at Benei Brak [in Israel]. A friend of mine was there. He was in the [Belzer] Rebbe's room, and a man brings in a kvitl to the Rebbe and he has the list of all his children. And when the Rebbe comes to one name of the daughter, the Rebbe stops. He was reading it and he says, "What's . . . ?" Then he says again, he doesn't want to read. The man grabs himself—oy vey, that was his daughter that died. He was always used to writing in the kvitl all his children, so he forgot that he wrote it in.

S, Klausenberg, E

Help Me (HA30)

Talking about the Belzer Rov, I'll tell you a story of a friend of mine, a very close friend. He didn't have any children for about twelve or thirteen years. And his wife went to the Belzer Rov, and she was there for about three months. And he never promised her anything. I mean you know it was always between the lines, but they knew already when he promised. Before Kol Nidrei the Belzer Rov used to go past by the woman's shul and used to wish a happy "before Yom Kippur." So she went just before that and she started screaming there and she did not leave him alone. She just stepped in front of him and started screaming, "Rebbe, you must help me. I don't have any children." She wasn't a young woman either.

And then the Rebbe asked the gabai to say what her name was. And then they knew already that that was it. So she gave her name and he promised her.

And she had a child. She came back, and three-quarters of a year later she had a child. That is the only child they have. I mean this is a very good friend of mine.[4]

S, Klausenberg, E

Kvitl (HA31)

I will tell you yet another story about the Belzer Rov. M. does not have any children either. And he went to the Belzer Rov. He went to Israel with the [Klausenberger] Rebbe about five years ago. The Rebbe then went to Israel. He went along with the Rebbe. So he came in to the Belzer Rov. So he had kvitlekh for himself, he had a kvitl for a friend of his who doesn't have any children in the United States, and he had a kvitl for G. who was mentally ill in Israel. And he put in all the three kvitlekh by the Belzer Rov. So with the

[4] The Biblical source of a birth resulting from a saint's prayer is I Samuel 1: 1–20. See also Ginzberg, *Legends*, 2: 220; 4: 59; 6: 217, n 11. See Noy, "Motif-Index," Motif T548: birth obtained through magic power; Motif T548.1: child born in answer to prayer; Motif T548.1+: child born after saint's blessing.

Belzer Rov there was a way of knowing—I don't remember how he told it—there was a way of knowing when he read a kvitl and he started to get like emotional about it, they knew that that person was helped. So he says by his kvitl he didn't see anything, by G.'s kvitl he saw something—G., she's living here in the United States. I mean she has a child already, just to tell you she was then seven years in a mental institution. And by her kvitl he said he saw that she was helped. And when M. came off this plane, he came over to me—"Is K.'s wife pregnant?" So I said "Yes."

I mean that was something there was no hiding. He was in our generation, the only one where you actually saw completely open miracles that you didn't see anywhere else. I mean it was just completely open. All Israel was flowing with his miracles. It was just like nothing. When he said something, they always knew it was that way. I mean if they knew people were sick and they came in, and they knew if he didn't wish it, it was finished.

S, Klausenberg, E

The Mistaken Journey (HA32)

There is another story I can tell you. There is Rabbi G. He had a son who was engaged to be married, and the son got a tumor on his brain. And he grabbed a plane and he flew to the Belzer Rov. And he walked in to the Belzer Rov and he says to the Belzer Rov his kvitlekh.

He says, "What are you doing here? Go right home."

And unfortunately on the way home the son was dead already. I mean he knew right away that it was hopeless.

S, Klausenberg, E

Cesarean (HA33)

I know for a fact that there is one of our young people, his wife's first child was cesarean. Now to have children natural is not too healthy for the mother. Yet the [Boyaner] Rebbe has told him each time he should do it natural. And thank God his wife is all right, and his children are okay. He has four more children after that. I mean they don't say it can't be done, but they say it's not good. And yet the Rebbe has told him each time they should let it be natural. And that's only one case.

W, Boyan, E

Adding a Name (HA34)

My brother once was very, very sick when he was a child. My father went into the Boyaner Rebbe. He told him then to change his name. There is a certain thing of changing—not changing—but adding on a name. That's what they do. And he promised him he would be better. He started getting better then.

S, Klausenberg, E

Foreseen (HA35)

My cousin went in to see the Satmarer Rebbe the eve of Yom Kippur for a blessing. The Rebbe leaned forward and said, "You should be healthy." My cousin was surprised and later he became worried.

A few weeks later he went down to make a sukkeh and he fell down and hurt his leg. Then he realized what the Rebbe had meant. The Rebbe had seen what would happen.

They said that he should go to the hospital, but the Rebbe told him to see Dr. K. and he went there.

K, Sziget, E

Children (HA36)

This is what happened to me. My wife did not have any children. I went to the present [Bobover] Rebbe's father and I told him. He said, "You'll have." And I had.

E, Bobov, Y

Jail (HA37)

When the [Squarer] Rebbe was cheated, he was told he could bring the man to court. He refused, saying, "I would never put another Jew in jail."

I, New Square, E

Fast (HA38)

Just the other week I saw a miracle by the [Bobover] Rebbe. On the Fast of Gedaliah, you're supposed to fast. The Rebbe's four-and-one-half-year-old son is learning the Torah, and the Rebbe told him he had to fast that day. And he told him, "Go into the office and ask M. what you're supposed to do today."

But he was shy and afraid to ask, so I went in with him and asked, and M. said, "Oh, I forgot! I had a cup of coffee this morning."

You know what that means? He knew. He knew. It's farsightedness.

HH, Bobov, E

No Way Out (HA39)

This story happened by my Rebbe, the Klausenberger Rov.

A director of the yeshiveh—I know him personally very well—he's a very fine young man, an American young man. I mean he is not young—he's probably in his mid-fifties. He's quite a successful business man, and he always used to come in and help the yeshiveh a lot. And he came in one day, Sunday, and was sitting by the Rebbe about an hour. They had a meeting about the yeshiveh, this and that. They had to raise money. I don't know what the particulars were. On the way out this man tells the Rebbe, "I don't know what to do. I have to meet a payment tomorrow of $5,000 and I don't see how it's possible for me to raise $5,000 by tomorrow. And if I don't have it tomorrow, my whole business can get ruined. And I really don't know what to do."

So he says to him—takes his hand, wishes him, "Don't worry, God will help you tomorrow."

This man walks out and forgets about it. He was quite worried. The next morning he was sitting in his business—he is in the fur business—and a man walks into his business. He never saw that man before. A couple. And they come in, they want to buy a fur coat—a very expensive fur coat. And they pick out a coat at five thousand dollars and some change. And the coat had to be altered and delivered. So he told them that it would be delivered the next week. So he says to this man—he never saw him before—but he says, "If you give me the check today I'll leave off the fifty or sixty dollars there."

He said, "Okay," and gives him the check.

And as that man was walking out, he asks him, "I just want to know—how did you ever get to me?"

So he says "I'll tell you. I'm from Chicago and a friend of mine bought a coat from you about eight years back. And I told him I was coming to New York to buy a fur coat. He told me go in to this man who treats you well."

So he saw this was something. I mean he never expected the customer or anything. So he takes the telephone and he calls up the Rebbe. He always used to call the Rebbe whenever he had anything to talk about. He calls up the Rebbe: "Rebbe, how did you know that this man was going to come in the next day? I mean how did you know it? I want to ask you." You know he's a very frank man, an American fellow who doesn't understand that you don't ask a Rebbe these things. But, "Rebbe, how do you know?"

So the Rebbe says, "I'll tell you. When you were over yesterday, I didn't know how you were going to get it. It's not a miracle. But we have a tradition handed down from the Baal Shem Tov that when a person is in a clamp, something bad is happening to him—as long as that person thinks, 'Well, I'll borrow money from him, I'll get money there, I'll do this, I'll do that,' whatever way he thinks that he will help himself—sometimes it works out and sometimes not. But when a person is in such a bad clamp and he knows there is no possible human way to be helped out of this clamp, 'The only way is that God is the only one who can help me in a supernatural way because I don't see how this can be helped any other way and only God can help me,' then it's one hundred per cent sure, a thousand per cent sure, that God must help him. When I saw you yesterday and you were telling me your problem, and you were saying that you had no way out—you don't know what's going to happen—I saw you had no other way. Only God had to help you. You had the faith in God; therefore, God had to help you. I knew that God had to help you."

S, Klausenberg, E

The Good Gabai (HA40)

The [Klausenberger] Rebbe had a gabai in Israel. A very good friend of mine. The Rebbe eats very late at night, so he brought in a meat meal. So after the meat meal, he tells the gabai to bring him in coffee. So the gabai brings him in coffee with milk in it. He understands coffee goes with milk! So the Rebbe calls in a couple of people that were outside and says "See, this is a good gabai. He knows you're not allowed to drink milk after meat, but if the Rebbe asks for it, he brings it in."

The Rebbe actually meant black coffee but he said, "Look, this is a good gabai! He knows I want coffee, so he brings in coffee."

S, Klausenberg, E

Measles (HA41)

A friend of mine's child got the measles and it went into the brain. I mean that is usually fatal. It was Passover and he ran to the [Klausenberger] Rebbe. And the Rebbe said, "Nothing to worry about. He's going to be healthy, a normal child, and everything will be okay." And it turned out that way.

I mean I've seen it many many times and it didn't come as a surprise to me.

S, Klausenberg, E

A Third Doctor (HA42)

Somebody needed an operation, and all the doctors said he needed an operation. And he wrote to the [Klausenberger] Rebbe. And the

Rebbe answered this person, "Go to a third doctor, and you would not need an operation." And it looks like this person will not need an operation.[5]

I mean you just happened to ask me, but I didn't think of it until a minute ago because it just came to mind. It's a natural thing by me.

S, Klausenberg, E

Dismissed (HA43)

Once one of the yeshiveh students caused a disturbance and the Klausenberger Rebbe warned him if it happened again he would dismiss him. Maybe he was playing ball or something. It happened again and the Klausenberger dismissed him.

A protest came to the yeshiveh and the Rebbe said: "I treat these boys as my sons. I take care of them and meet all their needs. If you throw your son out the door, he climbs back through the window. If he doesn't come back through the window, then he isn't worth keeping."

Z, Klausenberg, E

Blood (HA44)

One Shabbes I cut my finger on a nail on one of the chairs in the shul. A human being is not allowed to eat his own blood. I didn't know if you're allowed on Shabbes to drain the blood and spit it out. I walked in and just stood there in the office [of the Klausenberger Rebbe].

He said, "The Rabbis made a law that you cannot drain your blood on Shabbes."

He did not say good Shabbes to me. He just said it straight out. I have it written down, each instance.

U, Stolin, E

---

[5] Compare H14 and notes, in which three doctors are consulted and the opinion of the third contradicts the first two.

Study (HA45)

I was walking on the Shabbes. I walked from the Klausenberg yeshiveh to the shul and I had an argument with another fellow. I said he should give up working and go to the yeshiveh. He wanted to give up the yeshiveh.

The walk took fifteen to twenty minutes. We walked into the Klausenberger. He started giving a speech: "A person who wants to go to work and not learn, he should bang his head on a stone. He should study, not work." The boy's name was N. After that he stayed in the yeshiveh. There are witnesses. He couldn't have heard that before.

U, Stolin, E

Proof (HA46)

I know a rabbi who won't take any money from people who are not Shabbes observers and if the women do not cut their hair off.

A man came to a rabbi that I know. He was married thirteen years and he had no children. The Rabbi says, "If you cut off your wife's hair you'll have kids."

The people there say, "How can you prove this—that if this man cuts off his wife's hair he'll have children?"

"The worst that can happen is that she cuts off her hair and I'm not a rabbi."

In one year she had a child.

CC, Satmar, E

A Just Decision (HA47)

When two Jews have a difference of opinion, they don't go to court, they go to a rabbi for a judgment.

Two Jews having financial differences came to a rabbi. The rabbi saw who was right. Still, he could not say why, but subconsciously he wanted to judge in favor of the other one. He felt a certain pressure inside himself and did not know why.

After the judgment he put his hand in his pocket and felt money. This man had put money in his pocket and subconsciously this worked against the other man. The rabbi made the just decision, but he had not understood why he had the urge to judge in favor of the man who had put the money in his pocket.[6]

UU, Satmar, E

Simhes Toyreh (HA48)

There was a hasid who once dreamed that his previous Rebbe came to him in a dream and told him that one of his children will die. And so he became very nervous and disturbed, and he came to his Rebbe and told him the story and the Rebbe did not answer him. And he went home after Rosh Hashoneh. The whole time he was nervous and disturbed.

Simhes Toyreh came and all the Jews were dancing. And he was standing on the side and the memories of his dream kept returning—until he decided by himself: "Akh, it's Simhes Toyreh. All the Jews are dancing. I'll go also and dance with them."

Then he came back to the Rebbe and he spoke to him again, and the Rebbe asked him, "What did you do on Simhes Toyreh?"

And he answered him that on Simhes Toyreh everyone danced and so he danced also.

So the Rebbe said, "Think good and it will be good. Think good and it will be good." And of course if the Rebbe said so it will be good.

YY, Lubavitch, Y

The Soldier (HA49)

The old Rabbi was the first Rebbe who created the movement which we now call Habad. Now the Lubavitcher Rebbe lives in

---

[6] This is also told of the Apter Rov (see Buber, *Tales*, 2: 107).

Brooklyn. We are telling a story about this Rebbe. He should be well. One time a soldier went to the Rebbe before he went to Korea. This soldier did not know much about Jewish ways. The Rebbe told him that he should follow all the good deeds that he could, especially the mitsveh of washing before eating. Before a person eats he should wash his hands with a small glass of water and say a prayer. In the beginning the soldier did not know what the Rebbe meant.

And the soldier went to Korea. At that time there was a great big war and he did all the commandments that he knew and also the commandment of washing his hands before eating. One time all the soldiers were sitting around and they wanted to eat. Then all the soldiers took out their food and began to eat, and so did our soldier who went to visit the Rebbe. He took out a little piece of bread and he thought, "I haven't got any water here to wash my hands. What should I do?" It is told that in a person there are two ways—a good way and a bad way. One has nothing to do with the other. So the good side says, "The Rebbe told you to look for water. Go look!" He wanted to go and look as the good side told him. But the other side said, "No. What does the Rebbe mean? Should he look for water in the middle of a desert? The Rebbe thought that if there is a sink with water then you go wash yourself." Just as he was about to begin to eat he caught himself and he said, "If the Rebbe said that I should abide by this law and look for water I should go and look for water." So he went away.

In the middle of the wilderness it was not an easy thing to find water. He went a long way and he found water and he washed himself in order to eat. He ate a little piece of bread. After that he went back to his troop to be with his comrades. When he came back to all his comrades he saw a strange thing. Where all of his comrades were alive before there was now only smoke. Smoke remained. What had happened was that the enemy came and threw bombs on all the soldiers, and he who went away to look for water to wash his hands, he was the only one left alive. Now he realized what the Lubavitcher Rebbe had told him. He should perform all the commandments and the commandment to wash one's hands.[7]

XX, Lubavitch, Y

[7] See Weiner, "The Lubavitcher Movement I," *Commentary*, 23 (1957): 231. Compare H83. See the tale of the talmudic student in *In Praise of the Besht*, no. 53, whose initial sin was his failure to wash his hands.

The Mezuzeh (*HA50*)

Many people in the twentieth century are prone to deny that such
stories are true; so therefore I'll just tell you a few that I don't
think anyone can doubt. I certainly couldn't doubt it because the
person who was involved told me the story.

I was leading a group of children on a Shabbes in a shul in East
New York. After I finished conducting the celebration of the
Shabbes, one of the fathers who had brought the children to me
came up and said, "I suppose you're a Lubavitcher."

And I told him, "Of course. You've guessed correctly." Because
more or less most Lubavitchers look the same.

He told me, "Oh, you have a wonderful leader. Your leader is
truly a great man."

And I questioned him. I wondered what prompted him to come
up with such a spontaneous statement. So he told me, "Do you
know about seven years ago my mother lay critically ill in a
hospital after a brain operation. And my mother was not expected
to recover." He further told me that the doctors had given up hope
for any possible recovery since the operation was not successful and
his mother was in the ward which led up to the morgue. "Now,"
he said, "I was told by a cousin of mine about the Lubavitcher
Rabbi and about his blessings. So of course a drowning man grasps
on to a straw. So immediately, it was in the middle of the night, I
went to a mikveh because I realized that that would be necessary,
and immersed myself in the mikveh and came before the Rabbi and
asked the Rabbi his blessing that my mother would recover. Now
the Rabbi told me to take a mezuzeh and to wrap the mezuzeh in
two pieces of wax paper and to put this mezuzeh under the ear of
my mother. And the Rabbi told me not to advertise this, not to
publicize it, but to go through with it. And of course I thanked the
Rabbi and immediately ran to the hospital and placed this amulet
under the ear of my mother, and instructed the nurses that they
should forever leave that amulet there and under no conditions
should they take it away. And miracle of miracles, the doctors
noticed a faint trace of recovery in my mother until after a few
months she was well enough to come home. And of course we took
our mother home, but we forgot the amulet in the hospital. We

retraced our steps to recover it, and lo and behold we searched the hospital upside down and the amulet was no longer there." [8]

L, Lubavitch, E

Moyel (HA51)

I am a moyel. When I went to live in Israel the [Lubavitcher] Rebbe said to me, "I give to you the power to bless people. They should have a livelihood, good fortune from their children, and health." And so it has been, many times.

LL, Lubavitch, Y

What Can You Lose? (HA52)

A man who lived near me had a son who suffered from a nervous disorder. His hands trembled. I said to the man, "Come with me to my Rebbe [the Lubavitcher]." And he didn't want to. "What can you lose?" I said. "Come to my Rebbe. The Rebbe can tell what to do and he can advise you on the best doctors."

Finally, he came. I went in with him. He told the Rebbe what was wrong, and the Rebbe said, "First your wife must go to the mikveh." The man said that his wife would not go to the mikveh. He refused. The Rebbe pleaded with him but he would not. We were going out and he said, "It's too much to ask."

And the Rebbe said, "It's also too much to ask for your son."

If only his wife had gone. The boy is still sick.

EE, Lubavitch, E

I Saw It Happen (HA53)

I saw the Lubavitcher Rebbe take away cancer with his hand. A man came in and said that he had a cancer. The Rebbe said, "S'iz

---

[8] See *In Praise of the Besht*, no. 97, in which a prayer said before a Torah scroll results in the petitioner being cured.

gornisht" ["it's nothing"], put out his hand, and at that moment it was nothing.[9]

And the man walked in with a note from a doctor that he had a definite cancer. I saw it happen.

R, Lubavitch, E

The Writer (HA54)

The Lubavitcher wrote to a man he should visit somebody in Israel. The man he was to see is a writer. He said, "Go over to him and have a talk with him and remind him he should come back to real Judaism." The man was not orthodox. He said that he was not secure in his position and needs a push to go back. He told him, "Before you go there the man will have a dream. Tell him he had a dream that will remind him to go back to orthodox Judaism."

He went there and saw the man. He told him he should go back. The man turned white when he said he had had a dream. He said, "Yes, it's true."

I know the man. I don't know if he has become orthodox. I saw a copy of the letter.

Q, Tchortkov, E

Heart Trouble (HA55)

A man in Israel was very sick and they wrote to the [Lubavitcher] Rebbe here that he should give him a blessing. The Rebbe wrote back blessing him and telling him he should have his tefillin examined by a scribe.[10] The scribe found that in the saying, "You should love God with all your soul and serve Him with all your heart," [11] the word *heart* was completely missing. This is what the man had—heart trouble. The next day he was better.

EE, Lubavitch, E

[9] Compare to HA8.

[10] Every three years tefillin must be examined by a scribe to see if there are any imperfections (see *In Praise of the Besht*, nos. 14, 28, 93, 94).

[11] Deut. 11:13.

A Bad Scare (HA56)

Rachel had a very bad scare. She had a lump. She went to the doctor and the doctor said it was nonmalignant, but he said, just to be on the safe side, "It's positive, but it's going to bother you. Why not let us open it and take it out? Because otherwise it's going to be preying on the back of your mind. What if it's the one case in a million where we're making a mistake."

And they asked the Rebbe and the Rebbe said, "No. Don't cut."

Then it bothered her so much. And the doctor kept saying, kept advising her so strong that she asked the Rebbe again, and she could see the Rebbe was annoyed by the question again. And it passed and she went for checkups. And it was on the back of her mind. Finally she went to a bigger specialist. She went to one of the biggest specialists. "What are you talking about? I don't see anything wrong."

So she thought it was the Rebbe's blessing certainly.

She's one of those who asks the Rebbe for every breath she takes, literally—which bus to send the child to the country. If she's pregnant, should she travel by car or by plane.

AAA, Lubavitch, E

The Blessings (HA57)

When I was expecting my first baby at that time it was just the first year after we were married and we were going through a lot of economic settling, very hard times, and certainly since I'm expecting a child we let the Rebbe know first of all, and he sent in a very nice blessing. And it so happened all the time I was expecting her my husband had occasion to write in many questions about his own work, personal problems, livelihood problems, yeshiveh problems, and in every letter the Rebbe gave a very strong blessing that I should have an easy pregnancy, a child that should live and be well and be strong. Not knowing any better, it was our first child, we thought that's the kind of blessing that the Rebbe gave every time, and in fact I said, "Isn't that nice of the Rebbe. Did you mention my pregnancy to him in this particular letter?" He says, "No."

Well, when I entered the ninth month I had toxemia of pregnancy, a very bad case, and she was born 4½ pounds. So we feel it was the Rebbe's blessing. Later on, we weren't even aware at the time, a few years later, we sorted our papers, and we read the letters and it just stares you in the face—that I should have a child who lives and who stays alive. And it was certainly touch and go for me and for her. I went into a coma when she was two days old. I was very sick. So for myself and for her—she was in an incubator and then when she was three months old she had pneumonia and the doctor said if it had not been for penicillin. . . .

But my belief in the Rebbe is not contingent on that miracle. In fact, we weren't even aware of the miracle at the time, until a few years later we looked. "Look at those blessings." Later on, in different pregnancies, I never got such blessings from the Rebbe. Just when he heard the good news that I'm pregnant, "mazel tov," and then at the end when he was told I'm going into labor or when I had the baby. Mazel tov and a blessing, but not in every letter that you wrote about something else that mentions the pregnancy and the baby it should be well. We didn't realize at the time how unusual it was. We figured the Rebbe does that for everybody. The wife is pregnant and he gives a strong blessing. My family is a little closer to the Rebbe. We figured, that for us. . . . But now I believe she survived only because of him, only because the Rebbe was praying for us every step of the way. He knew I needed a blessing. It was a perfectly normal pregnancy until the end.

AAA, Lubavitch, E

WAYS OF HASIDISM

The Leaf, the Wind, and the Worm (W1)

The Baal Shem Tov and his disciples were traveling. While they were riding along the road a leaf floated down and settled upon the lap of the Baal Shem Tov. A bit further on a wind came and blew the leaf from the lap of the Baal Shem Tov to the ground; and there a worm came and crawled onto the leaf and used it for shelter and food. The Baal Shem Tov stopped the wagon and called his disciples. "Look here," he said. "When the world was created, even then did the Almighty decree that this leaf should fall on my lap and that a wind should come and take it from my lap and blow it onto the ground where this worm would use it for food and shelter." [1]

RR, New Square, Y

The Whistle (W2)

Before Hasidism the only way to show devotion to God was through prayer—standing in one place and praying.

According to law, you're not to whistle or play any musical instrument on the Shabbes. It was on Yom Kippur, the Day of Atonement, a shepherd suddenly ran into the shul where the Besht was davening and he whistled, a real long whistle, till his last bit of breath. Suddenly the Besht started smiling. When the people

[1] For other tales concerning the foreordained plan, see Buber, *Tales*, 1: 71; 2: 249; Newman and Spitz, *Hasidic Anthology*, p. 62, no. 6; p. 128, no. 3.

asked him the meaning of why he smiled he replied, "Before, I saw that there is a bad sentence passed for next year—but after that whistle I saw that somehow they changed it."

The Besht sent after him to find out what he did that night to bring about the change. "Why did you blow the whistle on Yom Kippur?"

"Rebbe, I don't know what's allowed on Yom Kippur. I didn't know how to serve God. So I blew the whistle to the last drop of breath. I did what I could."

The Besht said, "Now I know that it is not what one does but what his intentions are that count. According to the law he committed a sin. Whichever way you express your feelings it is accepted." [2]

CC, Satmar, E

Nothing Bad (W3)

There was once one misnaged who went to a Rebbe. He wanted to find out what's there. It's a fact that this misnaged came to this Rebbe, and he was there and he wasn't especially impressed. Before going away he says to the Rebbe, "I want to ask you a question." He says, "The Gemoreh says that a person is supposed to bless God for a bad thing as well as for a good thing, and just as happily." So he says, "You make a million dollars or you lose a million dollars. Can you tell me that you can really be that happy?" So he says, "I don't understand it. It's very hard."

So the Rebbe says, "I'll tell you. There's a young man, he's called Zusya." That was Reb Zusya. "Go in, he's in the besme-dresh. Go in and ask him."

So he goes in and asks who is Reb Zusya. He sees a young man sitting there. He walks over to him. And he says, "The Rebbe sent me to ask you a question."

"What does the Rebbe want?" he said. "Tell us the question." So then he says, "I'm sorry, you made a mistake. The Rebbe didn't mean me."

He says, "What do you mean?"

[2] Agus sees this tale as a revival of "the ancient legend of Hanoch (Enoch) . . . telling how he attained the rank of angelhood as a shoemaker, without the aid of mitzvoth, simply by praising the Lord with every blow of the hammer" (*Evolution of Jewish Thought*, pp. 342, 434).

So he says, "The Rebbe couldn't mean me."

"Why?"

"Because nothing bad ever happened to me."

So what does that mean? That means that if a person would really look, in every bad is something good. If a person loses money, it's probably something good. If something happens to a person, maybe he doesn't see it. Maybe twenty years later he'll see what the good was of it, and maybe he'll never see it. But God actually knows that it was for the good of the person.

S, Klausenberg, E

Two Holes (W4)

The Rebbe, Reb Motke Neshkhizer, wanted very much to have a talis koten. A talis koten is a four-cornered cloth with a hole in it that fits over one's head and is worn with tsitses—fringes. He wanted to have one very much from material produced in Israel, Palestine at that time. And being located in Europe, it was very hard for him to get material sent in from there. His hasidim were not very wealthy and they also found it hard. But they knew how much the Rebbe wanted it, so they tried with all their might and finally were able to procure one. When they finally got the material, one of the hasidim asked to be able to sew up the material for this article. However, he was in such a zealous mood and he wanted to do such a perfect job that he folded the material wrong, and instead of cutting one hole, he cut two holes through the cloth, rendering it useless. With his head hanging in shame, he brought it back to the Rebbe and said, "Look, I spoiled your talis koten."

The Rebbe said "No, a talis koten must have two holes: one hole for the neck to pass through and the other as a test to see if Reb Motke would get angry."

M, Stolin, E

The Three Trials (W5)

In Berdichev there was a Yid, a hasid of the Berdichever, whose name was Reb Haim. He was a rag handler—he dealt in old rags and he was a very wealthy man. When he died the Berdichever came to his funeral, and at the funeral he said, "Reb Haim had three law suits in my court, and he won all three of them." And he told of them.

"The first is: once a man was taken away to the service of the tsar's army. And he was there for forty years. Finally he was free. He had saved up ten thousand dollars and he figured he would get married, establish himself, and have something to get life started with. He had this money tied up in a red kerchief, which is the way they carried money in Europe. On his way home he traveled through the city streets of Berdichev during the day. At night he noticed that the kerchief with the money is gone.

"Reb Haim was an old man, and he took a walk early every morning by the river. He noticed someone standing there. The man got undressed, went to the water, and walked away from the water. He saw that something strange was going on. So he asked the man 'What's wrong?'

"He said, 'Oh, never mind, you can't help me anyway.'

" 'How do you know? Tell me.'

" 'No, you can't help me.'

" 'Perhaps I can. Tell me.'

"He says, 'I have lost my money and I have no use for living any more.'

"He says, 'Oh, you lost money? How was the money set up, and where did you lose it?'

"So he says, 'Oh, there was so and so many tens, and so many fifties, and hundreds. And it was wrapped in a red handkerchief.'

"He says, 'Sure. I found it.'

"So he says, 'Are you sure? You're not joking with me?'

"He says, 'No, I found it. Come to my house and I'll show it to you.'

"It was not true. Reb Haim did not find the money, but he took him home anyway and he went to his treasury and he took out the same amount of tens, fifties, and hundreds, and wrapped it in an old red kerchief. And he gave it to the man and he was very happy because it looked just like the packet that he lost. And he thanked him and he left.

"Meanwhile, the whole city heard about this person's tragedy and how nice and charitable Reb Haim was to return the money, and everyone praised him in the city. But the one who had actually found the money and did not return it started to feel guilty. It began to bother him that here he could have caused someone's death, and Reb Haim who did not find the money was kind enough to give him the money and saved the person's life. He felt very bad.

So he went to Reb Haim and said, 'I found the money. I'm returning it to you.'

"So Reb Haim said, 'I don't know you. I didn't take any money from you. I just saw someone that was going to kill himself and for ten thousand dollars I could have saved him. So I saved his life. If you want to return the money to him, go find him and return it to him.'

"So they came to my court and we judged Reb Haim to be right because he did not take any money from this person. If this person wants to return the money, he should find this ex-soldier and return it to him.

"In his second law suit there was a very poor teacher in this town, and he had no means of livelihood. He said to his wife, 'Perhaps I should go to a bigger city. I'll make money and be able to support you.'

"His wife said, 'No, don't go away, because as long as you are here, you do bring some money into the house. If you go away I'll have nothing to eat.'

"He kept pestering her and she did not let him go. Finally he decided to put her off. So the man leaves the house, and then he comes back and says, 'You know what? Reb Haim will give you five kopeks each week.'

"She says, 'Very good. Now you can go away.'

"It came Friday, and she went to Reb Haim and she asked him for five kopeks. So a woman asked him for five kopeks and he gave it to her. There was no agreement but he gave her the money. So every Friday she would go in and ask him, 'Please give me five kopeks,' and he gave her, and there were no questions and she was very happy.

"Meanwhile her husband had a good job, and he returned with a lot of money, and they were very happy. He said, 'How did you live this whole time?'

"She says 'What do you mean? Reb Haim gave me five kopeks each week. Didn't you tell him to?'

"The man reminded himself that he was just kidding to his wife, and he had not meant it. He never made an arrangement with Reb Haim. So they made an accounting of how much he had given her, and it was something like seventy-five to a hundred kopeks, and they went to Reb Haim to return it.

"Reb Haim said, 'You didn't ask me to give any money. Had you asked, I would have given it to you on your account. But here I gave on my own account, my own charity, so you have no right to repay me for my charity.'

"They went to my court, and we judged Reb Haim to be right.

"The third suit they had in my court concerned a rich person who took a turn for the worse and lost all his property. He became very poor. One day, early in the morning before davening, he came to Reb Haim and said, 'Please, I need five thousand dollars. I have a very good business deal, and I could set myself up again if I have this loan.'

"So Reb Haim went and gave him the money. As he was leaving, he said, 'God should bless you and should repay you for this kindness double-fold.'

"Reb Haim went to the synagogue to pray, and a Jew came in and said, 'Reb Haim, you must do something right now. You know what happened? Last night the nobleman was up the whole night playing cards and he lost all his possessions. He must sell his oxen in order to repay his debts.'

"So Reb Haim says, 'What do you mean? I am not a dealer in oxen. I don't know how to buy and sell oxen.'

"But the Jew said, 'No, you must do it. You could make a fortune without any effort at all.' And he kept on bothering him and bothering him.

"He saw that this is something out of the ordinary, and he went and he bought the oxen. He took them to market and he sold them, and in a short span of time he made ten thousand dollars profit.

"Meanwhile this man that he lent the money to was successful in his ventures, and he became rich again. And he came back to Reb Haim to repay him.

"Reb Haim said, 'No, because as you left, you said you're not going to repay me. You said God's going to repay me. And right there God paid me double-fold and I got back ten thousand dollars. Now you don't owe me any money.'

"They went to court, and I said Reb Haim was right.

"A person that wins three such law suits in my court is of such merit that I should go to his funeral and pay my respects."

S, Klausenberg, Y

A Sigh (W6)

They say about Moshe Leib Sassover that he was an extremely bulky person. He was very heavy. And they asked him, "Why are you so fat? Why are you so heavy?"

And he told them, "Because I never worry over anything. I never give a sigh."

"Why don't you ever give a sigh?"

"Because in the whole world, anything that's here, is not worth a sigh."

L, Lubavitch, E

Lust (W7)

This happened by the Baal ha-Tanya, the first Lubavitcher Rebbe. It's a story of a hundred and fifty years ago. He had a hasid who was a kibbitser, a joker. And the hasidim didn't consider him very highly because he was a very light person, but the Rebbe had a high regard for him.

So one time the hasidim were sitting and talking, and they were drinking a little shnapps. And the shohet was there and they brought in a portion of meat, cooked meat, to serve at the table. And the hasidim wanted to take the meat, and this joker took it away.

They said, "Please give it to us."

"I don't want to."

And they started, "Come on. Give it here already."

He said, "No, I don't want to."

And they were really getting angry, "Come on, give it."

So he went and took the meat and threw it into the garbage can. So they wanted to give him a treatment. They wanted to put him out on the table and paddle him, which was a hasidic way of putting someone in his place.[3] As they were ready to do it, someone rushed into the room and said he was just at the slaughter house, and the cow which this piece of meat was taken from was found to be treyf. So the meat is treyf. Now the hasidim wanted to paddle him again because, "Where do you come to know such things? You are not supposed to. I mean this is something which is reserved for the Rebbe. Where do you come to know what's doing here?"

He says, "Don't think I have any supernatural powers. It's just that I saw the lust that you wanted the meat, and it doesn't apply to

[3] See Maimon, *Autobiography*, p. 176, concerning a hasid paddled at the court of Rabbi Dov Baer for fathering a girl instead of a boy.

the hasidim to want to eat meat with such lust. I felt there's something wrong with it. So therefore I didn't let you eat it." [4]

M, Stolin, E

Hide and Seek (W8)

This story was told by the first Lubavitcher Rebbe. His son came to him crying and said, "I went into the forest playing hide and seek. I was hiding and my friends were supposed to seek me. But they didn't."

The Rebbe said, "How like that is God and the Jewish people. God hides from them and expects them to seek Him out. How terrible He feels when they do not."

TT, Lubavitch, E

Dance with Truth (W9)

Reb Areleh [5] said that in his hasides the Alter Rebbe [Rabbi Shneur Zalman] always spoke about how you have to make spiritual things from material things. One night he was speaking on this topic. There was a large group of hasidim around him. He forgot all about the law at that time, that nobody is allowed to go out on the street. So after he was done saying hasides, they were so engrossed by what he said—that there is no physical world—they all went out that night and of course police caught them. They saw men with beards and peyes and they asked one another, "What can we do with them?" One policeman said, "Make them dance."

So one of the hasidim said, "If we must dance, let us dance full-heartedly. Let us dance with truth, and not as a punishment."

LL, Lubavitch, Y

[4] Zevin, *Sipurei Hasidim*, Torah, pp. 301–2.
[5] Reb Areleh Strusseler (d. 1829) was a fellow student of the Mitteler Rebbe. Although he may be regarded as a follower of Habad, he was also a Rebbe in his own right.

Modesty (W10)

The Ropchitser told that when he was a young man he used to sit and learn all night. He never went to sleep at night. He used to sleep a half hour, an hour. So he used to sit by the candles by the table, sit and learn all night. One night he decided, "This is no good. Everybody is going to see the Rebbe." So he decided he was going to close the candles and he's going to. sit and learn in the dark. Nobody will see him learning. He'll sit and learn in the dark and nobody will see him.

So he figures what will happen—he tells the story himself. So he says, "What will happen if somebody walks in and sees him learning in the dark? He'll say 'Oooooh, we have really a great Rebbe. He doesn't even want anybody to know that he's learning. And he's a modest person.'" So he decided he was going to go into bed, and he's going to learn in bed. So the end is, he said, that he fell asleep. So he said, "Sometimes modesty is the idea of the Yetser Hora in order to trick him, to make him so modest that he shouldn't want to do anything." So he says, "If I have to sit and learn, let everybody see me sitting and learning."

S, Klausenberg, E

Fire (W11)

There is another story of the Strelisker Rebbe. All his hasidim were poor. He was the Rebbe of the first Belzer Rov. He was a very great Rebbe and all his hasidim were poor. It was terrible. This is the way the story goes.

One day his wife came in screaming to him, "Why are your hasidim so poor? Why don't you see to God that they should not be poor?"

The Strelisker hasidim were called "fire" because when they used to daven it was like burning. You could hear them miles away—I'm just exaggerating, miles away—you could hear them blocks away screaming and davening. They didn't know what was going on in the world. You could have dropped a bomb in there and they wouldn't know you dropped a bomb. So the Rebbetsn didn't leave him alone. He must see. So he said okay.

The next morning he comes in and when he says "David's Blessing" he said, "Anybody who will come over and grab hold of the talis will become rich." They started davening and they finished davening, and there wasn't one hasid who remembered in the middle of davening to go over to the Rebbe to grab hold of his talis.[6]

S, Klausenberg, E

The Present (W12)

There is a story that the Kotsker Rebbe had all poor hasidim. All his hasidim were poor. They didn't have what to eat. And he had one hasid that was very rich. So this hasid was by him and the Rebbe says, "Do you want a present from me?"

So the hasid says, "No!"

He knew the present the Rebbe would give him—poverty.[7]

S, Klausenberg, E

Sadness (W13)

There was a great rabbi, his name was Rabbi Teitelbaum. The great-grandfather of the man who was here. His name was the Yismah Moshe. "Yismah" means happy. They're usually called by the name of the book they wrote. He was a very great person. Every time before he went to sleep everything was ready for him—his stick and his clothes—so that if he hears the Meshiah is coming he shouldn't waste time looking for his clothes and his stick, he should be ready to jump down out of the bed and go. He was waiting every minute the Meshiah should come. He was also a misnaged. He was against Hasidism.

So he had a son-in-law who was a hasid, and you know the hasidim used to daven late. They used to learn before they da-

---

[6] Compare Langer, *Nine Gates*, p. 99, and **TA22**.

[7] Compare Langer, *Nine Gates*, p. 99.

vened. The misnagdim, they go up in the morning. They used to daven right away. He didn't like his ways—doing like a hasid. He became very mad at him.

So his son-in-law told him, "Why don't you try going once to see my rabbi? Maybe he'll make you understand."

The Talmud says if somebody wants to become good, God sends somebody and he helps him. If someone really wants to. So he was thinking, "I'm going now to the Lubliner and I really want to know the real way, which is the real way—my way, the way I'm going now, or the hasidic way. So I hope from God," that's what he begged, "that the Lubliner, this man, he should be the person to tell me my way is right or his way—he should be the messenger from God, he should show me the right way." That's what he thought. But the big question that he really had about Hasidism was that it says in the Bible that since the Temple was destroyed, nobody should show happiness on his face. He should be sad. That's what it says in the Bible. "You see, I see the hasidim happy the whole day, so how could they be religious people?" It was a big question. So he hoped that he should answer this question.

So all right. He went on his way and he went to the Lubliner, and the Lubliner knew that such a person is coming to him. So when he came in he gave a sholem aleikhem. "Why are you so sad?" he told him. "Why do you look so sad?"—right away as he came in. "You're such a young man." So the Lubliner started talking further: "Maybe in some things you are right that you should be sad. We know it says in the Bible since the Temple was destroyed you have to be sad. But I think you are mistaken. A Jewish person never should show his sadness on the face. Sadness should be in the heart. He should suffer because the Temple was destroyed, but on the face you have to show happiness." And he said further, "I shouldn't have to tell it to you, but it says in the Talmud that if somebody wants to become good they should send him a good messenger. So I'm the messenger." So he knew his mind—what he was thinking.

The Lubliner said further: "I am a student of Rabbi Shmelke from Nikolsburg, in Austria.[8] I was a student of this rabbi. He once told us a story: There was once a king in Russia and he had a war with another king. The other king became stronger and the king had to run away from his palace. So the king started running and running till he came to one of his generals who lived in another

[8] Rabbi Shmelke Horowitz of Nikolsburg, d. 1778.

city. The general saw the king coming, not in his palace, running like an ordinary person and he felt very bad. 'Look—my king!' he wanted to start crying. Then he reminds himself—'What! The king is coming in my house! I should cry? I should make a big parade!' So he threw away his sad feelings. Inside he felt very sad that the king is not on his own throne, that he's not in the palace, but he didn't show it to the king. He made a very big parade with songs and everything. So the same thing. When the Temple was in its place, God was there, that was His throne, that was His palace. The Temple was destroyed and so everybody should cry, 'Look, God is not in his palace!' But he says you shouldn't show it outside. You should keep it in your heart. That's why hasidim are so happy outside."

From then on he became a hasid.[9]

X, Bobov, E

Separation (W14)

Rabbi Akiba Eiger,[10] who was a misnaged and not a hasid, once attended a meeting of the heads of the community in Poland. Someone came who was not wearing a long coat. They all became excited and upset. The newcomer asked, "Why are you so worried? I follow all the laws of the Torah."

Rabbi Eiger answered him: "The Jews are likened to fire, the gentiles to water. If that is the case, then there is danger because, normally speaking, water extinguishes fire; however, if water is placed in a pot over fire the water boils out. That difference, that little separation, means that the Jew can exist."

F, Stolin, E

Their Psalms (W15)

He [the Dinover Rov] was sitting by the table saying toyreh and there were very, very plain people—the real common people, they

[9] Compare Langer, *Nine Gates*, pp. 162–63.
[10] Rabbi Akiba Eiger, 1761–1837, Rabbi at Posen.

didn't know anything. The only thing they knew was hardly how to daven. So he was sitting in the shul by the table, and he was telling toyreh, and upstairs in the back there, in the woman's shul, there were a couple of plain village hasidim. They were very plain people. They hardly knew any of them. And they were saying psalms. They started to sing psalms, and they were singing loudly, and they were singing loudly with their mistakes. You know you could see the way they said it that they didn't know what they were saying, but they were saying it so religiously and crying that they were making a lot of noise. So one of the people got angry at the table. They couldn't hear what the Rebbe was saying. So he gave a scream, "Shah! Be quiet there already."

So the Rebbe stood up and said, "How do you know their psalms are not worth more to God than my saying toyreh?"

S, Klausenberg, E

The Coat (W16)

The Satmarer Rebbe says the Sandzer was the originator of the idea that the hasidic movement is only temporary. When someone wears a coat and the coat starts to fade and you have no money to buy a new one, you give it to the tailor and he has it turned on the other side so that it looks like new. When it also wears, you turn back to the original side. Hasidism was injected into the Jewish nation until it gets back to the established rules. The Satmarer says Hasidism of such greatness was only understood by people of high morality as lived in those days of the Besht. Today you cannot do it.

SS, Stolin, E

Treasure of God (W17)

The Tchortkover Rebbe said: "Why are we called the treasure of God? Because we give everything to God. In everything we have we see God. Everything we have we bring near to God."

Q, Tchortkov, E

Grease (W18)

This is from a recent Rebbe, not from the past. Once the Rebbe said to his hasidim: "I will tell you a parable.

"Once a Jew was traveling and he came to a merchant and purchased there a thousand pounds of wheat. He bought a great many things. Before he left he told him, 'Come in,' he said.

" 'I need a little grease for the wagon.' And he gave him a little grease.

"The Jew started on his way. On the way he met another Jew.

"The second Jew said, 'Tell me, I need a little grease for my wagon. Where can I get it?'

" 'I got some from this particular merchant.'

"This Jew traveled farther. He arrived late at night and he knocked on the door, 'Sell me a little grease.'

"He said to him, 'I'm not a grease merchant.'

" 'You sold the other Jew grease.'

"He said, 'That other Jew came and bought wheat and fifty other things. He asked for a little grease and I gave him a little grease. You come in and ask for some grease. I haven't got any. I'm not a grease merchant. I don't give away grease.' "

Then the Rebbe said, "It is the same thing with hasidim. There was a time when a Jew came to the Rebbe he received the Rebbe's toyreh, learned a little Torah. Before the Jew left he said, 'Rebbe, I have no money. I have to marry off a daughter. Have you a little grease? But if you just come for grease then I am not a grease merchant.' "

S, Klausenberg, Y

Berel and the Klots (W19)

This is a good story and a short one. When there was a conclave of rabbis in Petersburg in the year 1927, all the rabbis stayed at a certain hotel. Reb Haim Brisker also stayed there.[11] And there was a young man who used to like to serve Reb Haim Brisker. The rabbi who wanted to serve was the previous Lubavitcher Rebbe. So

[11] See H68, n. 57, concerning Haim of Brisk.

Reb Haim Brisker told him a story, from his father, Reb Yoshe Baer: [12]

"In the city of Brisk, there was once a Jew who was arrested by the government. He was very rich, and they had to look for ideas to win his case. So my father acted in the following manner. As soon as the rich man came to him, my father became busy. He does not have any time. But he would lecture for two scholars: one they called the Klots [clod], the piece of wood, because he was always sitting and learning, and there would be a hole where he put his elbows as the result of his diligence; the other one was known as Berel the hunchback, because he developed a hunchback from sitting and learning hunched over.

"So he asked him when they did not want to let him in when he was learning with Berel the hunchback and the Klots, 'What are you learning with them? You are learning the section of the Talmud concerned with sacrifices, which in our day and age doesn't have any physical effect on our lives.'

"So my father answered him, 'Listen, I learn once a week with Berel the hunchback and the Klots, and in that shul where I learn with them, I learn every day a page of Talmud.' And he told them that in a different shul they learn mishnayes every day; in another shul they study *Ein Yakov* ["The Eye of Jacob"]. And then he started talking about the average people. 'These kind of people go three times a day to the synagogue. Then there are different people who go only once a day to daven, and there are other people that go only on Shabbes to pray, and there are other people that go only on holidays. And the son of the druggist fasts and goes to pray only on Yom Kippur. You do not see the practical side of my studying with Berel the hunchback and the Klots, but it has repercussions all the way down the ladder. That is the system which works from the top to the bottom and the bottom to the top, and a person should govern himself accordingly.' "

J, Lubavitch, Y

The Purpose of the Journey (W20)

The grandfather of the [Lubavitcher] Rebbe was taking a trip with a German scientist who asked him, "In olden times people

[12] Rabbi Yosef Baer Soloveitchik, Rabbi of Brisk (Brest-Litovsk), d. 1902.

witnessed the splitting of the Red Sea and so it's no wonder that they complied with the Torah. But there are no more wonders. If I could see one angel. . . ."

"Now, I'll tell you. Let's say we are three people traveling—ourselves and the coachman and horses are traveling. The horses know they're traveling to receive oats at their destination. The coachman is driving for his livelihood and is not interested where he's going. We know that we are traveling to meet influential people who may help the Jews. Is it any less a journey for the coachman and the horses because they don't know the purpose of the journey?"

C, Lubavitch, E

Appetite (W21)

There are two kinds of bitterness: pepper burns but does not give you an appetite; horseradish is bitter but it sharpens the appetite. If someone becomes bitter, downcast, he does not go any further. But some little things give one an appetite for perfection.

M, Stolin, E

Blessings (W22)

There was a woman going to one Rebbe after another. She came to the Stoliner in Israel. He said to her, "Are you collecting blessings? You'll remain with nothing. If you want me to add up the ones you went to, I'll do it. Go to one. Have belief. He is the messenger to God."

FF, Stolin, E

The Wheels of the Wagon (W23)

A Jew used to go far to buy at a big marketplace. Once everyone asked him to buy goods for them, and he returned with a wagon full of material. The wagon bogged down in the mud. The driver says, "We must lighten the load."

Throw out what he bought? His wife's yardgoods? What to throw out? "Throw off the wheels. The wagon will be lighter then."

A person has responsibilities. Cut down his car? No, he can't do it. He cuts down on Shabbes, charity, education. He forgets these are the wheels.

EE, Lubavitch, E

No Compromise Possible (W24)

The [Klausenberger] Rebbe was once in South America. A reporter from a very big network of South American papers came in to him to interview him. She asked a lot of questions. The last question she asked was this: "Why, if the orthodox Jews, especially the hasidic Jews, want to live and be together with all other Jews, why should they put up such big fights in Israel when it comes to do with something with religion? Why shouldn't they compromise? Why should they have demonstrations and fights and everything? Why should they fight so much? Why shouldn't they make some kind of compromise, something, so they should live together in happiness?"

The Rebbe answered her. It's from the Dubner Maggid but he brought out more what it means. There is in the Torah a story of Jacob's daughter kidnapped or taken away by Shechem, the son of Hamor. The son wanted to marry Jacob's daughter. And they came to Jacob, and he said, "Why shouldn't we become one nation. We should start living together and we should start being one with the other. I'll take your daughter and you take my son, and we'll live together. We'll become one nation." [13]

So the sons of Jacob said, "You are very right. But you know we are all circumcised, and anybody who isn't circumcised is a disgrace for us. So how could we live with you since you are not circumcised. If you will all circumcise yourselves the way we are circumcised, we can talk some business."

[13] Genesis 34. See Gaster, *Ma'aseh Book*, no. 49; Gaster, *Exempla*, no. 55. See also Babylonian Talmud, *Sanh.* 39a.

So they stress this. At the end they say again, "You should circumcise yourselves like we are circumcised." So why do you have to say again "like we are circumcised"? We are saying the whole time that we are circumcised. Why say again that we are circumcised?

So the Dubner Maggid explained what the Torah means: "If we are one nation it means that everybody should be the same. I mean, if you actually want to live together, not sects but one nation, one people, we all have to be together. That means I can't do something and you not, and you should do something and me not." So he said, "There's one of two ways. Either you should become circumcised as we are or else we should uncircumcise ourselves. Once we are circumcised, we can't uncircumcise ourselves. There's only one other point of view—that you should be circumcised, should become like us. We can't become like you because we are circumcised already."

So the same thing the Rebbe said now. He says, "I went ten days in the DP camp and I didn't touch a piece of meat. I didn't touch anything treyf. Why? Because I was afraid of God. I was afraid God would punish me. Let's say that the lowest form of religion is to be afraid for the fear of the punishment. The greater form is because you love God, which is actually the way it should be. But we will keep it the lowest form. It's because I fear God, I fear Gehenna. God will punish me. I can't help it. I can't go eat a piece of pig meat, because I fear God. I can't. You can push it into my mouth, I can't eat it." He said, "I was ten days in the concentration camp without food. I starved because I wouldn't eat a piece of treyf meat. Why? Because I fear God. I can't. I just can't go and start being treyf. I can't go and start working on Shabbes. I just can't do it. I can't even if you try to force me. I can't do it. Why? Because I believe in God, and I fear God, and I love God and I can't do it. It's something I can't do. But nobody told you that you can't eat kosher. The worst is that you will be uncomfortable if you just eat kosher meat. You wouldn't ride on Shabbes, you can only be uncomfortable with it. You don't fear to keep your Shabbes. That's the reason why these two groups can't get together. This orthodox Jew and this one, he can't be different. He can't compromise. He can't. And the only person that can compromise is the one who is not religious, because what is stopping him from becoming religious? Actually, he doesn't believe in it, I would say, but he has no fear of becoming religious. He isn't afraid that God will punish him because he's become religious. It's a free world. He can become religious. That's why—it's just one of those things."

S, Klausenberg, E

Adjusting the Environment (W25)

I heard this from the Satmarer at the Friday night meal.

The difference between Satmar and other Jews is this: once when the time came to put the Torah back in the covering it was too difficult to fit it in, and the man who was putting it in suggested that they cut the Torah to make it fit. Ridiculous? Of course. You have to cut the covering to shape. We will adjust our environment to fit the Torah and not the reverse.

CC, Satmar, E

NAPOLEON THROUGH

HITLER

Napoleon Will Fall (N1)

This story takes place in the Napoleonic war. The Rimanover Rebbe said, "Napoleon should win and then the Meshiah will come."

The other Rebbes said that the Russians should win because Paris is the symbol of modern things which would hurt the hasidim (like dancing).

There's a sentence in the Torah, "novol tibol—Thou will surely wear away." [1] God said to Moses, "Seek good men to counsel you because alone you will fall." That Shabbes, at the reading of the Torah, they read "Nofol tipol—Napoleon will fall." But it was read according to the Targum [2] and not the Torah.

CC, Satmar, E

The Strategists (N2)

When Napoleon took the city of the Rimanover Rebbe, he passed by the house of the Rebbe. Napoleon looked at his face and said,

[1] Exodus 18:18. See T53, note 42. See Pipe, "Napoleon in Jewish Folklore," *YIVO Annual of Jewish Social Science*, 1 (1946): 298, 301.

[2] The Aramaic translation of the Torah. The narrator apparently is mistaken. The reading "Nofol tipol" ("thou shalt surely fall") is from Esther 6:13. The Rebbe more likely read "Napol tipol" (Napoleon will fall).

"This is the man who commands my fight and is my strategist."
And he gave him a mantle for the Torah.[3] "I see his face whenever
I go to the front. He tells me where to start offensives and where to
make my defenses."

When Napoleon took the city of Lublin, he passed by the house
of the Lubliner Rebbe and saw him sitting there, and he said,
"This is the one that I see on the Russian front making strategy.
Let's capture him." But when the soldiers went in they couldn't see
him. They could only hear his voice.[4]

CC, Satmar, E

Matzot (N3)

When the Rimanover Rebbe was baking matses, he said for each
matseh, "One more Russian . . . one more Russian."[5]

CC, Satmar, E

Blood (N4)

The mothers of sons in the Russian army came to him [the Rimanover Rebbe]. "Why should Napoleon win?"

"Till here [pointing to ankle] I'm prepared to go in blood, and
grass should grow on graves. I'm prepared for anything to make
the Meshiah come."[6]

CC, Satmar, E

[3] See Noy, "Archiving and Presenting Folk Literature in an Ethnological
Museum," *Journal of American Folklore*, 75 (1962): 27–28. The Ethnological Museum and Archives in Haifa contains a parokhet (a curtain for the
ark) made from a French army parade mantle. The donor said it was given
by Napoleon to a Jew from Smolensk who showed the Emperor the correct
path to return to his army.

[4] A similar complaint was made of Rabbi Shneur Zalman. Pipe, "Napoleon in Jewish Folklore," p. 300, n. 21.

[5] See *ibid.*, p. 300, n. 22.

[6] See *ibid.*, pp. 300–301, n. 23, n. 26.

Napoleon's Snuff (N5)

Napoleon was short—not tall. One time in the middle of the night he woke up and he had a strong desire for snuff. And the snuff was high up on the top of the cupboard and he couldn't reach it. So he went to great lengths to bring over a table and a bench and he jumped until he finally jumped up high enough to bring down the snuff. When he finally had it and wanted to take a sniff of it, he said, "No, if my desire is so great that it is making me go to such great lengths to take it, I will stop the habit right now."

S, Klausenberg, Y

Sandz (N6)

I don't know exactly which war it was, but the Russians were in a war at that time and they came to about fifty miles from Sandz. And the Sandzer Rov hated the Russians. He always used to hate them. He called them fonyeh. That's what he called them. He used to call the Russians fonyeh ganev.[7] That's the way the Jews used to call them. I don't know the reason why. So they came and told him: "Fonyeh is coming toward Sandz."

So he says, "I won't let the fonyeh into Sandz."

So his son comes to him and says, "Father, they're about twenty miles away from Sandz."

He says, "I won't let them into Sandz."

It happens a few days later they were ten miles, they were five miles. "Father, they are at the entrance of Sandz and the mayor is going out to welcome them."

So the Sandzer says, "I won't let them in."

As they were standing there, the mayor was outside, there came a telegram from Petrograd—that was the capital of Russia then— that they should take a different route, a completely different route. That was when they were just getting those big tanks and they started carrying those tanks over the mountains and they had such

[7] A pejorative term for a Russian. It is the corruption of a Russian proper name and the Jewish word for thief The term is not uncommon. See Gross, *Maaselech un Mesholim*, p. 211.

a defeat then that he had a lot of pleasure. He wanted them to have the defeat then. And they had a defeat then in those mountains trying to get their big tanks over them.

S, Klausenberg, E

World War I (N7)

I heard there was very much talk about the war [World War I] before the war happened, I think. There was always talk they should leave Boyan because there was no use to stay there. If there would be a war so maybe they should get out before. So the Rebbe [Yitshok of Boyan] said he didn't want to leave because we believe that when you do something you bring it upon you. Whatever you do you bring upon yourself. If you don't do it then maybe the thing may not happen. But once you do something, for example, if you go away, you'd leave Boyan, so in other words you're going away because you fear that war is going to happen, so by doing it and fearing it, it's like bringing it upon yourself. Whereas if you'd sit still there's still a chance.

The thing is that we believe he has something to say in the matter. Even though Serbia and Germany or Austria were fighting among themselves, we believe that the Rebbe upstairs there had more to say about the war than some of these others had.

W, Boyan, E

Why Are They So Quiet? (N8)

Our Rebbe [the Stoliner] was in Israel and he came back to Europe in 1936 or 1937. And he said like this: "In Israel I went to all the holy places and I prayed and the Land of Israel is safe. America will redeem itself with charity. Why do all the tsaddikim—all the Rebbes in Europe—why are they so quiet? Why don't they try to save Europe?"

M, Stolin, E

Delaying the War (N9)

The [Stoliner] Rebbe held back the Second World War for two years. The Rebbe told the students in the yeshiveh that he held back the Second World War for two years. The world hinged on one or two people.

Can a person who says such things be a faker? We're not fools. Would he tell something he doesn't have the power to do? Things we can see him do? God gives power like that only to righteous people.

U, Stolin, E

They Cannot Last (N10)

Hofets Haim,[8] who was not a hasid but hasidim should be like him, said to Haimel Wasserman, his favorite student (who was killed by the Nazis and his head put in a store window), "Do you see all the yeshives? They are run on money contributed by people who earned it on Shabbes. They cannot last. They cannot last." [9]

I, New Square, E

Haimel Wasserman (N11)

This story is about Haimel Wasserman. He was one of the greatest scholars in Lithuania. He was not actually hasidic. And he was in the United States, and he was in England. I think it was 1939, and he knew already what was going on in Poland. And people begged him to stay, but he said, "No, I'm going back to my Jews. I cannot

[8] Hofets Haim: Rabbi Israel Meir Hacohen (1838–1933), known by his work *Hofets Haim* ("Desirous of Life"), was a talmudic scholar in Lithuania.

[9] See *In Praise of the Besht*, no. 148, concerning a mistake in a Torah scroll which could not be corrected because money for the scroll had been contributed by card players. In *ibid.*, no. 149, Rebbe Elimelekh throws away a ring, explaining that it was purchased with money gained from interest.

leave them alone in such a time." And he went back under Nazi occupation and he died with his whole congregation.

S, Klausenberg, E

The Lemberger (N12)

The Leipziger went to Israel before the war. After Hitler got all the power he went to Israel. But the other brother, the Lemberger Rebbe, the Lemberger Boyaner, he remained. He was killed by Hitler. Many people today still remember that during the war there were a number of times that the hasidim wanted to save him, wanted to give good money to get him out. And he said he didn't want to. He said he wants to be together with his people. He doesn't want to be saved—he doesn't want to be better than they. And many people who were saved remember how during the occupation how many people used to stay at his house and used to have where to eat and sleep by him.

W, Boyan, E

Debts (N13)

They say another reason why he [the Lemberger] didn't want to leave [Europe] was because he owed a lot of money. Why did he owe a lot of money? He used to borrow to give to poor people. And that's how he lived. He couldn't go without giving to poor people. He had to give. And to give even a little, a small amount, he couldn't always give either. I mean it wasn't in their nature. They felt that they'll be able to repay. They borrowed. They borrowed from here, they repaid here. But not for themselves but for the purpose of helping out these poor people. And so he had borrowed way over his head for this purpose, and he felt that if he'll save himself people may say that he ran away from the obligations; therefore, he felt he didn't want to have anybody have a bad word about him. So he remained with them and he didn't want to leave.

There was another reason that he didn't want to leave his

people. And he was killed by Hitler in the war. The Rebbe had a big part in the war, but I don't know. I haven't heard them talk much about it. They don't even know the day that he was killed.

W, Boyan, E

The Sacrifice (N14)

A lot of holy Jews that were killed were as sacrifices. Our Rebbe's brother [Abraham Elimelekh of Karlin] was in Israel in the early thirties. His family was in Europe. And as time came for him to go back to Europe he started talking about the dark clouds that are over Europe, and how he sees blood running in the streets. They thought he was a madman the way he was talking, describing Europe. But then the hasidim heard him talking so much so they said, "Maybe we shouldn't let him go back."

So he said no, he has to go back. He has to go back because he has to be with his people to see what he could do for them. He went back knowing that he would get killed, and he got killed. But they figured that getting killed is a very high way of dying. It is a very holy way of dying. And by his getting killed he could have saved others.

M, Stolin, E

Aaron (N15)

The [Stoliner] Rebbe's brother, Aaron, while he was hiding, the Nazis came there by his hiding place. They were torturing a woman. He came out to defend her and they killed him.

B, Stolin, E

Escape (N16)

When the [Stoliner] Rebbe ran away from Poland, he wouldn't go until the last minute, till actually nearby everything was on fire. In

the last minutes, he ran with a horse and wagon. Mendel doesn't
know till the present day how he was saved.

B, Stolin, E

The Trial (N17)

This story happened to my uncle.

The Sandzer Rov, Reb Shlomo Eliezer Halberstamm, lived in
Ratzferd, Hungary. Many people used to go to him. In Hungary
during World War II they used to take Jewish men and use them
as forced labor even before the concentration camps to dig
trenches. They were not treated equally, but like second-class
citizens. And so they tried their best not to pass their physical
exam. In the city of Kossa there was a doctor, a captain, who could
be paid off. My uncle had to go before the board of examiners.
Another uncle had a wholesale textile business that made embroi-
dered pillow covers. Somehow it came to the attention of the
government that this captain was bought off by the Jews. They
tried to find out who the middle man was and so they reexamined
all the men. They contacted my uncle because they saw his name
on a package and learned that he had paid him off. They looked up
the doctor's records and saw that my uncle was mixed up in it.
They checked the records in the post office and saw that he got
packages from my uncle. They found a few other men and they
held a trial. My uncle had a big textile business and had to
disappear because they would find him guilty before he was tried.
For one and a half years he lived incognito. He never came to his
home city. He had a lawyer and the lawyer always tried to post-
pone the trial because he didn't find a good panel of judges that
were not anti-Semitic.

Then my cousin's wife received a phone call from Budapest
saying that the trial was set and that it will be this and this date
when he comes up for trial. My uncle insisted that before he goes
to Budapest first he must go to Reb Shlomo Eliezer. He asked him,
"Do I have to go to the trial or not? Tell me."

The Rebbe told him, "Don't go."

He calls up the lawyer and says, "I won't go for trial."

The lawyer says, "Why not, Mr. L.? In ten years you couldn't find such a liberal panel. We'll win the case. Tell me why you won't go."

My uncle says, "Because the Rebbe says don't go."

The lawyer says, "I'm a lawyer, not a hasid. Who is responsible? Your lawyer, me, or the Rebbe?"

But my uncle says, "No, I won't go."

And the lawyer tells him, "Then I'm not responsible for your case. I'll keep the trial for the other fellows and you do what you want."

The same day when the trial was held—in the afternoon—he received a phone call from the lawyer. "Mr. L., I want to know your Rebbe. Where does he live? Where is your Rebbe?"

My uncle asks him, "Where, what happened?" He tells him, "In my practice this is the first time this has happened. Your name wasn't mentioned in the whole trial. Your whole documents are missing. You did good not to come because if you don't appear they won't know anything about you."

My uncle takes the first train to the Rebbe and tells him, "Rabbi, I am free." He cables to his parents that he is free, because for a year and a half he was incognito. After a week he received a letter from his father, my grandfather. "I am surprised that you didn't tell me that you are free. The Rabbi wrote me a letter that your son is free and I'm surprised that we heard this from the Rebbe and not from you." They never received the cable from their son—only a letter from the Rebbe. The Rebbe knows very well that the son cabled his father, but the Rebbe wrote because he knew that he never received it.

CC, Satmar, E

The SS (N18)

When the Jews were herded into wagons by the Nazis, the Nazis gave orders that everyone was to shave. Then the SS made an inspection. Rebbe Teitelbaum didn't shave, but the SS man said, "Ja, dieser Bart ist rein [Yes, this beard is clean]." And he let him keep it. The Rebbe was one of 15,000 Jews paid for by Kastner, who was later killed by terrorists in Israel.

UU, Satmar, E

The Bullet (N19)

The [Satmarer] Rebbe was reading and a German soldier fired through the window. The bullet lodged in the prayer book that the Rebbe was reading.

CC, Satmar, E

The Guard (N20)

There are hair-raising stories he [the Bobover Rebbe] tells about the concentration camp. Every man who was in the concentration camp can tell you he saw wonders. If they were standing by the guns to shoot them and then something happened to the guard, the guard fell down, he couldn't move. That is also a wonder, no? All the people saw with their own eyes.

X, Bobov, E

Where They Will Go (N21)

The Gerer Rebbe—not the one that is living now in Israel, his father—his father actually wanted that after he died, his sons should not be Rebbe—he had two sons—but he wanted his brother to be Rebbe after him.

His brother lived in Poland, and when Hitler came they took all the Jews and they sealed them up into wagons and they were taking them straight to the death chamber. So this Gerer Rebbe paid ten thousand dollars, I think—or more yet, they were very rich—that they should take his brother out from Poland. And they finally went so far that they paid one of the top SS men, and they stopped the train. The wagons were sealed so nobody could escape, and they broke open the seals and they opened up the wagons and they asked for him to come out.

So he came to the door and he said, "What do you want?"

They said, "Your brother—you're going to Israel to your brother."

He says, "Oh no, I'm not going. I'm going together with all the rest of my brothers and sisters, with all the rest of the Jews. Where they will go, that's where I will go." And he went back into the wagon. He refused to go with them, and he died together with his brothers.

S, Klausenberg, E

Auschwitz (N22)

This story I've heard from various people. I have never heard it directly from the person himself, but he's living here in the United States. It was known that in the gas chamber in Auschwitz they used to rotate the people that worked actually in the gas chamber. They used to rotate every thirty days. That meant they used to burn them and used to take new people, because they never wanted anybody to be able to go tell the world what was going on. So this young man was working there, throwing the remains of the people—taking them out, in and out, in and out. All of a sudden he sees a very old man. They've shaved off his beard and he still had his talis koten, his tsitses on. And he sees something in that man—something familiar. He didn't know what it was. He walks over to him and he asks him, "Who are you?"

He says to him "I am Sholem Leyzer, the son of the Sandzer Rov." He says, "I want a favor from you." This Sholem Leyzer says, "I know where I'm going to. I'm going to be burned. I promise you if you will see to it that while I'm being burned I should still be wearing my talis koten." They actually took them in there naked, but he wanted to be burned at least with one mitsveh on him, because actually when we bury a person, we bury him with his talis on. He says he wants to get burned with his talis koten. "If you promise that you will see to it that they should burn me together with my talis koten, I promise you that you will be saved and you will get out of here."

Even though he knew that it was impossible to be saved, naturally he tried his best, and he succeeded. He smuggled him through with his talis koten, and they burned him with the talis koten. And afterward that man, miraculously, he was able to escape and he lived to tell the story.

This story I heard about six or seven times from people who heard the person himself. I don't know his name. He is a Bobover hasid.

S, Klausenberg, E

The Escape of the Belzer (N22a)

When the [Belzer] Rebbe was escaping there were great miracles. The driver of the car said there was a cloud around the car. Once the driver stopped the car and went for a drink and he had a difficult time finding the car again.

The Nazis stopped the car and told the Rebbe to get out but he wouldn't. Then three men came and said to let him pass. He shaved and was in disguise because the Nazis wanted to catch him. They put his picture in the newspaper.

BBB, Belz, E

Rommel (N23)

In the Land of Israel there was the Hushatener Rebbe, the grandson of the Rizhyner. He was already quite old. He was in his seventies or eighties. He must have been in his seventies in the war. If you remember in Africa, Rommel pushed very close to Palestine, practically on the border. And at that time there was a yohrtsait of a big Rebbe, the Or ha-Haim.[10] So on this yohrtsait, the Hushatener Rebbe and a number of hasidim went—he's buried in Jerusalem—so they went to the cemetery to his grave, and he came to him to say psalms on the yohrtsait. At that time the Afrika Korps was right near. They were all worried. What if Hitler should come in to Palestine? They would all be stuck. So after he said this psalm, they asked him, the Hushatener, right here in the cemetery by this big tsaddik, he should pray, he should do something, see that

---

[10] Haim ben Atar.

nothing should happen. They say that he stood for a while. And then with these words he says, "He will not, he will not come here." In these words. And he walked away.

And it so happened that he never reached Palestine. They threw him back. That was the time they started the offensive back.

W, Boyan, E

The Blanket (N24)

The [Klausenberger] Rebbe tells many times very interesting stories about what happened to him in camp. For instance, there is a story that he told on Tishebov, the day the Temple was destroyed.[11] He told us this story. We were out in the country and he was telling us hundreds of stories that happened to him. We have a hotel and a camp, and he has about a half a mile from camp a bungalow for himself, and you know on Tishebov just before night he was telling this story.

He was telling the story that one day they were marching. It was Shabbes at Tishebov, and they were marching and everybody had to carry his blanket. It was terribly hot.

And they were all marching together and these blankets were very heavy. And it came out about Shabbes about carrying the blankets. You see he was very religious even in the worst times. So they figured out the best way to carry the blanket is to sew together two blankets and to use it like clothes. And he took a chance with another man, and once he carried it a half hour and then the other man carried it a half an hour. And that would be the best way according to the law and everything would be okay. So he tells, he's marching. And I have other friends from his pupils who were with him then when this story happened. They were marching together with him. And they're marching and there are about five thousand people marching. And he's taking chances with that man—the other man was a shohet. He carries it an hour and the other carries it for an hour. But the heat was so terrible that hundreds of people started throwing away their blankets because

---

[11] Tishebov (Tish'ah b'Av): the ninth day of the month of Av commemorating the destruction of the Temple.

they just couldn't take it. All of a sudden they stopped the march
and they say that everybody that doesn't have a blanket has destroyed government property and the verdict is death. And they're
walking around and they catch him. The Rebbe wasn't carrying
then; the other was then carrying the blanket. And they catch
about another twenty-five people that were without blankets and
they lay them down on the ground. There was the SS and the
Wehrmacht, the regular army. They were both there. And the SS
were going to machine-gun them down. He was the last one. He
says, "I don't know why God wanted me to stay alive. I don't
know."

But all of a sudden he sees a Wehrmacht goes over to him,
"What are you doing there?"

So he tells him, shows him, "What should I do?"

So he shows him, "Go back into that line."

He comes back and says he doesn't have to ask any questions. So
he runs back into the line and he goes back in. All of a sudden they
shoot at the nineteen and they count them over and there is one
missing. There are supposed to be twenty. So everybody stopped
marching and this head that caught them the first time, this SS,
goes around and he says "Will the person—the other person who
was supposed to be killed—will he come out."

So the Rebbe says since he wasn't such a patriotic German he
should come out, so he stood there. What could he do?

So he starts walking around looking everybody in the face. And
he was around the center, so he looked everybody in the face and he
comes to him and he recognizes him. So he tells him, "Why did
you run away?"

So he says that "Why did I run away? Because that man told me
to go back."

So they call over that man. He says he doesn't know what was
going on then. There was a big argument between them. And then
they gave him I think a couple of straps and they told him to run.
They used to tell them to run and they used to shoot after them.
And he runs and he runs until he gets into the line and they didn't
shoot him. So he just says that he just doesn't know, he can't
understand, but he was under the nails of death. God wanted him
to come to America to do this and to do that. That is why he was
left. He doesn't understand but that's the story that happened with
him.

S, Klausenberg, E

Milk (N25)

He [the Klausenberger Rebbe] has another story. He never ate a
thing that was not kosher in the camp. He fasted ten days at a time
sometimes, and he didn't have a thing maybe besides water. There
are pictures of him when he came out of the camp—he looked like a
skeleton. But he never ate a thing that was not kosher. So once
there came in milk. You know a Jew has to be by the milking;
otherwise, you're not allowed to drink the milk. That's the law,
although it's not in the Torah but was added later by the rabbis.
There is the law in the Torah and then the rabbis had power later
to make more laws. So they said that because we don't know—a
man might have a pig and milk a pig or who knows what and put
that milk into there—so if the Jew isn't there by the milking, even
though I may know positively that there is no unkosher animals in
that place, still he might have milked an impure animal and you're
not allowed to drink that milk. But that's a law where, let's say, if
I'm somewhere away and my child doesn't have other milk, I
would give him plain milk—which I wouldn't do with meat or with
something else. Because the thing is you can make it easier; that is
a thing that at certain times you can make it easier. It isn't as harsh
as something that is said in the Torah. So he figured to himself he
didn't have anything to eat in a few days and here they brought
him nonkosher milk. And the law is when you're bound to die,
you're allowed to eat pig, so why should he not eat this milk. So the
first day he started drinking a little bit of milk. That day, he
doesn't know, maybe because he didn't have food in his body, he
drank a glass of milk and his whole body got swollen. So he said,
"If I'm going to die anyway, why should I drink the milk?" So he
stopped drinking the milk and it went away and he lived through
it. That is another story that he told about himself.

S, Klausenberg, E

Purity (N26)

[In the camp] although the Stoliner Rebbe may have waited a long
time on line for food, if he saw a woman go on the line, he would
slip off the line.

F, Stolin, E

Out of the Ordinary (N27)

In camp, one man didn't know he was the Stoliner Rebbe. He always put people off the track so that he seemed like a simple person. He said he was a horse dealer. In the camp, they didn't know he was the Stoliner Rebbe. One man noticed something strange about him. He stayed up after everyone else was asleep. He saw the Rebbe get up and go toward the kitchen. "Ah, ha," he said to himself, "now I'll catch a thief." But he saw the Rebbe take out a book, read something, and go back to bed. And so he knew that here was a man out of the ordinary.

F, Stolin, E

His Voice (N28)

The brother of the [Stoliner] Rebbe in Williamsburg said after the war, "I know my brother is alive."

"Where?"

"I don't know. Only you can tell who he is because we have the same tone of voice."

They looked all over. They saw a Jew who held himself quietly, apart from others. Mr. T. of Agudas Isroel recognized him. He had the same voice. He asked, "Are you the Stoliner Rebbe?"

He didn't want to admit it. Even in camp he never said who he was. He would have been treated royally by the Jews.

He had his daughter with him. If he had a piece of bread, she would eat it right away.

In camp he never went to the Torah because he would have to say his name.

FF, Stolin, E

The Horse Dealer (N29)

During the war in the concentration camps he never said he was the Stoliner Rebbe. He said he was a horse dealer. His brother founded this shul, and when T. went to Europe, the Rebbe's brother sent him to the camp where his brother was held. The Rebbe despised the publicity. The man put up a notice for the Stoliner Rebbe, and then everyone was amazed when he appeared. Now you hear countless numbers claim to have slept next to the Rebbe.

F, Stolin, E

The Street (N30)

The [Stoliner] Rebbe once mentioned the name of a street in an offhand way. The war broke out and this man remembered the name of that street. He found the street and stayed there throughout the whole war. This was in Germany.

FF, Stolin, E

Suffering (N31)

Once, the past Lubavitcher Rebbe was asked why the European Jews suffered more than other Jews, when in fact the European Jews are the most orthodox, and Jews in countries less observant do not suffer.

The Rebbe answered, "When you give a person a smack, where do you give it to him? In his face."

V, Lubavitch, E

The Necessary Operation (N32)

There's an interesting story of a Rebbe who lives in Chicago, Rabbi Meisels. He was in a concentration camp. And he's a grandson of the Sandzer. He had a talis from the Sandzer Rebbe and he didn't want to give it up in going in to the concentration camp. So he had the talis cut down to a talis koten. And he carried that with him.

In the camp there was a Jewish officer in the camp—sometimes they were worse than the Germans—and after a shower they would search them to make sure that they didn't steal anybody's clothes—they weren't wearing more than the allotted clothes. He found him wearing this talis koten. He said, "What is this?"

So he said, "This is a religious garment. I wear it for religious purposes and not for warmth or anything."

He became incensed—the officer started beating him. He said, "What right do you have to wear religious clothing, believe in a God when you see what's happening to your people?" And he gave him an ultimatum, "Either you explain this to me—and if you explain it to me I'll give you free run of the camp—or else you're finished."

So he explained it to him like this: "Let's say a doctor has to make a heart operation. There's something wrong inside a person's heart that has to be cut out. How does the doctor get there? First he cuts away skin, and he saws through the rib bones, which are healthy bones and healthy skin. He cuts through layers and layers of tissue which are necessary for the person's life. He has to cut through in order to get to that part which is bad and has to be taken out. So any layman watching the doctor operate will say the doctor's a murderer—he's cutting the person there. They don't realize that the doctor must do that in order to save the person's life." He says, "By us Jews there is a certain segment that is spoiled, that has to be cut out. The operation also cuts through a lot of healthy meat to get it out."

M, Stolin, E

The Chosen Ones (N33)

The Klausenberger Rebbe said: "When I was in Warsaw in the ghetto under the Germans, a doctor came over to me and he asked me, 'How can you still say that we are God's nation if you see there's no other nation in the world where six million people have been killed like us?'"

So the Rebbe says, "Here I see that we are God's nation and that God picked us." He says, "I see that we're the ones that are being killed. We are not the ones that threw in six million people to be killed." He said, "If you can see that we are not the ones that are taking and killing millions of people and killing parents and children and everything. So you see that we are God's greatest nation. Throughout the whole civilized world people stand and look and see people killed and not open up their mouths, and most of them kill, but we Jews would never do such a thing. Here you see that we are God's greatest nation."

S, Klausenberg, E

The Arab War (N34)

When the [Stoliner] Rebbe was sick the last year of his life, a man stayed with him. Once he came in to the Rebbe and the Rebbe was in a sweat. He said he had been in the Heavenly Court. They had wanted to make war against the Jews. It was the time of the Arab war, but he prevented it.[12]

FF, Stolin, E

Gunfire (N35)

In Jerusalem, while the war was going on, the Arab-Israeli war, the [Stoliner] Rebbe had to go through. He had a mission to perform. He went right through gunfire. He said he had to go for a certain purpose. One man wanted to go along with him. He told him to lie on the floor. He shouldn't sit up like him because he was in danger. He came through without any damage. He wouldn't take anybody along if he was really in danger. He had a certain mission: God will protect. But the gabai had to lie on the floor. Mendel tells till the present day he doesn't know how they were able to get out of there.

B, Stolin, E

[12] Compare to N9, delaying World War II.

Tied (N36)

All I know was when the second Israeli war broke out—the second time, the Sinai campaign—usually everybody was walking around without a head. You know, what's going to happen? They were very afraid. And the [Klausenberger] Rebbe was then in such a good mood. And he said that they wouldn't be able to do a thing.

The next Saturday, we were talking. We were sitting by the table, and suddenly he says, "I don't understand. They have so many MIGS. They have so many of these Russian planes. They should be ashamed. They should take at least one plane and go and throw it down on Tel Aviv—throw some bombs. Why don't they do it? It just shows that it's a sign of God that they're tied, that they can't do anything, that nothing in the world will ever happen to Israel again. Israel was destroyed two times and we don't see anywhere that there will be a third destruction in Israel." And he was so confident the whole time.

S, Klausenberg, E

Sinai (N37)

The Belzer Rebbe knew beforehand of the Sinai campaign because two generals came to the Belzer Rebbe before the Sinai campaign to tell him that it's starting, that they were attacking. And that Friday night—it actually started Friday just before night—and that Friday night there's a prayer that God should protect the Jews and Jerusalem. So that Friday night the Belzer Rebbe started davening the evening prayer, and at the Eighteen Benedictions, that is, just before the Eighteen Benedictions, when he came to that place, he stayed I think for about six or seven hours. He didn't move. And he kept on just at that one point. And then afterward he davened the Eighteen Benedictions, and then he went into his room and he didn't even eat anything that night. He was seven or eight hours. They said that the hasidim who were there saw that they won the war at that moment. I mean it was something they never saw by the Belzer Rebbe, because the Belzer used to daven quickest of any other Rebbe. On Rosh Hashoneh the whole davening used to take him maybe two hours, or an hour and a half. He always davened very quickly. And he just stopped there and he was standing there by that one space. They saw where he stopped and he was staying there I don't know it was six or eight hours. Actually almost a whole night until morning. He just didn't move away from there at the Sinai action.

It is a known fact that it was not Moshe Dayan but the assistant of Moshe Dayan with another general who went to him a few days before to tell him that they are starting the Sinai action and that he should pray for them. Because the Belzer Rov was noted all over Israel. Doctors knew that when they had a hard case in the hospital and they saw it was an orthodox Jew, he used to go to the Belzer Rov. I mean it was so open by him that they knew one hundred per cent everything exactly. The doctors knew already that if the Belzer Rov says something, it is that way. And if they saw that it was an orthodox patient they would say, "Go to the Belzer Rov."

S, Klausenberg, E

They Will Fear You (N38)

Before the war [in Israel in June, 1967], the president, Shazar, called up the Rebbe and asked him what's going to happen.[13] The Rebbe gave him blessings and said that everything will come out all right.

The parents of boys studying in the yeshiveh asked if they should take their sons out, bring them home. The Rebbe said we're going to succeed against our enemies. The Rebbe was very sure of himself. We were certain that it meant either there wasn't going to be a war or if there was it was nothing to be scared of. Before, and in the middle of the crisis, not one student came back.

The Shabbes before, the Rebbe hinted about it all—something is coming up. The Rebbe said we could help in America by putting tefillin on with as many people as possible. He quoted from the Torah—who sees a Jew with tefillin, fear will arise in him. And all

[13] Shneur Zalman Shazar, third president of Israel. Just prior to the war Shazar was visiting the World's Fair at Montreal (see N39). See chapter 8, note 13.

the nations of the earth will see the name of God on you and they will fear you. It means the tefillin on the head.[14]

Also in Israel, Lubavitcher soldiers took risks to have soldiers put on tefillin.

One of our men got killed. Lubavitchers went into the army. One of them was killed at Suez. The friends, the group of soldiers with the soldier killed at Suez, came to pay condolences to Kfar Habad, a village of four hundred Lubavitcher families, "D. put on tefillin with us." The soldiers with him were not religious at all but they said they would put on tefillin for the rest of their lives.

XX, Lubavitch, E

You Will Surely Succeed (N39) *

When Shazar, the president of Israel, was in Canada—he came to Expo [the 1967 Montreal World's Fair] just before the outbreak of the war—the Lubavitcher Rebbe sent him two messengers. Shazar is a Lubavitcher hasid. The last time he came to bring him writings from the Mitteler Rebbe that the Rebbe had not seen. He [the Rebbe] told him: "You will surely succeed, but to ensure it try to see that the soldiers should wear tefillin."

The Necessary War (N40)

This story was told to me by a soldier in Galil. He lives in Tiberias. This person told me: "I am not frum [pious], but now I believe there's a God."

He was in the first line to go into the Syrian heights. The night before he had to go in he heard that the Lubavitcher Rebbe in Brooklyn said that this war is a milhemes mitsveh, a necessary war.[15]

---

[14] "And all the peoples of the earth shall see that the name of the Lord is called upon thee; and they shall be afraid of thee" (Deut. 28:10).

* Tales N39–N43 were collected by Rabbi S. Goldhaber in Israel shortly after the war in June, 1967.

[15] In rabbinical literature a distinction is made between two types of wars—a milhemes reshus (a permitted or voluntary war of offence) and a milhemes mitsveh (an obligatory war). The former designates wars under-

It's a mitsveh to go into battle. Therefore we will surely succeed.

"So I thought that if the Rabbi living in Brooklyn could have such faith, that one would succeed, I went into fire with less fear than what I have during maneuvers."

Three Soldiers (N41)

The settlement Habad, the village of Lubavitch, right on the border with Jordan, there was heavy fighting there during the war and Lubavitcher boys would rush down into the battle and grab the soldiers who were free at the time and have them put on tefillin. They tell a story of a group of three soldiers who were approached: one refused, one put up an argument but finally put on tefillin, and the other put on tefillin willingly. The outcome of the battle was—the one who refused was killed, the one who put them on reluctantly was wounded, and the other one was spared.

Shabbes Clothes (N42)

The Gerer Rebbe, Alter, told his hasidim—the mobilization was on Shabbes—he told them to go into mobilization, but they should not take off their Shabbes clothes. Normally they would go home and change to their uniforms. He told them to go in your Shabbes clothes and don't change until you come into camp.

Talis and Tefillin (N43)

A friend of mine, his name is S., he's a hasid and he was in Sinai. He was brought up on a bus and he had his talis and tefillin on the bus. He had a little time during the fighting and he thought he

---

taken to conquer territory, while the latter refers to wars of defense, to wars against the seven nations in Canaan, and to wars against Amalek. "In obligatory wars of defense . . . all must go to battle, even the bridegroom from his chamber and the bride from her canopy" (see Babylonian Talmud, *Sotah* 44b, *Sanh.* 20b; Deut. 25:19).

would be able to daven, and he came to take the talis and tefillin off the bus and his commanding officer didn't let him. He kept on telling him to come back later. Finally, he said, "I'll let you daven on the condition that you keep your talis and tefillin on the bus. We feel that as long as it's here we're safe."

WIVES AND HUSBANDS

Relatives (WH1)

The Baal Shem Tov had a son and he did not give his son his place after he died. Only the Maggid of Mezrich took over his place. They say a lot of things about the son: that he was famous, he went away, he was in Germany, he was a very hidden person, he didn't want to become a rabbi. His name was Reb Zevi.[1] And he had a daughter; the daughter's name was Edel. And this Edel left two sons: one was Ephraim [2] and the other was Borukh. And they were both big rabbis.

His daughter—she was like a rabbi. She saw very deep things. When she was at the weddings of her sons or daughters or grandchildren, she never went to the ceremony until her father came. He was dead already, but until she saw her father. . . . She stayed in a separate room and it sometimes took an hour and two and three.

Once it happened that she waited there about five hours. The people were ashamed. You know, people came from the whole world to the wedding and they are waiting and sitting, doing nothing, waiting till she's going to come out. Till suddenly she came out. She saw her father. So she asked her father, "What took you so long to come this time?"

So he said that she should never again do such a thing. "You should never take in the family persons that you don't know. You took a stranger, and you don't know who he is." So he said,

[1] Reb Zevi died in 1800. Concerning his failure to continue his father's work, see *In Praise of the Besht*, no. 249.

[2] Rabbi Moshe Haim Ephraim (d. 1800), author of *Degel Mahne Ephraim* (*"The Banner of the Camp of Ephraim"*). In his work Rabbi Moshe commented on hasidic teachings, cited dreams in which his grandfather had appeared to him, and noted some tales of the Besht.

"When I come to the wedding every time I don't go by myself."
Usually when you come to a wedding you take all the relatives of
the bride and of the groom. So now he said, "I came to take those
relatives of this groom. I didn't find them in Paradise. I had to pull
them out of Gehenna. That's why it took me so long."

X, Bobov, E

Tsaddikim (WH2)

So he [Motel of Tchernobl] used to call everyone tsaddik. Once he
was on a wagon, you know, with the driver. So he told the driver,
"Hey, tsaddik," that's how he called him, "when will we come to
this place?"

So he said, "Hey, rabbi, I'm a tsaddik and you're a tsaddik. I
have a daughter—you have a son. So let them get married."

So he says, "All right, you're a tsaddik and I'm a tsaddik. But
my son is going to get married with a tsaddik like I am, and your
daughter is going to be married with a tsaddik like you are."

X, Bobov, E

The Pledge (WH3)

I heard this story from a friend of mine. This story happened with
the Yeshuos Yankev, as he was called.[3] He was the Lemberger
Rov. He was the Rabbi of Lemberg. One day there was a man who
lived thirty or forty miles away from Lemberg in a small town. He
was a very wealthy man, but a very cheap man. And he was so
cheap he wouldn't give his wife anything to eat and he wouldn't
give his wife anything, so naturally his wife always fought with
him. And they were always fighting. One day he decided, "Well,
to divorce a wife is very expensive. The best thing would be if she
died." So he decides, "I'll go into the Rebbe with a kvitl and ask
him she should die."

This Rebbe knew the character. He knew the person. He comes

[3] Rabbi Yaakov Meshulem Orenstein (d. 1839), author of *Yeshuos
Yankev* (*Yeshuot Yaakov*, "The Salvation of Yaakov").

in to the Rebbe and says, "Rebbe, I want you to pray that my wife should die. She's a devil. She's no good. What use do I have from her? Let her die."

So the Rebbe says, "Listen, young man, we can't pray that a person should die. That's impossible. But I have an idea for you."

He says, "What?"

"I'll tell you. The Gemoreh says that if somebody pledges money for charity and doesn't pay it, his wife and children die. That's his punishment. So I have an idea for you. Go home. This Shabbes, go to your shul. Pledge a hundred dollars for the yeshiveh, a hundred dollars for the rabbi. Pledge a big sum of money and then don't pay. So she'll die."

The guy comes home. Shabbes, he walks into shul. They call him up to the Torah. All of a sudden the people looked at him—he must have gone crazy. He pledges two hundred—pledges a lot of money. Saturday night they run right away to him to collect. He starts laughing, "I don't want to pay you."

"He's crazy. Not only is he cheap, he became crazy too."

About six months pass by and this woman doesn't die. She's healthy, she's strong. So he comes in to the Rebbe, "Rebbe, I did everything you said, and I see my wife is growing stronger and stronger everyday. What should I do?"

So he says, "Well, I'll tell you the truth. The Gemoreh says it's a punishment. For you it wouldn't be a punishment because you want her to die. You hate her. So what kind of punishment is it? The Gemoreh says that if you donate money for charity and you don't pay it, your punishment is that your wife dies. But here this isn't a punishment for you. I have a great idea for you. You're here now in a big city. Go and buy your wife a beautiful, expensive gift. Then you come home, you give her the gift, she'll start being nice to you. She'll think something came over you, and she'll act nice to you and she'll begin loving you again and you'll love her, so then there will be a punishment. Because if you love her, she'll die."

"Mmmm, it's a good idea. I'll have to spend twenty-five dollars." He goes in. He buys a beautiful gift. He comes home. What came over him? And naturally his wife became very friendly to him, and all of a sudden he looks around he found he had a really wonderful wife. He just had to spend a couple of measly dollars and he had a wonderful wife. And they were living like two lovebirds. All of a sudden one day his wife gets sick. So he reminds himself, "Oy vey, I made a pledge and I didn't pay and now she's going to die. This is—this is something terrible." He loves her. He was madly in love with her. He never knew what a good wife he had. So he runs back to the Rebbe, "Rebbe, what should I do? I'm in love with my wife. Please, I don't want her to die."

So he says, "Now go pay."

That's a true story.

S, Klausenberg, E

Charity for the Rebbe (WH4)

The Sandzer Rov used to give away a great deal of charity. For his own family, his wife and children, nothing remained. In the beginning, when he first came to Sandz, there was a woman who came to him and said that at the end of the town there lived a Jew who sits and learns, a man with a wife and children, and they didn't have anything to eat. And she said that the Rebbe should give him money. He took out money and gave it for that woman and man and for the children. The woman then brought the money to the Rebbetsn. The Rebbetsn had something to talk about. The Sandzer Rebbetsn used to bring in that money.

Five or six weeks passed. The Sandzer Rov saw that the Rebbetsn didn't come to him asking for money. He took it upon himself to investigate and find out what it's all about. He found out for himself that each week the woman brought to the Rebbetsn whatever he gave her. She brings it back to the Rebbetsn. He became angry and never gave her any more.

S, Klausenberg, Y

Half a Soul (WH5)

This is told of the Rizhyner Rebbe. His wife had passed away. In those days they had a fund, a charity, for people in Israel who lived on it. The Rizhyner was the head of it. No one could go to Israel without his approval because they were dependent on him for support. It happened in the last year of his life, 1850. They asked him if he would go to Israel. He said he would go but half of his soul was buried here, and so he couldn't go with only half his soul.[4]

SS, Stolin, E

The Wedding (WH6)

There was a son born to one of the hasidim. He grew older, and he was normal in every way except that he was lame. So they went to the Maharash, and the Maharash said, "Marry him off right away. Find a wife and marry him right away."

They came back to their town, they found a wife for him, and they made preparations for the wedding. Since the boy's father was a shohet, they prepared all sorts of geese, chickens, meats. Another thing wrong with the boy was that he wasn't able to eat meat. The doctor said it was very dangerous for him to eat meat.

The day of the wedding, before they went to the wedding ceremony, the mother was carrying out a big plate of roasted meats, and the son smelled it and begged his mother to let him taste the meat. The mother told the son it was dangerous for him to taste it. He pleaded until she gave him a piece. He ate one piece first, then another. He felt very good. He went to the wedding. At the wedding he had to be held under his arms because he couldn't walk. After the ceremony was over he walked away just like a healthy man.

YY, Lubavitch, Y

The Promise (WH7)

Reb Israel [of Stolin], when he was born, his grandfather was there and his father. They have a custom, the night before the briss to go into the room where the baby is and say "Hear, O Israel." Beis ha-Aaron and Reb Asher came in with the child's mother. The Alter started to tell a story.

---

[4] After the loss of his wife the Besht said that he had only half a body and so could not rise to heaven in a storm as had Elijah the Prophet (*In Praise of the Besht*, no. 146).

One hundred years before, Yaakov Emden,[5] a big rabbi in
Europe, before the time of the Baal Shem Tov, married a second
time when he was eighty years old. He married a young girl. The
system is that first the groom goes to the wedding and then the
bride comes. He went to the wedding and he's waiting and the
bride doesn't come to the wedding. He's waiting and waiting. He
goes back and says, "Why haven't you come?"

The bride said, "I won't come unless you promise me that we'll
have a child."

So he said, "Okay." He promises they will have a child.

A year passes, and they have a child. They get ready for the
briss. All the men are waiting. The mother has to give the child
over to them. She doesn't give him over. He goes back to her.
"Why won't you give the child over?"

"I won't give the child unless you promise that we'll both attend
his wedding."

"I promise."

He went to the wedding. He was over ninety-five years. Right
after, seven days after the wedding, he died.

I'm not sure who it happened to—Yaakov Emden or Haham
Zevi.[6]

The Alter told the story and the next morning they made the
briss.

The wife saw that three years later he died, and then right
afterward the child's father died. Then she realized why he had
told the story—not give over the child until she had his promise.
Now it was too late. Certain times you're not allowed to say
things—only hint at them.

He [Reb Israel] became Rebbe when he was four years old.

M, Stolin, E

The Bridegroom (WH8)

A hasid from Tomashev was living in Lodzh and he married a girl
from there. The man's father continued to live in Tomashev. He

[5] Yaakov Emden, a talmudic scholar in Germany, 1697–1776. The Besht
died in 1760.

[6] The father of Yaakov Emden, the Haham Zevi, Zevi Hirsch ben
Ashkenazi, the Rabbi of Lemberg, d. 1718.

studied while his father-in-law supported them. The hasid's father asked him and his wife to come for Rosh Hashoneh and Yom Kippur. He went home to his father with his wife and said, "This is where my father lives," and he left her there and went back again.

What is the point? The point is the strong attachment of the hasidim. Though he was with his wife at his father's house for the first time, he just came to show his wife the house and leave her and then go back.

T, Ger, Y

Where Do I Live? (WH9)

There was a Kotsker hasid, Abe B., who had been born and who had lived in the city of Vilna. After having been in Khits two years he decided to return home. In those years the wives were the bread earners. They usually had little shops and they worked in them. After his visit to Khits he returned home. In the meantime, his wife had moved while he was at Khits. He went back to his old apartment, and since on his journey he hadn't been able to study Talmud too much, he had a small tenakh [the Hebrew Bible] in his valise. And he sat down for a few hours to study. The people who had moved into his apartment since his family left did not disturb him.

After he had learned for a few hours he opened his eyes. He asked the lady how she was. He was so immersed in his studies he didn't know it wasn't his own wife. They told him what had taken place and led him to his family.

What would you deduce from this story? He studied immediately after his trip. The family didn't disturb him. Afterward everyone called him "Reb Abe Where Do I Live?"

T, Ger, Y

The Grass Widow (WH10)

I heard a story from M. who was a teacher in Sosnitsa.

There was a rich Jew named Yosef Noah Lubinsky. He used to

go to the Maharash every year. He had a maid and the maid was a grass widow because of the siege at Plevna.[7] Most people have either an official letter stating that the person was killed or else the person comes home. She received neither a letter nor did her husband come home, and so she didn't know what happened to him. She couldn't get remarried. So she told her employer, "When you go to the Rebbe, ask him to advise me what to do." Every year he came back and he forgot to ask the Rebbe. So this time she told him, "How could you be so merciless to forget?"

So he said, "I have no excuse. I don't understand myself how I forget."

"This time don't forget."

This time as he came—the Rebbe didn't go away for vacations, but he used to go for rides in a small carriage—when he came to the Rebbe, the Rebbe was just going into the carriage. The Rebbe asked him if he wanted to come along for the ride. He went into the wagon with the Rebbe and he says, "I was sent here with a mission." He told him the story about this grass widow.

The Rebbe told him, "For grass widows you need my father [the Tsemah Tsedek]. He had luck with grass widows. I'll tell you something that happened in our house. We had a maid in our house. This servant was a distant relative of my mother's, and her husband ran away. And that's all. My mother used to ask the Rebbe to help her, and the Rebbe never made any mention of it. One time she really said, 'Why don't you have any pity on her?' And she said, 'For everyone else you take care of the whole world and for a relative you don't do anything.'

"He said, 'I have to answer you also? Look how many people are here waiting for me and bothering me. You have to ask me as well?'

"She answered him, 'If you can't do anything, you should tell the people and they wouldn't bother coming to you.'

"Most likely this happened between Rosh Hashoneh and Yom Kippur, since there were lots of people at the Rebbe's.

"He says, 'What's your rush? Is the river Dnieper burning? Wait till things calm down. We'll see what to do about it.'

"So when it came Sukkes, the Rebbe had hasidim from Moscow, and they used to come for the second day's holiday. They couldn't come for the first day, and so they came for the second day, for

---

[7] Plevna was besieged by the Russians twice in 1877 during the Russian-Turkish War.

Simhes Toyreh. So he told his gabai, Haim Ber, 'As soon as you see
this person come from this and this town you bring him to me.'

"And the person came a day before Hoshanoh Rabboh.[8] As soon
as he came into the Rebbe, the Rebbe said, 'I want you to go home,
and near where you live there's a hasid and I want you to give him
this letter. But give it to him immediately.'

"So he left soon with his three horses. As soon as he left he
encountered a terrible torrential rain. But he kept on going. He
came home past the holiday, and his wife took him in and gave him
tea and sat him down on the oven to thaw him out.

"The goy comes in and tells him that the black horse fell and
died from exhaustion. 'It should be a scapegoat for us.'[9] He is
warming himself and the goy comes in again and says that the
second horse died. He says, 'It's because it's Hoshanoh Rabboh!'
Another fifteen minutes pass, and another horse dies. So then he
reminded himself that he forgot the letter. He searched and found
the letter. It was wet, and he told the goy to take a horse and
deliver it. And the goy refused because he was wet. The goy didn't
want to go but he gave him a glass of shnapps and three rubles and
he went. And he sent along his own letter, saying that this letter is
from the Lubavitcher Rebbe and you should listen to whatever is
written there.

"The goy arrived early in the morning. The letter said to this
person that he should send his miller to Lubavitch for the holiday
immediately (there was one day left for the holiday). The miller
was still sleeping. So he woke him up, and he says, 'You're going
to Lubavitch for the holiday.'

" 'Why should I go to Lubavitch? I have nothing to do there.'

" 'You must go.'

" 'I won't go.'

"So he gave him a few smacks. 'If you don't go, you won't be
able to stay here!'

"So he says, 'How can I go? I don't have a talis. I can't pray
without a talis.'

" 'I'll give you mine.'

" 'I don't have a long kaftan.'

" 'I'll give you mine.' And he sent him off.

"The Rebbe told his gabai, 'If you see someone coming just
before the holiday, send him right in to me.' The man came and

[8] Hoshanoh Rabboh (Hosha'na Rabba): the day before Shmini Atseres.
[9] Hoshanoh Rabboh is considered a continuation of Yom Kippur and is
still part of the rites of forgiveness. The meaning here is that misfortune
should occur to his property rather than to his family.

was brought to the Rebbe. The Rebbe said, 'A nice guy you are—you leave your wife and you go away for so many years.'

"The man complained to him, 'I couldn't take her. She was too bad to me. She wasn't from the nicest people. Whenever I asked her for cream, she gave me sour milk. So I ran away.'

"So the Rebbe asked him, 'What do you want? A noblewoman? She's a Jewish girl and that's enough for you. You should keep her.' He said, 'Keep her. Take her. She's your wife.'

"He said, 'It can't last. I can't take her.'

"So he said, 'Give her more money and she'll cook you a better supper.'

"So he said, 'Where am I going to get more money from?'

"So he said, 'I'll write a letter to your boss and he'll give you a raise.'

"Meanwhile the Rebbetsn heard the noise and she came in and the maid also came in, and the Rebbe said, 'Here she is. Take your wife and go.' "

So the Rebbe said, "Such things my father was able to do. I can't do it. But I give you my advice that when you come home you should send a letter to the government in Petersburg. Write the story to them."

So Yosef Noah came home and wrote the letter, and he got an official document saying that he was killed.[10]

YY, Lubavitch, Y

The Missing Husband (WH11)

I heard a story about Z., the shohet. In that town there was someone called Avrom the lumber dealer because he sold trees. He had a sister-in-law who couldn't remarry because she wasn't sure her husband was dead. Whenever he went to the Rebbe to ask him what to do about it, the Rebbe used to tell him you have to look through the newspapers and things like that. They kept on going to the Rebbe, but nothing that they did and the Rebbe did helped. They didn't find anything in the newspapers.

Then the Rebbe said, "You have to go to a certain shohet. He could help you."

So they went to a big shohet who was also a relative of that

---

[10] Thereby enabling the widow to remarry.

woman, and the shohet asked, "What could I do?" And they started to think. They showed him pictures of the man. Now this shohet used to go to a certain town to sell meat and buy salt. He said that in that town someone looks like the picture of the man. "Next time I'm in that town, since it's a matter of life and death, I'll investigate."

The next time he went to that town he found that man and it was her husband. And he gave her a divorce so that she was able to get married again.

YY, Lubavitch, Y

More Bitter Than Death (WH12)

A man had trouble with his wife and was ashamed to tell the Rebbe. He went to the Rebbe, and the Rebbe answered him that if he knows the Bible and the Prophets it's written there that the Jews at that time did not observe the Jewish religion and they praised and worshipped other religions. And according to the Jewish law, if a Jew was warned that he should not do this kind of sin, to worship or to pray to other religions or to bend his head for the statues of other religions, and if he did it he would be killed. If two witnesses warned him and he still did it, according to the Jewish law he was supposed to be killed. And he has to live his life over thousands of times if he did so. Hannah with her seven sons had a choice like this. They warned her unless she worshipped before other religions she will be killed. He is supposed to have in his life a situation of servitude like this, and he should be killed for the Jewish religion to atone for this sin. He should have a choice what to do and he should choose to die rather than to pray to other religions. And in view of the fact that in such times the Jews could commit this sin maybe thousands of times, it means that such people should be reborn in this world a thousand times and to have this choice to be killed for the Jewish religion. And the world wouldn't remain for so many thousands of years; therefore, God provided this way to fix the sins: Solomon the King said in the Book of Proverbs, "More bitter than death is a bad wife." [11] And

[11] Eccles. 7:26 is probably the correct reference: "I find more bitter than death the woman, whose heart is snares and nets, and her hands as bands." The inspiration for this tale undoubtedly stems from the Babylonian Talmud, *Yebamot*, 63a–63b.

therefore he gave to such a person a bad wife. Every time when the wife is nagging him, he has a chance to redeem a sin for which he's supposed to be punished with death.

And he came to his home and every time when his wife started to nag him, he said, "Nu, I have one death less, and one death less." Until she asked him to explain this expression. And he explained to her what the Rebbe told him, and then after a little while she stopped bothering him.

V, Lubavitch, E

Divorce (WH13)

A man wanted to divorce his wife. She was always nagging him, screaming at him, and he wanted to go to the rabbi to ask him for a divorce. He went to the rabbi's house, and then decided no, he was ashamed to tell the Rebbe. He couldn't go in, and so he went home. And just as he stepped into his home, his wife started to scream at him and he made up his mind—he went back to the Rebbe.

He came to the Rebbe. The Rebbe is in the sukkeh. It was the seventh day of Sukkes. According to the custom of the Rebbe, they were eating a dessert of carrots. The reason is that in Jewish *ma'adan* means a delicacy, and in Aramaic *ma'adan ruvia* means multiplying.[12] You should multiply. We should have more and more from God. Therefore, the custom is to eat this kind of dessert. The man went over to the table and the Rebbetsn brought this dessert to the sukkeh. He felt that he wanted to sleep, and he's ashamed he's able to sleep before the Rebbe. He's ashamed, but he can't help it. He can't help it. He falls asleep and he has a dream that he came to the Rebbe, and he said the Rebbe must give him permission to divorce his wife. And the Rebbe tells him: "Be careful. How do you know the second marriage will be better than this one?"

But he said, "Rebbe, I can't take any more from this one. If I marry a second time I'll be very careful. I wouldn't marry so easy. I'll look the person over and find out all about her." And the Rebbe gave him permission to divorce his wife.

He looked for another one for a year, more than a year. And he

[12] I was unable to discover any Aramaic term carrying this particular meaning. The narrator's observation may be based on his knowledge of Yiddish: in Yiddish the plural form of the noun "carrots" ("mehren") is the same as the infinitive of the verb "to multiply."

found out from every angle that one woman would make a good wife. He married her. A year, two, she started the same thing as the first one, only ten times worse. And he's ashamed to go to the Rebbe again to tell him to divorce them. The Rebbe warned him before. But after another few years he feels he's at the end of his life. And so he repeated the same thing. The Rebbe told him stay with this one because he'll fall in again and get one worse than this one. "No, I can't. I must divorce."

"If you want to do it, all right. But remember, watch yourself."

So it happened he divorced the second one, and then later he married a third one. And also he waited and he found out from all kinds of sources about her, and everyone gave him the best opinion. And he stayed with her a few years, and then she started in worse than both of them. And he thought now he is lost. What he should do now? How can he come to the Rebbe to say he divorced once and then a second time? He was told he shouldn't do it and now he has the results. What should he do?

And the Rebbe told him: "Get up, you're supposed to say the prayer for the dessert. You're supposed to say a blessing over the carrots. Get up, it's a dream." And the Rebbe told him, "What's your opinion? You want to divorce your wife?"

He said, "No."

V, Lubavitch, E

THE SCHOLAR AND OTHER
HUMOROUS TALES

The Scholar (S1)

When the Berdichever was a young man, he was by his father-in-law.[1] And they wanted the honor of saying [the prayer] "Thou hast shown. . . ." on Simhes Toyreh. They give it to one of the nicest people. He was the son of a very rich man and they knew he was a very fine man. They told him to go over and say "Thou hast shown. . . ."

So he went over to the stand where the hazen stands. And he walks over to take the talis to put it on, and all of a sudden they see him taking the talis and then he puts it back. And then he takes the talis again and then he puts it back again. And then all of a sudden he starts screaming, "If you are so close to the Torah, you say it. Leave me alone." He walks back. That's the way he screams, and he walks back and he doesn't want to say anything. So naturally everybody looked at him very funny. What was going on there? And his father-in-law got very embarrassed. His son-in-law, something went wrong with him. So anyway they sent over somebody else, and he said "Thou hast shown. . . ."

That night, his father—he knew that his son really wasn't crazy. So he says to him, "Tell me, what happened tonight? Why did you embarrass me so?"

He says, "I'll tell you the truth. I went over to say Ato Horayso and the Yetser Hora came along and he wanted to say it with me. So I started arguing with him. I said to him, 'What kind of a relative are you to the Torah?'

[1] Rabbi Sholem Rosenfeld of Raveh.

"So he says to me, 'I always was together with you.'

"So I said, 'Did you ever learn the Torah?'

"So he said, 'Yes.'

" 'When I went to yeshiveh, did you come along with me?'

"He said, 'Yes, I was there with you.'

"And I said to him, 'When I went to my Rebbe, were you there?'

"He says, 'Yes, I was there with you.'

"So I got very angry with him and I said, 'If you yourself are such a scholar of the Talmud and you know so much, say it yourself.' I didn't want to say it." [2]

S, Klausenberg, E

Eighteen Dollars (S2)

Motel of Tchernobl was a rabbi in forty-eight cities. You know? Forty-eight cities. Maybe in all of his life he was twice in the same city. And he didn't go to a single place, not even one, that somebody didn't ask him to come in. He didn't go in the door before they had to give him some money. You know when we give a present to the rabbi, we also give money. Not because the rabbi needs the money—that's how it is. Because if somebody prays for you, you have to give him a pidyen, a donation.

So once, he took a trip. You know he had a big booth, and when he traveled he had everything in the booth—books and a kitchen, everything—because he used to go from one city to another far away. So once the booth turned over and he fell down. Blood was running. They ran to the nearest house to get some first aid and to take him in. So every place he had hasidim. A hasid came out and he took him on his shoulders. He was bleeding. He wanted to take him in the door, when he got a clop on the shoulder, "Hey, mister, eighteen dollars." He didn't even want to go in the room before he gave him the money.

X, Bobov, E

[2] See Buber, *Tales,* 1: 203–4.

Fifty-eight (S3)

Once Motel of Tchernobl was in a place and a woman came to him. She said she didn't have any children. She begged and prayed for him to help her to have children. So Motel of Tchernobl says, he starts to think and he says, "Give fifty-eight dollars"—whatever money was used then. "You'll have a boy and name him Noah. It's spelled 'nun-khet.' Nun is fifty and khet is eight—fifty-eight. Exactly like the name Noah."

So this lady was smart. She said, "I'll give you seven dollars, and I'll name him 'God.' 'God' is 'gimel-dalet.' Gimel is three and dalet is four. So it's seven. Why should I give fifty-eight?"

What is "God?" God.

So he says, "God says to give fifty-eight."

X, Bobov, E

Mazel Tov (S4)

There was a great rabbi—his name was Motel of Tchernobl. Motel is his name; Tchernobl is a city. His father had seven sons.

He was angry. You know he became very angry over every small thing. So people didn't like to stay near him. He didn't get mad if someone did something bad or didn't listen to him—told him to bring this and he didn't. He didn't get mad about those things. He got mad, let's say, if he said something in Talmud or something and someone didn't understand. He got very angry because he thought that everybody understands like him.

Once one of his hasidim had a child. So he called him to be the sandek, the man who holds the child when they perform the circumcision after eight days. They called him. He wanted to go to the other city, but nobody wanted to go with him. Because everybody was afraid that on the way he was going to say something they wouldn't understand and he would just slap them. He had to promise that he wouldn't do anything. So he promised. "I wouldn't even say one word."

"All right." So one man went there on the wagon.

They came near to that city, and it was on a farm, chickens. So one chicken went "aaawk." One chicken started making a lot of noise. So Motel of Tchernobl turned to the other man, "Do you hear?" There's no answer. He gave him a slap, right away a slap.

He didn't know what happened. He says, "You promised me that you wouldn't do anything."

So he says, "I couldn't hold myself back. You see, my wife was pregnant when I went away. Now the rooster said mazel tov [congratulations] to me. It's a girl. So if you didn't hear this, why shouldn't I slap you?" [3]

X, Bobov, E

Nails (S5)

You usually cut your nails on Friday before going to the mikveh. The Ropchitser cut his nails after the mikveh. A hasid saw him and said, "This must have a deep meaning." And he asked the Rebbe to explain.

The Ropchitser was a jokester. He told the man to fast two days, go to the mikveh, say so many psalms, and after he did these things, then he would tell him the reason why.

After the man did this he came back to the Ropchitser and asked for an explanation. The Ropchitser explained: "The reason why I cut my nails after the mikveh is that the water makes the nails soft and easier to cut." [4]

K, Sziget, E

The Cantor (S6)

The Ropchitser Rov used to say vertlekh [sayings]. We didn't understand everything he said. He was a student of the Seer of Lublin, the Lubliner, Reb Yankev Yitshok from Lublin. He always

[3] Concerning learning the speech of birds and beasts, see *In Praise of the Besht*, no. 237.

[4] Langer includes a similar tale about Reb Naftali of Ropchits' white trousers. After six days of fasting, his follower learned that the Rebbe bought white cloth trousers because they were the least expensive (*Nine Gates*, p. 76).

used to say those jokes. The Rebbe knew what he meant with the jokes, but once the Lubliner Rebbe told him, "Look, Ropchitser Rov," that is what he called him, "maybe you'll stop for a year. Why do you say so many jokes? Let me see you control yourself for a year and don't make any jokes."

So he said all right. He didn't crack any jokes.

Once he was at Lublin. All the students, all the big rabbis were there. The rabbi, the Lubliner, was standing for the Eighteen Benedictions. It was very long. They couldn't stand it. The Ropchitser calls over to his other friends and tells them, "You know why the rabbi stays so long saying the Eighteen Benedictions? He probably reminds himself of the day of the wedding." That is what he said. And so all of them start laughing. You know, it's a joke.

So then after the Ropchitser Rov said this he went over to the Lubliner and he sang a song in his ears, in the middle of the Eighteen Benedictions, and then right away he finished. As soon as he sang him the song, he finished the Eighteen Benedictions. And he turned around and he saw all of them were laughing. "Oh, you probably cracked a joke already. They're laughing." So he said, "You promised me you wouldn't crack a joke for a year."

In Jewish there's a saying: you say a year and a Wednesday. If somebody takes too long to tell something, you tell them it takes a year and a Wednesday. "It's not my fault if the Rebbe stays for the Eighteen Benedictions a year and a Wednesday. The Rebbe told me only one year I shouldn't say any jokes. The Rebbe stays for the Eighteen Benedictions a year and a Wednesday."

So then he asked, "Why are you laughing?"

So they told him, "The Ropchitser said that you reminded yourself of the day of the wedding."

"He knew what he was talking about." So he told them in the middle of the Eighteen Benedictions there came a man, a man who sings songs at weddings. He was not a good person. So in the other world they didn't want to allow him in Paradise. So he came over to the Lubliner, and he begged him he should do something for him here—pray for him they should let him in.

So he says, "I didn't know him."

So the man says, "I sang at your wedding."

"So I don't remember."

The Ropchitser Rov came to his ear and sang what he sang him at the wedding.

X, Bobov, E

The Meal (S7)

The Ropchitser Rov was by the Lubliner once, by the meal on Shabbes, when you sit together. They used to eat together like here we eat together with the Rebbe on Shabbes. The Lubliner liked him very much. The Ropchitser gave him his pipe every time he used to smoke. The Lubliner didn't smoke, only one time he found one of his students had a pipe. He took the pipe, gave a couple of puffs, and gave it back. He took it from him and he used to hold it the whole day. That's how much he liked him.

So in the middle of the meal he gave a pudding. There was a lot of people pushing, and he said, "The Ropchitser Rov." He called his name. He wanted to give him pudding but he couldn't reach him. So people passed it over their heads one to the other until it came to him. But one was very hungry so he grabbed it off and had a plate.

After the meal the Lubliner asked him, "How did you like my pudding?"

He says, "The one above knows." You could take it in two ways: the person that took it off, and the One on top [the Almighty].

X, Bobov, E

Good, Pious, and Smart (S8)

The Ropchitser Rebbe said: A Jew has to be good, pious, and smart. Because good alone is a fool, pious alone is a priest, smart alone is a thief. A Jew has to be all three.[5]

UU, Satmar, E

One, Two, Three (S9)

The Kaminker Rov was a student of the Ropchitser Rov. He was a friend of the Sandzer Rov. (He is the Bobover Rebbe's great-grand-

---

[5] Compare Langer, p. 262.

father on one side. The Rebbe's grandfather was a son-in-law of the Kaminker Rov.) Both were students of the Ropchitser Rov. He also used to say those jokes, just like he took it over from his Rebbe.

The Divrei Haim [the Sandzer Rov], he didn't say even one joke, and they told him, "Why does the Kaminker Rov make jokes?"

So he says, "What he says are all high things. He doesn't say any jokes. I'll tell you what he said once. One time a student came to him and wanted a drink, to make himself lively. 'Why do you want to drink? For three reasons I don't want to give you any whiskey. One, you don't drink. Second, you drank. Third, so why do you need it?' That's what he said. What did he mean? 'One glass of whiskey you never drink. You drink more. That means you drank two already. So why do you need a third one?' "

X, Bobov, E

Am I Worse Than the Shoemaker? (S10)

The Sandzer Rov had a son, the Gorletser Rebbe, whose name was Reb Borukh. Once he came in to his father with a problem: he must marry off his daughter, the Sandzer Rov's granddaughter, and he has no money. And he asked his father for money for the wedding.

His father said, "I don't have any."

A few days later he noticed four or five of the Rebbe's rich hasidim come to visit the Rebbe. And he knew how much they gave: this one gave two hundred rubles, this one gave—well, he knew how much each one gave.

Later, after the rich hasidim left, he went into the Rebbe, and asked him again, "Father, give me money for my daughter's wedding."

And the Rebbe said, "I don't have."

He said, "But this rich person was here, and this rich person was here. What do you mean you don't have money? They surely left you money."

The Rebbe answered him, "The shoemaker came in and he has to marry off his daughter. I gave him the money."

So he said, "Am I worse than the shoemaker?"

He answered him, "You have an old father with a white beard. I don't have a drop of Torah. I don't have a drop of wisdom. And I don't have a drop of fear of heaven. I have only a drop of charity, and you wish to take this away from me also? You could go to Hungary and other countries and say that you are the son of the Sandzer Rov, and people will give you money."

So the son answered him, "Father, please don't repeat what you told me. If people will learn how lowly you are, they won't give me any money."

S, Klausenberg, Y

The Rabbi and the Officer (S11)

Reb Sheah Tamishav's father [Yosel] was a very great rabbi. He was a great rabbi too. The generations get weaker and weaker and so the rabbis get weaker and weaker too. At Mt. Sinai all the people were stronger. We consider them as the wisest.

Reb Sheah Tamishav said once, "My father, who was a very great rabbi, was standing on the street and an officer of the tsar came to him. His fringes were hanging out, and the officer took Yosel Tamishav by the hand and said, 'What is this?'

"The officer had a sword by his side, and my father took it in his hand and asked, 'What is this?'

" 'A sword. With it I can defend myself.'

" 'Well, this is my sword.'

" 'Well,' the officer said, 'Let's have this out and have a duel.' He grabbed his sword, but he was paralyzed as he drew it out of the sheath. He apologized and everything was all right."

And the Rebbe said, "The same thing happened to me. I was standing and an officer came to me and said, 'What's that?'

"And I pointed to his sword and said, 'What's that?'

" 'A sword. With it I can defend myself.'

"It's repeated. 'Let's have a duel.'

"And can you imagine? I got beaten up terribly."

And it's true too.[6]

UU, Satmar, E

[6] Compare Gaster, *Ma'aseh Book*, no. 18; Babylonian Talmud, *Shabbat* 30a.

Melody (S12)

There was once the Rebbe Yavyones. Do you know who the Rebbe Yavyones was? The Rabbi Yehoynisen Eybeschütz.[7] He wrote a lot of famous books, like *Kreisi u-Pleisi* and *Urim ve-Tummim*. This is what the High Priest used to wear on his heart.[8]

He used to have arguments with the priests all the time. So once—you know in the Torah there are certain dots on every word, because when you say Torah, you say it with a certain melody. So the priest said, "Why don't you read the Torah like you usually do? Why do you have to make this noise, this melody?"

He didn't answer him anything. "It's a very good question," he told him.

The next day he came over to him, and he took out a small snuffbox with silver, gold, and diamonds. He said to the priest, "If you want it, I'll give it to you."

"Sure, it's a very nice thing."

He didn't give it to him. He just said so. Then two minutes later he said, "If you want it, I'll give it to you?" So the Rebbe Yavyones said, "Look, I didn't change my words. I just changed my melody, and it's another meaning. So now you can understand. In the Torah you just change the melody and it's another meaning."

X, Bobov, E

Quiet (S13)

Here's another story. One priest asked him [Rebbe Yavyones], "Look, tell me why when you come in our church it's so quiet, you hear every word, everybody's quiet, and you come in your shul everybody's making noise? You pray so loud."

So the Rebbe answered him. "You asked a very good question, but I have a very good answer. You see, your God is a young man.

---

[7] Rabbi Yehoynisen Eybeschütz, German talmudist, ca. 1690–1764.

[8] *Kreisi u-Pleisi* (*Kreti u-Phleti*) signifies the bodyguard of David; *Urim ve-Tummim* was the breastplate of the High Priest.

He has good ears, so you don't have to scream. We have an old, old God. So He should hear us, we have to scream to Him."

X, Bobov, E

Respect (S14)

When the Dzikover was a small child, he was known as a genius. Everybody was talking about him, a kid of six years, a genius. He learned with all big boys when he was six years old. He knew everything. So his father took him once to a Rebbe when he was small. So after the father went out, the kid, the Dzikover, said to the Rebbe, "Rebbe, *ikh vill di solst mir benchen*—I want you to bless me." In Yiddish you don't say *di* to an older person. You should say *ir*.

So the Rebbe says, "How about a little respect? Why do you tell me *di?*"

So the Dzikover answers, "Listen, do you merit more respect than God? When you pray to God you say *Borukh Atoh* [Blessed art Thou]. What does *Atoh* mean? *Di*—you. To God I should say *di* and to you I should say *ir?*"

X, Bobov, E

Cookies (S15)

His [the Dzikover's] mother once cooked cookies with chocolate. She put it on the top shelf so nobody could reach it, the children shouldn't eat it up. So his father found him as he was on a ladder eating the cookies. So his father says, "What are you doing?"

So he says, "I'm doing the same thing as Moshe our rabbi did."

"What did Moshe our rabbi do?"

So he says, "There's one portion that starts, 'Vayakehel Moshe—Moshe gathered the people together.' So the Targum says 'ikh nash.' " So he says, "Moshe our rabbi nashed, so I nashed too."[9]

X, Bobov, E

[9] In Aramaic, the language of the Targum, "ikhnosh" means "he gathered," as does the Hebrew "vayakehel." In Yiddish "ikh nash" means "I nibble."

The Watchman (*S16*)

In Europe, every night somebody else had to be a watchman in the city. And the rich people naturally took a man, and they paid him to be watchman so they would not have to go. So once the Ropchitser Rov was walking on the street at night and he sees somebody, and it's the watchman. He asks him, "For whom are you watching today?"

So he said, "I'm watching for this and this person. For whom is the Rebbe watching today?"

He says, "Nobody special, but I want to see you tomorrow. Come tomorrow to my house. I want to see you." Then he took him as a gabai because he saw he wouldn't see what he's doing. He wouldn't be able to tell what he was doing. Not that he was hiding anything, but they used to want to hide their greatness that nobody should see it.[10]

S, Klausenberg, E

Sheah (*S17*)

You see the tsaddikim used to have their gaboyim, those people that go with them and serve them. Not a secretary—he gives them their meals. He's more like a servant, you might say. They used to take such people that had very little sense, because if they would take people with sense they would understand what the Rebbe is doing, the hidden things. He does very high things for God, so they used to take people that had very little sense.

So the Ropchitser Rov, that's the [Bobover] Rebbe's great-grandfather, he was a very hidden man. You just saw him like this—he talked, made jokes. You could crack from his jokes. You know, later on people thought they figured out every word that he meant with the joke. So the Ropchitser Rov was once outside on a winter night and he was rolling naked on the snow. That's one of the things you do, if you commit sins, one of the things to have the sins forgiven. We don't believe the Ropchitser Rov did those sins.

[10] This tale is also told of the Ropchitser. Newman and Spitz, *Hasidic Anthology*, p. 319, no. 1.

He was a great tsaddik. But even if he doesn't do those sins, he does the same thing. It's not done now because the people are very weak. It used to be done.

In those times, every night somebody sent out a man. Let us say in every apartment house five people lived. So every night somebody has to stay outside and watch the house. The rich people they didn't want to be up all night to watch the house, so they gave money to poor people and they watched for them.

So the Ropchitser Rov's gabai was named Sheah. So how did he become his gabai? Once, when the Ropchitser Rov was rolling in the snow, so Sheah didn't understand what he was doing. He thought the Rebbe was hot. "It's hot. He's going outside in the wintertime to roll in the snow." So he says, "Rebbe, for who are you watching now? Whose house are you watching?" He thought he's watching a house.

So the Rebbe saw, "This person is good for me. He has a lot of sense." So he goes over. "Listen, Sheah, how much do you get paid?"

He says, "Five cents an hour."

So he says, "Listen, I'll take you with me, and I'll pay you whatever you make for a whole year, and you'll be my gabai."

So he said, "Okay."

"Don't call me Rebbe," he says. Call me balebos—boss. I'm your boss." The hasidim used to laugh at him. The hasidim used to call the Rebbe, the Rebbe. He says, "The balebos goes to the meal. The balebos goes here." He used to call him balebos.

X, Bobov, E

Carrying Water (S18)

Once the Ropchitser Rov looked out of the window and he sees Sheah carrying water from the city pump. He says, "Sheah, what's wrong with you? We have a pump right here in the yard. Why do you go there?"

So Sheah answers, "Rebbe, I thought you'd have sense. People say where the Torah is, there's wisdom. I thought the Rebbe has sense. Don't you know why I go there? Because if I take water from the city pump I have three chances to rest, but if I'm going to take it from the yard, I'm going to have no time to rest."

X, Bobov, E

Four Gaboyim (S19)

The Sandzer Rov had four gaboyim when he was young. When he was older he had only one. So they asked him, "Why is it now you have only one when before you had four?"

He said, "Well, now I'm an old man and I cannot serve four people."

X, Bobov, E

Getel (S20)

He [the Kaminker Rov] had a gabai also. His name was Getel. He was a very old bachelor. In the olden times, even now, if after the wedding they don't have any children for a long time, they go to the Rebbe he should pray for them. The Rebbe would do a miracle and they would have a child. So people knew—go to the Bobover Rebbe, to the Belzer Rebbe, to any Rebbe—have a child.

So the Kaminker Rov said once, "Getel! Why don't you get married?"

Getel knew that if you get married you're two people, so Getel said, "Why does one person need a wife?" He knew if you have a wife you're two persons. "I'm one person. Why does one person need to have a wife?"

So he answered, "Because you need to have children. The Torah says you must have children."

"I need to have children? So what do I have to get married for? I'll go to the Belzer Rebbe. Then I'll get children." He knew that when you go to the Rebbe you get children. "So why do I have to get married?"

X, Bobov, E

Yoyel (S21)

The Bobover Rebbe's father, he also had a gabai. His name was Yoyel. When you looked at him, he looked to be the most impor-tant Rebbe. He had a big white beard. You know, he looked like a holy man. But he wore the fringes on the wrong side. He didn't even know how to pray. They used to call him Yoyel.

After he got married, the second night right after he got married, he ran away from his wife. He said, "I have to feed the chickens at the Rebbe's in Bobov. I can't stay with you any more."

X, Bobov, E

Sending the Moon (S22)

Once the Rebbe, our Rebbe's father, went to a summer place, Marienbad. It's a city in Germany. And this Yoyel, he remained in Bobov. You know, when a new month begins, you go outside and renew the moon. You pray, so you have to see the moon bright and nice. He went out with a handkerchief, waving to the clouds. He says, "I'm sending the moon to the Rebbe to Marienbad. The Rebbe should have the moon there." He really meant it. "See, I'm shaking with the handkerchief, the moon should go over there."

After two months the Rebbe came from Marienbad to Bobov. So Yoyel was the first one to the train. He said, "Rebbe, did you get the moon over there?" That's Reb Yoyel.

X, Bobov, E

Moshe Gendarme (S23)

The Rebbe's father had a gabai—Moshe Gendarme, Moshe the Policeman. The Rebbe used him for many strange things. On kiddish levuneh, the seventh day after the new moon, when it was cloudy, he would have Moshe whipped. Then the moon would come out. It's common to make the moon come out. "Makhen a levuneh" is to give someone a hit.

M, Stolin, E

Stomachache (S24)

The [Stoliner] Rebbe took him [Moshe Gendarme] one day into someone's house. It was on a Monday. He asked the person's wife if she had horos [a dish of potatoes, barley, and beans] left from Shabbes.

"Yes."

"Warm it up."

And he made Moshe Gendarme eat it all up. The reason why? The woman used to make it on Shabbes and make her husband eat it the whole week. He would get a stomachache and come running to the Rebbe. So the Rebbe made Moshe eat it up.

M, Stolin, E

The Interrupted Journey (*S25*)

Once Moshe was going with the Rebbe to a wedding, and the train stopped at a station in the middle of the way and the Rebbe said, "Get off."

He didn't ask any questions and he got off. Right away he meets another Stoliner hasid, and the man asks him, "What are you doing here?"

"I don't know. The Rebbe kicked me off."

"I know why already," the man says. If someone has a rupture, sometimes it gets out of place, this Moshe knew how to treat this. Someone in town was suffering and he had to go help this person.

Some say that these people are great also, but give up their greatness helping the Rebbes. Some say that the Rebbes need them to bring them down to earth.

M, Stolin, E

Not So Obvious (*S26*)

A rabbi went out in the morning and met the chief of police. The chief of police asked the question, "Where are you going?"

He was obviously going to the synagogue to say the morning prayers. He had asked the question in a friendly spirit, but the rabbi had no answer except to say that, "I don't know."

The police chief was antagonized. He says, "You could have answered. It's obvious where you were going." He throws him in prison.

The rabbi says, "See! When I left the house this morning I thought I was going to shul, but I ended up in prison."

QQ, Square, E

The Dream (S27)

A hasid came to a Rebbe and said: "I had a dream that I became a Rebbe."

The Rebbe answered him, "If you dream that you're a Rebbe, it isn't anything. But when hasidim dream that you're a Rebbe—then you're going to be a Rebbe."

Y, Munkacz, E

The Gangsters (S28)

Some goods of the Rebbe were stolen, and the hasidim went to the head of gangsters and said, "Look, steal, all right, but not from the Rebbe. Please find out who did it and have it returned."

The gangster chief said, "Okay, if it's one of my hasidim who did it you'll get it back, but if it's one of your hasidim, you'll never get it back."

SS, Stolin, E

How Awful Is This Place (S29)

A Polish rabbi met a German rabbi, and the German rabbi asked him, "Why are our shuls so nice and clean and painted fresh, and your shtiblekh are always in a state of disrepair—dirty?"

So he answered him, "When Jacob left his father's house and was traveling, he had a dream and he saw the angels going up and down. And he woke up and he said, 'Ma norah hamakom hazeh—how awesome is this place.' [11] '*Norah*' has two translations.

---

[11] "How full of awe is this place! This is none other than the House of God" (Gen. 28:17).

It means, 'How *awesome* is this place' and it also means 'How *awful* is this place.'

"So he [the hasid] translated it as 'how awful is this place.' It's so terrible, it's in such a state of disrepair that it could only be a shtibl."

M, Stolin, E

Davening (S30)

After prayers the hasidim drink a little whiskey. The misnagdim learn prayers for mourning. So why do the hasidim drink? The misnagdim are doing better.

The misnagdim don't daven lively. They're like dead people. In mourning you learn mourning prayers for your father's soul. You had a dead davening. So the misnagdim study them.

The hasidim have a lively davening and so drink brandy.

C, Lubavitch, E

Belief (S31)

Two Jews meet and they're both a little drunk. They like to drink.

One says, "When the Meshiah comes, everything will be wonderful. The Red Sea will be brandy."

The other says, "Why not the Mediterranean? If you're going to believe in something, why believe in so little?"

CC, Satmar, E

His First Wife (S32)

A man came to the Rebbe and said, "It's three months after the wedding already and I didn't have any children. So I want you should pray for me I should have children."

So the Rebbe says, "What do you want? It's only three months after your wedding."

So he says to the Rebbe, "I'll tell you the truth, I think this is a sickness of the family because my father didn't have any children either."

So the Rebbe asked him, "What's wrong? How were you born?"

So he said, "That was from his first wife."

X, Bobov, E

Potatoes (S33)

When Hitler invaded other countries in Europe, wherever he came he took away the licenses of Jews for business. There were no more businesses. So one Jew decided to go to the United States. He's on the ship and a big storm comes up. He doesn't know what to do, the ship's in danger of sinking. He sees the captain goes on deck, and he sees a sack of potatoes and throws it overboard thinking to lighten the ship. Two hours later, the ship is still sinking. He sees the Jew sitting with his Book of Psalms and he throws him overboard with the book. They go a few more miles, and they're still sinking. He sees a woman with a shopping bag. He throws her into the sea.

In the Atlantic a whale comes along and takes these things into its stomach and then goes to the coast to digest its food. In the United States, a fisherman went out and spied the whale. They caught it, and cut it open. Inside they found the Yid sitting reading his psalms. He had the sack of potatoes and the lady with the shopping bag was coming to buy from him.

Y, Munkacz, E

The Rebbe Looks at the Kvitl: I (S34)

A woman comes in for a kvitl. She writes her name, her mother's name, and her problem. The Rebbe doesn't look at a woman. The gabai—the Rebbe's secretary—lets her in.

The woman says, "My husband left me."

The Rebbe says, "He will come back."

The gabai lets her out and says, "Your husband won't come back."

"How can you say that? The Rebbe just said that he will."

"He didn't look at you."

UU, Satmar, E

The Rebbe Looks at the Kvitl: II (S35)

The story is this way. The woman came in to the Rebbe. Her husband disappeared and never came back. So the Rebbe says to the woman, "He will come back."

So the gabai says, "No, he won't."

Afterward the woman walks out, and the Rebbe says, "Why did you embarrass me? I said he would."

"The Rebbe looked at the kvitl. I looked at the woman."

S, Klausenberg, E

The Dybbuk (S36)

I don't know exactly how long ago it was, but when the Satmarer Rebbe was in Israel a Yemenite from Yemen came with his daughter. First they went to the Belzer Rebbe. He claimed that a dybbuk entered into her and he's bothering her, and she has pains and she talks with a strange voice, and it's very painful for her that something talks out of her. It's not her natural voice. It might be a dybbuk. So he went to the Belzer Rebbe and the Belzer Rebbe took him into his room and he told him he hopes that—there is a version of the story that the Belzer Rebbe commanded the dybbuk to leave the person alone and to go. But anyhow, she didn't feel any better, and she came to the Satmarer Rebbe. So they thought that the Satmarer Rebbe will do some miracles there, say something and the dybbuk will disappear. So the Satmarer Rebbe said, "I think it's a mental case. Better go to a good psychiatrist and leave me alone." [12]

CC, Satmar, E

Questions (S37)

A man asked Rabbi Schneerson two questions—one personal and the other—"How do the angels conduct themselves in heaven?"

The first he answered, and for the second he said, "What business is it of yours how the angels conduct themselves in heaven?"

C, Lubavitch, E

[12] Compare H86.

A MISNAGED'S TALES AND

OTHERS

Horses (M1) *

Someone came to a Rebbe and complained that he has no parnosseh, no means of making a living. And the Rebbe said, "Go and
start a business with horses."

He did so and he became prosperous. Then he went back to the
Rebbe and he said, "Praise God first and then you, Rebbe. Thanks
to both of you, I'm prosperous. But how did you know? Why did
you tell me especially to start a business with horses. Why did you
give me that advice?"

So the Rebbe answered him simply, "Because I know myself
from my own experience, I deal with horses and I make out very
well. And I figured so will you."

ZZZ, Y

Prophecy (M2)

A lady came to a Rebbe and she brought a deaf and dumb boy, the
Rebbe should help that he should be able to speak. The Rebbe said
to the child, "Good boy, I ask you, do it for your mother's sake.
Start talking." And he told him again and again, until at the end
the Rebbe told him, "I see you are stubborn. I am commanding
you, you should talk!" And the child still didn't talk. So the Rebbe

* The six tales in this section were not collected from hasidim. They are
included because they furnish comparative examples.

saw that he was still dumb. So the Rebbe said, "I see that you are a stubborn shaigets [gentile]. For that reason for your entire life you'll be deaf and dumb." And so it was.

ZZZ, Y

Fish (M3)

There was a Rebbe, a faker, and he was visiting a town and there was no fish. And the Rebbe said, "I must have fish for Shabbes. To honor the Shabbes I must have fish." Still they couldn't find any fish. So the gabai realized the situation, and he took a cab and he went into a big town and he bought a big carp, a live one, and then he came back and threw it into the well.

Well, later on the Rebbe asked the proprietor of the house, "What about fish? I must have fish for Shabbes."

The proprietor said, "I can't help it. I don't have it."

So the Rebbe said, "I don't care what you say. Stay here at the well a whole night, day and night, but catch me a fish. I must have a fish for Shabbes."

So the proprietor told him, "Impossible. There were never any fish in this well. You wouldn't find any fish. Impossible." But the Rebbe persisted, and so he stood there and finally they caught the big carp that was thrown in by the gabai. It weighed seven to eight pounds. Then gossips started to say that he performed a miracle. So people came running to the Rebbe and they gave him large amounts of money.

ZZZ, Y

Hershele Ostropoler (M4)

Hershele Ostropoler walked around town and it was toward the end of the day that he noticed smoke from a chimney.[1] And as tired and hungry as he was he thought that this was a good place to go into. Well, he knocked at the door and told the lady of the house that

---

[1] The famous "court jester" who is said to have been at the court of Rabbi Borukh of Mezhibezh.

he's hungry and he needs lodging too for the night. She agreed to it and gave him something to eat and then put up a place for him to sleep. But he didn't sleep.

When he asked what's cooking in the oven, because he saw the chimney and the smoke, she said she put laundry in there, in the earthen pots in the old-fashioned European oven. She said she put in laundry to boil there. When everybody was sound asleep Hershele Ostropoler got up quietly and went to see what's cooking in the oven. Instead of laundry he found a big pot of kreplekh. He ate to his heart's desire, had a nap, and at dawn walked out not saying anything to anybody. And he thought to himself what nice people there were.

YYY, E

Hershele's Cloak (M5)

Hershele Ostropoler walked around town dressed up in a black satin cloak, but the back of the cloak was full of holes and patches. And people while facing him admired him the way he was dressed up, but then when they turned back after they passed him they saw the cloak was so shabby and full of patches of different kinds. So they turned back to him and tried to ask him why is it that way that he's dressed up just facing him and not the back. So he said, "In front I see people so I got to be presentable. But in back I can't see myself."

YYY, E

The Burned Hand (M6)

I recall a story that happened to a little boy in Czechoslovakia and how evil tried to get him. This little boy lived on a farm and right near the farm there was a cemetery and in the cemetery every night little lights would flicker above the graves. Well, this little boy wanted to know what these little lights were. He asked his mother and his mother told him not to worry about them that they weren't harming him so he should not harm them. But one night this little boy decided that he was going to find out what these lights were. So he went near the cemetery and picked up a stone and threw it and the flickering lights all seemed to come together and came at him. He got very frightened and started running to the house, and as he got into the house he slammed the door. And just as he slammed the door there was a great noise against the door. He told his parents what he had done and everyone was too frightened to go outside and see what had happened until daylight would come. So when the day had come everyone went outside to see what had happened and there was no sign of any damage. But as the boy's mother turned to go inside she was horrified to see a burnt hand imbedded in the door.

JLH, E

IN OTHER TIMES

The Pasha (11)

When the Jews were living in the Land of Israel under the Arabs they would go out of shul after Shabbes to bless the new moon. And when you bless the moon you say, "David, the king of the Jews, continues to live." The Pasha went by and heard this and he said, "David is your king? I am your king. For this rebellion I don't want to see a Jew in the city." He gave them a certain time when they're all supposed to be out.

So they appointed two of the most holy members to go to David's grave. And they came to the grave. The grave is a series of rooms. And they came into the innermost room and they saw David the king sitting there with a golden crown, and they told him of their plight. So he gave them two apples. He said, "A half of one apple you should give to a man sitting outside the city. He is my Rebbe." David had studied with him. "And one-half apple each of you should eat. Keep the remaining half."

The next day the Pasha's daughter became deathly sick. And the Pasha dreamed that a half apple of the Jews would cure her. So he came begging for this half apple and they gave it to him on condition that he nullify his decree.

I heard this story sixty-five years ago.

BB, Slonim, Y

The Blind Man (12)

Maimonides [1] was the Sultan's house doctor. He said it was possi-

[1] Moses Maimonides, the Rambam, philosopher and physician, 1135–1204. In Jewish tradition he is the hero of myriad legends, exceeded

ble to heal a blind person, but he said that someone who was born blind could not be healed. Some of the doctors were jealous of him and wanted him removed, and one said that he could heal someone who was born blind. The Sultan said, "Make a test." The doctor said he will bring someone who was blind from birth. He arranged with a man who was actually blinded later on in life to say that he was blind since birth. He succeeded in restoring the man's sight.

The Rambam said it was impossible. Moses took out a handkerchief and said, "What color is this?"

The man said, "Red."

"Then he was not born blind."

That's a legend about the Rambam.

UU, Satmar, E

Cat and Mouse: I (I3)

They once asked the Rambam, "What is God?"

He answered, "If I knew what God is I would be God."

The Rambam once had an argument with other smart people in his town in Egypt. They said, "You can teach any animal to act like a man."

The Rambam didn't agree.

"We'll bet you we're going to do it." They took a kitten, taught her to bow when a man comes in, to walk on two feet. The cat ate with a fork and spoon. It wore a suit like a real man. It used to wear a suit, you know, like anybody.

So it grew up. They made a whole party. They won. They taught a kitten to be like a man.

"Maybe you're right. We'll see about it."

In the middle of the party, they said, "See how the kitten sits on a big chair and acts like a man."

"Okay, you've won. For that I'm going to give you a present." So he took out a small box, and put it on the table. Everybody was interested in what the present was. So he opened up the box and a mouse flew out of the box. As soon as the cat saw the mouse he

---

in number only by the tales of Elijah the Prophet. See Noy, "Archiving and Presenting Folk Literature in an Ethnological Museum," *Journal of American Folklore*, 78 (1962): 24.

jumped on the table, threw all the plates down, and he went running after the mouse.

"See!" he said. "That's how you can teach a cat how to be a man."[2]

X, Bobov, E

Cat and Mouse: II (14)

A priest challenged a rabbi to a religious debate. The rabbi was preparing to go to the debate, and he had his tobacco pouch there and a mouse jumped in.

He went and they talked. The priest said, "You say an animal is an animal and can't act like a man. He brings in a cat. He's dressed like a man. He sits down at the table and he eats like a man. The rabbi is thinking how to answer him. He opened his pouch and the mouse jumped out. Oh, the cat chased him. "See. You can't train a cat to be a man."

EE, Lubavitch, E

Ten Ducats (15)

Rabbi Ibn Ezra, in the Rambam's time, was very poor.[3] He heard that the Rambam was a very great doctor and he wanted to test him. The Rambam lived in Morocco and he lived in Europe. The afternoon hours of the Rambam were devoted to giving free service. Lines of people came to him. The Rambam was too busy to see him. So he got in line with the sick people. And when the Rambam examined him he gave him a prescription for the pharmacy. He was laughing on the inside because he knew he was healthy. When he reached the pharmacy the prescription was for ten golden ducats.

UU, Satmar, E

---

[2] See Aarne and Thompson, *Types of the Folktale*, type 217.

[3] Ibn Ezra, Abraham Ibn Ezra, ca. 1093–1167. There are many tales of encounters between the Rambam and Ibn Ezra. See for example, Noy, *Moroccan Jewish Folktales*, no. 58, pp. 144–47.

The Son-in-law (16)

The Bakh had a daughter of marriageable age, and his wife was always bothering him to pick a son-in-law.[4] So one night when she was particularly annoying he said, "Tomorrow I'll choose the first person that comes into the house as a son-in-law."[5]

The next morning, the Bakh was very late in coming to shul and the people were getting restless, and so they sent the shammes to call him. When he came into the house the Bakh fainted. But he had to keep his word. So he asked him, "Do you want to be my son-in-law?"

He said, "I will, if you promise me three things: One, that I should be able to sleep on the oven; two, you should give me meat every day; and three, that before the engagement I should have a half hour to speak with my bride." His reasons were these: he wanted to sleep on the oven because the Bakh used to learn there and he wanted to hear him learn. The meat was so he should have strength. And the half hour was so that he would be able to tell his bride that he was as learned and as scholarly as her father, except that his way was to keep everything to himself and not to show the world. She heard this and she was very happy.

It was Thursday night before the Great Shabbes.[6] The Bakh was preparing his talk by the oven and the son-in-law was sleeping on top. The Bakh went outside for a while and the son-in-law wrote a note that upset the whole lecture. It contradicted and disrupted the complete lecture. He came back and saw this note, and he surmised that it came from heaven. It bothered him very much and he walked around in the room trying to answer it. While he was walking around, the son-in-law wrote another note with the answer and put it down on the book. He came back and saw the second note and he was very happy. It was a very good answer. So he went and gave the lecture on Shabbes.

[4] The Bakh: Rabbi Joel Serkes (1561/62–1641), commentator on the codex *Turim*. His name is derived from his book *Bayit Hadash* ("The New House"), abbreviated Bakh.

[5] This is a common motif in folk literature. See Thompson's *Motif-Index*, motif T62 (princess to marry first man who asks her). See also Aarne and Thompson, *Types of the Folktale*, type 900. In *In Praise of the Besht*, no. 40, a match is made with the first person to arrive.

[6] The Shabbes before Passover. On this Shabbes every rabbi gives a homily called the Great Shabbes talk.

The custom was that after the lecture all the scholars would come to the rabbi and he would give them cake and shnapps. The son-in-law told his bride to ask her father for some cake and shnapps for him. But her father told her that since he's not a scholar he doesn't belong in this group and he has nothing to do with us. She came back and told him, and so he said, "Tell your father that heaven doesn't send any notes."

So she told him and he said, "So he's the one that sends the notes." He brought him over and kissed him.[7]

BB, Slonim, Y

The Thief's Confession (17)

Rabbi Bakh—he lived 150 years before the Besht—wrote a book but it wasn't printed. They asked the printer why not.

He says, "Megaleh Amukos says no."[8]

They go to Megaleh Amukos to ask and they get a flat no. He is asked why wouldn't he even give a recommendation to the book. He said because he knows that when the book is printed the Bakh will die shortly thereafter and he's trying to prevent it. Megaleh Amukos was said to confer with Elijah the Prophet.

Rabbi Bakh says, "Don't worry, I'm here for a certain purpose." The book comes out. Rabbi Bakh gets very sick and has to judge cases in bed.

In one case a man comes and says he owes six hundred guildens. There is a signed note. There are witnesses. He says it's all a lie. The judges say they can't help. The Bakh looks at the note and says, "It's false. The man is a thief. The witnesses are thieves." He says, "Leave me alone with the man." He tells him if he confesses he will be in Paradise with him. The man confesses.

Soon after, the Bakh dies. He asks God to send him to purgatory. He looked for a sin to send himself. He found a minor point. Once his Shabbes clothes scared horses. He was sent to purgatory and there he raised souls.

P, Bobov, Y

[7] The son-in-law of the Bakh is called the Taz, after his book *Turei Zahav* ("Golden Towers"). In the book he often contradicts his father-in-law.

[8] Megaleh Amukos (Megaleh Amukot): Nathan ben Solomon Shapira, kabbalist, 1585–1633.

The Bells (18)

Shmuel Eliezer lived over 300 years ago.[9]

In this town the church was built over the main thoroughfare of the town, with an arcade running through the church. And the only way to get from one end to the other was to go through the church. Whenever there was a funeral and the Jews would have to go through the church, the priest would ring the bells of the church.

So Shmuel Eliezer said, "At my funeral, when they start ringing the bells, lay me down on the ground."

So when his time came and they were taking him in the funeral, when the bells started ringing they obeyed his command and put him down inside the arcade of the church. And they noticed that the church was sinking. It began to sink. So they hurriedly took him out and the church sank halfway down into the ground and remained so. It forced the people to carve out a new road around the church, and the church remained always halfway sunk into the ground.

B, Slonim, Y

Graf Potocki: I (19)

Graf Potocki[10] was a talented son and his father wanted to teach him everything that he could be taught: Latin, Greek, and he also brought in a Yid to teach him Hebrew. The Yid said he will come in on one condition: he be given one hour a day locked in solitude.

The boy was attracted to his teacher and wanted to know what he did in this hour. Before he came he hid in his room and he saw him putting on talis and tefillin. "What is this?" He told him what it was. "If that is so you have to teach me everything about Yiddishkait. If not I'll tell father what you're doing and have you killed."

[9] Solomon ben Eliezer ha-Levi, Turkist talmudist, 15th and 16th centuries.

[10] Count Valentine Potocki (Pototzki), a Polish nobleman said to have been burned at the stake at Vilna on May 24, 1749. His teacher was said to have been Menahem Man ben Aryeh Loeb of Visun, who was also executed.

He taught him and the boy decided to run away. He ran away and became a very holy person.

His father offered a great reward for anyone that found him. He told the detective looking for him, "My son has great taste in lacework." The detective saw a bearded man standing in front of a store admiring the lace. He caught him, took him to his father. That was the son. He gave him the choice to reconvert and all will be forgiven or else he would be put to death.

So there by the stake he mentioned why it is that people convert: "Actually God didn't go to the Jews right away with the Torah. He went to other nations first, but they said no. Some were willing but most didn't want it, so God couldn't give it to those nations. But those souls who were willing to accept the Torah still preserve his holiness in their souls for generations. Later it happens that they want to convert. The same thing is true of Jews. Since some didn't want to accept the Torah but the majority wanted it, generations later it turns out that some convert to Catholicism."

Then he said, "The taste that a poor Jew has on Shabbes is better than all the great balls and dinners that a nobleman has." [11]

M, Stolin, E

Graf Potocki: II (110)

There was a noble family in Poland, not Jewish, named Potocki. They were princes and were called Graf Potocki. One of their children became a Jew, and the family was upset. They cried, "Why does he disgrace us? Why does he become a Jew?" This happened about a hundred years ago. They had a family emblem, an eagle, and one nail of the eagle is broken off because one of the men of the family left the faith. They were staunch Catholics. They were so ashamed.

His mother asked him, "What do you see in the Jews? I could give you anything. You know we're so rich I could give you anything."

He said, "The taste of fish on Shabbes to a plain Jew—this taste you couldn't get any place." That's what he said.

And when they took him away to burn—they burned him, the

[11] Compare H10, H12.

Catholics burned him—they built a fire and they said to him, "You could still change your mind—you could still repent."

He spoke with his mother and the whole family before they threw him in the fire and they told him, "You could still change your mind. You have no sense."

And he praised God and he said, "Listen, my soul is Jewish. It draws me only to the Jews. I know I'll go up to heaven. But I was born by too many goyim. I wondered how is it possible to be purified? My soul is very holy. It comes from God, but the flesh was not born in a pure place. So how could I purify it? How could I make it holy? I can't make it holy. I went around every day wondering what to do. I could purge myself of my body—but this is not allowed. A Jew is not permitted to do this. So God helped me. You're doing me a favor. You're burning out the flesh. You're purifying it. Why shouldn't I thank you for this? This is the greatest gift you could give me." That is what he told them.[12]

X, Bobov, E

Graf Potocki: III (I11)

There was a man named Graf Potocki. He was a Catholic and he converted to Judaism. His family was very wealthy, and his father searched all over for him and finally they found him. He was given a chance to reconvert or be hung, and he preferred to remain a Jew. He said, "The taste of fish on Friday night to a Jew is more than all the pleasures of this world." And so they hung him.

H, Stolin, E

The Man in the Sack: I (I12)

Reb Shimon Shmuel went to a village and there was a problem. In this town there was a woman whose husband was missing. She did

[12] Rabbi Akiba's martyrdom was also considered to be a purification (see Newman and Spitz, *Hasidic Anthology*, p. 4, no. 13). Sanctification by fire was not an altogether unusual wish for the mystic believer. Joseph Caro, the sixteenth century mystic of Safed, recorded visions that his soul would be purified by burning (see Schechter, *Studies in Judaism*, pp. 245–46).

not know where her husband was. The custom is that a woman cannot marry again until it is established that her husband is dead, and two witnesses are required for proof. A man came along who swore that her husband was dead. What to do? How did he know? Was he sure?

This man had been on a ship that was captured by pirates. The pirates took him and put him on an island. And there was another Jew. They told each other about their lives, and this other Jew was this woman's husband.

One day the husband came and said that he was going to be killed. He was a shepherd for the pirates and he had lost one sheep. The pirate said if he did not bring back this sheep in three days he would kill him. The man said it was impossible. He would not be able to get the sheep and he would be killed. He told the man to come by in the evening before the third day and he would tell him for certain. So on the third day he went and he had not found the sheep, and he was going to die. And the man the next day, should bury him and bring back word to his wife.

The next day he went and saw a man dressed like a Jew lying dead, all beaten. He assumed it was this man and he buried him. And he came back and told this woman.

What should they do? It seemed clear that the man was dead, but it was a complicated case. So they took it to Reb Shimon Shmuel and Reb Shimon Shmuel said, "Wait ten days."

"Why? What for? This man saw the body."

"Wait ten days."

Because it was Reb Shimon Shmuel they waited. So they waited, and in ten days the man appeared. The husband returned. So the other man must be a liar. "How could he say he saw you dead?"

"No, he's telling the truth. Here's what happened. When I came to the pirate chief he took me to a hut, threw me on the floor and tied me up. Then he went away. While I was lying there a goy came along and asked me what I was doing there. I told him that a king wanted me to marry his daughter but because I was Jewish I didn't want to, and so he tied me up and was forcing me to marry her. So the man untied me and changed places with me, and when the pirate came back he first started hitting him and he beat the man into unrecognizable shape." [13]

KK, Lubavitch, Y

[13] See Aarne and Thompson, *Types of the Folktale*, type 1535 V (fatal deception); see also types 1525A, 1737. See also Thompson, *Motif-Index*, motif K842.

The Man in the Sack: II (I13)

There was once a great gaon. His name was Rabbi Yaakov Emden. When he was a young man, right after he got married, he had a good friend, and they didn't work, they sat and learned, and their fathers-in-law, both his and his friend's, supported them. So once they were sitting and learning. At that time there were the Cossacks. They used to go around and if they'd just find a man on the street, they'd take him and sell him for a slave. So they caught those two students and they sold them for slaves. They sold them to farmers for slaves. Reb Yaakov they sold to one person, and the other, his friend, to another. They were not too far off so they met together every day. They learned the whole night.

Reb Yaakov's owner used to go with the sheep to feed them, so he saw in the morning that Yaakov goes and he sleeps. So he knew that he meets with his friend. He's up all night. That's why he doesn't sleep. So he says, "If I see you meet him again I'm going to kill you." That's what his owner told him.

So the next time he met with his friend he told him, "Listen, I can't come no more to you. I have a very bad master." Reb Yaakov said to him, "I don't want to shorten my life. If I don't give in to him maybe he'll kill me. If you don't see me for a couple of days, maybe he's killed me. You'll look for me and you'll give me a Jewish burial. You'll bury me as a Jew is supposed to be buried."

So once the boss caught him again and he was sleeping. He tied him up, took him to a tree and said, "Now I'm going to kill you." So it happened that his owner tied him to a tree, and gave him a little time. "I'll give you a half a day of life." He went back. "I'll come back and I'll kill you."

Reb Yaakov untied himself, and he asked another guy who worked there for this man, a goy, he said, "Listen, do me a favor. Let me change with you for once. I want to see how I look in your clothes." So he changed his clothes. Now he looked like a goy. He gave him his long suit with a beaver hat. So Reb Yaakov started running away.

The owner comes back, sees him still there, sees him tied up, didn't even look who it is. The other one screamed. He said, "Shut up." He closed his mouth, took him to the tree, killed him. Didn't even bother with it. Just killed him.

A couple of days passed and his friend didn't see Reb Yaakov.

He went to the place and he saw his friend lying dead with the clothes and everything. He had told him to bury him according to the law, and he buried him with his clothes.

A couple of months passed, and Reb Yaakov's friend's master freed him and he went home. He came home and told the whole story. He said, "I saw my friend Reb Yaakov dead and buried him." His wife was not allowed to be married to someone else, but since he's a witness, he saw him and buried him, and you need only one witness, the rabbi gave the wife permission to get married.

So now we go back to Reb Yaakov. This Reb Yaakov went from town to town. He didn't have any money. He came to the city close to his town. He came up to the Rebbe. The Rebbe didn't want to let him in, didn't know who he is. So he started talking with the Rebbe in Gemoreh and learning, and the Rebbe saw that he is a very learned man, he knows how to learn, and he said, "Let him be with us."

He's eating and sleeping there by the Rebbe, and he saw the Rebbe is getting ready to go someplace. So he said, "Where are you going?"

He said, "I'm going to the next city. There's going to be a wedding tomorrow night." He told him this certain widow is getting married.

So he said, "What's happening here?" His wife is getting married. So he said to the Rebbe, "Take me with you."

At first the Rebbe said, "I have no place." But at last he took him with him.

There are two kinds of stories close together, one with a bride. I'll tell you some other time.

So he took him to the wedding, and everything was ready. The poor people sat at a separate table, and they sat with the poor people. They came before the wedding ceremony. He didn't want to make it into a bad thing, so he got up on the table. He said, "You can't go to the wedding ceremony before I see the in-laws, before I see the bride's father."

"What? Are you crazy?" they say. "A poor man like you? What are you opening your mouth for? Sit down."

He said, "I'm not going to let them go to the wedding. Call the father."

And he said to the father, "You should know that it is not true—your daughter's husband didn't die, and I'm the husband."

First he started laughing. "Somebody was a witness. He buried him."

Then he said all the personal things he knew from his wife.

Then from this wedding they made a big celebration, "Thank God he lived."

X, Bobov, E

The King and the Restaurant Owner (114)

See, I remind myself now of a story of a king.[14] I heard it also from the Rebbe. It doesn't have much to do with Hasidism, but I think it's a nice story if you want to hear it.

There was once a war, also a war between two kings. The same thing. The Russian army was called the Cossacks. They had a war with Poland. And the Cossacks became stronger, you know, and they started winning the war. And the king saw they're probably going to take his whole land away from him and he started running away. Right away he came to a Jewish person that had a restaurant in another city. So he told him, he begged him, "Listen, now you have to help me. Hide me someplace because they're going to look for me. They want to catch me. Hide me in a good place so they shouldn't be able to find me." So the Jew saw the king is there so he found a good place where nobody would think a person is there. He hid him in a good place, he gave him to eat, and to drink.

After a few days, those Cossacks knew something was suspicious. They knew the king ran some place around here. So they came in to all the people. They told them, "We saw the king run into this room. You'd better give him up to us."

So, "I don't know nothing about it. You're very mistaken. I'm very sorry, I didn't see the king. If I would see him, I would give him up. I don't like him." But they were suspicious of him. They started hitting him. They gave him blow after blow. He didn't say a word. All right, they saw that he doesn't say anything so they went away.

Then the wheel turned and the Polish people got stronger and they knocked back those Cossacks. The king heard that his land is free already, so he went out. He was free. He went back to this palace. They made a big parade. Before he went away he said to the Jew, "You know you did me such a great thing, you saved my life, I want to give you something back."

[14] This tale was told immediately after W13.

The Jew said, "I'm very sorry, it is enough that I had the opportunity to save the king. The king's life, this is a big gift for me. I don't need any more." And he says, "I have children, and I make a nice living. What else do I want? What do I need with millions? Or what? That's enough."

So the king gave him a letter and he said, "Any time when you need something you just come to me and I'll give it to you." All right. The king went away.

A few years passed. The mayor of the city where the Jew lived was a bad person. Once he got drunk. He told this restaurant keeper, the Jew, "I don't want you in this restaurant any more. I want you to go away unless you bring me $300,000." He named a very big amount of money that he wouldn't be able to pay.

So he said, "Now comes a time when I have to go to the king. Till now I didn't want to ask him, but now I have to." So he went to the king. He came to the door—they wouldn't let him in. He took out the letter and showed it was from the king. They let him in right away.

The king saw him and was very happy. He says, "Listen, I haven't decided yet what good thing I should give you." He didn't even let him talk. "Come in tomorrow at twelve o'clock. Tonight we'll have a committee with all the generals and decide what to give you. But now go away, and come tomorrow."

So he said okay. He slept overnight. He came in the morning to the same room where the king was, but the king wasn't there. Instead a big general was sitting on a chair by a table. And he called him over. He said, "Listen, yesterday we had a meeting about what we could give to a person that saved the king's life. We decided that we can't find any better thing than being only second to the king. But the thing is, the one second to the king can't be a Jew. So you have to convert, become a Christian, and if you don't accept this, if you don't want to be second to the king, we'll have to kill you."

"But for saving a king's life you kill? That's the good thing that you give for saving?"

"I'll tell you why. Because if you won't take this, to be a second to the king, the king is going to have a reputation as a bad king. They'll say about the king—look, somebody saved his life and he doesn't care, he doesn't give him anything. You understand? So you have to accept all—become second to the king and become a Christian, or if not we're going to kill you so no one will know about you. Everybody'll forget about you because you won't be alive any more. Then they won't say anything about the king."

So the Jew said, "Give me time to think, I can't decide such things so fast standing on one foot." All right, he gave him a couple of hours to think. Then he came and said, "No, I'm not going to become a Christian."

So you know before a Jew dies he confesses to God all the sins he did, God should forgive him. So he begged him he should be able to confess. So then he took him to a special room where you kill people, and he put his head on a stone, and there was one guy with a sword standing ready, and as soon as he lays down his head he's going to knock off his head. He put his head down on the stone and he fainted right away. Because he knew he was going to kill him, he couldn't maintain himself. He fainted. And the person laid down the sword. It was from silver paper. It wasn't a real sword. Just put it down and nothing happened. He just fainted. Then they put him in a bed and they washed him and put him in clothes like a fine man should wear, and they gave him something to eat—you know, so he should recover. He opened up his eyes. He didn't know if it was Paradise or what. He didn't know. Where is he? Where is he? They killed him. They killed him. What happened to him? Then suddenly the king came in the room so he saw he was in this world.

So he says, "You're wondering probably what happened. So I'll tell you." This is a story that shows how in olden times the kings were smart too. He said, "You saved my life, right? I have to pay you something for that. So I knew what could I give you? Let's see, give you a whole city? One bomb comes—no more city. Give you a million dollars? Nothing will stay." So he says, "I know with you Jewish people the greatest thing that a man could do is he should die for God, die in God's name." And he says, "What a great thing it would be that a man should die for God and he should be living. You'll never find a greater thing. I gave you a gift you should die for God because you were ready to die just like you died. And now you live. Could there be any greater thing? So now you can tell me what you want." So he told him and the king gave him money and everything and he sent him away.[15]

X, Bobov, E

[15] See Aarne and Thompson, *Types of the Folktale*, type 1736A, in which a man is to be executed unless his sword turns to wood. A similar tale is told of Napoleon and a Jewish tailor who hides him in his bed (see Noy, "Archiving and Presenting Folk Literature in an Ethnological Museum," *Journal of American Folklore*, 78 [1962]: 26). For another treatment of the theme of choosing death rather than conversion, see WH12.

The Treasure (115)

There was once upon a time a Jew who had a dream. There lies at the top of a mountain a large treasure that lies there under a stone. The Jew had the same dream several times. He thought to himself that when he sees a poor person he will go to him and see what he could do. So when he went to it he noticed that he could not dig out the treasure and he knew for certain that it was lying there. Around him there were soldiers and they asked him what he's doing there. So the Jew told them the whole story. So the soldier said, "The same thing happened to me. I dreamed the same story. And I dreamed that in the city where you live, under such and such a tree, there lies a big treasure." And he had the same dream several times. When the Jew heard this he went back to his town, and right under the tree where the soldier told him the treasure lies, he found it.

This story has been told by different rabbis. Different rabbis have different versions. It is a parable about the ways of the Almighty in that what is hidden will later be revealed. When you do something even though you do not understand it, it later has meaning for you.[16]

D, Lubavitch, Y

Guilty (116)

A nobleman in Poland accused a Jew of a crime, and the Jew was given a choice by the nobleman to choose between two cards, one saying "go free" and the other saying "guilty"—he should be killed. But the one who marked the cards was an anti-Semite and he marked them both guilty. The rabbi knew this and he took one and ate it and said, "See what the other one says. This one is the opposite."

YY, Un., E

[16] See Aarne and Thompson, *Types of the Folktale*, type 1645. Compare Langer, *Nine Gates*, pp. 247–48.

Handsprings (117)

I'm not sure this story is true. I haven't heard it among hasidim, but I've heard a few versions of this story. It's been told by various rabbis, various students, but not by hasidic rabbis. The story goes as follows. There was a great rabbi and everyone recognized his greatness even in his early days. When he was ten years old once a day he would go into a room by himself for one hour and nobody ever knew what he did in that hour in that day.

Once upon a time somebody asked him, "Now tell me one thing. What do you do in that hour when you're by yourself?"

This boy was only ten years old, don't forget. And so this ten-year-old boy answered them, "In that time I do handsprings and I jump around just like an acrobat."

And the people were wondering. This ten-year-old boy had so much wisdom and he was such a serious boy the whole day, and all of a sudden he would go in for a whole hour and do handsprings and act like an acrobat. They asked him, "What is the meaning of all this?"

And he answered them, "Well, sometimes I have to do some things that a ten-year-old boy does."

XX, Lubavitch, E

APPENDIX A: STORYTELLERS

The tales were collected from fifty-nine hasidic informants from thirteen different courts. Nine tales included for comparative purposes were collected from four other persons (those listed last).

Narrator	Court	Age	Occupation	Tales
A	Stolin	28	teacher	T24, TA4, TA9, H13, H23, H73, H77, H79, HA14, HA26, HA27
B	Stolin	50	storekeeper	TA12, TA14, TA18, TA19, TA20, H22, H64, H65, H71, H72, H95, HA5, HA7, HA9, HA12, HA22, HA23, HA24, N15, N16, N35
C	Lubavitch	38	rabbi	W20, H53, H85, S30, S37
D	Lubavitch	21	student	TA1, H8, H11, H24, I15
E	Bobov	45	unknown	HA36
F	Stolin	30	teacher	TA3, TA6, TA7, W14, H17, H18, H75, H76, HA4, HA8, N26, N27, N29

Narrator	Court	Age	Occu-pation	Tales
G	Lubavitch	40	ritual slaughterer	T56
H	Stolin	30	musician	I11
I	New Square	35	principal	HA37, N10
J	Lubavitch	60	unknown	T34, W19, H29, H83, H87
K	Sziget	60	salesman	HA35, S5
L	Lubavitch	20	student	W6, HA50
M	Stolin	30	adminis-trator	T18, T58, T59, T59a, T63, TA5, TA8, TA10, TA11, TA11a, TA13, TA15, TA16, TA17, W4, W7, W21, H12, H21, H25a, H37, H45, H64a, H64b, H69, H75a, H96, HA3, HA10, HA11, HA15, HA16, HA18, HA19, HA21, HA21a, HA25, HA28, N8, N14, N32, WH7, S23, S24, S25, S29, I9
N	Lubavitch	50	unknown	H25
O	Lubavitch	60	fund raiser	T11, T12, T13
P	Bobov	50	unknown	H81
Q	Tchortkov	50	rabbi	T2, T6, T54, T55, W17, H34, H50, H66, H67, HA54
R	Lubavitch	45	rabbi	TA21, TA25, TA26, HA53

Narrator	Court	Age	Occu-pation	Tales
S	Klausenberg	35	diamond dealer	T7, T14, T36, T42, T52, TA22, W3, W5, W10, W11, W12, W15, W18, W24, H32, H48, HA42, N5, N6, N11, N21, N22, N24, N25, N33, N36, N37, WH3, WH4, S1, S10, S16, S34
T	Ger	65	retired	H59, H60, WH8, WH9
U	Stolin	25	student	T27, T60, H74, H78, H93, HA6, HA17, HA20, HA44, HA45, N9
V	Lubavitch	60	teacher-rabbi	T16, T17, T61, H26, N31, WH12, WH13
W	Boyaner	30	adminis-trator	T5, T45, T62, HA33, N7, N12, N13, N23
X	Bobov	22	teacher	T3, T22, T23, T26, T28, T29, T30, T31, T32, T33, T43, T57, TA24, W13, H7, H10, H28, H31, H49, H61, H62, H63, N20, WH1, WH2, S2, S3, S4, S6, S7, S9, S12, S13, S14, S15, S17, S18, S19, S20, S21, S22, S32, I3, I10, I13, I14
Y	Munkacz	40	storekeeper	S27, S33
Z	Klausenberg	45	rabbi	T49, HA43

Narrator	Court	Age	Occupation	Tales
AA	Lubavitch	60	unknown	H82
BB	Slonim	70	retired	T46, T53, H3, H33, H55, I1, I6, I8
CC	Satmar	30	factory worker	T20, T21, T25, T35, T37, T39, T50, T51, W2, W25, H47, H54, HA46, N1, N2, N3, N4, N17, N19, S31, S36
DD	New Square	unknown	unknown	T4
EE	Lubavitch	50	storekeeper	W23, H16, H56, H89, HA1, HA52, HA55, I4
FF	Stolin	30	unknown	TA2, W22, HA13, N28, N30, N34
GG	Stolin	70	retired	H5, H15, H91
HH	Bobov	15	student	HA38
II	Lubavitch	unknown	unknown	H35
JJ	Belz	30	principal	H84
KK	Lubavitch	38	principal	H42, I12
LL	Lubavitch	60	circumciser	W9, H2, H27, H30, HA51
MM	Lubavitch	unknown	unknown	H43
NN	None	45	rabbi	TA23
OO	Lubavitch	unknown	unknown	H38, H39, H44
PP	Lubavitch	60	unknown	T1
QQ	Square	35	rabbi	T9, S26
RR	New Square	60	unknown	W1
SS	Stolin	40	diamond cutter	T15, T40, T41, W16, H70, H92, WH5, S28

Narrator	Court	Age	Occu-pation	Tales
TT	Lubavitch	22	student	W8, HA2
UU	Satmar	30	watch repairer	T38, T44, HA47, N18, S8, S11, I2, I5
VV	Lubavitch	unknown	unknown	H9
WW	Lubavitch	55	unknown	H1
XX	Lubavitch	23	teacher	T8, T10, T47, H14, H90, HA49, N38, I17

YY   Six unidentified storytellers: T48, H4, H6, H19, H20, H36, H40, H41, H51, H52, H57, H58, H68, H80, H88, HA48, WH6, WH10, WH11, I7, I16

Narrator	Court	Age	Occupation	Tales
ZZ	Stolin	unknown	unknown	H80
AAA	Lubavitch	37	housewife	HA56, HA57
BBB	Belz	21	student in England	N22A, H86A, H86B
YYY	Misnaged	66	retired	M1, M2, M3
ZZZ	unknown	69	housewife	M4, M5

JLH   Retired Czechoslovakian-American, age 75: M6

APPENDIX B: REBBES AND
OTHER HISTORICAL FIGURES

The spellings of the names of Polish, Russian, and Hungarian place names follow generally accepted forms in English language Judaica. Because of the historical, linguistic, geographical, and literary precedents which have established spellings for certain words and terms, the orthography used in this work is a compromise between consistency and comprehensibility. Variant spellings of place names in eastern and central Europe sometimes make identification problematical. The town of Sandz is spelled elsewhere Zans (in Buber's *Tales*) and Tzanz (in Newman's *Hasidic Anthology*), among other variants. Mezrich is also spelled in other works Mezhireche, Mezeritz, Mezhirich, and Mezritch. In deference to established spellings, Shabbtai Tsevi is spelled Sabbatai Zevi. Berdichev (so spelled in the *Columbia Lippincott Gazetteer of the World*, ed. Leon E. Seltzer, New York, 1962) and Lubavitch have the same *ch* sound; however, the currently accepted spelling of Lubavitch retains the *t*. The name of the Russian town of Skvir has been Anglicized by the hasidim themselves to "Square." The previous Lubavitcher Rebbe spelled his name Schneersohn; the present Rebbe spells it Schneerson.

Aaron I of Karlin: *see* Karliner, the

Apter, the: Abraham Joshua Heshel (1765–1822), disciple of the Lizhensker. T22–T25, T40, H34

Baal ha-Tanya: Shneur Zalman, author of the *Tanya; see also* Lubavitch

Baal Shem Tov: Rabbi Israel ben Eliezer, the Besht (1700–60); founder of Hasidism. T1–T7, T60, H1–H11, H50, W1, W2, WH1

Belzer, the Sholem Rokeah of Belz (1779–1885): Disciple of the Lubliner. H83

Isoskher Dov (1854–1927): grandson of Sholem Rokeah; during

World War I he left Belz and settled in Ratsfeld (1914–18), and then in Munkacz (1918–21). H84

Aaron Rokeah (d. 1957): H85–H86b, HA29–HA32, N22a, N37, S36

Berdichever, the: Levi Yitshok (1740–1809), disciple of the Mezricher. T15, T16, T40, H16–H20, W5, S1

Besht, the: abbreviation of Baal Shem Tov (Be–Sh–T); *see* Baal Shem Tov

Bnei Isoskher: *see* Dinover, the

Bobover, the: Shlomo Halberstamm (d. 1905); grandson of the Sandzer Rov. T56, H61

Ben Zion Halberstamm (d. 1941): T57, H63, H81, S21, S22

Shlomo Halberstamm (1905–): present Bobover Rebbe. TA24, HA36, HA38, N20

Boyaner, the: Yitshok (d. 1917); son of Abraham Yaakov of Sadeger. N7

Mordekhai Shlomo Friedman (1890–): son of Yitshok, present Boyaner Rebbe. HA33, HA34

Dinover, the: Zevi Elimelekh Shapira, Bnei Isoskher (1785–1841); son of Pesakh Shapira (brother-in-law of Elimelekh of Lizhensk), disciple of the Rimanover and the Lubliner. T42, W15

Divrei Haim: *see* Sandzer, the

Dov Baer: the Maggid of Mezrich, the Great Maggid (1704–72); disciple of the Besht, leader of the hasidic movement after the death of the Besht

Dov Baer of Leovo: son of the Rizhyner. H50

Dzikover, the: Eliezer (d. 1861), son of the Ropchitser. T29, H49, S14, S15

Elimelekh of Lizhensk (1717–87): brother of Zusya of Annopol. T8–T10, H14

Gerer, the: Yitshok Meir Rothenberg (Alter), (1799–1866)

Abraham Mordekhai (d. 1855): H59

Yehuda Leib (1847–1905): author of *Sefat Emet* ("Lips of Truth") and *Lukutei Emet*. H60

Abraham Mordekhai (1866–1948): the Yehuda Reb. N21

Israel: the present Gerer Rebbe in Jerusalem

Gorletser, the: Borukh (d. 1900), son of the Sandzer Rov. S10

Halberstamm: *see* Bobover, the; Klausenberger, the

Hushatener, the (1852–1948): grandson of the Rizhyner. N23

Kalever, the: Eisig (d. 1829), disciple of Rabbi Shmelkeh. T39

Kaminker, the: Sholem (d. 1875), disciple of the Ropchitser Rov. S9, S20

Karliner, the

   Aaron I (1736–72): Reb Aaron the Great, disciple of the Mezricher. H12, H13

   Shlomo Karliner (1738–92): the Holy Karliner, disciple of Aaron I

   Asher of Stolin (d. 1827): the Great Stoliner, son of Aaron I

   Aaron of Karlin (1808–72): Beis ha-Aaron, the Alter Rebbe; son of Asher, Rebbe in both Karlin and Stolin. H45, H46, H80, WH7

   Asher of Stolin (d. 1873): the Yunger Rebbe, son of Aaron of Karlin; he was Rebbe at the same time as his father. T60, H45, H46, WH7

   Israel (1868–1923): son of Asher; called Yenuka ("Child") because he became Rebbe at the age of four; also called the Frankfurter since his grave is in Frankfurt. T58–T60, H69–H79, H82, H91, H92, WH7, S23–S25

   Sons of Israel of Karlin

   Abraham Elimelekh of Karlin (1892–1942): killed by the Nazis

   Moshe of Stolin (d. 1942): killed by the Nazis. T63, H64, N14

   Asher of Warsaw (d. 1942): killed by the Nazis

   Aaron of Warsaw (d. 1942): killed by the Nazis. N15

   Yaakov (d. 1946): came to America in 1929 and lived in New York. He died while on a visit to Detroit and is buried there. TA2, N28, N29

   Yohanan (1900–1955): Rebbe in Lutsk, Poland; after the war he went to Israel for two years and came to the United States in 1947. TA2–TA20, H93–H96, HA3–HA28, W22, N8, N9, N16, N26–N30, N34, N35

   Borukh Meir Yaakov Shochet: grandson of Yohanan, b. 1954.

Klausenberger, the: Yekutiel Yehuda Halberstamm, the present Klausenberger Rebbe; he moved to Israel from Williamsburg in 1959. T49, TA22, TA23, HA39–HA45, W24, N24, N25, N33, N36

Koretser, the: Pinhes Shapiro (1726–91), disciple of the Besht. T46

Kotsker, the: Menahem Mendel (1787–1859), disciple of the Lubliner and Simha Bunam of Pshiskha. W12

Kozhenitser, the: the Maggid, Israel (1740–1814); disciple of the Mezricher. H28

Leipziger, the (d. 1951): brother of the Boyaner. T62, N12

Lelever, the: David (d. 1918), disciple of the Karliner. T37, H64a, H64b

Lemberger, the: brother of the Boyaner; killed by the Nazis. N12, N13

Lemberger, the: Yaakov Meshulem Orenstein (d. 1839): author of *Yeshuot Yaakov* ("*The Generations of Yaakov*"), WH3

Lubavitcher, the
  Shneur Zalman of Ladi (1745–1813): the Tanya. T17, T34,
    H24–H27, W7–W9
  Dov Baer (1773–1827): the Mitteler Rebbe. T34, H29
  Menaham Mendel (1789–1866): the Tsemah Tsedek. T47, T48,
    H38–H40, H42–H44, WH10
  Shmuel (1834–82): the Maharash. T47, T48, H41, H52, H53,
    H56, WH6, WH10
  Sholem Dov Baer (1860–1920): T61, H56–H58, H68
  Joseph Isaac Schneersohn (1880–1950): the Alter. T61, TA1, H68,
    H87–H89, HA1, HA2, HA48, W19, N31, WH11
  Menaham Mendel Schneerson (1902–): present Lubavitcher
    Rebbe. TA25, TA26, H90, HA48–HA57, S37
Lubliner, the: Yaakov Yitshok Horowitz, the Seer (d. 1815); disciple
  of the Mezricher. T19–T21, T30, H23, N2, S6, S7

Maharash, the: *see* Lubavitch
Matevicher, Moshe: son-in-law of Abraham of Slonim. T53
Mezhibezher, the: Borukh (1757–1811), grandson of the Besht. T18,
  T21
Mezricher, the: *see* Dov Baer
Mitteler Rebbe, the: Dov Baer, second generation of Lubavitcher
  Rebbes; *see also* Lubavitch
Munkaczer, the: Haim Eleazer Shapiro (1819–83). TA21

Neshkhizer, Mordekhai (Motel, Motke) (1747–1800): disciple of the
  Zlochever. W4

Oheler, the: Moshe Teitelbaum, the Yismah Moshe (1759–1839);
  disciple of the Lubliner. T35–T38, H62, W13

Premishlaner, the: Meirl (1780–1850), son of Aaron Leib. H36, H37

Rimanover, the: Menaham Mendel. Disciple of the Lizhensker. d. 1815.
  T21, T26, N1–N4.
Rimanover, the: Hirsch. Disciple of M. Rimanover. 1778–1847. T41
Rizhyner, the: Israel Friedman (1798–1850), great-grandson of Dov
  Baer of Mezrich. Israel had six sons, among them Abraham
  Yaakov of Sadeger, David Moshe of Tchortkov, and Dov Baer of
  Leovo. *See* separate entries. T43–T45, T62, H34, H35, H37,
  WH5
Ropchitser, the: Naftali (1760–1827), disciple of the Lubliner. T10,
  T20, T28–T30, T33, W10, S5–S9, S16–S18

Sadagerer, the: Abraham Yaakov (d. 1883), son of the Rizhyner

Sandzer, the
> Rabbi Haim Halberstamm: the Divrei Haim (1793–1876). T49,
> T52, H47–H49, W16, N6, WH4, S9, S10, S19
> Sholem Eliezer (Leyzer) Halberstamm: son of the Sandzer; killed in
> Auschwitz. N17, N22

Sassover, the: Moshe Leib (1745–1807), disciple of Shmelke. T13,
T14, W6

Satmarer, the: Joel Teitelbaum, the present Satmarer Rebbe. TA21,
H47, HA35, W25, N18, N19, S36

Shimshen, Yaakov: *see* Spitovker, the

Shinyaver, the (d. 1899): son of Haim of Sandz. T49, T52

Shmelke Horowitz of Nikolsburg (1726–78): disciple of the Mezricher. W13

Shpoler, Leib: The Zaideh ("Grandfather"), (1725–1811), disciple of
Pulnoer. T27, H21, H22

Slonimer, the: Abraham (1804–84), disciple of the Kobriner. T53,
H55

Spitovker, the: Yaakov Shimshen of Spitovk (d. 1800); disciple of the
Mezricher. T24

Squarer, the: Yaakov Yosef Twersky, the Squarer Rebbe (d. 1968).
HA37; *see also* Tchernobl, the

Stoliner, the: *see* Karliner, the

Strelisker, the: Uri (d. 1826), disciple of Shlomo Karliner. W11

Szigetter, the: Yekutiel Leib (d. 1883), grandson of the Oheler,
grandfather of the present Satmarer Rebbe. T37, T39, T40, T50,
H54

Tanya, the: Shneur Zalman; *see* Lubavitch

Tchernobler, the: Mordekhai (Motel) (1770–1837), son of Nohem
Tchernobler and son-in-law of Aaron of Karlin. He had eight sons
who founded dynasties, among them Tchernobl and Square. H30,
H31, WH2, S2–S4

Tchortkover, the
> David Moshe Friedman (1827–1903): son of the Rizhyner. T54,
> T55, W17
> Baer Friedman (1882–1936)
> Israel (1854–1933): H65–H67
> Nohem Mordekhai (1874–1946)
> Shlomo (d. 1960)
> Heshel Avi: the present Tchortkover Rebbe in Israel

Teitelbaum, Joel: *see* Satmarer, the

Teitelbaum, Moshe: *see* Oheler, the

Teitelbaum, Yekutiel Leib: *see* Szigetter, the

Tsemah Tsedek, the: Menahem Mendel, third generation of Lubavitch; *see* Lubavitch

Vitebsker, the: Menahem Mendel (d. 1788)

Yampoler, Yoseleh (d. 1812): son of Yehiel Mikhel of Zlochev. T12, T13.
Yismah Moshe: Moshe Teitelbaum; *see* Oheler, the

Zalman, Shneur: *see* Lubavitcher, the
Zbarazher, the: Zev Wolf (d. 1800), son of the Zlochever. T31–T33
Zlochever, the: Yehiel Mikhel (1726–81), disciple of the Besht. T11–T13, T24
Zusya of Annopol: Meshulom (d. 1800), brother of Elimelekh of Lizhensk. T8, H14, H15, W3

OTHER HISTORICAL FIGURES CITED
(For additional information, see the notes to the tales)

Akiba: Rabbi Akiba ben Yosef (c.50–c.132). T40
Akiba Eiger (1761–1837): W14

Bakh, the: Rabbi Joel Serkes (1561/62–1641). I6
Brisker: *see* Haim Brisker, Yoshe Baer

Caro, Joseph (d. 1575)

Dubner Maggid, the: Yaakov Krants (1741–1804), disciple of Elijah Gaon

Edel: daughter of the Besht. WH1
Emden, Yaakov (1697–1776). WH7, I13
Eybeschütz, Yehoynisen (1690–1764). S12

Haim ben Atar (1697–1743): T4, T5, N23
Haim Brisker: Rabbi Haim Soloveitchik of Brisk (Brest-Litovsk), (d. 1923): H68, W19
Haim Rappaport: *see* Rappaport, Haim
Haim Vital: *see* Vital, Haim
Haham Zevi: Zevi Hirsch ben Ashkenazi (d. 1718), the Rabbi of Lemberg. T1, WH7
Hasam Soyfer: Hatam Sopher (d. 1839). H32
Hofets Haim: Rabbi Israel Meir Hacohen (1838–1933). N10

Ibn Ezra: Rabbi Abraham Ibn Ezra (1093–1167). I5

Kopuster Rov, the (19th century): T47

Lubliner Rov, the: Meyer Shapiro (d. 1934). H66

Maimonides: Moses ben Maimon, the Rambam (1135–1204). I2, I3
Megaleh Amukos (Megaleh Amukot): Nathan ben Solomon Shapira
    (1585–1633). I7
Moshe Al Sheikh (1507–1600): H33
Moshe Haim Ephraim (d. 1800): the grandson of the Besht. WH1
Moshe of Kitov (d. 1738): T2.

Nosen: brother of Elimelekh of Lizhensk and Zusya of Annopol. T8

Ostropoler, Hershele: "court jester" at hasidic courts during the latter
    half of the 18th century. M4, M5

Pnei Yehoshua: Rabbi Joshua Heshel ben Falk (d. 1648). T1

Rappaport, Haim: the Lemberger Rov (d. 1771). H14
Rashi: Solomon ben Isaac (1040–1105). T7
Rosenblatt, Joseph (1880–1933): T57

Sabbatai Zevi: the false messiah (1626–76). H4
Shazar, Shneur Zalman (1889–): third President of Israel (1963–).
    N38, N39
Sheah Tamishav: S11
Shimon ben Yohai (2d century): T34
Shimshen: Reb Yaakov Shimshen Spitovker (d. 1800). T24
Solomon ben Eliezer (16th century): I8

Tvuos Shor (Tvuat Shor): Rabbi Ephraim Zalman (d. 1634). T1

Vital, Haim (1543–1620): T3

Wasserman, Haimel (killed by the Nazis during W.W. II): N10

Yaakov of Yanov (17th–18th centuries): H12
Yehuda ha-Nosi (Judah ha-Nasi) (c.135–c.220): T42
Yosel Tamishav: S11
Yoshe Baer: Yosef Soloveitchik (d. 1902), Rabbi of Brisk. W19

Zevi, Rabbi: the son of the Besht (d. 1800). WH1

GLOSSARY

The spellings generally follow the pronunciation of the informants; however, since the informants come from several different geographical areas, complete adherence to this principle would have resulted in too many variant transliterations. In general, the spelling is in accordance with the Polish and Volhynian-Ukrainian dialect of Yiddish. Sefardic spelling is retained for some literary and ritualistic words; transliterations from the Sefardic are also presented in parentheses in the glossary. The Hebrew and Yiddish consonant *heth* is spelled as *h* (e.g., haleh) and the harder *khaph* as *kh* (e.g., brokheh); however, for the sake of pronunciation and clarity, Bah has been spelled Bakh and Pesah has been spelled Pesakh. In some words an *h* has been added after a final *e* to ensure that the *e* is pronounced.

Alter (Yid.): elder; older

Apikoyres (*pl.* Apikoyrsim) (Greek *Epicurus*, i.e., Epicurean): skeptic; unbelieving Jew

Ashkenazim (Heb.): Jews of central and eastern Europe

Balebos (*pl.* balebatim) (Heb. *ba'al bayit, pl. ba'aley batim*): householder; boss; proprietor; man of means

Balebosteh (Heb. *ba'alat ha-bayit*): housewife; mistress of the house

Bar mitsveh (Heb. *bar mitsva*): confirmation at age thirteen

Batln (*pl.* batlonim) (Heb. *batlan, pl. batlanim*): idler—an adult who is supported by others so that he can study

Beit din (Heb.): rabbinical court

Beit ha-Kneset (Heb.): synagogue; shul

Besmedresh (Heb. *beit ha-midrash*): house of study; place of prayer and study

Boher (Heb. *bahur*): young boy; unmarried boy

Briss (Heb. *brit*): circumcision

Dalet (Heb.): fourth letter of the Hebrew alphabet

Daven (Yid.): to pray, customarily with a slight rocking motion

Din toyreh (Heb. *Torah*): law suit in a rabbinical court; court

Dybbuk (Heb.): soul of a dead person that returns to inhabit the body of a living person; metempsychosis

Einhora (Heb. *'ain ha-ra'*): evil eye

Erev (Heb.): evening, eve; Erev Pesakh, the eve of Passover; Erev Shabbes (Erev Shabbat), Shabbes eve, Friday night

Esrog (*pl.* esroygim) (Heb. *etrog*): a type of citrus fruit that is part of the festival bunch composed of a piece of myrtle, a piece of palm tree, a piece of willow, and a piece of esrog

Farbrengen (Yid.): hasidic gathering (farbreng—to spend time)

Fringes: see Tsitses

Gabai (*pl.* gaboyim) (Heb. *pl.* gabaim): Rebbe's assistant

Ganev (Heb. *ganav*): thief

Gaon (*pl.* geonim) (Heb.): great scholar; formerly, head of rabbinical academy in Babylon

Gartel (Yid.): belt worn during prayers

Gehenna (Heb. *gehenom*): hell

Gemoreh (Heb. *Gemara*): that portion of the Talmud which discusses the laws in the Mishna

Gesund (Yid.): health

Gilgul (Heb.): reincarnation

Glat kosher (Heb., Yid.): unquestionably kosher, the most rigid standards of kashrut

Goy (*fem.* goyeh; *pl.* goyim) (Heb. *fem.* goya): gentile, non-Jew. The word has a wide range of shades of meaning. It can be used simply to stress the otherness of the referent or as a generic term for non-Jews or it can include derogatory implications for non-Jews and Jews alike. A single passage may contain one or all of these aspects

Great Shabbes: see Shabbes ha-Godel

Habad: abbreviation of *hokhma* (wisdom), *bina* (understanding), *da'at* (knowledge); the Lubavitcher movement founded by Rabbi Shneur Zalman

Hakire Sforim (Heb. *sifrei hakira*): term referring to any philosophical books

Haleh (Heb. *hala*): festive Sabbath loaf

Hanukeh (Heb. *Hanuka*): holiday celebrating the victory of the Maccabees

Hasides (Heb. *hasidut*): teachings of Hasidism, philosophical exposition

Hasideshe (Heb. *hasidi*): hasidic

Haskala (Heb.): enlightenment; the movement espousing secularism

Haskoras neshomas tish (Heb. *azkarat neshamot*): memorial meal

Havdoleh (Heb. *havdala*): the ceremony marking the end of the Shabbes and the beginning of the week

Hazen (Heb. *hazan*): cantor

Heilige oygen (Yid.): Holy eyes

Homets (Heb. *hamets*): leavened food and dishes unfit for Passover use

Hoshanoh Rabboh (Heb. Hoshanah Rabbah): the sixth day of Sukkes;

a day in which, according to tradition, the ultimate fate of each Jew was decided in the Heavenly Court

Hoyf (*pl.* hoyfen) (Yid.): court; the Rebbe's residence

Hupeh (Heb. *hupa*): wedding canopy

Kaddish (Heb.): mourner's prayer

Kaftan (Polish): long coat

Kaleh (Heb. *kala*): bride

Kapote (Yid.): long black coat

Kashrut (Heb.): the dietary laws

Kehilleh (Heb. *kehilla*): community; the community council which dealt with community matters

Keinhora (Yid., Heb.): no evil eye

Kibbitser (Yid.): joker; one who offers unsolicited advice

Kiddish (Heb. *Kiddush*): benediction over wine

Kikhlekh (Yid.): cakes

Kimpetsettel (Yid.): childbirth amulet

Kislev (Heb.: month of the year during which Hanukeh occurs; usually coinciding with November–December

Kol nidrei (Heb.): prayer ushering in Yom Kippur, the Day of Atonement

Kosher (Heb. *kasher*): ritually pure

Krekhtsen (Yid.): groaning

Kreplekh (Yid.): dough filled with meat or cheese

Kugl, Kigl (Yid.): a baked, sweet pudding, usually of noodles

Kvitl (*pl.* kvitlekh) (Yid.): petition presented to Rebbe which contains the names to be blessed, the request, and the name of the mother of the petitioner; it may also be left on a tombstone

Lag Baomer (Heb.): thirty-third day in the time of Omer, i.e., the counting of the days between Passover and Shevuos (the Feast of Weeks)

Lehaim (Heb.): toast; to your health, to life

Levoneh (Heb. *levana*): moon

Likkutei Torah (Heb.): work by Shneur Zalman containing sermons on portions of the Holy Scriptures

Litvisher (Yid.): Lithuanian; normally synonymous with misnaged

Lulev (Heb. *Lulav*): palm branch used in celebrating Sukkes

Maggid (*pl.* maggidim) (Heb.): itinerant preacher

Mairev (Heb. *ma'ariv*): evening prayer

Maisseh (Heb. *ma'asia*): story, tale

Mashgiah (Heb.): supervisor of religious laws in the preparation of kosher food products

Matseh (*pl.* matses) (Heb. *matsa, matsot*): unleavened bread eaten especially during Passover

Mazel tov (Heb. *mazal tov*): good luck; congratulations

Mehatunim (Heb. *mehutanim*): in-laws

Melaveh malkeh (Heb. *malka*): literally, "escorting the Queen"; the fourth meal of the Shabbes (actually takes place after the Shabbes has ended)

Mentsh (Yid.): man, person

Meshiah (Heb. *Mashiah*): Messiah, the anointed one

Mezuzeh (Heb. *mezuza*): amulet placed on doorpost which contains two Biblical judgments, Deut. 6:4–9, 11:13–21

Mikveh (*pl.* mikves) (Heb. *mikva, mikvot*): ritual bath

Minheh (Heb.): afternoon prayer

Minyen (*pl.* minyonim) (Heb. *minyan, minyanim*): required quorum for public prayer of ten Jews over age thirteen

Misheberekh (Heb. *mi she-berakh*): a blessing made before the Torah

Mishna (Heb.): the codex of laws by Reb Yehuda ha-Nosi (second century C.E.)

Mishnayes (Heb. *mishnayot*): portions of the Mishna

Misnaged (*pl.* misnagdim) (Heb. *mitnaged, mitnagdim*): opponents of the hasidim

Mitsveh (*pl.* mitsves) (Heb. *mitsva, mitsvot*): commandment, precept, good deed

Moyel (Heb. *mohel*): circumciser

Moyfes (Yid.): miracle

Nahes fun kinder (Heb. *nahat*, Yid.): joy from one's children

Nign (Heb. *niggun*): song, melody

Nu? (Yid.): so?

Parnosseh (Heb. *parnasa*): livelihood, earning a living

Pelts (Yid.): fur coat

Pesakh (Heb. *Pesah*): Passover

Peyes (Heb. *pe'ot*): earlocks

Pidyen (Heb. *pidyon*): literally, "redemption"; money given to Rebbe when visiting him

Pidyen shvuyim (Heb. *pidyon*): redemption or ransom money, often collected to pay fines for those taken into jail or to pay back taxes for those in debt

Rabbi (Heb.): man ordained to judge matters of the law; in this work, when spelled with a capital, it indicates the chief rabbi of a town

Rebbe (Heb. *rabbi*): literally, my teacher, my master; the leader of a hasidic court; tsaddik

Rebbetsn (Yid.): Rebbe's wife

Rosh Hashoneh (Heb. *Rosh Hashana*): Jewish New Year

Rosh Hoydesh (Heb. *Rosh Hodesh*): the new moon; the beginning of the Jewish month

Rov (Heb. *rav*): rabbi of the community or synagogue

Sandek (Heb. *sandak*): the man who holds the child during the circumcision ceremony

Sefardim (Heb.): Jews of Spanish and Portuguese origin; non-Ashkenazi

Seudeh (Heb. *seuda*): the festive meal

Shaa (Yid.): be quiet

Shabbes (Heb. *Shabbat*): Sabbath

Shabbes ha-Godel (Heb. *Shabbat ha-Gadol*): the *Great Shabbes;* the *Shabbes before Passover*

Shadkhen (Heb. *shadkhan*): matchmaker

Shahris (Heb. *shaharit*): morning prayer

Shaigets (Yid.): young gentile; also has the pejorative meaning "arrogant Jew"

Shaikhus (Heb. *shayakhut*): connection

Shaitl (Yid.): wig worn by women after marriage

Shalehseudes (Heb. *shelosh seudot*, actually *seuda shelishit*): the third meal of the Shabbes

Shammes (Heb. *shammash*): beadle

Shatnes (Heb. *sha'atnez*): garment made of a mixture of wool and linen forbidden by law (Lev. 19:19; Deut. 22:11)

Shekhina (Heb.): divine spirit

Shema Yisroel (Heb.): Hear, O Israel; the first words of the central prayer of Judaism, the profession of faith

Shevuos (Heb. *Shavu'ot*): Feast of Weeks, commemorating the giving of the Torah

Shikker (Heb. *shikkor*): intoxicated, drunkard

Shiraim (Heb.): remains of Rebbe's meal shared by his followers

Shmini Atseret (Heb.): the eighth day of Sukkes

Shmoneh Esreh (Heb.): the Eighteen Benedictions, said in daily prayer services first silently and then read aloud by reader

Shnapps (Yid.): brandy

Shohet (*pl.* shohtim) (Heb. *pl. shohatim*): ritual slaughterer

Sholem aleikhem (Heb. *shalom*): literally, "peace to you"; greetings

Shtetl (Yid.): town

Shtibl (*pl.* shtiblekh) (Yid.): house of prayer of hasidim, usually consisting of a single room

Shtraiml (Yid.): fur cap worn on the Shabbes

Shul (Yid.): synagogue

Shulhan Arukh (Heb.): compendium of Jewish Law made in the sixteenth century by Joseph Caro

Siddur (*pl.* siddurim) (Heb.): prayer book

Simheh (Heb. *simha*): happiness

Simhes Toyreh (Heb. *Simhat Torah*): Festival of the Law; the last day of Sukkes celebrating the end of the yearly cycle of reading the Torah

Slihes (Heb. *slihot*): prayers asking for forgiveness recited during fast days and during the week before the New Year; also the days between Rosh Hashoneh and Yom Kippur when the slihes prayers are recited

Slihes nakht (Heb. *slihot*): the night when the slihes prayers are recited

Sofer (Heb.): scribe who writes the Torah scrolls

Sukkeh (Heb. *sukka*): booth; a wooden hut covered with branches in which all meals are taken during Sukkes

Sukkes (Heb. *Sukkot*): Feast of Tabernacles, begins four days after Yom Kippur

Talis (*pl.* talaysim) (Heb. *talit, talitot*): prayer shawl

Talis koten (Heb. *talit katan*): fringed ritual undershirt worn by men

Talmid (*pl.* talmidim) (Heb.): student

Talmid hokhem (Heb. *hakham*): learned man

Talmud (Heb.): the oral law; the Mishna plus the commentaries on the Mishna

Tanna (*pl.* Tannaim) (Aramaic): the teachers of the Mishna

Tanya (Aramaic): Exposition of Hasidism by Rabbi Shneur Zalman. The actual title of the book is *Likkutei Amarim*, but it is known by the first word in the work, Tanya. It is often used to refer directly to Rabbi Shneur Zalman—"the Tanya" or the "Baal ha-Tanya" (Master of the Tanya)

Targum (Heb.): the Aramaic translation of the Bible

Tefillin (Heb.): phylacteries (two leather cases which are bound by attached straps to the forehead and the left arm during the morning prayer; the cases contain parchment on which are inscribed Exod. 3:1–10, 11–16; Deut. 6:4–9, 9:13–21)

Tish (Yid.): table; a communal meal at the Rebbe's table

Tishebov (Heb. *Tish'ah b'Av*): ninth day of Av commemorating the destruction of the Temple

Tmimim (Heb.): synonym for hasidim; the perfect ones, men of pure hearts

Torah: the Pentateuch

Toyreh (Heb. *torah*): Rebbe's teachings, usually given at a Shabbes meal

Treyf (Heb. *taref*): unkosher; impure; not permissible to eat; not prepared according to the ritual law or found to contain some defect

Tsaddik (*pl.* tsaddikim) (Heb.): a righteous man; synonymous with Rebbe

Tsaddik nistor (Heb. *nistar*): the hidden righteous; one of the thirty-six hidden righteous who are said to sustain the world

Tsitses (Heb. *tsitsit*): fringes sewn at the four corners of the talis and the talis koten as reminders of God's commandment. See Deut. 22:12; Num. 15:37–41

Wakhnakht (Yid.): the eve before circumcision when protective psalms are read

Yarmelkeh (Yid.): skullcap

Yeshiveh (*pl.* yeshives) (Heb. *yeshiva, yeshivot*): school of religious study; rabbinical school

Yetser Hora (Heb. *Yetser ha-Ra*): the evil inclination; the evil urge; Evil

Yid (*pl.* yiden) (Yid.): Jew

Yiddishkait (Yid.): Jewishness; Jewish way of life

Yihus (Heb.): lineage; status based on lineage as well as learning and position

Yizkor (Heb.): prayer for the dead; commemoration of the dead

Yohrtsait (Yid.): anniversary of day of death

Yom Kippur (Heb.): Day of Atonement

Yom tillim (Heb. *tehilim*): psalms designated for each day of the month, especially for those unable to study the Talmud

Yontev (Heb. *yom tov*): holiday, holy day

Zaideh (Yid.): grandfather

Zohar, the (Heb.): mystical writings of the thirteenth century, compiled by Moses de Leon (1250–1305); legendary author said to be Shimon ben Yohai (second century C.E.)

SELECTED BIBLIOGRAPHY

Aarne, Antti, and Thompson, Stith. *The Types of the Folktale*. 2d rev., Folklore Fellows Communications No. 184. Helsinki: Academia Scientiarum Fennica, 1961.

Agus, Jacob B. *The Evolution of Jewish Thought: From Biblical Times to the Opening of the Modern Era*. New York: Abelard-Schuman, 1959.

Aeścoly-Weintraub, A. Z. "Le hassidisme." In *Introduction à l'étude des hérésies religieuses parmi les Juifs*. Paris: P. Geuthner, 1928.

Asch, Sholem. *A Passage in the Night*. New York: Putnam, 1953.

Babylonian Talmud. 18 vols. English translation edited by I. Epstein. London: Socino Press, 1948–52.

Bascom, William. "Verbal Art." *Journal of American Folklore* 68 (1955): 245–52.

Benedict, Ruth. *Zuni Mythology*. 2 vols. Columbia University Contributions to Anthropology, vol. 21. New York: Columbia University Press, 1935.

Boas, Franz. "Tsimshian Mythology." *Thirty-first Annual Report of the Bureau of American Ethnology*. Washington, D.C., 1916.

———. *Kwakiutl Culture as Reflected in Their Mythology*. Memoirs of the American Folk-Lore Society, vol. 28. New York: American Folk-Lore Society, 1935.

Buber, Martin. *For the Sake of Heaven*. Translated by Ludwig Lewisohn. 1953; reprinted New York: Meridian Books and the Jewish Publication Society, 1958.

———. *Hasidism and Modern Man*. Edited and translated by Maurice Friedman. New York: Horizon Press, 1958.

———. "Interpreting Hasidism." *Commentary* 36 (1963): 218–25.

———. *The Legend of the Baal-Shem*. Translated by M. Friedman. New York: Harper, 1955.

———. *The Origin and Meaning of Hasidism*. Edited by M. Friedman. New York: Horizon Press, 1960.

———. *Tales of the Hasidim*. Translated by Olga Marx. 2 vols. New York: Schocken Books, 1947–48.

———. *The Tales of Rabbi Nachman*. Translated by M. Friedman. New York: Horizon Press, 1956.

Budge, Sir E. A. Wallis, translator and editor. *Baralam and Yewasef.* Cambridge: Cambridge University Press, 1923.

Code of Jewish Law (*"Kitzur Schulchan Aruch"*). Compiled by Rabbi S. Ganzfried. Translated by H. Goldin. Rev. ed. New York: Hebrew Publishing Company, 1927.

Di Yiddishe Heim 1 (1959).

Dresner, Samuel H. *The Zaddik.* New York: Abelard-Schuman, 1960.

Dubnow, Simon. *Geschichte des Chassidismus.* Translated by A. Steinberg. 2 vols. Berlin: Jüdischer Verlag, 1931.

———. *History of the Jews in Russia and Poland.* Translated by I. Friedlaender. 3 vols. Philadelphia: Jewish Publication Society of America, 1916–20.

Eggan, Dorothy. "The Manifest Content of Dreams." *American Anthropologist* 54 (1949): 471–85.

———. "The Significance of Dreams for Anthropological Research." *American Anthropologist* 51 (1949): 177–97.

———. "The Personal Use of Myth in Dreams." *Journal of American Folklore* 68 (1955): 445–53.

Fischer, J. L. "The Position of Men and Women in Truk and Ponape." *Journal of American Folklore* 69 (1956): 55–62.

Fishman, Judah Loeb, editor. *Sefer ha-Besht* (*"Book of the Besht"*). Jerusalem: Mosad ha-Rav Kuk, 1960.

Frazer, Sir James George. *Folk-Lore in the Old Testament.* 3 vols. London: Macmillan, 1919.

Gaster, Moses. *The Exempla of the Rabbis.* London: Asia Publishing Company, 1924.

———. *Ma'aseh Book.* 2 vols. Philadelphia: The Jewish Publication Society of America, 1934.

Gaster, Theodor. *The Holy and the Profane.* New York: W. Sloane Associates, 1955.

Gersh, Harry, and Miller, Sam. "Satmar in Brooklyn." *Commentary* 28 (1959): 389–99.

Ginzberg, Louis. *The Legends of the Jews.* Translated by Henrietta Szold. 7 vols. Philadelphia: Jewish Publication Society of America, 1909–38.

Gross, Naftoli. *Maaselech un Mesholim* (*"Tales and Parables"*). New York: Naftoli Gross, 1955.

Gulkowitsch, Lazar. *Die Grundgedanken des Chassidismus als Quelle seines Schicksals.* Tartu: Universitatis Tartuensis, 1938.

———. *Der Hasidismus.* Leipzig: Eduard Pfeiffer, 1957.

Hand, Wayland D. "Status of European and American Legend Study." *Current Anthropology* 6 (1965): 439–46.

Hirsch, W. *Rabbinic Psychology: Belief about the Soul in the Rabbinic Literature of the Talmudic Period.* London: E. Goldston, 1947.

Horodezky, Samuel Aba. *Ha-Hasidut veha-Hasidim* (*"Hasidism and the Hasidim"*). 2 vols. 3rd ed. Tel-Aviv: Dvir, 1951.

Horodezky, Samuel Aba. *Religiose Strömungen im Judentum*. Bern and Leipzig: Ernst Bircher, 1920.

In Praise of the Besht (*"Shivhei ha-Besht"*). Translated and edited by Dan Ben Amos and Jerome R. Mintz. To be published by the Indiana University Press.

Jacobs, L. "The Concept of Hasid in the Biblical and Rabbinic Literatures." *The Journal of Jewish Studies* 8 (1957): 143–54.

Jacobs, Melville. *The Content and Style of an Oral Literature*. Chicago: University of Chicago Press, 1959.

"Jewish Materials." Partly unpublished interviews and notes, Columbia University Research in Contemporary Cultures, 1947–49.

Kahana, Abraham. *Sefer ha-Hasidut* (*"The Book of Hasidism"*). 2d ed. Warsaw: L. Levin-Epstein, 1922.

Kardiner, Abram, with a foreword and two ethnological reports by Ralph Linton. *The Individual and His Society*. New York: Columbia University Press, 1939.

Kardiner, Abram, with the collaboration of Ralph Linton, Cora Du Bois, and James West [pseud.]. *The Psychological Frontiers of Society*. New York: Columbia University Press, 1945.

Kluckhohn, Clyde. "Myths and Rituals: A General Theory." *Harvard Theological Review* 35 (1942): 45–79. Reprinted in Lessa, William A., and Vogt, Evon Z., editors, *Reader in Comparative Religion*. Evanston, Ill.: Row Peterson, 1958, pp. 135–51.

Kranzler, George (Gershon). "Chosid from the Left Bank." *Orthodox Jewish Life* 22 (1955): 32–36.

———. *Williamsburg, A Jewish Community in Transition*. New York: P. Feldheim, 1961.

Langer, Jiri. *Nine Gates to the Chassidic Mysteries*. New York: David McKay Co., 1961.

Lehrman, S. M. *Jewish Customs and Folklore*. London: Shapiro, Vallentine & Co., 1949.

Levin, Meyer. *The Golden Mountain*. New York: Behrman House, 1932.

Löhr, Max. *Beiträge zur Geschichte des Chassidismus*. Leipzig: N. W. Kaufman, 1925.

Loomis, C. Grant. *White Magic*. Cambridge, Mass.: Medieval Academy of America, 1948.

Mach, R. *Der Zaddik in Talmud und Midrash*. Leiden: E. J. Brill, 1957.

Maimon, Solomon. *Autobiography*. Translated by J. C. Murray. London: East and West Library, 1954.

Malinowski, Bronislaw. *Argonauts of the Western Pacific*. 1922; reprinted New York: E. P. Dutton & Co., Inc., 1961.

———. "Myth in Primitive Psychology." In *Magic, Science, and Religion*. 1926; reprinted New York, 1948, pp. 93–143.

Marcus, Ahron [pseudo., Verus]. *Der Chassidismus.* 3rd ed. Harburg: S. Marcus, 1927.

Minkin, Jacob. *The Romance of Hassidism.* New York: Macmillan, 1935.

Morgan, William. "Navaho Dreams." *American Anthropologist* 34 (1932): 390–406.

Newman, Louis I., and Spitz, Samuel, eds. *The Hasidic Anthology.* New York: Bloch Publishing Co., 1944.

———. *Maggidim and Hasidim: Their Wisdom.* New York: Bloch Publishing Co., 1962.

Noy, Dov. "Archiving and Presenting Folk Literature in an Ethnological Museum." *Journal of American Folklore* 78 (1962): 23–28.

———, editor, with the assistance of Dan Ben Amos. *Folktales of Israel.* Translated by Gene Baharav. Chicago: University of Chicago Press, 1963.

———, editor. *Moroccan Jewish Folktales.* New York: Herzl Press, 1966.

———. "Motif Index of Talmudic-Midrashic Literature." Ph.D. dissertation, Indiana University, 1954.

Parker, Seymour. "Motives in Eskimo and Ojibwa Mythology." *Ethnology* 1 (1962): 516–23.

———. "The Wiitiko Psychosis in the Context of Ojibwa Personality and Culture." *American Anthropologist* 62 (1960): pp. 603–23.

Peretz, J. L. *In This World and the Next.* Translated by M. Spiegel. New York: T. Yoseloff, 1958.

Pipe, Samuel Zanvel. "Napoleon in Jewish Folklore." *YIVO Annual of Jewish Social Science* 1 (1946): 294–304.

Poll, Solomon. *The Hasidic Community of Williamsburg.* Glencoe, Ill.: Free Press, 1962.

Rabinovich, Wolf. "Karlin Hasidism." *YIVO Annual of Jewish Social Science* 5 (1950): 123–51.

Rabinowicz, H. *A Guide to Hasidism.* London and New York: T. Yoseloff, 1960.

Raddock, Charles. "The Sage of Sattmur, Hassidism and Israel Politics." *The Jewish Forum,* May, 1954.

Ringelblum, Emmanuel. *Notes from the Warsaw Ghetto.* Edited and translated by Jacob Sloan, New York: McGraw-Hill, 1958.

Schacter, Zalman. "How To Become a Modern Hasid." *Jewish Heritage* 2 (1960): 33–40.

Schauss, Hayyim. *The Lifetime of a Jew throughout the Ages of Jewish History.* Cincinnati: Union of American Hebrew Congregations, 1950.

Schechter, Solomon. *Some Aspects of Rabbinic Theology.* 1910; reprinted New York, 1936.

———. *Studies in Judaism, A Selection.* 1896–1924; selected and reprinted New York, Meridian Books and the Jewish Publication Society, 1958.

Scheftelowitz, Isidor. "Das Fischsymbol im Judentum und Christentum." *Archiv Für Religionswissenschaft* 14 (1911): 1–53, 321–92.

Schneersohn, Joseph I. *Lubavitcher Rabbi's Memoirs.* Vol. 1. Brooklyn: Otzar Hachassidism, 1956.

———. *On Learning Chassidus.* Translated by Z. Posner. Brooklyn, 1959.

———. *On the Teachings of Chassidus.* Translated by Z. Posner. Brooklyn, 1959.

Scholem, Gershom G. "Baal Shem." In *Ha-Entsiklopediyah ha-ivrit* (*"Encyclopaedia Hebraica"*) 9: 263–64. Jerusalem and Tel-Aviv, 1958.

———. "Devekuth, Communion with God in Early Hasidic Doctrine." *The Review of Religion* 15 (1950): 115–39.

———. *Major Trends in Jewish Mysticism.* London: Thames and Hudson, 1955.

———. "Martin Buber's Hasidim." *Commentary* 32 (1961): 218–25.

———. *Shabtai Tsevi.* 2 vols. Tel-Aviv: Am Oved, 1956–57.

Sobel, Bernard. "The M'lochim: A Study of a Religious Community." Master's thesis, New School of Social Research, 1956.

Steinberg, Yehudah. "Sipurei Hasidim" ("Hasidic Stories"). *Kol Ketavi.* Tel-Aviv: Devir, 1959.

Steinmann, Eliezer. *The Garden of Hassidism.* Translated by Haim Shachter. Jerusalem: World Zionist Organization, 1961.

Thompson, Stith. *Motif-Index of Folk Literature.* 6 vols. Bloomington, Ind.: Indiana University Press, 1955–58.

Tishby, I. "Bein shabta'ut le-hasidut" ("Between Sabbatianism and Hasidism"). *Knesset* 9 (1945): 268–338.

Tishby, I., and Dan, J. "Hasidut" ("Hasidism"). In *Ha-Entsiklopediyah ha-ivrit* (*"Encyclopaedia Hebraica"*) 17: 756–821. Jerusalem and Tel-Aviv, 1965.

Trachtenberg, Joshua. "The Folk Element in Judaism." *The Journal of Religion* 22 (1942): 173–86.

———. *Jewish Magic and Superstition.* New York: Behrman's Jewish Book House, 1939.

Unger, Menashe. *Die hasidishe velt* (*"The Hasidic World"*). New York: Hasidus, 1955.

———. *Hasidus un lebn* (*"Hasidism and Life"*). New York, 1946.

———. *Sefer Kedoshim* (*"Book of the Martyrs"*). New York: Menashe Unger, 1967.

Vansina, Jan. *Oral Tradition: A Study in Historical Methodology.* Translated by H. M. Wright. Chicago: Aldine Publishing Company, 1965.

———. "Recording the Oral History of the Bakuba—I. Methods." *Journal of African History* 1 (1960): 43–51, 257–70.

Wallace, W. J. "The Dream in Mohave Life." *Journal of American Folklore* 60 (1947): 252–58.

Waxman, Meyer. *A History of Jewish Literature.* 5 vols. 2d rev. ed. New York: Bloch Publishing Co., 1936–60.

Weinberger, Bernard. "The Miracle of Williamsburg." *The Jewish Observer* 2 (1965): 16–19.

Weiner, Herbert. "The Lubavitcher Movement I." *Commentary* 23 (1957): 231–41.

———. "The Lubavitcher Movement II." *Commentary* 23 (1957): 316–27.

Weinreich, Beatrice S. "Genres and Types of Yiddish Folk Tales about the Prophet Elijah." *The Field of Yiddish, Studies in Language, Folklore, and Literature.* Edited by Uriel Weinreich. The Hague: Mouton & Co., 1965, pp. 202–31.

Weiss, J. G. "A Circle of Pre-Hassidic Pneumatics." *The Journal of Jewish Studies* 8 (1957): 199–213.

———. "Contemplative Mysticism and 'Faith' in Hasidic Piety." *The Journal of Jewish Studies* 4 (1953): 19–29.

———. "The Great Maggid's Theory of Contemplative Magic." *Hebrew Union College Annual* 31 (1960): 137–48.

———. "The Kavvanoth of Prayer in Early Hasidism." *The Journal of Jewish Studies* 9 (1958): 163–92.

Wertheim, Aaron. *Halakhot ve-halikhot ba-hasidut ("Rites and Ceremonies").* Jerusalem: Mosad ha-Rav Kuk, 1960.

Wiesner, Naphtali. "Faith and Suffering: A Study of the Impact of Concentration Camp Experiences on Moral and Religious Attitudes." Ph.D. dissertation, New School of Social Research, 1950.

Ysander, Torsten. *Studien zum B'eštschen hasidismus in seiner religionsgeschichtlichen sonderart.* Lund: A.-b. Lundequistiska bokhandeln, 1933.

Zborowski, Mark, and Herzog, Elizabeth. *Life Is with People.* New York: International Universities Press, 1952.

Zevin, Solomon Joseph. *Sipurei Hasidim ("Tales of Hasidim").* 2 vols. Tel-Aviv: Avraham Tsioni, 1956–57.

Zimmels, H. J. *Askenazim and Sephardim.* Jews' College Publications, New Series, No. 2. London: Oxford University Press, 1958.

INDEX